The Ivory Fount

Other Works
by Johann M. Moser

Verse

Most Ancient of All Splendors

Late Autumn at Dumbarton Oaks
And Other Poems

Farewell . . . and If Forever
And Other Poems

Prose

Love of the Blossoming Hills
New England Stories and Sketches

Tutelary Presences
And Other Stories

The Song of the Eternal Aeons
A Phantasmagoria

Translations

O Holy Night
An Anthology of Classic Nativity Verse

Devoutly I Adore Thee
Prayers and Hymns of St. Thomas Aquinas
(with Robert Anderson)

Johann M. Moser

The Ivory Fount

A Novel

The Diamond Ledge Press
Sandwich, New Hampshire

For more information, please contact us at:
https://diamondledgepress.com/

978-1-964001-12-8(hardback)
978-1-964001-13-5(paperback)
978-1-964001-14-2 (ebook)

Library of Congress Control Number: 2024904675

How but in custom and ceremony
Are innocence and beauty born?
Ceremony's the name for the rich horn,
And custom for the spreading laurel tree.

William Butler Yeats

To love is the great amulet
which makes the world a garden.

Robert Louis Stevenson

Contents

Part One

I shall never fully understand the reasons that drew me, initially, to that most curiously sequestered of offices—office and domicile, as I would soon enough discover—of Theodore Besserman. He would adduce, as he did eventually, my reasons for coming—had adduced them already, he would later assert, even before I arrived that first time; and he may have been right about that, as he usually is about most things. If he has a way of being right, finally, about most things—often to my bemused, if delighted, annoyance—he also has a way of being, according to his own admission, always "incomplete" (so he says) and hence "probative" in whatever account he has to give of whatever it is that needs accounting for. Such an account is never fully satisfactory; all the facts are never quite in; something is always left over, even as it should be—not as a painful block of ignorance discouraging any further concern but as an enigma still inviting inquiry both patient and tentative, still waiting to be resolved, if it ever should be resolved. In any event, I did decide to accept his invitation, as unexpected and as inscrutable as it was, to make my appointment and to visit that—as I perceived it at the moment—all too sequestered office. And that's what, in the end, mattered ... matters now, has mattered ever since.

After all, how often does one, sitting in one's law office in an oversize, glassy, shapeless, even soulless building of a kind all too familiar and all too consonant with our age, receive a note, rendered with a fountain pen in an elegant though sportive hand, delivered by a courier—yes, by a courier and a somewhat elderly one at that, unannounced and without introducing himself, garbed in the most improbable Burberry tweed cape and most decorously capping his heart with (could it actually be?) a derby hat in his right hand and, with a suede-gloved but broad-knuckled left hand, presenting me with the missive, after which he bowed and vanished as promptly and as mysteriously as he had shown up? The note bore a return address that, to my surprise, was located in the heart of the business district, only about a five-minute walk from my office, yet on a street whose name had, for some odd reason, never registered in my consciousness. That in itself would have provided a sufficient ground to spur me on to answer the summons and, a week later, to attend the interview it had proposed. There were other grounds as well, as I have already indicated, but of a more complex nature; but, where action is required, how often do we act on what is the simplest motive, the easiest to apprehend, even if not, as in this case, the most central or critical that may be involved.

I located the street easily, a short and narrow cul-de-sac that led, as far as I could see, nowhere in particular. I recognized that I had hurried by it a thousand times over the years on the way to and from my office, without much more than a glance down it, jumping to the conclusion that it could have nothing of interest to draw me in. What I found, as I entered the street, was not unlike what I had expected it might be: one of those shabby backwaters of an immense contemporary city, a locale somehow missed by the cyclopean upheavals of modern megalith building, a tiny remnant of what was, or must have been in its time, a paragon of a modestly nurtured urbanity belonging to another age. A row of once, no doubt, comely townhouses, four or five stories high, lined each side of the street; most of them, it was clear, had been converted into flats, presumably a long time ago. They looked out on the street through dusty windows and tangled blinds, with the occasional potted plant or pallid, malnourished cactus stationed on a cluttered sill and with assortments of misshapen glassware and ceramic knickknacks sometimes suspended from upper-window frames by rawhide straps. Here and there along the street a fire escape had been, in later times, incongruously tacked on to some now defaced and forlorn Ionian façade. The bottom floors of the houses had obviously been witness to the proliferation, several decades earlier, one could assume, of an adolescent commercial culture whose unkempt boutiques, to all appearances, had declined directly from flamboyant youth to premature dotage without having passed gracefully though any of the intermediary stages. A sorry prospect it was, an empty, lonely street, so replete with that flavor of disconsolate human wreckage that the concourse of a great city in our time all too often harbors in its very bosom.

Except for . . . ! Even well before I saw the brass plate affirming that I had reached the point of my destination, I had been astonished by a slender five-story building, situated about halfway down the street. Its façade was executed in a Venetian-Gothic style, very "old-world" at that, but it glowed in those spare shafts of morning sun that managed somehow to slant through the glassy skyscrapers that towered over the secluded street. Tall, leaded, multipaned windows, adorned on the higher floors of the edifice with rows of stained-glass medallions, added both a richness and a simplicity to its comportment, its delicate tracery, its finely rendered arches and motifs. And as old, even as ancient, as the building appeared to me, it also had a palpable newness about it, a sense that it had been born that very day, blossoming afresh out of the city pavement just moments before I first gazed upon it.

This must appear foolish, I know, but, having found my destination, I likewise found myself, after a momentary break in my stride, strolling right past it, following the street down to where it terminated in a small cluster of vegetation that was frail and stunted, perhaps by a lack of light and nourishment but certainly by the frigid effects of a mid-February morning. Here an iron railing, now speckled by blistered rust and contorted into a dozen entangled shapes, set off a little park, or what looked like a little park—once genteel, no doubt, but now little more than an unruly patch of weeds and brush and a few skimpy trees barely surviving amid the dank shadows cast by the buildings around it and littered with old newspapers, cigarette butts, and a twisted umbrella whose spiny supports, jabbing here and there through its fabric, attested eloquently to what must have been its brusque, if not positively apoplectic, abandonment. I stood there for a moment, contemplating in a distracted way this assortment of debris, and then retraced my steps.

I can assure you that I don't normally do this sort of thing—at least not since the time when, while still in law school and being interviewed for employment at a variety of firms, I always needed a ready pretext to delay my entrance. One did require, didn't one, just a little more time to recollect one's thoughts, have another breath of fresh air, size up an unfamiliar milieu, and review what little one had learned about a potential employer. Further, one cannot help but think that the physical appearance of the venue where one's ordeal will occur provides some indispensable clue to its moral character, and this information, however inchoate it may be, must be duly processed. Of course, in this instance, I had no need for anxiety. I was already employed, as satisfactorily as one gets employed in my line of work, at a "white-shoe" Boston firm, old-line, established, as substantial as the bedrock upon which its new mighty redoubt, however thoroughly modern it was, was indubitably planted. I had neither ambitions nor specific motives to move on. Yet here I was, submissive to a summons as obscure as it was fortuitous, standing before an arched doorway with its carved granite threshold, its brass plate inscribed, in large Gothic letters, "Besserman and Davidowitz, Attorneys at Law."

Naturally, I had done some research. I always do my research. As a partner in a prestigious law firm, I had all the research facilities—and research assistants—I needed at my immediate disposal. Nevertheless, this research called for some effort, only because more "dated" materials get shipped off to storehouses where, after having been meticulously boxed, labeled, stacked, and catalogued, they are, for most purposes, lost forever. How could it be otherwise? The sheer magnitude of what we can produce to preserve records of the past—in this case, paperwork—is so vast that it perversely buries the past under its bulk, makes it more and more inaccessible to us. It's as if the past doesn't matter; it's as if the past didn't even happen. But, for all that, I discovered what, at this point, I needed to discover; in hindsight, though, I think I knew in advance what it was I would discover, and that in itself was enough of a wonder, enough of a provocation—not only the intimation I had already divined, but how I had divined it in the first place.

For, from the beginning, from the very entrance of that courier into my office, I detected a scent of something so marvelous, something so treasured in its own way that I could scarcely express what it portended for me. It is curious how, in the course of our lives, the random visit to an attic, or an old barn, or a forgotten nook somewhere among the unsurpassable wealth of all this world can rivet attention on an otherwise trivial object from the past—a toy, a book, a garment, a simple tool—whose presence precipitates a spontaneous inundation of richly sensuous imagery that surprises and overwhelms us. How curious, too, to use a word like "scent" to describe what is indeed not merely olfactory, if olfactory at all, but, beyond that, so visceral, so embedded in the composite denseness of our corporeality, that no other word will do, no reference to any other sense perception, under the circumstances, will be sufficiently versatile. Sure, such instances are memories, usually, of childhood and hence of childish things; yet of such things whose fullness for us at the time made promises to which a goodly part of our adulthood, either overtly or covertly, either wisely or foolishly, has been devoted to seeing replenished. In the moment when that courier entered my office, I detected already, in that same curious "epiphanic" way (if I may call it that), warm, tranquil dinners after Saturday matinees in winter; Christmas centerpieces on festive dining-room tables; lively Easter baskets and trays of rich, dark, aromatic chocolate; jovial papier-mâché Halloween pumpkins brimming with brightly colored orange and lime confections. Some persons might deplore that all too often, in our times, enchanted memories are associated with brand names and with the paraphernalia of a modern commercial civilization. Be that as it may, I have no regrets about the objects and phenomena that bestowed color and vivacity upon my childhood. At the time, when I was a child, I could hardly have been expected to know that I was experiencing the prolonged autumnal years of what amounted to almost a civic institution in its day, for it is now long gone—as vanished now from modern urban America as if it had never existed.

One could say that I knew little about Theodore Besserman, but I knew one vital thing, and that was one of those more complex reasons that enticed me into his lair: he was the director of what is known, at least to a small circle of people who occupy the Boston investment and philanthropic scene, as the Schefflin Foundation. And the name Schefflin said everything that needed to be said. I knew—I knew in my sinews, in my bones, in its veritable "scent"—that a carefully proffered plenitude presented itself to me as one of the most richly fragrant memories of my life. That Gothic portal, so delicately capped by its slender ogee arch, might well be identified as the office of those quondam law partners Besserman and Davidowitz; but

I knew that it also led into an entity of singular import: the home office of the Schefflin Foundation itself.

Hence I recur to what my research, in the more conventional sense, told me. Theodore Besserman had been, originally, a partner in his own firm with another attorney, Samuel Davidowitz. Much of the legal business of the firm eventually became apportioned entirely to serving the manifold needs of a single client, so much so that its offices were moved into a building erected by the client to house some of its ancillary operations. The client was Schefflins and Son, a corporation that was founded in the late nineteenth century as a simple manufactory and emporium of confectionary goods by Benjamin and Marlena Schefflin and which, in the early part of the twentieth century and under the direction of their son, Frederick, burgeoned into one of the largest producers of fine chocolates in the world and provided both title and management for an array of dining facilities initially in Boston and later for an extensive network of urban restaurants in the northeastern United States. What began as a one-room Viennese-style *konditorei* or café attached to a candy emporium was transformed gradually into a complex amalgam of luncheonettes and soda fountains, British tearooms and Parisian *patisseries*, prodigiously formal restaurants and informal grills, all collocated under the trade name of Schefflin's, a brand inscribed in the baroque curvature of a late-Renaissance calligraphy and displayed regally on all their products and over the cordial entrances of their multifarious retail and dining establishments.

After the death of his partner, and later, after the demise of Frederick Schefflin himself, Theodore Besserman had confined his work to managing several trusts established by Frederick Schefflin; among these, as I have said, was the Schefflin Foundation, which, if recognizable to those who are able to access the public records of its activities as one of the more substantial charitable trusts in the city of Boston, is also one of the most unknown to the general public, for it protects its anonymity with something like a relentless vigilance. I also learned that Theodore Besserman, now well advanced into his eighties, managed these trusts with the assistance of a staff by and large about as elderly as he was and that eventually—which is to say, in regard to such an important trust as the Schefflin Foundation, the sooner, the better—he would have to arrange for a new associate who would be partner and then, if all looked propitious to this end, a successor in the trusteeship itself. I surmised that the object of my visit, though never stated in Besserman's note, was in some fashion connected to this matter. Besserman and I, if my conjecture turned out to be true, would need, as it were, to test the waters; to probe the territories we would reconnoiter together; though I could not help but wonder, as things turned out, if the waters hadn't been, in some way, tested already and the territories, tentatively but tactfully, surveyed in advance.

I took a small measure of odd comfort in the fact that I would not be meeting Samuel Davidowitz. I knew he was deceased—a long time ago; but it was not that fact that I took comfort in, nor in anything personal about the late Samuel Davidowitz himself, about whom I knew close to nothing at all, but rather, that I would have, under such unusual circumstances, only one personage to contend with. I have to say, in retrospect, that my intuition about this matter was not wholly without merit. Besserman would be enough to contend with, although, in no sense, either then or anytime since then, have I ever had to "contend" with him in any real meaning of that word. To the contrary, Besserman is one of those people one has somehow always known, as if they unveiled, amid the particularities of their age and place, the lineaments of a venerable historical prototype that one is born, for some strange reason, already familiar with. Their character unfolds before one's gaze in a curiously predictable way—a way that is always full of surprises, yet these surprises are ever more surprising because one anticipates them and then is all the more perplexed when they occur just as they should. It is rather like visiting a rare place—a city in Italy, perhaps, situated in a mountain valley somewhere—where in the first few minutes of one's acquaintance it passes through one's mind: Why do I know this place so well already? Why do I feel at home here, as if I lived here once, relishing over a whole lifetime its sunny days and olive-groved slopes and vine-leafed verandas? I won't try to explain such recondite experiences; it would turn out to be a similar sort of thing for me in this case, with the old Gothic edifice that arose before me, with Besserman himself, and with all that would unfold in the months ahead of me. I approached the carved oaken door and rang the doorbell.

A tall, slightly bent, lean old gentleman answered the door. He wore a pair of striped pants, a white shirt and black bow tie, and a green waistcoat with gold buttons. If I had just opened the pages of a nineteenth-century novel, I might have been prepared to meet him; in reality, I was not . . . in a way. What strange attire, one would immediately think! Yet could anything else have been, at the same time, more appropriate? It matched, in motif, if not in tone as well, the handwritten note, the elfish courier in his Burberry cape, and the façade of that marvelous edifice itself. "Mr. Schofield?" he queried, even before I had the chance to speak.

"Yes, Edmund Schofield," I replied.

"Come in, Mr. Schofield. We have been expecting you. It is so nice of you to come." He ushered me into a modest vestibule and asked me if he could take my coat. He took it and hung it on a coat rack in a narrow room to the side of the vestibule. At the far end of the room was a chair and a desk and an old brass lamp over which was suspended a board for organizing keys and other equipment pertinent to the function of a porter or a concierge. On another wall was deployed an assortment of lists and announcements, prominent among which was a large poster showing the coming year's schedule of the Red Sox at Fenway Park. Next to the poster was a small religious icon of some sort. The room, despite its functionality, had a supremely "lived in" look, as if, over long years of use, it had taken on the character of its habitué and become richly imbued with his presence. I had a sense, not of glancing into a cloakroom, but of peeking into someone's most private retreat.

From the vestibule he showed me into a wide, airy, polished marble foyer, lit dimly by four brass sconces at each corner of the room and by a massive brass and crystal chandelier that hung high above an intricately inlaid marble floor. To my right was a door, left ajar in this instance, which led into a brightly phosphorescent modern office. I could make out, through the door, desks and typewriters, computers and filing cabinets. Several people were busy at their tasks. To my left was an ornate marble staircase and balustrade that led upstairs in an ascending series of right-angle turns. In the stairwell of this monumental ascent was an open, wrought-iron, utterly transparent elevator shaft; and, waiting all too ominously for me was one of those tiny glass elevators one sometimes still encounters in Europe, a crystal-cut jewelry case with large, finely cut glass panels that are etched with a variety of floral designs. At the far end of the foyer, facing the entrance doors, was the most extraordinary thing of all—a huge, shimmering glass wall, the entire expanse of which was backed by a complex grid of curvilinear iron tracery. A single glass door led into a small garden beyond—a garden, but I am almost tempted to say a cloister, for along the three sides of the garden was an arcaded gallery of delicately pointed apertures. The garden was crisscrossed by two diagonal gravel paths intersecting one another in the center, marking out four triangular flower beds. At the center, where the paths met, was a small fountain—four or, at most, five feet high and made of a travertine masonry perhaps, more baroque than classical in its series of basins and spires and runnels, one surmounting the other and peaked by a delicate, acanthus-leaved finial at the top. The flow of water, I quickly discerned, had been turned off—ostensibly for the winter season. The outermost or lowest basin of the fountain was rimmed by a broad marble band that formed a kind of bench, where I imagined one could, if one had the leisure to do so, sit by the fountain and, when it was in operation, watch its waters play before one's eyes. There was evidence there of a luxuriant growth of water lilies, now dormant. It was perhaps, in most contexts—and certainly I have seen many—a fairly ordinary sort of garden adornment; luxury hotels and casinos seem to compete with one another in how grand they can make these things. But, in this case, at so much more modest a scale, each of its basins exhibited its own rather special moldings and designs, and its soft, presumably travertine masonry was tinted a soft ivory tone and was varied by such mellow strains of violet and amber over its slightly uneven surface that the whole piece looked vaguely like some rich and delicate blossom in the half light of the garden.

The concierge, Mr. Dougherty, as I later learned his name was, conducted me, as I expected he would, to the elevator and told me that Mr. Besserman's office was located at the top, or fifth, floor. I confess, to my embarrassment, that I was somewhat diffident about entering that ethereal little wrought-iron box with its crystal panels, that spindly looking "contraption," as I came, over time, to think of it, having considered proper elevators as being spacious and secure compartments made of stainless steel or other materials that were run by pushing innocuous buttons and that shot at high speeds upward through immense, durable shafts and whose mechanisms modern technology, had, politely and antiseptically, rendered invisible to one's eyes. Here I would have to operate, at my own initiative, a door and a latch and a grate and a handle. I would actually have to drive this thing, if one could call it that, though admittedly there was nowhere else to go but up. Here I would also have the dubious pleasure of watching the antique and thoroughly exposed system of pulleys and cords, as attenuated as they looked, slowly revolving in little circles above my head and drawing me upward, with the occasional hesitation now and then and with the momentarily slight—and ever so unnerving—swing, as I moved from one floor to the next, reminding me that I was actually suspended from something or other over an ever deepening abyss below me. But my misgivings were premature. In fact, no "contraption" of any sort could have been better outfitted for a passage up through that lavishly ornamental staircase and from one superbly appointed landing to another, each one with its own décor, each presenting a fineness that I found, for reasons I certainly cannot wholly explain, inviting, humane, and reassuring.

On the fifth and final floor, I came to a stop, opened the grate, and stepped out of an elevator with which I was now on the best of terms. The lobby of the fifth floor was the finest of all the landings I had seen, with especially high ribbed ceilings, covered with frescoes of orchids and parrots and, surprisingly, the occasional head of a giraffe, its parded neck and nubby-horned head angling up through the foliage and its lustrous black eyes peering quixotically at me through fronds of billowing palms. Something, someone whimsical had had a hand in this; there could be no doubt of that. At the far end of the landing was a ponderous oaken door. I knew it was Besserman's office. There was no secretary there to announce my presence by making the appropriate call or pushing the appropriate buzzer. I tapped at the door.

My introduction to Theodore Besserman was remarkably informal. After all, the circumstances of our meeting seemed most attuned to some ceremonious reception, replete with formal salutations, delivery of properly inscribed and validated credentials, even, if so required, the submission of an imperial baton, or whatever. But later reflection confirmed that there was no disharmony here. I had simply not understood, at the time, the genre of ceremony we were engaged in; for, as I would learn again and again, Besserman's life was ceremony itself, a register of protocols so deep, so many-faceted, so flexible and responsive to particularities in their assiduous exercise that one would have thought that what appeared to be informality itself had been enshrined as the most studious of social disciplines. Thus, if our ensuing chatter was chatter, more or less, it was also a prelude, necessary and indispensable, to whatever followed. I had been marshaled into a somewhat low-slung but comfortable divan, its thick fabric well-worn with usage and facing directly toward a huge hearth. Above the hearth was a large, elegantly framed portrait of a man dressed in the formal attire of at least a half century ago. Around me in a high, cavernous, oak-paneled chamber were disposed a variety of tables covered with framed photographs, drawings, and other items, and, further off, were bookshelves and display cases filled with old albums, mementos, and more photographs and drawings of many kinds. In a glass case I noticed a violin, highly polished and mounted prominently on an ebony support.

I recognized immediately, of course, that I had entered a sanctuary, a very precious one at that, whose bountiful inventory would have, and did have, as it turned out, many a marvelous story to tell. Besserman himself sat opposite me, resident—I am tempted to say—in a tufted leather winged chair drawn up close to the hearth but tilted outward at a slight angle. It was colossal enough to make him, colossal as he was, look diminutive by contrast. One was, at first impression, inclined to think of him as a short man, yet he was of about medium height—as tall as I am, in fact. It's just that his breadth, his massive horizontal conformation, as rectilinear as a block of wood; his wide, large-featured, swarthy face, the capacious lateral expanse of his forehead capped by silvery gray hair streaked with black; and a broad-shouldered, brownish, out-of-date double-breasted suit with impossibly splayed lapels—all conspired to cancel out whatever was remotely vertical in his figure. Add to that the steep Gothic lines of that high-arched mansard chamber, the tall mullioned lancet windows with their glittering red and blue and violet stained-glassed medallions, a fireplace big enough for the average person to stand upright in, an array of richly napped oriental carpets spread here and there, and that well-seasoned leather chair that towered over him, and he looked, by contrast, like a gnome, beneficent and serene, occupying for the time being the domain of a friendly giant. Despite his advanced age, his eyes were attentive and warm, and his thick, gnarly hands moved quickly and precisely as a kind of rhythmic supplement to his speech, as if he were a choirmaster conducting an *a cappella* piece that he himself was performing. The whole tenor of his face and physique evinced the most unflagging vitality. The only sign of age—if indeed it were that at all—was the occasional implication in what he said and how he said it that I was not the only person he was speaking to at the moment, as if there were others present in that magical chamber whose needs and interests had to be addressed as well.

I have already pointed out that he struck me then, as ever afterward, as a prototype I had always known, though I don't know from what source I would have drawn that knowledge. But something even further was involved, something at the time even more mystifying: I seemed to recognize him in some curious way, as if I had seen him before—seen him not as a prototype but as an individual. Had I passed by him one day on the street, or in a hallway of the Suffolk County Courthouse, where the pathways of briefcase-bearing attorneys could be expected to cross from time to time, or in some situation where his physical appearance had left a permanent, if evasive, imprint on my mind? Or did he look like someone I knew when I was a child—perhaps like the Lebanese grocer whose image was dimly implanted somewhere in me and whose lettuce and eggplants, flatbreads and hummus, back in those days of little corner stores, my parents were all too happy to purchase? I could not, for all my efforts, place him.

So, as I said, we chatted. Did I know so-and-so? Were his father and mother still alive? When did my company change its law offices to the new high-rise building we now occupy? Why on earth did it do that when it had such a nice place already? How is this person's health, and is that person retired yet? How is my family—my wife and my children? How are my parents? My siblings? He asked that as if he had known them personally. But how could he have known them personally? And so forth. I had the strange presentiment that he knew all the answers already. The way he asked those questions seemed to indicate that he did. So what was he doing?

I had expected to find a recluse; and a recluse he was. Yet he was a recluse who knew everything that was going on around him; he was a hermit whose hermitage gave him an uncluttered vista of the complex world that scurried blindly up and down the alleyways of a metropolis too preoccupied to trace or to understand its own movements—rather like the amused observer of the activities transpiring on a frenetic anthill spread out beneath him. Meanwhile, as the conversation continued, it occurred to me that any really formal business between the two of us was to be deflected to another day—that, after all, could wait. It could wait because there were more important things to do and also because I realized that Besserman had made up his mind about me. I did not come as a postulant for anything. But I did come as a person already assumed to be, *in potentia*, an associate—that I did not know. In time, I would find out, again and again, how very much Besserman knew and, despite his perpetually probative and tentative disposition, how very much he had resolved, long before one would have thought he had, what was propitious to arrive at as a resolution. I perceived then, out of all that chatter, that I would never have received that note in the first place if Besserman did not already have access to all the sources necessary for my recommendation. He had decided; and he assumed, with the usual astuteness of his assumptions, that my reply to his inquiry was the mark of my decision to accept whatever arrangement he had in mind. I arrived, in that respect, in an unusually receptive mood. As far as he was concerned, I am sure, why would anyone in my position refuse? And he was correct. I had made my choice as well. Our small talk was, in this sense, not prior but posterior to a decision that we now realized we both had made, even though the terms of the decision remained not so much to be negotiated as to be deciphered.

In another sense, our chatter did anticipate something really important—something that I realized I was expected to initiate. It was not long before I did so; it simply took an unintentional, perhaps, moment of distraction, a shift of the eyes to that large, full-length portrait that hung over the mantelpiece of the great hearth. Besserman, calm in his manner, settled into an even deeper calm. I now knew that mere social graces were to be set behind us. "Ah," he exclaimed, "I see you have noticed. That is him. That is Frederick Schefflin."

I learned quickly that morning that to gaze upon the portrait we had turned to see was to apprehend not simply the image of a man but, rather, the features, however obliquely suggested by the painter's brush, of a legacy of intellect and character so intrinsically textured that it would take Besserman no little effort to reveal for my benefit even partially its variegated shades and subtle modulations of meaning. I saw that Besserman held his old friend and colleague in the highest esteem—an esteem that, I became convinced, must have been reciprocal, for it was of the kind, fecund and generous and many-sided, that only equals can confer upon one another and that can be fostered only within a relationship as mutual as it is deep. Yet there was more than esteem involved here: one detected the presence of a task enjoined and a task fulfilled, and consequently of a fealty (if I may be permitted to use such a chivalric word) so profound that, even in his resplendent mastery of things, Besserman was, in every sense of the expression that has ever really mattered, truly "the good steward."

The portrait itself, suspended over the hearth in a gilded frame, is a full-length depiction of a tall, raw-boned, heavy-limbed man in his early fifties, with short, flaxen hair and uneasily, ruggedly perhaps, attired in a dark blue suit with a white, high, round-collared shirt and a narrow golden tie pin carefully secured into place under the knot of the tie. The portrait is muted and dark, for the most part—a combination of deep blues and blacks, except for an intense light that seems to radiate from the face and hands and that endues the entire piece with an aura of luminosity. The right hand, muscular and gnarly, rests casually at the side of the figure, while the left hand seems to repose against a bronze statuette, a mounted horseman, perhaps, on a small pedestal of black marble and positioned on a dark mahogany desk or console table of some sort. The face itself is oval in shape, distinctly plain, without any especially marked feature, almost—one might say—bland to a fault except for the tenderness and penetration of the light blue eyes. Something in that portrait, perhaps the focus of the eyes outward from the portrait and directed to a distant object somewhere, makes one think, oddly, of a lumberjack or a forester or a ship's pilot, one who is accustomed to ranging through open spaces, or to gazing into a perpetual glare of sun and snow and seascape, or to broaching, with utmost tenacity and utmost trust, sustained opposition and the challenge of starkly elemental forces. The portrait emanates the most rarefied blend I have ever seen of energy and composure, of confident but unassuming self-possession.

Besserman studied the portrait for a few moments, as if there was something there in that image already so familiar to him yet which he needed to refresh his memory about or to consult before we could proceed any further. Then he interjected into our silence the single comment: "He was relatively young when he died—it was in his late fifties. It happened while he was on one of his many journeys to Italy. He came down with an influenza that rapidly metamorphosed into a fatal pneumonia. He died in Florence."

I acknowledged this pronouncement with a nod, and we were silent again. But I found it peculiar that Besserman would begin what was clearly to be a narrative—what would be, indeed, a narrative of a very complex order—in just this way. For the tone of the pronouncement implied several things: an untimely event that came, in Besserman's view, I assumed, too early and thus it must have, in some way and among other sufficiently grave matters, left an intangible substratum of unfinished business; yet, at the same time, it was a termination of a life in a distant locale that, in one respect, made such unfinished business impossible to conclude under those circumstances, even as it, in another respect, rendered such a conclusion, as precipitate as it had been, as "fitting" as assuredly it was. I decided at once to pursue what was apparently a significant aspect of the second implication, figuring that it gave easier access to whatever else needed to be considered. "I presume then," I said, "that Frederick Schefflin enjoyed Italy and visited it often."

Besserman responded immediately to this anticipated overture. "Yes, he did love Italy. There were many things he loved about it, and he went there as frequently as he could. But I think he especially loved the architecture. As a young man he had wanted to be an architect, though constraints in his early years hindered that intent. Nevertheless he was well-versed in the works and the treatises of the great Italian architects, in Alberti and Bernini and Palladio. Ruskin's studies of Venice had impressed him deeply at a young age. And, in later years, he studied Sebastiano Serlio's treatise on domestic architecture. For that he had to consult original documents stored at Columbia University in New York. Though his ambitions to be an architect were to be, as we shall see, displaced by other obligations, he did have several opportunities to exercise his architectural proclivities, and architecture became one of several avocations he pursued earnestly in his life. He had an important hand in the design of many of the edifices that housed the Schefflin enterprises; he designed his final residence at Madison Street in the Newton suburbs, and one jewel of his work is this very building in which you sit at this moment.

"Now, is not this, in itself, a perfect marvel? And doesn't it make you think of Ruskin's Venetian reveries?"

"I regret to say I am not familiar with Ruskin's 'reveries,' as you call them," I answered, "but it is, as you say, a perfect marvel. And, no doubt, a somewhat whimsical one at that!"

"Whimsical?" Besserman retorted.

"I am thinking of the giraffes in the foyer, the ones depicted overhead in the frescoes, their heads tilted coquettishly in the fronds," I explained.

"Ah, those giraffes! Those delightful giraffes! How curious it is that when one lives with something for long periods of time, one sometimes no longer particularly notices them. But whimsical? Well, yes—whimsical indeed. There's an explanation for that, even a rather complex one, which we will get to in time. I should note, at the moment, that in everything Frederick did, there were other sensibilities that had their say, that made their presence felt, and that Frederick loved and nourished as his own. But more about that later!"

And it was, I could acknowledge, despite my impatience to know it all at once, a perfect marvel, too, that my acquaintance with the revered memory of Frederick Schefflin should begin on this note. For Besserman was anything but a garrulous old gentleman bent upon detaining a younger man with disparate, if perfervid, recollections of a long-deceased companion. Here, as with everything, he had his purposes; and the order in which he put them, though often inscrutable at first—even, if I may repeat the word, whimsical in its own way—was precise and to the point. As important as the charitable trust he represented was, it was most important to the degree that it stood firmly, if flexibly, within the *sensus largior* of a legacy grounded not, finally, in the bounteousness of Frederick Schefflin's resources but in the bounteousness of his character. It was this legacy that, as piecemeal as the process must be, Besserman felt himself obliged to illuminate. The marvel, doubly retold in view of the considerable resources of the trust and of the effort and skill obviously requisite for the original mustering of these resources, was that Besserman rarely, on this first morning or in the many colloquies that were to follow, dwelt on or even made much of a point of Frederick Schefflin's prowess as a man of commerce. That much he took for granted, even as he similarly took the trust for granted—as if such matters were not, at least for him, what was exceptional in this case but were, in the last analysis, sufficiently ordinary within their own province as to be scarcely worthy of too much reflection. Boston alone could, undoubtedly, boast a thousand men and women who had done as much in their own distinctive domains. What was exceptional, what was not ordinary at this juncture anyway, was Frederick Schefflin himself. I would learn, and learn soon, that there was great deal more than Frederick involved, but Frederick was, in a way, a threshold one had to cross or a portal one had to enter before other marvels could be revealed.

I also would learn why this was so. Besserman, in all our acquaintance thereafter, would never attempt to define in explicit terms, in clearly delineated concepts or propositions, what Frederick's legacy really was, and that's why it came as piecemeal as it did, in a sequence of anecdotes and details, even more tellingly, perhaps, in the barest adumbrations of an attitude—yes, a persistent attitude that marked Frederick for who and what he was. Maybe that is why the portrait was so important. It is the bearing in that portrait, in the way the figure seems to be "holding" himself, not a "holding in" but a "holding forth," a gesture of generosity, a conferral—not of goods simply—but of a good that could evoke, out of the depths of the beholder, a promise, both germane and beneficent to that beholder, that entailed a task and a responsibility. In this light, in this very luminosity itself, those who lived and moved within his ambiance and were responsive to what he held forth before them in so many ways were, in and of themselves, the Schefflin legacy in its essence. It is that—that "beautiful legacy," as Besserman in time would call it—which I most needed to know about. It is that which, ever more fully and significantly, I would realize, I, too, needed not simply to know but also, if it were in my power to do so, to become.

"You understand," Besserman went on, "he never intended, initially, to go into his parents' business. Nor was he intended to do so. If he became, in the course of time, as many would agree, a *chocolatier extraordinaire*, it was more by default than by calling. His parents saw his unusual gifts and, as was true in so many immigrant families, were bent upon seeing those gifts directed toward, and perfected in, one of the learned professions. Consequently, while he was still very young, they made no motion for him to consider the business, to apprentice himself in its skills, nor even to expend much effort in helping out in his spare time. But the latter, as one might well expect, he did willingly and abundantly, even over the protestations of his parents, though all the while maintaining his vigorous resolution to be, as the intimate community of friends and associates who surrounded the Schefflins liked to call him, the 'young scholar.' Benjamin Schefflin also, in the early years when things had settled for a while and before Frederick was born, had requisitioned from the old country a treasured heirloom saved for him by his parents: a fine and richly toned cello. The young Frederick took to this instrument as if he were born to play it and achieved, early in life, a mastery of its musical qualities that he was never to lose.

"So, as you can see, the business itself did not have prime importance for him. One can equally conjecture that never in his life did it have prime importance for him, despite the wealth of intelligence and imagination he poured into it. His music, his travels in the search for and appreciation of architectural beauty, his nexus of devoted familial and social relations, his later civic projects and commitments, even the trust he would found as a memorial for his parents and which I now am privileged to administer—all these had priority for him. His sudden and premature death in Florence, as saddening and even as shocking as it was to all of us, nevertheless had the stamp of a curiously fitting conclusion, there amid all that artistic splendor that so occupied his life and mind.

"The business itself was naturally, at first, a rather small operation and was located on the first two stories of a narrow three-story building tucked away in a crowded street not far from the old South Station. The section of the first floor that faced the street was a shop, a *konditorei*, you could call it, managed by Marlena and, as I have been told, was invariably charming, with its warm aromas and colorful displays of candied fruit, assorted old-world pastries, and chocolate confections of many types that began to draw customers from all over the Boston area. The loveliness of that setting would provide the model for the innumerable emporia, the Viennese-style cafés, and ultimately the full-scale restaurants that would follow in the course of time. The back part of the first floor was a kitchen where Marlena made those delectable pastries. The floor above was the domain of Benjamin Schefflin, and what a domain it was! Here, among simmering copper kettles and cast-iron ovens, the cocoa beans were unloaded from the burlap bags shipped in from Central America or the west coast of Africa. They were toasted and crushed and blended into the chocolate that acquired, in its day, such an illustrious reputation. Benjamin and Marlena formed, as we would express it nowadays, the perfect manufacturing-marketing team. What he so expertly produced, she just as expertly sold.

"The third floor of the establishment was the apartment where the family lived, where, amid the abundance of its days, Frederick studied his books and practiced the cello, and, from where, when he could spare the time, he would issue down into the purlieus below to assist with a bulky burlap bag just arrived by horse cart from the nearby wharves, or to assist his mother in setting out some Easter display in the one show window they had at the front of the building, or to run off to the flower market and hoist back on his shoulders panniers of the spring lilies with which she festooned her glassy counters and smoothly lacquered shelves. Frederick, as she told me many years later, was fascinated with the enterprise, and he came to know it with thoroughness and precision. Though it was hard work, she assured me that it never constituted any kind of drudgery for them. They delighted in it, taking it on in the lively spirit of entertainers regaling the tastes and predilections of their clientele, and were infinitely pleased with every innovation they could contrive and which they thought their customers would enjoy, whether it was a new flavor for the center of a fine chocolate or a new presentation—perhaps a lemon frosted rabbit—for an Easter cookie. Their lives, one might say, were filled with experimentation: collecting and devising new recipes, revising old ones, and refining the extraordinary and complicated techniques (and the technologies they required) involved in producing the kinds of items they made. Frederick, you can be sure, was always the first to taste whatever fresh concoction his parents had come up with; and, with such culinary mentors, you can be certain that he developed at an early age a fine palate for what did and didn't work.

"Old Benjamin, of course, had it 'in his blood'; although he was the descendent of lumbermen who had lived and worked in the steep woodlands of the Vosges and the Black Forest for generations, part of his lineage also comprised prosperous innkeepers and master confectioners whose professional habitat extended throughout much of the region, through contiguous portions of Switzerland and Alsace and the Grand Duchy of Baden-Württemberg on the thither side of the Rhine. He brought generations of that tradition, all that experience and know-how, with him when he first unloaded his meager belongings on the wharves of Boston harbor."

Besserman interrupted his monologue, tilted forward out of his massive chair, stood up, and ambled slowly over to the leaden glass windows, where he stood for a minute or so in silence, as if studying the street below. The morning light from the window flooded in around him so that I could see him only as a massive silhouette against the multicolored surface of the panes. He turned toward me again and rested back against the window embrasure. Small, brightly colored splotches of light slanting through the stained-glass medallions played over the surface of his brown suit in little harlequin refractions. He raised one hand, indicating some small shift of subject. "Then there was the mother's side of the family. Marlena took readily enough to the business that Benjamin had founded; but her background was different. She was an extraordinary woman — forceful, dedicated, decisive. I knew her personally in her final years, well after Benjamin's death. These years were devoted to memories, and she found in me an eager audience, if I might say so myself. I was very young at the time, freshly emancipated from the tiresome juggling of night-school law classes and daytime jobs and eager to be 'part of things' in a growing firm that accidentally found me and found the services provided by the minuscule backroom office I had set up with my partner, Samuel Davidowitz, useful for some limited legal footwork and then kept us on for reasons altogether obscure to us. I think we fit in well with the rough-shod aura of the enterprise, the pioneer atmosphere of something like a Conestoga wagon lumbering, however adroitly and resolutely, into unknown prairies.

"I wanted to know its history as well as I could. It was from Marlena that I learned about the early years of Frederick and about their lives, for Frederick was a taciturn man and was little given to talking about himself. Marlena had arrived in Boston about the same time as did Benjamin but independently, for they met here in the city for the first time and were married. She was, to some extent, a political refugee. I do not think that Benjamin's immigration was motivated by political concerns. If he found himself disaffected with the *ancien régime* of his homeland, I suspect it had to do with little more than the inconveniences of permits and regulations that potentially made the decoration of a wedding cake a legal process of interminable complications. On Marlena's side of the family, in the province of Swabia, matters were different. Her people had been pastors and schoolteachers, wandering scholars and musicians, jurists and choirmasters—modest enough employment in such epochs, but embedded, as little else was, in learnedness, in moral gravity, in enough detachment from the immediate exigencies of social and economic life that one could observe, and reflect upon, the conditions in which people attempted to sustain their lives.

"And the conditions were not easy. Frederick grew up infused during many a dinnertime conversation with the legends of recalcitrant forebears and especially of a maternal grandfather who carried on, as the story went, unremitting psychological and legal contention with the local barons. He was a schoolmaster and an organist in a small village known by the colorful name of Drachenstein, or Dragon's Rock, who used his spare time to hunt through the intricate and long-standing web of feudal rights and privileges, often difficult to find among the ancient ledgers where they had slumbered from time immemorial and, just as often, granted their archaic language, difficult to interpret. But they still exercised, in principle, a kind of authority over the communal life of the people and the various 'estates' into which they were divided. I say 'in principle' because many of these statutes, these contractual agreements, were hundreds of years old, had either fallen into disuse or forgetfulness, and had, consequently, been eroded and usurped over time by the personages who had the power and interest to do so. His purpose was to discover them, to renew them, and to reassert the rights of the village communes to land and resources long denied them. The task was neither easy nor without peril. The rights to the water from a remote well could necessitate interminable litigation. He had, of course, many hair-raising scrapes with the local authorities—the stuff of legends, one might add, though sometimes lamentably comic, slapstick even, in their own spectral way. One escapade involved the preposterous scenario of hiding valuable barnyard fowl in the church's choir loft and the fortissimo rendition of a Buxtehude fugue to disguise from rapacious tax-collectors the irrepressible quacking of some refractory ducks. Well, I shall not go into all the details of this matter, but, if it seems rather remote to you, Mr. Schofield, I would ask you to place it in a context of the frequent destitution and famine that the peasantry often faced when crops failed or when some military expedition or other saw fit to strut through its territory on the way to a princely engagement and to despoil ruthlessly its herds and granges—from which blight it often took years to recover. The rebellious schoolmaster, courageous as he was, certainly had his work cut out for him.

"In any case, Mr. Schofield, there was another tradition to uphold—at least in principle. I suppose it were to belabor a point to insist that, in one sense certainly, Marlena's somewhat visionary impact on the young Frederick may have been more significant than the more toilsome and focused influence of Benjamin. Yet the two sources would fuse—fuse fruitfully and permanently, as events turned out. As I said before, both Marlena and Benjamin agreed that the pursuit of a learned profession, rather than business, was most appropriate for Frederick. Even when Frederick graduated from high school two years too early to advance to college, his parents consented to his devoting of the intervening time entirely to the study of the cello. He never became equal to a true professional in the exercise of this skill; but he certainly aspired to, and achieved, a standard of excellence few amateurs realize, especially in the narrow range of eighteenth-century music, which he so enjoyed. Then, in his sixteenth year, he prepared to go to college. But it never happened. This happy concordance of things was irrevocably altered."

Besserman paused and once more traced his steps back to the hearth and resumed his seat in the lofty armchair beside the fireplace. As I watched him,

I felt some strange, barely perceptible somberness of mood come over him. It was so strange indeed, so strange in its subtlety, that I am still not able to characterize it accurately, even though I was to experience it again, later that morning, in another context. "Tragic," if one means anything serious by that word, would be immeasurably too strong to do it justice; yet it was the only word that, at the moment, I could find to interpret this change of demeanor and to solicit from an abruptly solemn Besserman whatever contrivance of events it was that had countered such a "happy concordance of things" and had incurred, even in remembrance, his corresponding distress. But Besserman was not disposed to the word either, and when I mentioned it, he rejected it out of hand.

"No, not a tragedy," he dissented, "The Schefflins were not a tragic people, nor were the events of their lives so grand or so catastrophic as to merit such a designation. The Schefflins were too prudential a folk for that kind of thing, too organized, too cautious. They lived too fully in the awareness of peril to be ever surprised by it, and even less overwhelmed by it. They were always prepared for any eventuality—had backup resources aplenty, had lifeboats stocked and ready to launch, knew what to do, knew not, in any case, to panic. To detect the presence of an immediate danger was, for them, but to shift, ever so slightly, their ordinary stance. It was, I think, their disposition to recognize how things are generally not under one's own control that allowed them to master, as they did, those few things that are, and to use those latter things, as best as one can and as the occasion demands, to tack to windward through all the varied and haphazard resistances that events inevitably confront us with. It was this recognition that lay at the roots of their courage and magnanimous dexterity.

"Here I cannot claim that I know exactly what happened. I can only frame such conjectures as give some minimal coherence to what I heard from Marlena and what I would hear from others and see unfold, in its manifold consequences decades later, around me. I have never had reason to believe that the stability of the business was ever directly compromised. To the contrary, the peril that arose was centered in the milieu in which the Schefflins lived and worked, and in which, under often troublesome circumstances, they had managed, together with an intimate circle of friends and associates, to create a haven of modest prosperity and cultivated repose. In this respect it didn't really matter what activity compelled their attention at a given moment: the conduct of business over a lunch of beer and bratwurst at Jakob Wirth's, a picnic on some breezy day at one of those many beaches north of Boston, a gymnastics exercise at the local *Turnverein*, a canoe excursion into the wilderness of northern New Hampshire, or a Sunday afternoon devoted to Bach, to Telemann, to Haydn, to so many others—yes, one of those so-called continental Sundays celebrated with plentiful food and drink by their peers and regarded with such dour misgivings by the more traditional, old-line denizens of Boston. But it all bespoke such measured resilience of days and seasons, it was so very much their own, that even here the illusion of its permanence could undeniably assert itself. But matters did deteriorate around them, matters induced as much by the vagaries of a robust but remorseless economic moil with its dips and rises as by anything else. Naturally, they were aware of all of this, but it had not encroached on that sanctuary of leisure they had fashioned so assiduously over the years.

"Now, Mr. Schofield—Edmund, if I may call you that—in all my ruminations on this matter, collating this and that from my conversations with Marlena, I have never been able to specify what catalyst in particular served to bring the emergency directly before their eyes. As the business grew, they needed to bring additional staff into its operations; and from that source, if not also from a multitude of others, they would hear a great deal and would take seriously what they heard. Then there was the sudden illness and consequent debilitation of old Benjamin himself, with the more immediate effect of bringing Frederick into the business and displacing, for the meantime, as was initially envisaged, his other plans. But all of that was enough to act as a prism through which what was undefined and hence ignored at the onset became sharply focused and variously clarified into its component elements. It would have been difficult for them, ripened as they were in the experience of immigrant life, not to feel the incommensurable hurt that seemed to engulf their favored enclave. For Europe was pouring forth a tidal wave of its impoverished upon the shores of the Republic, and what awaited so many of these impoverished was further impoverishment. The Schefflins were well aware of what it was like to stand on a strange wharf, trying to absorb a chaos of warehouses and lofts and smoky factories, knowing scarcely a word of the language, struggling with roots that still clung to a foreign soil, suffering from the acute loneliness and sense of abandonment induced by moving from a settled, if constrictive, social ambiance to a freewheeling, disruptive environment where one really was on one's own, and having just enough money in one's pocket to get through another week or two, if one was lucky. Moreover, the city of Boston was, at the time, declining into serious, endemic, and periodically recurring economic recession, sometimes of considerable severity. It is difficult to imagine such conditions in our time, since Boston's economic recovery, having, at this point, occurred so long ago, has restored an opulence and an industry that we tend to take for granted as its natural and permanent condition.

"But there were other factors involved as well: it was not simply the deluge of immigration that posed such a problem; something else had emerged as never before. They had known it all the time and had made with it, however disconcerting it had been for them, whatever accommodations had been required. But not until these crucial years did they become alerted to the magnitude of its force or the pain of its coercion. For America had its barons too: precinct bosses; city commissioners in the pay of this or that group; organized crime gangs; corporate interests and trusts that were busy diverting immense investment assets from Boston to more immediately profitable sectors of the country; those who found it useful to exacerbate, from one direction or the other, the strains between labor and capital or to stoke anger and resentment between the older population and the newcomers, who were thought of as piling up like unwelcome ocean chaff upon their shores.

"Indeed, it would have been easy enough for the Schefflins, at this point, to escape from this deluge, to pull up stakes, abandoning their familiar quarters of the city and striking off for new horizons, as so many enterprising folk were doing, and for very good reasons. But to have done that would have been to abandon not only their own small group of workers but others who, in those intricate webs in which we find ourselves in our lives, depended upon them as well. They decided to stay. One could not contain or even oppose successfully that scope of events that faced them. But they could ride, as it were, the vectors of its energy, and snatch from its turmoil, at least for a portion of its multitudes, a communality of life that was both measured and good. And if a portion could be salvaged, its repercussions for others might very well be both profound and enduring.

"Three years later, when Frederick was twenty, the ailing Benjamin died. Several days before his death, reclining on his bed like a great white-bearded Isaac, he summoned his sole heir to his bedside. Not even Marlena, who stood by the door during this final colloquy between father and son, could ever bring herself to disclose the words that passed between them. But one can be reasonably sure that no mandate of any kind, no injunction, was imposed; only a pointing occurred—a pointing in a direction that, with the weight of a firm and benevolent sagacity behind it, could enjoin little else but the fullest exercise of one's freedom. And such freedom meant, as I think it has always meant, to accept a burden from another's hands, to walk the second mile, to fulfill a promise, to take on as one's own the uncompleted task. I tell you, if such a conferral happened, it was not, and would not turn out to be, the last time that Frederick should act accordingly in his life. Another's task became his own, and the fruit it bore was the fruit of both. It is hard to know, in such circumstances, just who the giver and the receiver are. The roles are interchangeable. Frederick himself so often maintained a principle, one that we try to observe here in the Foundation, that the prime purpose of giving is to enable another to give; to give freedom to the person who receives by allowing them to give back, in a sense, what becomes his or her own.

"In the end, Frederick never, finally, went to college. One might say that such a project was deferred until it would be more advantageous to follow that course of action. Instead, he had chosen to set aside several years of his life in order to help steady the business and to assist his parents before moving on to other things. Naturally, with the death of old Benjamin such a need became ever more pressing. One cannot help but wonder what kind of loss may have been entailed here. Perhaps there was not much of a loss at all. It is difficult, in our time, when we are all too eager to pass on the education of our offspring to institutions only partially qualified for that task, to understand how important the family and its multifarious connections once were in the mediation of a high humanist tradition and of the judicious assimilation of intellectual, civic, and artistic legacies: to appreciate its ability, and its ability alone, to foster a community of memory and to sift through and conserve the dialects of our origins, dialects that exceed the power of articulation itself, for they speak to us out of both the conviviality and the sufferings of our shared experience. This, you might say, was the keystone of Frederick's education.

"What more can I say? Can you imagine the surprise of the two Rubashevsky brothers, Igor and Pavlov, when the young Frederick entered their ramshackle establishment on Haymarket Street with his shoulders slightly rolled forward like a lumberman preparing to stoop and heave up a log on his back—a characteristic gesture of his when he was at the threshold of some momentous decision. The Rubashevsky bank was little more than a storefront operation, an immigrant bank in the best sense of the term. It has since, of course, metamorphosed into a major Boston financial institution, bearing one of those innocuous and somewhat pretentious names that banks are so fond of and that you are, I am sure, familiar with. But at that time it was a single disorderly room, jammed with files and papers and a ponderous black safe, where the portly brothers sat at their desks like a brace of ruffed grouse nested amid piles of manila folders and stacks of ledgers. In a cashier's cage, the young Simon Arcadevitch fluttered back and forth rather like a timorous parakeet, his wispy pate already in an advanced stage of molting. The brothers were accustomed to Frederick; they had done business with his father for years, and they knew Frederick as a frequent emissary, fetching deposits and payrolls back and forth from the Schefflin establishment to the bank. They realized, even before Frederick had a chance to speak, that something decidedly confounding was about to take place.

"And their reaction! Simon Arcadevitch liked to tell of it so many years later, having observed it all in stupefied alarm from his ungainly perch in the cashier's cage. What exclamations! What shuffling of papers and thumping of desks! What raising of hands and slapping of foreheads! What excited brandishing of extemporarily clasped paper bouquets in front of the calm face of Frederick! The vociferous protestations! The impossibility of it all! But Frederick successfully, proficiently, presented his case. He was thoroughly prepared, had considered the not inconsiderable risks, was ready to answer every objection, and understood the implications of what he was proposing with clear and succinct insight. The Rubashevskys, on their part, had always been tough players, were accustomed, through long experience, to see through the occasional *luftmensch,* however well-intentioned, showing up periodically at their doors, though they knew from the start that Frederick was anything but that. But, through a miracle upon a miracle, as they insisted, they provided the financial backing Frederick had sought. That was a great deal of money to hand over to a very young man whose primary collateral was his character.

"Shortly thereafter, a steamer arrived from Europe carrying the special equipment Frederick had designed and ordered. The machinery had been manufactured in England by the only tooling companies in the world prepared at this time for this kind of work. It was set up in a rented loft building near the Charles River. Raw materials in copious amounts arrived from Africa, from the sugar refineries of Louisiana, from the cherry groves of Oregon, from all over the world. A substantial workforce, mostly Irish and Italian, was hired and trained for the multitudinous tasks that needed to be carried out. Soon enough, Schefflin's, the new enterprise, was in business.

"From this point on, does not the story unfold in its manifold way like some wonderful blossom from a soil whose depth and richness surpass our ability to pay it sufficient homage? One cannot but wonder at the vision that inspired the young Frederick and with which he was able to inspire others. Partly it had its roots in some deeply buried memory of those guilds that thrived in the 'free cities' throughout medieval Europe with their devotion to craftsmanship and to a ceremonial and communal way of life that accompanied it. Partly it was invested with what Frederick had learned, and would continue to learn throughout his life, by studying and visiting, here and abroad, corporate interests that had made an erstwhile effort to fashion a genuinely communal project out of its work. And then there was that sense of civic obligation, the observance of a common good whose demands must, in the end, help to direct the particular goods of all other social projects, public and private, precisely by limiting their authority and curbing their claims, and which we are all bound, in our own fallible ways, to observe. It was the surpassing achievement of Schefflin's to create a modern industrial enterprise in which all of its members could participate in its integrity and fruition. For Frederick, the 'bottom line,' as they say, was the value of the human energy and intelligence vested in the work of the corporation, the prospering in every individual involved in that initiative that, among other things and however limited it may be in many cases, gives to an individual a sense of place and importance in this world. In the end, the employer worked primarily for the employees, kept in intimate contact with them at all times, and gave primacy to the welfare and integrity of the workforce. And the employees, in turn, worked for the customers, whose highest expectations they would always strive to fulfill.

"Be that as it may, within a decade of Frederick's entrance into the Rubashevskys' bank, Schefflin's had become a major industry with its own complex of buildings, which produced a wide variety of goods for its ever appreciative customers and which also flourished internally with a host of associations: with a dramatics club and a musical society and sports teams, with medical and legal services, with mutual aid funds and a credit union and educational programs, and with participation in many forms of civic and religious life that extended far beyond the confines of the corporation itself. I should add that the purpose here was not to turn the company into the center of people's lives—far from it; but rather it was to create contexts in which the tonalities of a full human life could resonate and echo from one portion to another, each preserving its own distinctive and independent character. Eventually, as you know well by now, the company expanded into other goods and services for its clientele—the cafés and restaurants, the confectionary goods and ice creams—that spread to New York City and then to many other eastern cities. It was a distinctive virtue of Schefflin's that it could appropriate as it did the multitude of skills and traditions brought to its operations by diverse immigrant groups with their sensitivity to seasonal festivals and how to commemorate them in colorful displays. As such, it was a vibrant testimonial to the manifold ways in which the Old World was not left behind but rather flowered in the New World with ever resurgent vigor. During the Christmas season, for example, a large portion of the factory grounds were thrown open for a Christmas celebration to which the surrounding neighborhoods were invited and which looked like a curious combination of a Christkindlmarkt in Strasbourg or Munich and a festival in Palermo or a fair in Galway or Vilna. I should add that, though the primary market of Schefflin's was largely a prosperous urban middle class, it attempted to appeal to all sectors of American society—the rich and the working class as well. If a well-heeled lady could feel comfortable being driven by her chauffeur to one of the luncheonettes for a light but leisurely repast with her friends, it was equally a place where that same chauffeur and his wife could go to dinner that evening and know they could afford it and be served gracefully and unpretentiously by a young waitress who had arrived from Ireland only four weeks before."

Besserman paused for a few moments before he recommenced his line of thought. "I grant there are many for whom an account of any enterprise of the commercial world must seem an exercise in what is only peripheral at best to the greater and presumably more perdurable achievements of mankind. I find this, in some respects, a shortsighted view, unappreciative of many of the fine things that human beings accomplish, even if such accomplishments are necessarily transitory. But allow me, even in my best moments, to hobnob with the master chefs of the world, the brewmeisters, the vintners, the distillers of well-aged scotch and liqueurs, the makers of automobiles and airplanes and ships, the craftsmen, the publishers of fine books, the fabricators of so many of the accoutrements that make our lives commodious and gracious, to say nothing of the myriads who, through their work, make this productivity possible and make available to us through all those services whose mediating functions are indispensable—grant me all of that and I shall be, for the nonce, a contented man."

"And what about that maternal forebear of his, the schoolmaster who took on the barons? Was Frederick ever compelled to emulate his activity?" I asked.

"Well," Besserman replied, "I hardly think that Frederick ever needed to resort to the more arcane researches or extravagant adventures of his esteemed ancestor, but he did need to weave an intricate course through the many and duplicitous obstacles erected by the new adverse 'barons' of his own milieu. He did it in his calm, methodical way, scrupulously utilizing all that is good about the knowledge and the power of the law, protecting his colleagues at every level and the integrity of their persons and their work, and keeping at bay the potential predatory forces that circled around them. I, and my former partner, Samuel Davidowitz, were involved, naturally, in this effort, and we were very gratified to be part of it. Samuel, I should say, to his immemorial credit, could spot a snake in the grass from a hundred paces away and dispatch it before it had even occurred to it to strike."

"But it was primarily to Frederick's credit—" I tried to interject.

"It was to a point," Besserman countered. "I try at times to think about it the way Frederick may have thought about it, and I think he would have been a great deal more modest than the rest of us in his assessment of what actually was achieved, or, at least, what in that achievement could be credited either to him or to anybody else. Frederick would be the first to acknowledge that the conditions of his life, at the beginning and throughout, were advantageous for the sorts of things he did, very highly advantageous indeed, and, if he attained meritorious results, it is to a large extent because he had meritorious reserves to draw from and meritorious persons at every level to work with. If he brought something special of his own to what he did, I have often thought it was because he had a soul in concord with a world of values, things useful and things to be enjoyed for their own sakes, measuring every pitch, every shade of sonority with a most flexible vibrato of touch, and coaxing, as it were, out of the variable inflections of things—of persons, of abilities, of opportunities—their most clearly accentuated purity of tone."

I could not help but interpose again, "But what happened to it all—to Schefflin's? How could it simply have vanished? It was such a loss—especially to those of us who had, in some way, come to depend on it."

Besserman deliberated with himself for a moment before he spoke. "That, clearly, is an enigma. That the company thrived for nearly a full generation or more after Frederick's death attested, more than anything else, to the soundness of its conception and the stability of its design. Those who had known Frederick and who had worked with him were able, within limits, to perpetuate his vision and maintain his standards. I think sometimes that the essence of Frederick's genius as a man of commerce was his ability to arbitrate judiciously among the inherent tensions and conflicting claims that mark any kind of institutional life, pressures that arise both from interior and exterior pressures. But a later generation had a much greater difficulty sustaining the kind of delicate synthesis that he had attained. One could argue, as it has been argued, that Schefflin's market changed, and Schefflin's didn't change with it: that the critical mass of its clientele, the urban middle class, departed for the suburbs, and the urbanity of Schefflin's simply could not be retooled for suburban life; that the leisurely pace of Schefflin's service did not and could not adjust to a new and more hectic pace of city life; that it became too expensive to deliver such quality at moderate prices; or that its relatively tame cuisine could no longer compete with the extravagances that proliferated at either end of the culinary spectrum—so-called fast food at one end and the high gourmet at the other. There is the terrible irony that, until the day that Schefflin's closed its doors, its establishments were so crowded with patrons that one could scarcely push one's way in, and its goods were in such demand that its outlets could not deliver them fast enough. However, in the end, it could not pay its bills or meet its payroll. It collapsed overnight into bankruptcy. So much was lost! Who can understand such things? I know that I cannot.

"Could Frederick, had he lived long enough, have done anything about it? I think that, if he could have observed what happened, he would not have been especially surprised by it. He was sufficiently compassionate with what is fragile and impermanent in human nature and in the course of events to understand the limitations of any project and to exercise generosity toward its inevitable shortfalls. He often reminded me how totally, how utterly, what human beings have built up, sometimes over centuries and generations, could be destroyed in the flickering of an eye. In setting up the Schefflin Foundation, named after his parents, he was specifically providing for some extension, as limited as it would be, of part of what had been fruitful in the enterprise, when that enterprise finally, as he knew it must, would find its natural terminus. We who represent the trust, do, of course, what we can in that regard, and I think he would be well pleased. He would be just as well pleased by the stories—let's call them, the Schefflin's stories—that still circulate as a kind of folklore in some of our great cities about the benign impact that his enterprise made on so many lives. I even know of one rather enterprising hobbyist who has spent part of his life tracking down and collecting, as it were, any and all literary allusions to Schefflin's to be found in the corpus of modern American literature.

"Ah, Edmund, how you do let me go on!" Besserman bewailed, lifting his hands as if in supplication to some tutelary embodiment of good hospitality. "And we are getting ahead of ourselves! Since it is so late, please do me the honor of joining me in a simple lunch. On the mezzanine floor downstairs we have a small restaurant for the staff—actually it is modeled as a miniature replica of one of the original Schefflin's establishments. We employ a young Vietnamese fellow there by the name of Tram who can put together a devil of a sandwich. I can send for some to be delivered up here. He has this 'specialty' he makes that is well worth giving a try. I won't try to describe it. It is beyond description."

"I would be delighted to try it, Theodore," I replied, "if I may now switch to first names. But frankly, I find its apparent ineffability more a cause for alarm than a recommendation for its consumption."

"You will love it. And I will order some tea and coffee. Eventually I would like you to meet the staff, but I think that would all be too much for today. We have plenty of time for that. You have already met Mr. Gleason, our courier, our indispensably supple and elusive envoy without whom I couldn't do half of what I do."

"Indeed! I didn't learn his name at the time, but how could I ever forget him?"

"He always gets through somehow, gets the right message into the right hands, faster than any postal service can do. He manages to pass through any barrier that confronts him. I think his rather chimerical garb convinces others that he cannot possibly exist, so he passes through obstacles, in a way, paradoxically noticeable and unnoticed at the same time."

"I did wonder how he breached our much-vaunted multiple layers of watertight security."

"And I trust you have met Mr. Dougherty, our concierge."

"I have."

"Expect to hear a great deal about the Red Sox from him."

"I will prepare myself for that."

"He knows a great deal about them, indeed everything that has happened to the team since its original founding, I imagine."

"I could ask him about a game I saw at Fenway Park when I was nine years old, about which I can remember nothing at all, except for the hot dog my soon-to-be-horrified father purchased for me, which made me very ill with immediate and untoward consequences."

"Rest assured. He will remember every detail—of the game, I mean!—and will be more than glad to fill you in, if you let him. He has a prodigious memory for that sort of thing. Did you say nine years old? I'll try to jog his permanent mental file. He also knows every detail about this building, about every wire and pipe and joist and building stone. He has been with us, I think, for fifty years or more. He actually knew Frederick himself. He occupies a small basement apartment in this building, underneath the sacrosanct enclave of his cloakroom. I am the only other permanent occupant. After my wife, Martha, passed away, I moved into some simple lodgings arranged for me on the floor below, adjacent to our library. It restricts my daily commute to a flight of stairs. So the two of us, as it were, haunt this dwelling as guardian spirits, though it is so replete with other guardian spirits of a less corporeal nature anyway that our efforts are largely superfluous."

"I assume, then, that you do not follow the sports world the way Mr. Dougherty does."

"I hardly need to. He keeps me well informed. But, except for dabbling with tennis when I was young, I have never been much of a sportsman."

"And Frederick, what of him?"

"He loved his camping, his fishing, his occasional mountain climb. Splitting firewood was one of his more favored avocations. A different technique for every species of wood, he liked to boast, with a twinkle in his eye. It all looked pretty much the same to me. But I have to admit that he occasionally drafted me into being an umpire at the annual championship softball game between the chocolate and the shipping departments, the two departments that always seemed to field the best teams. Their rivalry was ferocious. Once a year, during the summer, the entire Schefflin operation was shut down for a day and the workforce, en masse, was bused out to a beachside resort on the South Shore for a communal picnic and barbecue and a dance and competitive events of all kinds. That's where I had to be the umpire. And I assure you, I cannot tell the difference between a ball and a strike. I needed all my legal skills to mediate between the contentious parties that I had inadvertently created! Well then—I must make some arrangements. Do make yourself at home while I am absent. You might be interested in looking about somewhat. I have, I must confess, indulged the fancy of an old man, Edmund, by deploying around me here some of my most valued mementos of the past."

We arose, and Besserman accompanied me across the room to a large table where several dozen photographs of various sizes were disposed; many were neatly arranged and mounted in silver and gold frames. At first, I rather dreaded the prospect of being introduced, one by one, to each of them—I have never been a "family photograph" sort of person and have always felt shy about having to respond with trite comments to images suddenly imposed upon me by a doting father or mother or paramour. But Besserman spared me that ordeal and departed without another word, his wide, rectangular shape just barely clearing the horizontal dimension of the tall vertical door through which he passed, and left me to my own devices.

I saw, right off, photographs from many different times, each with its own style of how figures were posed or how the film was developed. Brownish tinted daguerreotypes showed stiffly posed figures sitting upright in chairs or by tables with flower bouquets resting on them, or standing behind a seated figure with a hand on that person's shoulder. Others, black and white, were more informal and showed holiday events—sailboats, picnics, men in flat straw hats and women in jaunty jazz-era cloches, rickety-looking bicycles that belonged to another age altogether; meanwhile, a disorderly spread of color photographs depicted people who were not posing at all but were caught spontaneously laughing or sitting around crowded restaurant tables. I knew I had a century of history in front of me.

I noticed a younger but recognizable Besserman standing next to a woman of about his age: both were holding tennis rackets, and I assumed the woman was his wife, Martha. There were several other photographs of the same woman, one of them as a bride. I also recognized Frederick—the same man, the same expression as in the portrait—holding up a large trout with a north-woods landscape in the background. A number of photographs depicted a small chamber orchestra, each member of which was rather dramatically posed with his or her instrument. In one of them, the woman whom I took to be Martha sat with a violin poised demurely in her lap. Frederick was there, a cello nestled in the hollow of his left arm and a bow held loosely in his right hand and rested across his knee. Framed by Frederick's ample limbs, the cello seemed almost tiny by comparison. It was, I assumed, the ancestral cello to which Besserman had referred earlier in our conversation. I looked closer at the photograph and was surprised to find Besserman there as well, in the background, as if he were not a usual participant in this scene. He was holding on to—what was it?—a flute I figured, though it was difficult to make it out in the faded picture. I noted several photographs of Frederick with a woman—his wife, I deduced. Like Frederick, she was rather plain-looking, almost as tall as he was, with resolute eyes like his and her long, what I guessed to be brown or ruddy hair (as far as one could ascertain from a seriously faded black-and-white photograph) scooped up into a wild and eccentric bun clinging precariously more on the side of her head than on the back and with tufts escaping here and there. She faced the camera with a gamesome, dare-me, genial look—her eyebrows slightly raised and head poised at an angle.

There was another woman too, just one photograph of her. She looked like the person I had assumed to be Frederick's wife: her sister, maybe, from the family resemblance—the same eccentricity, the same wryness and audacity of expression but perhaps without the same warmth of character, yet, in contrast, immaculately beautiful; she was standing next to a bicycle, in an elegant, expensively tailored white gown drawn up at the knees as if thereby adapted to the exigencies of riding a bicycle, though hardly constituting a proper riding habit in any case. Her hair was bound up in a coiffure faultless in its deportment, and she resembled a model posing in front of a professional cameraman. The bicycle, to all appearances, was merely a prop in a lovely, if somewhat dramatized, composition. Her hair was dark and, I posited from its intensity of darkness, probably black.

The center of the table was given over to a small, delicately colored portrait rendered in oils, surrounded by an antiqued gilded wooden frame and supported on a pewter stand: an adolescent girl sat on the outer rim of a fountain in a small, enclosed garden. She, too, was beautiful, very much like the woman who looked like a model in the photograph and with similar (and what I could now see unmistakably in this instance) jet-black hair, which cascaded voluminously over her shoulders and contrasted so strikingly with the whiteness of her complexion and the startling aquamarine of her eyes, though those eyes, unlike the eyes of the model, were deep-set and penetrating. But she had none of the eccentricity or the professional veneer of the other woman. She had a curious bearing, I thought, almost like . . . almost like what I had found in the portrait of Frederick Schefflin: the same composure, earnest and pliant, the same modest but unassuming self-possession. I also couldn't help but detect the presence of someone else here—a stranger, gazing at me out of the striking depth of those glowing but sad blue eyes. As I studied the portrait, I suddenly remembered the fountain: it was the fountain downstairs that I saw when I entered the building. It was depicted in rich ivory hues, veined here and there with delicate amber and mauve shadings while crystalline waters overflowed from basin to basin. In the bottom basin was a flourishing growth of water lilies, capped here and there with snow-white flowers. But the garden in which the girl reposed was not the same garden I had seen below. I pondered this anomaly for a moment, then shifted my attention to other things in the room.

There I was able to take in a great deal: old Schefflin candy tins, handsomely shaped and embossed, one of which, the renowned so-called Golden Casque, I could recall from my childhood; a framed menu from a café; a tennis ball with some signatures on it; a wide silver ashtray with an inscription; a goodly number of books and musical scores; and a dozen other items distributed here and there on shelves and over tabletops. I noted again the crystalline showcase in which was displayed a violin and, now that I could see it more closely, a bow, brightly polished and obviously revered as embodying an important memory of a beloved person. Martha's violin, I immediately concluded.

As I studied some of the titles of books and albums on the shelves, I was slightly jolted by coming across a single photograph backed up into a shadowy gap between some books. It faced outward into the room almost exactly opposite the great portrait of Frederick. It showed the face of a young man; he had soft, wavy, light hair, combed directly back from a high forehead, a firm male visage, tender but almost upsetting in its sculpted finesse, with dark, deep-set eyes, attentive and tragic at the same time. Yes, tragic; the one tragic note amid all this glorious amplitude; I couldn't avoid thinking, at this moment, of those Arthurian knights of the old Celtic legends, whose very prowess and grace rendered them "fey" (as the legends would have it), rendered them doomed somehow to precocious extinction, as if, in regard to such a perfected bloom of life, life itself could not abide permitting it to flourish for too long. I also couldn't avoid thinking of the portrait of the young woman by the fountain—by happenstance, certainly, those same passionate eyes so affixed on some melancholy vista one could hardly begin to broach. The photograph gave me the impression of a charitable and compassionate man, waiting anxiously and with resignation for another to speak to him, another to address him out of the depths of his or her deeply occluded anguish, as if his own sorrow were the most fitting receptacle for all the suffering this maculate world produces in such profusion. And then this position of the photograph in the room, facing the great portrait on the other side, as if some special bond and some special division, a parity and a distinction, existed between the two of them! Who can he be? I thought to myself. He is so set apart, so hidden in a way, yet again is so much at the center of it all, gazing out from his recessed enclave with an expression of such infinite sadness. How odd that what appears partially to hide him serves as well to enshrine him in a numinous grotto whose very isolation confers upon him the utmost sign of reverence.

Who could he be?

"Ah, Edmund," Besserman exclaimed as he brushed through the door, holding a tray covered with the most exotic of fare. "I see you are well advanced in your explorations. That's as it should be. But it's time now for lunch." He set the tray down on a small table near the hearth, between his winged chair and the divan.

"Tea or coffee?"

"Tea," I replied. He poured some tea into a Russian tea glass inserted neatly into a silver-gilt wire basket and handed it to me, along with the sandwich. He took coffee in a wide, shallow cup, almost as if he were drinking from a saucer.

"This sandwich looks more like a float in a parade than something to eat," I declaimed.

"Indeed it does," he confirmed, "but you will find it delicious. I admonish you that when you first bite into it you may think it is alive, but I assure you it isn't. It just has a way of shifting around unexpectedly. Enjoy yourself."

We discussed family matters again as we ate. I spoke about my wife and children, what they were doing, where we went on vacations, what college my oldest son was going to, and so forth. His nods, accompanied by contented grunts and sighs, seemed to signify that he knew everything already. To my surprise, he even corrected me about one or two dates in my family history, once again arousing in me the suspicion that I may have had some contact with him earlier in my life. Then he spoke about his wife, about Martha—they had had no children, he told me, gazing at me somewhat pointedly and regretfully as he said that. She was a fine violinist, had taught the violin, had performed professionally now and then in the greater Boston area, and was part of Frederick's chamber group in its later years. I asked about him and his flute. He was a little taken aback by the question. Then he must have realized that I had seen it in the photograph. He chuckled. "I was really never very good at it," he commented. "But I did get a chance to 'toot' it now and then at some opportune—or maybe inopportune—moment. Everyone was rather forgiving under the circumstances."

He addressed Frederick's family—his marriage with Agnes—and he pointed out her pictures. I had guessed that much correctly. "She was a bewitching woman," he observed with a laugh, "always doing the unexpected thing, playful and—um—whimsical, to use your word." He leaned toward me as if to whisper. "She is the source of your quizzical giraffes in the hallway, since you want to know! I think Frederick never ceased to wonder at the bizarre things she could come up with. She was never directly involved with the business—had too many other things to do, but many of the novelties Schefflin's was famous for had their origin in her ever prolific ingenuity. Her sister Bernice—well, we always said, 'Aunt Bernice'—was different. An actress, or an actress of sorts, wouldn't you know, from her photograph." He indicated the photograph of the beautiful woman posed so expertly like a model next to the bicycle. It was difficult to take one's eyes off the contemplation of that exquisite visage, its rarefied features so perfect in their poise and luster, and I found myself almost embarrassed by how my gaze lingered upon her.

I turned my attention to the portrait of the young woman sitting by the fountain. For some reason I was a little embarrassed by gaping at that picture too, so I hoped to approach it indirectly by asking about the fountain. "I have seen that fountain. It's downstairs in the courtyard."

"So it is."

"But this is not the same garden."

"No, not at all. The fountain, the 'ivory fount,' they used to call it, was originally in a small walled garden off the breakfast room at Madison Street—the house I mentioned to you that Frederick designed and built for his family on Madison Street in Newton in the mid years of his life, although it was as much Agnes's project as it was his own. Agnes always insisted they come up with some suitably literary name for the house, something derived from a Russian or an English novel or a poem, something like 'Sparrow Hill' of Tolstoyan provenance, or "Penshurst," or the 'Appleton House' of Marvell's wonderful poem, but nothing was ever decided in that regard, and the house was called, ever so prosaically, just by its address and remained Madison Street ever after. Years later, after the death of Frederick and, a decade later, of Agnes, the house was donated to an order of Catholic nuns who use it and its grounds for a small women's college, Saint Hroswitha College. At the time of the donation, the 'ivory fount' was transported from the breakfast garden at Madison Street to the garden downstairs, where you can see it now."

"And who is that?" I had been dying to ask all the while. "I mean the young woman in the portrait."

"Oh yes, do excuse me. That is Cornelia—Cornelia Schefflin, now long known by her married name as Cornelia de Quevillon. She married a French military officer and has lived in France most of her life, though she comes to the United States usually once a year to visit old friends and relatives and look after the various international projects that she participates in. Her children are grown up now and also live in France. From this office we manage not only the Schefflin Foundation but a variety of other minor or subsidiary trusts as well, one of which Frederick set up for Cornelia. But we will get to all of that in time. You will have the opportunity to meet her someday. She is, I should mention, a member of the board of trustees of the Schefflin Foundation and attends our meetings when they coincide with her annual trips to the United States. She is a remarkable woman and has led an extraordinary life."

"She is, then, I take it, Frederick and Agnes's daughter."

"Well . . . of course . . . your assumption makes sense," Besserman replied.

"And who, then, is that—that extraordinary figure who looks at us from out of the sheltered recess?" I pointed to the photograph on the adjacent bookshelf.

Besserman delayed his answer. "You don't miss a thing, do you, Edmund?" he said a moment later. He finished his sandwich and drained his final saucer of steamy coffee. He meditated the remains of my half-eaten repast. "I guess you are the traditional 'ham and cheese on white' kind of fellow," he complained, "and with mustard, no doubt. You know, Edmund, you do want to jump ahead to things. I like that, but I can't always be expected to jump with you. There are many things to be understood here, and we need to approach them in an appropriate order."

"You still haven't answered my question," I protested.

He hesitated. Then he declared, "His name was Aloysius Fitzgerald—Dr. Aloysius Fitzgerald, for he was a physician, a doctor of medicine. But he was known as 'Uncle Aloysius' to Cornelia, and, in the course of time, we all more or less picked up that same name for him. We all called him Uncle Aloysius."

"Uncle Aloysius," I repeated. The name had fallen with such somberness from Besserman's lips that I knew it must have been a very special name among the Schefflins, that it bore with it some incalculable weight of remembrance. "So he was Cornelia's uncle?"

"He died young, at a very young age—in his mid-thirties," Besserman continued, evading my question. "Against all well-intentioned counsel and well-informed prudence, he insisted on an almost heroic expenditure of himself in ministering to the sick when a typhoid epidemic raged among the textile workers in the great mills along the Merrimack River in New Hampshire. He lived in Concord—the New Hampshire Concord—and that's where he died when, exhausted by his efforts and exposed by the risks he took, he contracted the disease himself. He was married to Bernice, or Aunt Bernice, as I have already called her, Agnes's sister, whom you have noticed in the photograph. She is the one who was the actress. The two of them, I can assure you, made the world's most beautiful couple. The loss of Uncle Aloysius was deeply felt by the Schefflins and everyone in his circle, and especially by Cornelia, who was fourteen at the time of his death and was very close to him. He was, I should say, a most extraordinary man: a true chevalier of the heart, I would call him, invoking some old chivalric mode, a man of gallantry, honor, grace. I hope to tell you about him someday."

"Did he . . ." I muttered.

Besserman raised his hand, like a traffic cop in the midst of a busy intersection. "I apologize for interrupting you, Edmund. There is a great deal to be said about Uncle Aloysius. There is a great deal to be said about many things. But it is perhaps most just to all of us to measure out how and when we say it. I think we have made a good start, and I hope I have enticed you to want to know more about us. Let us arrange for a meeting next week, and we can continue our conversation."

I was glad to meet these conditions. We made the suitable arrangements, and I said goodbye to Mr. Besserman. I knew that I needed time simply to assimilate what I had already heard. I could also do some more of my "research." On the landing outside his office, I stole a brief glance at the giraffes in the frescoes above (who appeared to be stealing a brief glance back at me) and decided to forgo the crystal elevator that still stood—though friendly enough—where I had left it. I then glided down the various flights of polished marble stairs, finding the differences in style from one high-arched landing to another very worthwhile to meditate upon as I descended.

The building was vast and quiet and solemn, like a library or a monastery or a basilica secreted away among the back streets of an ancient and forgotten city, though I could sense that there was a goodly portion of activity going on around me, and at one point a young woman carrying a sheaf of manila folders hurried up the stairs past me and greeted me as she went by. On the second, or mezzanine, floor I could detect the fragrance of coffee and various other culinary aromas emerging from the room that had been set up as a miniature version of the traditional Schefflin's café. When I actually saw it as I turned a corner, it was something of a shock, for it brought back such a flood of memories, especially of my mother, who so relished our visits to the Boylston Street Schefflin's on Saturday evenings for dinner after a matinee in downtown Boston. When I finally descended to the entrance foyer on the bottom floor, Mr. Dougherty was waiting for me, coat over his arm;

obviously he had been informed by intercom that I was on my way out. As he helped me with my coat, he asked me about that game when I was nine years old. I was a little taken aback that he knew about that already. Clearly Besserman had mentioned it to him on the intercom. I gave him the date of the game, and after a few moments of recollection, he told me regretfully, as if still in mourning about it, that the Red Sox had lost to the Yankees, despite a spectacular home run in the ninth inning. I could remember none of that.

Before I left the building, I turned for a moment to view the fountain at the center of the garden. The "ivory fount," I thought, remembering Besserman's words. Temperatures had warmed up somewhat outside, I guessed, for the fountain had been turned on. The sun now, just after the noon hour, slanted down at a steep but cheery angle into the courtyard and was refracted into a miniature rainbow by the spray of water emerging from the acanthus finial at the top of the fountain and was reflected, in a dozen directions, by the glimmering surfaces of the basins. The water curled over the ivory-tinted marble rims of the basins in glassy, wavering sheets that broke into glistening ripples as they met the waters below. I took pleasure in watching it and took pleasure in knowing that I would soon return to see it again. Mr. Dougherty thrust open the huge wooden door for me, and I made my departure into the busy metropolis that lay beyond those portals.

Part Two

"You must come!" Besserman insisted. "Soon! Tomorrow, if possible. Important news; important ground to cover. Please come—at one o'clock. I'll have Tram prepare us a lunch."

He hung up the phone before I had a chance to answer. Did he assume I would have no other engagements for the day—and, if I did, that I could break them off at such short notice? As it turned out, I didn't have any appointments for the afternoon. I had put aside time to work, peacefully and unhurriedly for a change, on the rewording of a contract whose deadline was still several weeks away. It was difficult not to have the shadow of some freakish qualm pass through my mind that he knew this already about my plans. Yet, as ever, I was eager to go, to drop whatever else I was doing, especially since his summons was delivered with such apparent urgency. I would have preferred to have had a chance to respond, however; I mean, not so much about the appointment but about the prospect of lunch. I did like Tram very much, but I was not, and still am not, acclimatized to his rather excessively flamboyant sandwiches.

We had had, of course, meetings subsequent to our initial conference. It is difficult to characterize these meetings in general terms, the three or four of them over a span of several weeks, ranging from mid-February through much of the month of March, paralleling, in some curious way, their own unfolding buds of illumination with the succession of variegated spring flowers that began to meet my eyes each time I passed through the central foyer of the Schefflin Foundation and gazed at the neatly laid out parterres in the courtyard garden. But I will do my best. Their purpose is most adequately summarized by their being, as the first meeting was, an effort to open before me a kind of loose and informal compendium of attitudes, measures, policies, and reminiscences, for my consideration and approbation. We approached these in the manner of personal, even casual, conversation, as if we were still, for all purposes, two strangers, thrown together in a dining car on a train and mulling over, meditatively, what had been and was still important in our lives. There was nothing overtly determined or resolved between the two of us—even despite my sense that, at some deeper level, so much had been determined and resolved already; our discussions were explorations, and, if Besserman did most of the talking, he did it with the purpose of allowing me to explore myself in relationship to what he was saying, to find my way into it, if "into it" was where I could go and settle to some extent and thrive. That was distinctly, at this stage, my task, and I was more than pleased to abide with that intention. I would find out, soon enough, that the terrain being opened up for my exploration would branch off into totally unexpected regions, some aspects of which would be left to others to divulge. But that would come, as it did, in time, and much sooner than I had expected.

Those early conferences had ventured into questions pertinent to the guidance of a substantial charitable foundation. There is no need to rehearse what all of these were: Besserman discussed at length, for example, the kind of investment policies that the Foundation pursued and how important it was to keep these policies in line with original principles without, at the same time, ignoring genuinely new features of the investment scene. He emphasized how difficult it was to chart a course through those ominous and capricious fashions that sweep periodically through the world of high finance. I found these discussions informative, though not especially remarkable, for Besserman was simply describing the kind of policies that any prudent person would endorse under the circumstances.

If I felt somewhat perplexed at times by these observations, perplexed by their rather "ordinary" stance, I didn't mention it: the law firm in which I was—still am, technically—a partner and which is so titanic that I have come to know personally over the years only a mere handful of its associates seemed to be perpetually buffeted by those fashions and the consequent "bubbles" that Besserman alluded to, however indirectly. But, as in so many things, many of my compatriots were invariably rewarded for being at the "cutting edge," even if the "cutting edge" was also, at times, the edge of a precipice. In my department, we were, of late, being pressed to write contracts for mergers, acquisitions, and hostile corporate takeovers so multitudinous that the queue for our services virtually "stretched around the block," as the saying goes, bringing untold millions into our coffers even as we sutured together industrial mammoths whose incompatibility would soon enough, it seemed likely, demand our services to separate them once again. What we soldered together, multiplying with unbridled sophistication and nuance our stock of representations and warranties, we took no little relish in presaging that nobody other than ourselves would be qualified to pry asunder. I have little doubt that Besserman was not already cognizant of these activities and of the not altogether gracile acts of legerdemain that sometimes may very well accompany them. His "litany" of the ordinary, in this respect, was perhaps intended to illustrate to me, by implicit contrast, his awareness of the extraordinary—the extraordinary in such matters being commensurate with the parlous and irresponsible.

He also addressed, now and then, and in the desultory manner to which I was growing accustomed, the many problems involved in making charitable grants to institutions of various kinds. He enumerated the principles that the Foundation attempted to follow, mentioning how fallible even these principles could be in various situations. "Generosity without discrimination is a weapon of incalculable destructiveness," he liked to say, and the process of spreading largesse was at least as treacherous as the investment side of the Foundation's work, if not, in its own way, more so. He might add, "We give to institutions, not individuals: to give to institutions is, by the very nature of institutions, to suspend a piñata above a crowd, and what happens to the contents of that piñata after it bursts can never be predicted aforethought or satisfactorily explained afterward. We demand thorough accountability but are not so naïve as to think that we get it. We simply need to live with those limitations." I think he had at least a dozen apothegms of like nature to impart to me and to illustrate with stories both amusing and appalling. But he praised his associates, "in the ship's hold, down below," the keen-eyed, sharp-eared garrison of his staff who protected and guided him on a hazardous voyage. Although my prior research had already informed me about the Foundation's work—it was all a matter of public record—Besserman reaffirmed for me that the primary interest had been the support of medical delivery services in rural communities. He also mentioned strong secondary interests in advancing musical education—especially in conservatories and dance academies—and in helping to found and to build up collections of fine art in small municipal museums; wildlife refuges and nature conservation were also a matter of interest.

All of that was perhaps, over this month or so, a preface to even more important matters he wished to address. I assumed that the peremptory summons I had received to this most recent meeting indicated that such a threshold had been reached, a threshold determined not simply by the internal dialectic of what had already transpired in our conversation but by an external event, the presage of which demanded some immediate response. As usual, whatever that event would turn out to be, and it turned out to be portentous enough, its announcement was delayed and our discussion ancillary to it proceeded by steps oblique, if methodic, on the way to its final articulation. Further, I knew already by experience that Besserman, in one way or another, would induce me to coax it, as it were, out of him. It would be left to my initiative, if I may use an analogy borrowed from football, to bring him down before he had the chance to cross the line of scrimmage.

So it all began with lunch, as it had been so fatefully, for me, preordained, Besserman once again calling upon Tram to produce several of his spectacular, though rather intimidating, culinary masterpieces. At the end of our lunch, Besserman had the irony, or maybe it was audacity, to refer to our repast as "abstemious fare."

"Abstemious?" I repeated. I recalled the festively festooned sampan I had just devoured, with, I did not doubt, something like a full-grown crocodile encased in its crusty hull. Well, I can hardly say it was a crocodile, but, whatever it was, it was long and scaly. And I still wasn't sure, at that moment, whether I had consumed the sandwich or the sandwich had consumed me.

"Well, perhaps not so abstemious then, if you insist. But you did survive it this time around, didn't you?" Besserman laughed. "You actually managed to finish it—not like some of the previous times, you recall."

"Indeed I did," I allowed. "It's just that I like to know what I am eating. It seemed to be a rather inscrutable thing."

Besserman laughed again. "Inscrutable, to say the least. I spend so much of my life asking questions that there are occasions when I would rather not ask them at all. Sometimes it's good to live with a puzzle. As for the sandwich, all I can guess is that it was a tentacle of some sort. Beyond that I don't especially wish to know. The sauce was delicious, that you must concede, to say nothing of its fulsome leguminous garniture." I conceded with a nod, vowing inwardly to avoid ingesting all future "tentacles," no matter how festively festooned they might be in whatever kind of greenery and no matter how sumptuously garnished with whatever kind of sauce.

During lunch we had talked about music. He expressed some measure of embarrassment about the Foundation's lack of support for larger musical institutions in recent decades. He spoke of how important music had been in the life of the Schefflins and of how they had been of signal importance in the support of the Boston Symphony Orchestra, to say nothing of other musical institutions in the greater Boston area. But then they were personally active in that sphere of private and civic enrichment and, understanding music as they did, they understood what they were doing and how to assess the worth of what was being achieved. Further, he could always depend upon Martha's expert advice. Besserman expanded on this point: "We don't—I don't—have that kind of discernment available anymore, regrettably, and even if we did, that whole world has by now grown so much more complicated in the scope of its financial and social ramifications that we feel that we could hardly cope with that. But what of you, Edmund? I assume you have an interest in music, am I correct?"

I hesitated. "Well, I do . . . I mean . . . well, I suppose not in your sense."

"Not in my sense? Now, what can that possibly mean?"

"I enjoy, perhaps most of all, certain kinds of American folk music—I mean the real thing, not the many variants of simulated folk traditions that have proliferated in commercial guises. I have a special interest in Cajun music. But it's not the same thing as—"

"Well, yes and no," Besserman interrupted. "One is blind not to acknowledge important differences. But, then again, one is equally blind not to acknowledge what really is the same. And there is a great deal that is the same. Can you perform it? Can you play an instrument?"

"If you consider the ability to strum about a half dozen chords on the banjo as being able to play an instrument, then perhaps I can claim to be able to perform something, though it is only accompaniment to 'Red River Valley' and 'Home on the Range' and other items that my children enjoy, or did enjoy when they were younger. Anyway, I stick with my fairly monotonous strumming and my handful of cowboy songs. I can also venture to play a Cajun piece or two. But they are more complex."

"I should find nothing amiss with that. My father, bless his soul, brought a rather scraggy concertina with him from Kiev. He was what one might call a 'one-tune' musician, his entire repertoire consisting of a single old Russian melody that he must have played a thousand times, over and over again, in his life, but always with the same gusto as if he had never played it before—and we reacted accordingly, never tiring of it, for some reason."

I concurred. "Yes, my father—I guess I should also say, 'bless his soul'—was likewise the enthusiastic impresario of a single work. He knew one Longfellow poem by memory. I am afraid we were not so generous in our appreciation of his tormented and tormenting recitations, often delivered, to our chagrin, while he was driving us to some destination to which we were not particularly eager to go. To this day, I can never make the drive from Boston toward Lexington without hearing the insistent galloping of Paul Revere's horse and the even more insistent galloping of my father's rendition of Longfellow's hexameters. It was all rather awful, in a way. And funny too, I won't deny. But I assume that your musical circle, or perhaps I should say the Schefflin musical circle, was pretty close to being professional in its accomplishments."

"That would be something of an exaggeration, Edmund. Actually, some of those who joined us from time to time were indeed professional—Thaddeus Holzteufel, for example, who taught the viola at the Conservatory, or Margit Stolnitkaya, whose harp concertos were worth dropping anything else to hear. Walther Goedkoep loved to come by and play on Frederick's magnificent pianoforte, a concert grand custom-made by Steinway for him. If we were especially lucky, a vocalist would join us and Walther would accompany him or her in the performance of *lieder* by Schubert or Hugo Wolf. Some members of the Boston Symphony, if they were free on a late Sunday afternoon, might come with their instruments and join in now and then. And, of course, Martha was a 'regular,' provided that an occasional concert with one of several string quartets in the area did not call her—and me, as her most devoted aficionado—away at the time.

"So we were partially professional, you could say, though it was ever a potluck affair and depended on who could show up. We never knew until the last moment. And there was always, one might add, an appreciative audience for these recitals: erudite and cosmopolitan, eccentric in their own way and multilingual, inclusive of dealers in Egyptian antiquities, to learned Jesuit philosophers from nearby Boston College, to a pensive, if not also loquacious Talmudic scholar from Lviv, to a quirky Hungarian baron notorious for his bushy red mustache and his rather vertiginous archaeological excavations high in the Andes, or to a black-robed archimandrite fresh in from the Ethiopian highlands. This was potluck too; one never knew what strange or familiar personages might be there, for the Schefflins maintained an 'open house' principle of hospitality.

"Frederick himself had close to a professional competence in that range of music with which he was most familiar. But that range was limited—to the eighteenth century primarily; he didn't have the versatility of the true professional. Furthermore, one could not put a fresh piece of sheet music in front of him and expect a creditable performance right away. It might take him several days of practice to get to that stage, and even then his capacity was constrained to accustomed modes of harmonic and melodic registers: a Haydn trio, for example, but certainly not a work by Stravinsky. At times he had simply to back away from active performance and listen to what others could do. However, I think I learned to love the cello more from him than anyone else. It is the only instrument about which I would say, even if I must stoop to a rather conventional set of phrases, that its tone is 'delicious,' rather like the bouquet of an aged and mellow wine. How we loved to listen to him play, then, in solitude, often after many of the others had left, after the musicale had, in a sense, officially concluded, performing on his ancestral instrument one or another of Bach's solo suites for the cello.

"How supremely alone, yet not lonely at all, was that somber braid of tonal modulation we attended to; and, in both its supreme aloneness and in the finesse with which its variant themes parted and converged, how it seemed to entwine together the hidden and intimate threads of all we knew and nurtured in our lives. Frederick would sit by himself, arcing his glistering bow over the carnelian loom of his revered instrument in the semidarkness of the long winter twilight as his family and his few remaining guests gathered close to the great hearthstone in Madison Street, watching the final embers of the fire glowing among the brassy andirons and being woven by that strand of melody into the evening like the golden filaments embroidered into those old Renaissance tapestries that hung so close around us. Even the commodious walnut sideboard, now littered with empty salvers and decanters, with crumbs and shards and rinds of a repast now finished, shone with that same burnished cheer, that same measured rapport with which it had initially invited us to partake of its redolent offerings, with which it now blended into the even greater resolution of a gesture brought to a perfect finish, of a repletion most enrapt in its own consummate depletion. Can I actually have been so favored, Edmund, as to have experienced such a wondrous thing? Could anything in life have been better than that?"

How does one answer questions like that? It's simple. One doesn't. But I had my own questions nevertheless. "About Agnes, about Aunt Bernice and Uncle Aloysius—did they have anything to offer these musical occasions?"

"I think their souls were filled with music, Edmund," Besserman replied. "But they didn't make music themselves, at least not in the way we conventionally think of it. Uncle Aloysius and Aunt Bernice lived far enough away so that their presence was not always possible at these events, but they seemed to enjoy them when they were available. Agnes lived around and through and perpetually enthralled by the music bequeathed by the Schefflin household of old, and she could, occasionally, be persuaded into giving a creditable rendition of an ancient Gaelic ballad. But her skills were more visual. She was a gifted amateur painter—you have seen some of her work already. Her tropical frescoes on the hallway ceilings outside our door represent her in her more or less ephemeral 'Michelangelo' period—you know, working on teetering scaffolds and doing frescoes up on ceilings while making sarcastic remarks to people who were watching from below. She loved all the visual arts and spent much of her time collecting and restoring pieces of antique value. She was also, more than anyone else, the literary person in the family. I will have much more to say about that in the course of time.

"Aunt Bernice, on the other hand, not infrequently displayed some impatience with music. Fine music is not for impatient people; one must be willing to put everything else out of one's mind—even those grandiose fantasies that some music can inspire, and must take up residence, as it were, inside the music itself, attentive to every modulation in tonality, however slight—a task not for people who have somewhere to go and something else to think about. In reference to Aunt Bernice, she was always impatient with everything. Nevertheless, I have always thought that persons with such refined articulation of words as she had, such rhythm and beauty of voice, must have a wellspring of music in them somewhere. Her every movement, every gesture, a tilt of a wrist or the position of a hand, seemed to have an unheard melody that went with it. If she did have music in her soul, which I believe she did, I never had the chance to experience it. But then, she always seemed to be in a hurry to go someplace else, as if she was late for an appointment. But there was no appointment that I was aware of, and she wasn't late for anything. I could never fathom what was stirring in her."

"She was perpetually diverted, perhaps, by something."

"Yes, but by what, I wonder?"

"She herself may not have known—just one of those longings people can never define."

"Perhaps something she felt obliged to do but could never get herself to do it?"

"And Cornelia . . . after all, being a Schefflin . . . ?"

"Well . . . yes . . . of course . . . a fine pianist, fostered on that magnificent piano itself, which skill has stood her in good stead on many occasions in her life. She has, like Frederick, made music a cornerstone of her family activities. One of her sons, Gabriel, is an outstanding professional violinist and performs now and then with some string quartet, in Geneva, I believe. Her daughter, Giselle, is a budding cellist, working as she does with the original Schefflin instrument."

"So the instrument has completed its pilgrimage to the New World by returning to the Old. In any event, they have continued the Schefflin tradition."

"I guess you could put it like that. How could it be otherwise? And yet . . . and yet."

"'And yet!'" I echoed Besserman. I looked at him as he sat magisterially in his encompassing chair, his eyes shadowed in thought, in reminiscence, his head bowed just slightly, his hands now at rest and folded across his waist. I repeated the phrase: " 'And yet.' Is that all you have to say, Theodore, when you are scarcely ever at a loss for what to say; meanwhile, you hover on something else to say, something that you have been both withholding and not withholding from me all this time. You bombard me with hesitations."

"Another story, if you will, Edmund," he replied, "that needs must be told if . . . if . . . "

"If? Another story, another hesitation? If what?"

"If you are going to understand us, who we are . . . where we have been . . . where we are going."

"Proceed, though I have already divined what this is all about. You are not good at keeping secrets, Theodore."

"Ha!" he blurted out. "One can't be good at everything, can one? Anyway, it's not a secret in the usual sense . . . just a placing of one's cards on the table in the proper order. Some things must come later. Sometimes they must come years and years later. Sometimes they must come centuries and even millennia later. I wonder how often things are like that. Providence, I am told by those who presume to know, deals its cards in its own good time; keeps things partial until the time is right to make them full. I don't wish to compare myself to something as plenipotentiary as that, but, in any event, no one can argue that I don't share good company. Tell me what you have divined, Edmund, and that shall be our starting point."

"So I shall be the one who begins your story—or this story anyway?" I asked. I knew that something of this order was bound to take place.

"What could be more appropriate? Since the story in time will become your story as well, who could be better than you to set the terms?" he answered.

"The terms? I don't understand."

"Every story worthy of the name has a central point, a soul, a heart of the matter, which establishes, around it, its limit, its circumference; what we might call the mutually interactive centripetal and centrifugal forces that define its tensions. To define the center and to discern the limit in the nexus of their reciprocal relations is, I propose you could say, to set the terms."

"Then I am not sure I know how to set the terms."

"Of course you do. Our conversation would not have taken the turn it has unless you did."

"Then I shall state what I know or, in any case, what I feel must be confirmed or denied."

"As good a place to begin as any!"

Well, another long hesitation—on my part this time. I felt simply too diffident to begin where I knew I had to begin, to put myself out on a limb that could be most ignominiously lopped off if I was wrong, yet it was a limb I knew I had to edge out on because I knew that I was not wrong and that, in any case, Besserman was forcing me to "set the terms."

Finally, I asserted, rather obstreperously, as if stumbling over a stone and warning someone that I was falling in his direction, "Frederick and Agnes Schefflin were not the real parents of Cornelia. They were her adoptive parents, were they not?"

"Indeed!"

"Is that an affirmation or a denial?"

"Neither, at this point. Anyway, what is so exceptional about that? People often adopt children."

"But this is an exceptional case."

"So what is exceptional about it?"

I took a deep breath. "Her adoptive parents were her uncle and aunt. Frederick and Agnes were Cornelia's uncle and aunt. Her real parents were Uncle Aloysius and Aunt Bernice. Now that, you must admit, is an exceptional case."

"And how do you arrive at this extraordinary supposition?"

"Because you have evaded several questions I have put to you, Theodore, which you are still doing, by the way, and because of your 'and yets.' The supposition I have made is the only logical connection that binds such a miscellany of prevarications together. What else could I think?"

"Then I shall have to be more circumspect about my—how did you call them?—'prevarications' in the future, at least with you, Edmund. You obviously can read some of the cards before they have been flipped over. But that is good. Frankly, I figured you might be able to do that. But you still have not set the terms of the story."

"The terms? We come back to that?"

"Yes, the terms. The outer limit, the circumference, the beginning and the end, provided that anything in life has a beginning and an end; let's say an onset and an offset; that which positions the heart of the matter clearly at the center and no place else. What will determine that?"

"A question, I assume."

"A question?"

"The question. More significant, Theodore, than your prevarications were that you prevaricated at all. I cannot see what loss would have been incurred by your simply telling me outright the facts of the case. From everything you have told me so far and from the inferences one can make, I can only guess that your not putting all the cards on the table at once perpetuates a set of understandings among the original participants in this state of affairs; and those understandings entail an agreement to withhold disclosure—for the time being, however that 'time being' may have been defined—of all there was to be disclosed. I rather suspect that these understandings, in some way, still obtain today, even as you talk to me and even though most of the parties privy to these understandings are now deceased. I guess one could ask many questions about all of that, but there is only one question, at this juncture, which really counts for me."

"And that question would be?"

"Was Cornelia ever informed about the arrangement? Does she know about it now? Does Cornelia know who her real parents were? Does she know who Uncle Aloysius and Aunt Bernice really were?"

"So that is the heart of the matter?"

"If confidences have been imparted, and one needs to understand what these are, one needs to know the crux of what is being held in confidence.

Further, your big prevarication, more than all your little prevarications, implies that there is unfinished business involved here. I suspect rather strongly, Theodore, that my question is also your question."

Besserman raised his folded hands to his lips and held them there for a moment. Then, spreading his fingers upward and outward like the petals of a flower and lowering his hands, he exclaimed. "I am glad, Edmund, that you are not a trial lawyer and that, thereby, a multitude of plaintiffs, if not also defendants, have been spared your cross-examinations. I have been arraigned and convicted. You are right, of course. You are absolutely right. You are right about everything."

"So you affirm my suppositions?"

"I do."

"And would you have finally told me, even if I had not made the suppositions?"

"Probably not. I had to wait for you to advance your hypotheses before I could confirm them."

"So could I make the further supposition that your prevarications were calculated to elicit exactly that result?"

"Perhaps. But not, in any event, 'calculated.' After all, how could I know 'exactly' how you would take things? Nor am I quite that devious. Let's call them 'inducements'; I could hardly know that, or how, or even when, you would decide to follow up on them."

"But why did I have to be the first to say these things, Theodore?"

"As you have correctly assumed, Edmund, there is unfinished business here, and my attendance upon your initiative is part of that unfinished business. A portion of those original understandings involved in this case differentiating between what one could advance on one's own initiative and what one could respond to at the initiative of another. You are also correct about the key question you have posited. I know it must seem almost preposterous to you, but, in any rigorous sense at all, I do not know the answer to the question."

He lowered his hands again into his lap. "I am glad, Edmund," he resumed, "that the terms you have set for me, more or less, and perhaps without your fully realizing it, hinge on what is for me, as I have said, a real question.

Too often the questions we have are merely ruses, gauged to produce the answers we already think we know. But this is a real question for me. I say this because, to this day, and for complicated reasons, I do not know the answer. I can make some reasonable conjectures, have made reasonable conjectures, possess a wealth of circumstantial evidence to support those conjectures, but I do not have the direct evidence to confirm the answer, and, until I know the answer, I do not feel at liberty even to air those conjectures with anybody except—under these special circumstances—with you. For, Edmund, you have hit the mark; I am bound by just those understandings you mention not to speak of it to Cornelia. In all my dealings with her over a long period of time, I have come to the intimation that, if she herself knew, she has had similar grounds for reticence, similar obligations conferred upon her, no doubt in generosity and benevolence, obligations to hold in reserve the mystery she bears in her heart; and, if I am correct about this, she will observe those obligations until the end of her days. We enter here, not upon secrets, but, as I have said, upon a mystery, and it is this that we must, as much as we can, attempt to plumb even as we persist in revering at the deepest level what very well may be, and what we may come even more to fathom as, the inviolateness of its fidelity. As Frederick would say, the unspoken gives us a task—not necessarily to translate it into speech but to discern what it bids us to do. I do not know whom we are most bid to serve in all of this, Edmund: all of those originally involved, I imagine, in one way or another. But at the center of it all is the one whose blessed but tragic image impelled you at the beginning into this inquiry."

"Uncle Aloysius," I said.

"Uncle Aloysius it is," Besserman affirmed.

Besserman shuffled out of his colossal chair like a winter bear emerging from its hibernal den, stretching its powerful limbs, and shaking out its shaggy pelt. He shambled around the inner sanctum of his "hilltop citadel" for a minute or two, stopping to bask momentarily in the latticed rays of the early afternoon sun, arcing downward through the lancet windows and fixing his gaze on the stained-glass medallions that shimmered like many-bejeweled diadems in the keen sunlight. He then edged over to our luncheon table, stacked its various items on a tray, and hoisted the tray out to the landing to be picked up by the waitstaff later on. He closed the door and returned to his chair where he sat again, reposing, aloft and serene, his arms held evenly on the armrests, like an ancient king upon his royal dais.

"So where did he come from, this Aloysius Fitzgerald, this Dr. Aloysius Fitzgerald, I should say?" Besserman uttered with a slight flourish. "How did, for example, Uncle Aloysius and Aunt Bernice, originating in such different worlds as they did, ever find one another? And beyond that initial meeting, what drew them into such a close bond together, a bond both infelicitous and fruitful at the same time, that would have such manifold consequences, that would touch so deeply the lives of others? Yet this kind of thing happens all the time and remains, for all that, as much an enigma as ever, despite all the chatter it produces regarding it, the sort that typically generates the inevitable question: 'Now whatever did those two see in one another?' Heavens, how should I know! Yet I want to know. And I am not afraid, up to a certain point, to ask.

"He appeared one day, without advance notice, Agnes once told me, standing next to, and perhaps a little behind, Aunt Bernice on the bow of small sailing yacht that hove to a dock out of a sunny mist that lingered over the ocean's surface. Frederick and Agnes, at Aunt Bernice's urging, had driven out to Marblehead to view a sailing regatta and partake of a picnic that would follow. Some recent acquaintances—Aunt Bernice didn't mention who—had entered a modest yawl in the competition; she would join them, ostensibly as part of the crew, though if Aunt Bernice knew anything about sailing it would be quite a surprise to anyone who knew her. But the sea was calm and there was little wind, and the light mist so obscured the visibility on the bay that, though it was a lovely, balmy afternoon, one could see fairly little into the distance, and the regatta never got seriously underway. Then, as Frederick and Agnes waited on the dock appropriated for the afternoon's festivities, into this tranquil prospect floated, on some indiscernible breeze or tidal swell, a vision, almost, as it were, gliding on a shaft of sunlight, of that insouciant and vivacious beauty, framed by the flocculent cascade of her raven hair; just to her side and framing her in his own gilded aurora, was Aloysius Fitzgerald, Uncle Aloysius himself. The two of them stood together in silence on the bow of that airy, slack-sailed sloop, each attired in the sporty linen suits still considered fashionable in those days for boating events and meditating with somber but tender eyes the dipping and rising of the limpid surface of the bay as they approached the landing.

"Well, Edmund, my source for this account, as I mentioned, was Agnes, whose perfervid imagination, I would think, did what it could to provide the occasion with the apposite literary embellishments. But in her own way too, and I give her credit for this, she may have caught, at that moment, what would be the tenor, then and thereafter, of this remarkable confluence of two human beings—a confluence oddly seamless and solitary and noble and sad. The spell of this almost mystic luminosity, she went on to tell me, was broken soon enough as the scene became more animated. Uncle Aloysius leapt onto the dock, holding a line and guiding the craft into place as others emerged from the hold and the stern, Uncle Aloysius's medical school friends, as they turned out, fetching from below the canisters of well-iced wine and baskets of savory fried chicken. The boating party that followed was pleasant and affable, though subdued, perhaps because the regatta had been a disappointment, or perhaps because Frederick and Agnes, to say nothing of the medical friends, were finding out for the first time that any social affair that included the young physician and his glorious inamorata was doomed to fall into a penumbra cast by the incandescence of this inimitable pair. When the two of them were together, everyone else was relegated, by some inscrutable law of nature, into the status of a stupefied and dumbfounded spectator.

"About Uncle Aloysius, this much I can conjecture. There are men, I think, whose appreciation of feminine beauty runs so deep and so far beyond what the ordinary man is capable of that, in itself, it constitutes a kind of genius—and I assure you, Edmund, I use that word advisedly, for of all the words of our language I doubt there are few more systematically abused and more persistently invoked to expound a condition all too often approximately opposite to the sort of inference being claimed. But I do not think I am being presumptuous if I observe that Uncle Aloysius had a unique disposition in this regard—the sort that few can understand, except perhaps by analogy, and, because few can understand it, like any genius it is all too often disparaged. Also, like any genius, it is as much a liability as an asset.

When it is given to a singular human being to see something with the sharp, penetrating eyes of the angelic intellect—for, if there is anything such as the angelic intellect, that would be, I take it, its distinguishing mark—such a person must necessarily be led down roads obscure to us and possibly perilous to him or herself, for inevitably his or her perspicuity on one hand and our obtuseness on the other must, in the end, discover its terminal and sometimes fatal collision.

"It is strange how persistently this remarkable propensity gets figured forth in the literature of the world, as if fiction were the only vehicle possible to express what most people, of custom and necessity, can consider, or can apprehend finally, only in a fictive guise, though they take this fiction, ironically, as a reality, even as they dismiss the real thing as an improbable fiction. Consider the knights of medieval romance whose capacity to discern beauty in a woman was extolled as being as much a mark of distinction in their character as their military prowess, though this capacity was also fatal, in the end, to them all. Consider the figure of Alexandros in Homer, who began as the judge of the goddesses for their beauty and ended up, rightfully so, in a sense, as the consort of Helen, the most beautiful mortal woman the world had ever known; how easy it was for the chieftains of the opposing hosts, even the chieftains of his own side, to disparage him for this. Yet how misplaced that critique was! After all, one side was ready to sacrifice everything to retain her, while the other side was willing to sacrifice everything to get her back. Except, of course, for Achilles—the greatest of them all! But even here, for the sake of his own Briseis, he was willing to allow his own comrades in arms to be massacred, almost as if there were a measure, disproportionate in the ways of the world but proportionate in itself, terrible and finally doomed, between a man's capacity to engage the highest order of the cosmos, to converse almost as an equal among the gods, and his worship of an exceptional woman. I think of the ill-fated McDiarmud and his illustrious Dierdre; I think of Lancelot, equally ill-fated, and his matchless Guinevere; I think of Tristan on the storm-tossed wastes of the Irish Sea . . . ah, but I do go on. I hope you will forgive my somewhat excessive literary excursus here. Agnes would have prized it so. Good for Agnes! Who knows how much she may have understood in her heart about all of these matters!

"So here was a man drawn to a woman's beauty and, because of her beauty, to all of those things that made her who she was; her tone of voice, her mode of dress, the way she would raise her eyebrows when she was surprised, the kinds of books she read, her particular tastes in food, her quirks, you might say, became objects of devotion for him. Don't we all do this, Edmund, in our own lesser, more dispassionate ways? Haven't you done this? Haven't I done this? Indeed . . . how could I forget . . . indeed, how could I ever forget? Yet, I dare say, he just did it so much further than we do or are capable of doing. I might add that her theatricality, if I may call it that, was a source of fascination for him too, for she knew how beautiful she was, and she knew how best to show it off and make the most of it. And he knew that. He knew she was doing that primarily for him; that, however much she craved an audience, he, in the end, was the sum and substance of all her audiences, and he welcomed and loved that mark of distinction.

"Now, as for Aunt Bernice, it is infinitely more difficult to say. It is only natural that the motives of the other sex in relation to our own are always obscure, if for no other reason than that it is impossible for us to live, or to have lived, through any of them. That Uncle Aloysius was an imposing man you can see readily from his photograph. He was vigorous and clear-eyed, intelligent and kind and in no manner parading around that self-assuming character, that 'I own everything' pretentiousness that mars so many men of his caliber. I would maintain that any woman would appreciate such features in a man, though, having seen, in the course of my life, so many inexplicable aberrations—or at least what I think of as aberrations—in this matter, I confess myself still pretty much in the dark about what it is, after all, a woman looks for in a man. Moreover, I would guess that Aunt Bernice realized in him this unique capacity to apprehend and appreciate her beauty. She may have thought—and she was probably dead right about this—that there could never be a more appreciative audience for her than he—not just in the intensity of appreciation but in the fact of the appreciation being conferred by someone possessed of such perspicacious qualifications to do so. It is noteworthy perhaps that, after his death, as far as we know, she never sought another.

"More than that, she understood that the two of them made an extraordinary-looking couple. He not only framed, he set off, her own beauty in the way that the quintessence of a *premier danseur* incontestably resides in his ability to enhance and enrich the finesse of the *première danseuse*. It is her dance, the dance of the prima ballerina, after all, that really counts. And when she takes one of those dazzling leaps, she must trust, trust in the depths of her being, that her male consort has the agility, the timing, and the strength to catch her on the way down, and to catch her in such a way that it is she, and not he, who remains the focus of the dance. It takes an unusually virile power to do that—a combination of strength, of steadiness and resiliency, and, most of all, of a willingness to realize and to put oneself at the disposal of what is, and can only be, a uniquely feminine disposition.

"There was something strangely concordant about their physiques so that, when they moved even in very ordinary circumstances, they moved in a kind of harmony together, a rhythmic grace that flowed from one to the other, but all very naturally. In this regard—and I saw this myself, Edmund, many a time—it was difficult for them to enter a public place, let's say a restaurant or the foyer of a theater, without a sudden quiescence falling over the crowd, or a gasp, or a puzzled murmuring about who they might be and why they were there. That they might be—and were mistaken as—putative 'stars' of the 'silver screen' was a frequent occurrence, and not a few eager fans sought out their autographs, until they discovered their error. One could claim that they looked more 'the part' than the real thing generally does, whose actual appearance, divested of the magic of cinematic art, all too often disappoints. I might add that, if this were true in more ordinary circumstances, you can imagine what it was like when they took the floor together at a nightclub, or a hotel ballroom, or a country-club tea dance. It was never long before the other dancers slouched off the floor, mortified by their own delay, as if their clumsy and sluggish lingering defiled a space that had become consecrated, for the moment, by such votaries from the temple of beauty itself.

"For all this, I don't think that Uncle Aloysius was particularly cognizant or heedful of this response in others, or did anything deliberately to provoke it—he was simply too absorbed in her; but Aunt Bernice certainly was aware, did all she could to elicit it, and enjoyed every minute of it. Curiously, though, it was all rather 'natural' in its demeanor and not, by and large, an artifice: I have known couples who like to make a very big production about their 'coupleness,' who take prodigious pride in celebrating themselves in front of others constantly; who make lavish public displays of their mutual affection; who are living exemplars of what the French call *l'égoïsme à deux*. There was little of this sort of thing in Uncle Aloysius and Aunt Bernice; their unity was all the more striking because of their differentiation, and if both stood on the opposite sides of a room, they were never more together than in that situation.

"There may have been something else, too, between them, and I can hardly venture to say what it was. It was not artifice, as I have said, but it goes well beyond the merely natural. You know, Edmund, when one considers the Schefflins, and I include Agnes under that aegis, one is impressed by their intelligence, their skill, their industry, their social affability, their modesty; but all of these attributes are, in the end, common in a sense, or potentially common to us normal human specimens, if and when we put our minds to it. But Uncle Aloysius and Aunt Bernice shared something that went beyond all of that and cannot adequately be described by those terms. This is not to say that they did not possess some of these attributes as well—as so exceptionally they did; it is to say that they were gifted by something almost preternatural in its register—not a possession but a being possessed by something outside themselves, a being possessed by a daimon or a tutelary divinity that the ancients would have readily described as having 'flashing eyes' and an awe-inspiring aureole of light emanating from it. I am not describing just an appearance as such but rather an '*esprit*' that flowed from them, an aliveness or an energy that enlivened their every movement and gesture and word. I think this is what brought them together—an energy perhaps even somewhat auspicious in the potential sunburst of its mutual impact."

"So when you speak of the Schefflins, you include Agnes in that particular circle," I interjected. "But Uncle Aloysius and Aunt Bernice occupy their own special circle—their own enchanted circle, as you seem to describe it. And about Cornelia . . . ?"

"Cornelia? Cornelia? Well, she . . . she is an exceptional case altogether. She is her own circle . . . yes, her own circle," Besserman mumbled softly, as if talking to himself. "We are about to get to that. All of these circles intertwine at the end, I assure you."

"Intertwine in Cornelia, perhaps?" I appended.

Besserman stared at me. "Yes ... of course ... that's it. That's it. Again you anticipate me."

He folded his hands in his lap, appeared to ready himself, to initiate a new movement, a new cantata perhaps, a shift in key, a rhythmic variation, I couldn't say.

"Yet, Edmund," he recommenced, "you should not be precipitous in concluding that I am describing what was necessarily a happy relationship—one of those irresistible affinities, you know, 'made in heaven' or something like that. I am even reluctant to define what happiness and unhappiness can mean in such matters. Can one and the same thing be most sublimely fortunate and most sublimely unfortunate at the same time? I think it can—it happens all the time, not just in affairs of the heart but in everything else that suffering mankind must endure. Here again one must be cautious, for, if gliding in the buoyant air of another's joy may be subject to its limits, sounding the depths of another's sorrow is boundless in the tenebrous spaces it cannot begin to plumb. I did have, as you must realize, many a conversation with Aunt Bernice on social occasions of various kinds and sometimes, though rarely—and usually at someone else's behest—concerning her financial and legal affairs. She was an entrancing interlocutor, lively and imaginative and fun. The only problem was that, at a certain point, one could hear the downward rush of a stage curtain descending on the scene, a shuffling of props, the clicks as new lighting switches were activated and old ones turned off, and she was gone, or rather, one was gone, the scene was over, and a new one had started somewhere else with someone else. One had been a character, a *dramatis persona*, for an interlude and not a real person, and that's what she had been too, all the while. Heart did not meet heart; soul did not meet soul. There was, I believe, no matter what else went on in her life, no matter what role she scripted for herself from scene to scene, little real capacity in her for a heartfelt intimacy with other human beings, or at least with those of us who did not command her exceptional attention. She had limitless capacity for passionate admiration—yes; for passionate gratitude in being admired—yes; but for passionate intimacy—perhaps no. If I am correct about this, Edmund, and I say all of this with a great deal of forbearance, the consequences must have been beyond all our ability to speak of it. For Uncle Aloysius—the devoted physician, the healer, the inveterate lover—was tenderness itself in all its multitudinous dimensions. I doubt there was a more intimate man in this world than Uncle Aloysius.

"You may have deduced, I would think, that there was initial and even some sustained opposition to their union. When they married, as they finally did after many years of a kind of a vague and unofficial 'betrothal,' it was a private affair, an elopement, in effect, a surreptitious event with no family present at all. Now, that fact suggests that, for some reason or ensemble of reasons, it was best not to have families involved. We could speculate at length about those reasons, and perhaps we will get to that in the course of our account. It is natural for parents to be protective of their children and to look out for their interests; and nowhere is this protectiveness more evident than in matters pertaining to marriage. But such a defense is not always benign, for it may be that the values being defended are not benign in themselves or the parents are defending themselves rather than the child. I do not think that either of these possibilities were overtly the case in the relationship of Uncle Aloysius and Aunt Bernice, though I think the situation was complicated. On the surface and to the casual spectator, it could have looked like the clash, as clichéd as these matters so often seem to be, yet nonetheless pernicious for all of its clichés, of cultural and religious allegiances. Aunt Bernice came from a decidedly Belfast Presbyterian background. By 'decidedly' I mean that it was pronounced and combative at some time in its remote past. Agnes, often in a spirit of humor, used to tell me about its more extreme manifestations. I don't know how much of this background still assumed an important role in the life of her extant family members; it certainly, as far as I know, had little further role in either her or her sister's life; they had distanced themselves from it, and that is why they could treat it in the somewhat comic mode that they did. Furthermore, I am not sure how much of a family was left anyway. Many of them had been military people. Agnes once told me that the Civil War had been a bottleneck from which her once involuted ancestral lines emerged seriously decimated.

"Uncle Aloysius, on the other hand, came from a large and proliferating Irish Catholic family, of much more recent emigration, tenacious in its loyalties and aggressive in its efforts to overcome the discrimination encountered in every sphere of life. Uncle Aloysius's father was a physician, perhaps the first professional man in his family's history and, I have heard it reported, one of the first Irish Catholics to be admitted to Harvard Medical School. That was an achievement, given the ferocity of prejudice that existed then and even until much more recently than we are always willing to acknowledge. Uncle Aloysius followed in his footsteps. I do think he revered his background and tried to live aspects of it, but what he was able to live of it was alone and apart from his liaison and later marriage with Aunt Bernice.

"You can see here, Edmund, spread before us all the right ingredients for the sort of clash I have intimated above. That does not mean that there ever was such a clash, at least of this kind. I never met the parents, or any other family members of Agnes or Aunt Bernice. Their father was deceased, and their mother was something of a recluse, living by herself in a rundown house in Medford with a few thousand dog-eared old books stuffed in every nook and cranny and entertaining her daughters, on the rare visits she allowed them, with fine old stories from the past and the potent blackberry liqueur she distilled herself from the wilderness of scraggly brambles that crowded up against her house. She did have a flower garden of sorts, more noteworthy in its neighborhood for its spectacular weeds than for its withered and withering blossoms. By contrast, I came to know over time many of the Fitzgerald clan, a tumultuous lot with an addiction for picnics and sports and horse racing and strutting around in ceremonious processions, holding up banners of one kind or another, and in not-so-ceremonious parades, sporting silk top hats and striped bandoleers, and flocking to these religious events they called 'novenas' at the local parish church whenever they came up.

"Good enough! Now, I really don't have the impression that Uncle Aloysius's mother and father were somehow against his prolonged courtship of, and eventual betrothal and marriage with, Aunt Bernice, nor that Aunt Bernice's reclusive mother cared about much of anything at all except her privacy, her books, her garden (whatever its shortcomings) and her blackberry liqueur, and she would have been the last person to put her foot down on some principle that she, or at least her ancestors of recent vintage, had ceased to care about a long time ago. But some parents in that situation are wary, and perhaps rightfully so. They know that there may be shadowy figures in the backdrop, the distant or maybe not-so-distant cousin or uncle or whatever of the spouse in question, who will not let old grudges pass, though incurred centuries earlier; that even the well-disposed have deposited deep in their psyches, like hard little snags of shrapnel, tactless expressions and insidious attitudes they may hardly be aware of but that do have a way of popping out of their sullen troves at unguarded or stressful moments; and that, even under the most advantageous of circumstances, the projected union will involve, inevitably, ineluctably, renunciations that one or the other or both spouses may find difficult to abide. Yes—all of that, in addition to whatever other factors may be relevant.

"I doubt very much that Aunt Bernice's mother gave the matter much thought. Her Bernice could marry anyone patient enough to endure her impromptu scenes and excessive preening. That one could have never succeeded in dragging her mother off to an Irish Catholic wedding is, in this context, immaterial; one could have never dragged her off to any wedding of whatever stamp, and even the strudels and quiches, *choucroute* and apple wine and *kirschwasser* and other Alsatian and Black Forest delicacies dished up at the wedding of Agnes and Frederick could not dislodge her from her bucolic, if shabby, retreat. But it was a different matter for the parents of Uncle Aloysius. If they were familiar with a life of renunciations, and the religious rhetoric that justified those renunciations, they were equally disposed to regard some renunciations as ones that human beings had no privilege to make. To all appearances, they liked, enjoyed, and admired Aunt Bernice (who couldn't?) and respected—even understood and marveled at—Uncle Aloysius's devotion to her. Devotion—this, in their heart of hearts and soul of souls—they understood. They lived in a world in which devotion perhaps counted for more than anything else. But early on they may have detected the reserve in her, her apparent narcissism, most of all her lack of warmth, which, if carried over into her spousal relationship, they knew their son would eventually miss dearly. Also they feared in their hearts that their son's choice would involve possibly some of those inadmissible renunciations—renunciations, finally, severe and calamitous in their consequences. These renunciations implied renunciations for themselves as well, though their projected effects on an esteemed son were the real locus of their concern. And, I regret having to acknowledge this, their fears were not wholly ill-founded.

"I have said that they would not be opposed to a marriage, but I would be remiss if I did not add that they would have deeply regretted such a prospect. It was clear from the start—when the time came, and it would be a long wait before the time did come—that Aunt Bernice would not suffer herself to be married according to the rites of the Roman Church. She probably didn't say as much, but she was interested, eventually, in marrying Uncle Aloysius, and not interested in marrying his family, or his Church, or a thousand years of the tortuous and tormented past of his people. Most of all, she was not interested in marrying a set of commitments and undertakings that she dreaded her future spouse might take seriously if he actually made vows to uphold them while standing before a high altar of his faith and that she, in no unequivocal terms, was unable to countenance without a modicum of dread. Aunt Bernice, one got the impression, took some obverse pride in fancying herself and her sister—not incorrectly, in a way, but shortsightedly, in another way, as it would turn out—as the final blooms bestowed by an otherwise prolific nature upon the terminal florescence of a perishing stalk. For her, the trajectory of her family line was sinking into a melancholy demise. What a wonderful role it was to partake of that distinguished company designated as the 'sole survivors' or the 'last of the something or other,' silhouetted against the sunset or poised in a plaintive gesture beneath a slowly falling curtain! Such a delectable denouement must, of necessity, be accoutered in all the livery most requisite for the 'dying swan' and its inimitable, heartrending song. In contrast, poor Agnes did not share this perspective, though her aspirations, as we shall see, were sadly disappointed—though ironically fulfilled, partially anyway, precisely by her sister, whose vision of a wistful *grand finale* Agnes did not entertain, nor was entertained by, in any sense at all, but whose obsession with that vision would provide Agnes with the child she had always desired in the depths of her being.

"Now, to the contrary, the Fitzgeralds' perspective, the father and mother of Uncle Aloysius, could not have been more radically different, for they thought of themselves as the fecund seedbed of vibrant generations to come;

and in this perspective they embodied not only their own attitudes but those of their clan and neighborhood. Moreover, there was for them a question of some social accountability vis-à-vis these same constituencies, a warranty of honor they needed to secure against the potential disappointment or even disapproval of the community, or at least a need to provide explanations to those whose convictions they shared and whose prospects they supported. At a deeper level, you must recall, Edmund, that the time about which we speak was not as latitudinarian in its attitudes as we are today. Rites and customs, as ancient and venerable as they were, were held as conferring a kind of absoluteness and finality upon the events they helped to mold. Our contemporary negligence, if not positive derision, of such scruples in the past may sometimes justly discern that secondary concerns were often confused with the primary while, at the same time, we succeed, from a different angle, of course, in perpetuating the identical confusion, and primary concerns are relegated to the secondary. But I shall not dwell on this—well, not at the moment. In any event, Uncle Aloysius's parents did not, as far as I know, blatantly object—after all, they could find comfort in assuring themselves that not all the facts were in. They urged delay. Aunt Bernice could change her mind; their relationship could shift and settle in the gradual seismic way that relationships often do; new considerations regarding a prospective marriage could make their entrance and have their effect. Time could alter, and alter substantially, the landscape that at this point was so distressing to their social sensibilities and their moral consciences.

"Uncle Aloysius, however, never wanted delay. But Aunt Bernice did, and I think it is safe to say that it was Aunt Bernice who, in the end, always choreographed the moves and measured out the pace of their relationship together. Aunt Bernice and Uncle Aloysius, as I have indicated, were not to be married for many years—not technically, not legally anyway. They were, or they seemed to present themselves as, 'betrothed' in some archaic, some Old World, primeval way, a 'betrothal' that for all purposes was tantamount to a vow of marriage without the formalities and blessings of a final union but with, according to some lights, the conferral of selected privileges consonant with a union that had been irrevocably agreed upon. I will not try to unravel here, Edmund, what this was all about, whether such an arrangement had authentic grounds and precedents in the vast reservoir of human experience over the ages, or whether it was one more dramatic ploy deftly contrived by Aunt Bernice to ensure the preservation of her options while, at the same time, casting Uncle Aloysius into a supportive role that may well have been a burden on his conscience and involved compromises that both affirmed and violated the deepest attachments of his heart. But what I am trying to tell you, Edmund, no matter how one chooses to define it, is that Aunt Bernice succeeded in attaining what she wanted. It was her intention to bind him to herself by a liaison that she knew, counting on his integrity, his sense of honor, even his fidelity to a tradition whose injunctions she did not affirm, he would regard as the effective consummation of a *de facto,* though not a *de jure*, marriage, one from which he would never have even remotely considered himself at liberty to disengage, even if he had wanted to. And I am convinced that he never wanted to; never even remotely wanted to."

"And Aunt Bernice's options," I interrupted to ask, "what were these?"

"Simple enough, Edmund," Besserman replied. "I don't wish to presume too much about her motives, but to all appearances she wished to sustain her relationship with Uncle Aloysius, to 'lock it in,' one could say, even as she safeguarded the mobility she needed to take advantage of opportunities in her calling as these unpredictably and fortuitously presented themselves. She knew that his own calling, the practice of medicine, particularly of what today we would call 'family medicine,' would be demanding on his time and resources and would, in a comprehensive way, tie him down to a very specific region and circuit of people. A family physician, after all, cannot arbitrarily walk away from patients or from the community in which he settles himself. She was not ready for that level of 'localization' and may have, arguably, never been ready for it unless, in time, it could be somehow configured—and I supply the somewhat implausible analogy here—like a revolving stage in a circular theater whose revolutions, while centered in one place, left her the freedom to redirect the purview of the stage and reorder the scenery and props as she deemed necessary. I don't wish to disparage Aunt Bernice in any way by making these observations, and I hope I haven't; she was an enormously intelligent and gifted woman and knew what she was about. The deeper problem may have resided with Uncle Aloysius. How could a man as devoted as he was to this woman renounce her when he knew very well that she was committed to him and tenacious in this commitment; and when that 'betrothal,' that exchange of promises, in whatever guise that had assumed, had taken place inexorably, irrefrangibly, between them?

"This is not to say that they took up residence together through all those early years of their liaison until, as would eventually occur, they officially married. Social discretion, appropriate to its time, was exercised with care. Early in his professional life, after completing an internship and residency in Boston, Uncle Aloysius was offered a partnership in a medical practice in Concord, New Hampshire. An old friend of his father had developed this practice over a half century; now, advanced in age and no longer having the energy to provide adequately for his patients, he needed a younger associate to work with him and, if everything looked propitious to this end, to assume the practice upon his retirement. Uncle Aloysius, at the urging of his father as well as being attracted to Concord and its surrounding area, accepted the invitation and moved to Concord, where, as it would turn out, his predecessor soon retired, and he assumed responsibility for the entire practice, which would occupy him for the rest of his brief life. Aunt Bernice remained in Boston, where, at one and the same time, she was a short train ride from Concord and also had easy access to a variety of New England cultural centers, to its many summer-stock companies, and, of course, to New York City, with its robust theatrical life. Their time together, from what little we know about it, was confined to the occasional vacation, to their sudden and startling appearance at family dinners and celebrations, to a variety of more or less sensational public events at which Aunt Bernice, with Uncle Aloysius as her inimitable escort, so supremely triumphed, and to Uncle Aloysius's dedicated and often strenuously engineered arrivals at opening nights for the few 'gigs' at small and generally rural theatrical productions that Aunt Bernice was able to muster for herself during that time. It seemed such a fanciful and sporadic affair, the two of them together, like flashing, transient sunlight on the ripples of a pond, like a darting pair of fireflies when the moon peers from behind a lattice of clouds and the two points of light move in tandem, move apart, splendidly one, splendidly in consort together, no matter how distant from one another they seemed. One could almost be tempted to say that such an *ad hoc* set of arrangements itself assumed the mantle of a finely orchestrated panorama of formalities.

"Yet one might very well be deceived in such a judgment. I knew Uncle Aloysius well during these years—we were about the same age—and he was a deeply anguished man. He did not regard any of these arrangements as 'formalities.' They were uneasy and tenuous adjustments he made to bridge an abysmal cleavage in his soul, a cleavage between a set of deeply ingrained loyalties on one hand and, on the other hand, his faithfulness to a woman he loved more than his own life. Still, one might very well conjecture that Uncle Aloysius would one day 'come to his senses,' come to some kind of realization that the situation was untenable. But then something unexpected happened—something that did inevitably limit both of their options, though in a way thoroughly unconventional, and, in the last analysis, thoroughly predictable."

"Cornelia," I said.

"Exactly," Besserman said. He smiled as he gazed down into his hands, smiled to himself, smiled inwardly as if at some deeply imperturbable source of satisfaction that irradiated throughout the very center of his physical being; then he looked up and smiled at me.

"How often," he murmured, in a tone both tender and jocose, "is a stroke of bad luck the best luck there is, so much so that it was never bad luck to begin with? What greater gift, what more wine of astonishment, what more boundless largesse could we all have had bestowed upon us than what ensued at this moment of our lives, with all its consequent manifold of extraordinary convolutions! Yes, Cornelia—Cornelia herself.

"It is best, Edmund, to begin where it began with me. It was early autumn, and I had accompanied Frederick and Agnes to New York City on what was intended to be a mixed business and pleasure trip. The Schefflins often managed to combine the two, wherever they went. Martha sometimes used to accompany me on these New York trips, but on this occasion she was too tied up with her violin students—an impending recital, I recall. However, it was even more of a trip than that: it was, for the Schefflins, the first leg of an extended journey to Europe, for they were to embark in a few days at the New York wharves on a French steamer and sail out for Cherbourg.

Agnes spent those days frequenting the artistic and literary places she loved so much, while Frederick visited many of the Schefflin establishments, conferring with managers and interacting in that companionable way he had with chefs and waitresses and soda jerks whose fealty he was always so successful in evoking. I had the somewhat more mundane task of spending my time at the branch Schefflin offices in downtown Manhattan and of gobbling down untold quantities of their glorious Danish pastries while studying leases and contracts pertinent to a number of recent initiatives. Of course, we enjoyed evenings together and managed to take in an opera at the Met—Bizet's *The Pearl Fishers*, if I remember correctly. After several days of this and before I returned to Boston, I was to join the Schefflins for a brief bon voyage party in their stateroom aboard the *Mauritania*.

"I was already familiar with the kind of stateroom the Schefflins usually procured for themselves: it would be located at midship usually and, if possible, would have its own entrance that led directly out to one of the upper decks. It would consist of two rooms: a bedroom and an adjoining sitting room—not a luxury suite, by any means, but spacious, spare, and comfortable. I was not disappointed by what I found when I arrived. But I was nonplussed, immeasurably so, by entering the stateroom and finding, in stark contrast to the gaiety bubbling over with confetti and champagne bottles popping on the surrounding deck, a tense atmosphere, full of suppressed alarm and taut concentration. Unexpected and unannounced arrivals among us of Uncle Aloysius and Aunt Bernice were common enough, but I was surprised to see them there. Uncle Aloysius stood by himself in one corner of the stateroom, his physique at something of a half angle toward us. He was uneasy and shifted his position slightly from time to time, sometimes glancing at us, sometimes gazing through the portholes that opened out to the deck. Agnes sat on a sofa that rested against the wall on the far side of the stateroom that faced the door. She sat upright at the edge of the sofa, her head lowered but tense, her body held firm, her arms looped tightly around her knees and her hands clasped together. Frederick was pacing back and forth in front of the door; his shoulders were rolled slightly forward in that woodsman's way of his, and his face, ordinarily so calm, was now uncharacteristically distraught. He was clearly confronted by a dilemma of a kind he had never experienced before.

"The stateroom itself was a shambles—so unusual for a Schefflin venue of no matter how brief an occupation: coats, hats, and valises were strewn here and there, a sadly ignored bottle of champagne tilted sideways, unopened, in its silver ice bucket, and the nearby table, with its tall stemmed crystal and its parsley-garlanded sandwiches and pink- and lemon-frosted petit fours, stood as yet unmolested. Several bouquets of lilies and roses, nested in dripping ferns, still lingered, wet and mournful in their delivery boxes and wraps. The center of the stateroom was occupied by a stack of capacious, well-worn leather portmanteaux, not yet unpacked or even deployed to their proper storage repositories. Enthroned upon this stack, sublime, regal, unassailable, was Aunt Bernice herself—Aunt Bernice assuming for the moment what was perhaps the most captivating role in her life. Her head was held high, her lustrous sapphire eyes glowed with pleasure, her shoulders were thrown back and supported by her arms and hands, braced behind her against the tops of the trunks, while a torrent of shiny black hair tumbled down over her shoulders in great, undulating curls. Her legs were crossed beneath her full-length skirt, the tip of one high-heeled pump poking upward jauntily—and, yes, I would add defiantly—from underneath its gaily embroidered folds.

"I could think of a half dozen grand masters of the art of portraiture who would have loved to have been there at this moment, Edmund, with brush and easel, palette and canvas at their instantaneous disposal, though it might have taken all half dozen of them to do justice to such a spectacle. And could one have expressed anything about Aunt Bernice other than a blazon of boundless praise for her grandeur at this moment? It was she who was in the midst of us, or as they might chant among the misty highlands of the East, it was she who was the 'jewel in the lotus'; it was she, I would soon find out, who, *enceinte,* bore the nascent miracle of life within her being; it was she, enrobed in all the glitter of her raiment, who was a lotus herself enfolding the jewel that would change our lives forever.

"So what was I to do, Edmund, what was I to do? You cannot imagine my consternation. Had I blundered into where I should not have gone? Had I obtruded into a scene as a person who now was suddenly a stranger among the oldest of friends? I was expecting a celebration; I stumbled into what looked like a catastrophe. I had almost bumped into Frederick as I entered.

He jerked to a stop when he saw me. Everything was dead silence. All eyes in the room momentarily alighted on me. The atmosphere was so palpably tense that it bordered, ironically, on a kind of repressed exhilaration.

" 'Theodore,' Frederick assailed me, 'Theodore, you have come just in time!'

" 'In time?' I quavered, 'in time for what?'

"I didn't know what I dreaded, but I dreaded, in any case, what he might say to me next. I didn't let him answer, as if to put off what might be too dreadful to hear. I rushed in with the first irrelevant banality I could think of: 'The celebration? What about the celebration? What about that bottle of champagne?' I clamored stupidly.

"Frederick's face brightened and immediately resumed its usual unruffled demeanor. 'You are right, Theodore, our celebration first and foremost! Thank you for reminding us. We must have the greatest celebration ever.'

"The stateroom burst into inexplicable laughter—long, sustained, spontaneous, joyful laughter. Aunt Bernice laughed, and Agnes laughed, and Frederick playfully grappled my shoulders with his powerful lumberjack's hands and pushed me deeper into the room. 'Now you get working on that bottle of champagne, Theodore, since you mentioned it, while I attend to some matters with the ship's steward,' he said as he turned to go. Even Uncle Aloysius now faced us, still anxious and reserved, but smiling and making an effort to enter into the sudden eruption of festivity.

" 'What are we celebrating?' I cried at last, satisfied that my original statement, though not particularly redounding to my credit, had been neither irrelevant nor banal.

" 'The most wonderful thing in the world!' were Frederick's parting words as he stooped through the door and vanished into the hail of confetti and the boisterous crowd on the deck.

"I dwell rather a while on this extraordinary scene as I have—that scene incised on my mind less as an unfolding action, which it was, to some extent, than as a sequence of gestures chiseled in time, or even, as I have proposed might have been appropriate in its own way, as a painting, as one of those paintings, perhaps, from the High Renaissance, wherein a powerful current of anticipation, of inchoate rather than enacted movement, molds the attitudes of all the figures present into a single coherent image of strain, of flexed and prodigious energy bent to a common and ever so urgent purpose. And if I dwell on that state of suspended action, I do so only because I have spent much of my life since then attempting to elucidate its dimensions, exploring in my mind all that it was saying without saying it. There was little doubt in my mind about who had blocked out the original 'cartoon' in broad charcoal strokes, who, to change my figure of speech, had drafted the outline of the script. The artist was Aunt Bernice, who presided over it all, who presided from her eminent perch upon that leathern mound of time-worn portmanteaux, and who had every right, in a sense, to preside, to be the center, to be the one who, up to a point, assigned each person his or her appointed role. I even wonder, in my more fanciful interpretations of that *tableau vivant,* if she could possibly have predicted that I would flounder in at the just right moment and so inadvertently, though indispensably, rupture the lid of tension that forestalled the exhilaration that was now upwelling from below. But, having said all that, it was Frederick who circumscribed the periphery and who, in time, would fill in many of the details. As such, it was a characteristic achievement of his: leaving things unsaid was his way of doing things, not simply by virtue of his taciturnity but because he felt that by leaving something unsaid, it was left to others to say it. And when they said it, in some way, they became it. Or is it the other way around: When they become it, then do they have the authority to say it?

"And here I prevaricate again, Edmund, not because I am withholding my cards but because the hand I was dealt at that time in my life involved levels of complications that still succeed in casting over me a spell of something; I don't know if it is awe or intimidation, or something in between. I am glad that through the prime of my life I had Martha as my companion in my ruminations over this matter, a patient listener, a willing contributor to whatever trains of thought engaged our review and analysis. She knew the protagonists in these events about as well as I did; and that was a great relief and consolation for me because I was never able, and never did, discuss the matter with those same protagonists. Our silence together was part of our understanding. Nevertheless, I thought at that time, still do, and Martha had always confirmed me in my conclusion, that on that early autumn afternoon, in that stateroom on the good ship *Mauritania*, mere seconds before I made my brash and lumberly entrance, all decisions had been made and resolutions affirmed. I came in as, and remained, a belated and puzzled witness to what had already transpired.

"What more can I say of Aunt Bernice at this juncture? I have told you that she exulted in the role that both nature, primarily, and she, secondarily, had devised for herself, the focus of attention on her, the complex set of human interactions that she had set in movement and that now had to be sorted out by others while she could sit back and watch with pleasure as they struggled with the issues that placed her, again and again, as the source and center of everyone's concern. How marvelous to write a script in which she was the one who made all the difference and yet could simultaneously retreat backstage and watch what others now had to do! Of course, it could be reasonably protested that a significant part of her eminence in this situation—and I don't think it is preposterous to imagine that she was also very much aware of this—flowed from the irony that, unlike the other people in that room, as we have mentioned before, she had consigned herself to being the sweet and efflorescent denouement of her lineage. Now everything had been reversed. Among those whose ardent aspirations to generational fruitfulness had failed, for all the inscrutable and sad reasons such aspirations fail, she herself had become, miracle of miracles, the springtime of life and renewal. I do not doubt that precisely such an awareness was at the basis of the demands she had made and had known, in advance, would be met.

"Further, I wonder sometimes if it was not the idea of all of this that intrigued her, more than the reality; that, not only did she take pride in her foreknowledge of how others would rise to the occasion presented by her apparent dilemma but that she sheltered in her heart in some way the romance of motherhood, the image of it as culled from the theater, from the opera, from poetry, from soft and deeply affectionate portraits and icons that so often depict it in the most touching of emotional shades. It may have been, indeed, the strange abridgment of affection in her own being that impelled her to think that the experience of motherhood itself would somehow provide, if not the essence, then at least the foundation for a compelling mimesis, a simulation, of an exalted state that otherwise she could never hope to fathom. Could one act a role one had never had in the real course of events? Obviously, one can, and it is done all the time. But one cannot be too sure how carefully Aunt Bernice was thinking this matter through. As I have said, it was the image rather than the reality that she may have rejoiced in; for, as much as she took delight on this occasion, and on this occasion alone, in the novelty of bringing a child into the world, she immediately set about both divesting herself of her responsibility for taking care of that child as well as delivering it over to those in whom she knew she could reposit, without the slightest misgiving, the maximum trust possible to carry out that task for her. To give her child up for adoption by the Schefflins was to guarantee, as much as was humanly possible, the salubriousness of its future. How could one raise an objection to this prospect? How could she have been, given the obduracy of her premise, more totally astute in exercising her judgment toward the fitness of her conclusion?

"To be sure, the Schefflins had to be willing to accept. I am reasonably certain—and how often Martha backed me up in this thought—that the consent of the Schefflins, both Frederick and Agnes, to an adoption was assured as soon as it was proposed, though it was one of those decisions, as determined and almost conceded as it was right from the start, that required, nevertheless, a convoluted process of deliberation before the grounds of its preordained conclusions could be suitably explicated. I suspect that is a way of saying, in accordance with some sages of old, that the only free decision is the reasonable decision, and that our exercise of freedom is disclosed not always in the decision itself but in the process of recognizing its reasonableness, as long as such recognition does not, as it often does, provide a mask for a not-so-reasonable rationalization. Here again, I must be cautious in my effort to grasp what various motives may have had an impact on what occurred, for there is not a great deal that Frederick would tell me about in later years, though we did discuss the matter from time to time—always with reserve, always rather indirectly, leaving a great deal to be inferred rather than said.

"Agnes, I dare say, was probably less distinctly 'cerebral' in her approach. Aunt Bernice was her sister, her childhood companion, a shoot from the same root, one whose life she had shared as intimately as it was possible to share an intimate life with Aunt Bernice, one whose sunny girlhood had been unremittingly fanciful in sportive concourse with her sister. That she would have recoiled for a moment from consenting to her sister's bidding is inconceivable, as singular as this bidding, in a sense, was. Further, we only need to remind ourselves that much of Agnes's married life had been consumed by the desire to have offspring, a desire that more and more seemed incapable of fulfillment. Frederick had shared in this hope and in this disappointment, and they had already considered adoption, on a number of occasions, as an option for their parental aspirations. To be presented, suddenly and without the ordinary complications, the opportunity to nurture a young life in their household was like having the proverbial 'gift from heaven' dropped into their arms. For Agnes, the case was closed, right from the start. Her affectionate heart, her undaunted and imaginative spirit, vaulted clear over any hurdle that might have intruded itself into these deliberations. Agnes prided herself, indeed, not on mistaking the woods for the trees, or the trees for the woods, but on seeing everything at once, as it were, from the treetops. It is difficult for us to know with any precision what Agnes saw from her vantage point, but we can surmise that what she may have seen, with transparent and immediate lucidity, was who her sister was and what she could and could not be expected to do. To such a prospect, there was only one logical, irrefutable answer.

"For Frederick, if the ordinary technical complications of adoption may have been absent, the extraordinary moral complications of this adoption were irrevocably challenging. Like Agnes, he could not help but be moved by the deepest aspirations of his heart. But he was wary about allowing aspirations to define obligations. Further, for him, methodically, though in this case swiftly, ruminating over the proposal in his mind, as he always did with any proposal, the decision to adopt, if it meant anything at all, was tantamount to the decision to bring up as one's own what, clearly, was not one's own; and this decision demanded, provisionally at least, that one would have to resort to those measures requisite for securing the conditions most conducive and germane for that endeavor. What did such conditions require? It was difficult to assess such a move in the few minutes afforded to making such an assessment. He did know, in any case, that it would entail some measure of cocooning the situation into a protective husk of confidentiality—of making only an inner circle party to the compact that must inevitably be formed and that must be kept secluded, as far as that was possible, from a garrulous and tendentious world quick to judgment, quick—despite its sometimes best intentions—to suspicion and contempt.

"It is needless to say how much such a prospect could possibly go against Frederick's grain, against his commitment to an irreproachable probity in all his affairs. Anything that even hinted of artifice where human relations were concerned was adverse to his nature. Yet what had to be weighed in the balance?—a multitude of considerations arguably too serious to be ignored, each of whose imperatives was, in its own way, just as obligatory as the others and which demonstrated that one's reluctance to artifice had to be partially waived by both justice and discretion—to say nothing of discreetness itself where this embodies the safeguarding of others' confidentiality and privacy. But justice, more than anything else, had to be served—justice, with its conflicting demands and obscure directives. And what order of importance, what priority could one attach to any one of those imperatives when all of them appeared to have equal say in what was required?

"The child, for example. Shouldn't the child be brought up within the context of a settled marital accord and be spared the confusion of parentage should an array of contradictory asseverations reach its innocent ears at too young an age? On the other hand, no matter how well woven the confidentiality, or how faithful the parties to the compact might be in observing it, did there not threaten, in the course of time, arrival at a crossroads where the agreement must, if not of its own weight and duration, then of the weight and duration of events themselves, cease to be in force anymore; and would not the disclosure consequent upon this inevitable pith of contingencies produce its own painful renunciations, the most painful of all possibly being the renunciation of one's own prized, even if in a sense 'deputized,' parenthood itself? Such a consideration reinforced the thought that whatever was settled upon would have the character, at best, of the provisional and that one would have to trust to time itself as the final arbiter as to when its limits had been reached. In any event, one could prepare oneself, to say nothing of preparing the child, to be resilient enough in the future to welcome the positive, as well as fend off the more negative, consequences of its inevitable disclosure when the time arrived for that.

"Then there was Uncle Aloysius to be considered. Where would he stand in all of this? Frederick could not be too sure. That Uncle Aloysius, despite whatever apparent stoical complacency he showed at the moment, was immeasurably distressed by the situation was certain. The biggest part of that distress would be the resignation, in effect, of his own paternity and of the subsequent paternal relationship it would be possible to have with his child. But, to the side of that, perhaps in a sense running parallel with it but without assuming the same gravity, would be the enormously difficult relationship engendered with his family. How could he explain to his parents, to his sprawling and prolific clan, the nature of the dilemma he found himself in? How could he protect his own child from the pall of illegitimacy that might be cast over its birth from the very start; or how protect his beloved parents from the scandal or even the ridicule conferred by those whose moral fidelities in one case, or moral obtuseness in another case, would hardly allow them to understand the situation in anything like the complexities it embraced? How, especially, if the adoption did not take place, or even if it did take place and became known that it did take place, could Uncle Aloysius shelter his betrothed, his future spouse, from the ignominy and rejection she could possibly draw down upon herself within his family circles? And how, under any of these circumstances, would he manage to preserve, in whatever faltering way, some shred of his own dignity, not only in his own conscience but also before the censorious eyes of the world—consequences that would necessarily affect not only himself but, infinitely more importantly, the future of his child and of his relationship with that child, regardless of what form it might take?

"Frederick would not have much difficulty ascertaining all of this. I think, Edmund, that he saw in Uncle Aloysius, somehow right from the onset of this crisis, his counterpart, his compatriot: one who must pass on his burden to him, one who would, in spite of everything and in the long run, share his paternity, share his responsibility, be a comrade in arms, for whom he must requisition that indispensable 'cover' in the heat of battle, a fellow trooper whose ramparts were unbearably exposed and whose maneuvers, however courageous and dutiful they might be, were tragically vulnerable.

"If we turn to Uncle Aloysius himself, it is difficult not to think that the thoughts we have ascribed to Frederick would not have been on target. Here, naturally, we can make only the purest of conjectures. Could Uncle Aloysius have been anything less than deeply anguished by the arrangement? I think we can appreciate the weight of his consent to the compact made in that stateroom only if we understand the weight of those forces that must have compelled that consent. There was his family, as we have already considered, and his entire familial circuit, for whom a knowledge of a child born out of wedlock could have been inexorably crippling, and not just momentarily but also permanently. Uncle Aloysius was not one to hold too lightly the consequences that would ensue in that regard. His parents, whatever happiness accrued to them from the other progeny provided by their burgeoning family and even the happiness they would experience, though in perplexity and distress, in the child born to him and Aunt Bernice, would have to live out their days with this much sadness in their hearts, this much disappointment in what they had most expected to be an unalloyed source of joy. Uncle Aloysius could be expected to foresee all of that and to desire to spare them that pain. Then there was the child. It would have been extremely difficult for Uncle Aloysius to envisage a childhood for a son or daughter that might occur in a household not yet established and in a parental framework not as yet defined, for there would be the entire question of the child's awakening consciousness of who he or she was amid shifting and unstable conditions. So passionate was Uncle Aloysius for the parentage of his child that he, out of his own sense of parentage and against the deepest longings of his soul, was willing to sacrifice that parentage itself and give it over to another.

"Further, there was his relation with Aunt Bernice. His devotion to her now as mother of his child would only increase that much more exponentially; now, more than ever, as one united to her incarnate, as the 'two in one flesh' of what he already knew to be a single vibrant life, he would feel bound to her and observant of her priorities. It is difficult to say how much Aunt Bernice would have cared about that sort of perspective, with its implicit metaphysical overtones. But she, let's be frank about it, had all the chips in her corner. It was her decision, and she made it the way she made it, and there was nothing he could do about it. I need not point out that they never did have any children in their eventual marriage—Aunt Bernice knew where to draw the line, and, for the one child they did have, they had, under the terms of the compact, to disclaim their parentage. Can you envisage that, Edmund—the spectrum of anguish upon those moral heights: a man, born to be a father, renouncing his fatherhood—and not just the fatherhood that he would have hoped for but the one he had been gifted with, and gifted with from just that woman, alone among all the women in the world, from whom he had most desired it—from just that woman, and none other, in whom he wanted to transmit, not life, but a specific and singular life that would conjoin the two of them forever? Under the circumstances, there was nothing he could do but choose to live, as honorably as possible, within the perimeter of this . . . this disconsolate enigma that would mark, of dire necessity, the rest of his days.

"Well, Edmund, perhaps I have excessively belabored my effort to extrapolate from that still all-too-vivid *mise-en-scène* into which I stumbled that autumn afternoon, those conditions that would shape the years that followed. And perhaps you will forgive me for presuming too much about those persons whose lives would unfold according to the provisions set by a solemn compact, the terms of which, clearly, had been defined before I had entered that stateroom and had managed to deflect their attention away from what had assuredly been a momentous negotiation and over to that coyly uncorked bottle of champagne. But precisely because I was not party to the original compact have I felt the compulsion, both at that moment and over the long years that have passed, to deduce from what I knew and from what others were willing to impart, some of the aspects that went into its formation. I was, at best, a kind of witness, after the fact, not so much to the transaction itself but to the fact that a transaction had occurred. I could guess at some of its terms, and some were directly told me.

"Once Frederick returned to the stateroom, a steward in tow with a cart loaded with comestibles of various sorts and with vases for the flowers, we set about properly adorning the room for a celebration. Agnes was quickly at work with the flowers; Aunt Bernice surrendered her throne upon the leather portmanteaux and, uncharacteristically for her, began doing something or other with arranging the food, I don't know what, while Uncle Aloysius and Frederick hauled off those aforesaid portmanteaux into the bedroom, where they belonged for the moment; coats and hats and valises were stored in closets; and the stateroom was soon spacious, buoyant, filled with light and charm. And I, yes I, Edmund, fulfilled my destiny of being the one appointed from the veritable foundations of the world itself to pop the cork of that patiently—or was it impatiently?—waiting bottle of champagne.

"But I still didn't know, as you must realize, what we were celebrating. I knew it was not anymore just the voyage abroad. I found out soon enough. Frederick drew me aside to tell me. He didn't tell me everything, but he told me enough so that I could understand that altogether curious mode of jubilation that was going on around me—jubilant, yet restrained; joyful, yet reserved; the welcome relief of mountaineers when a fog has finally lifted and the climb may now recommence, though the climbers themselves must scale what are still, certainly, treacherous heights. Uncle Aloysius, naturally, was the most reserved of us all; his gracious good humor upon this, upon indeed all occasions, resembled that of the disabled bird in story and fable who, unable to fly from its bough, awaits the crouching cat while singing its heart out in melodious praise.

"When our brief but somewhat subdued festival was over, Uncle Aloysius and Aunt Bernice departed for wherever they were going. Agnes disappeared into the bedroom and began unpacking what was necessary for the voyage. Frederick invited me out for a stroll on deck, which was now reasonably clear of its former celebrants. He discussed a few business items with me about as dispassionately as if nothing much had happened out of the ordinary in that stateroom. It was not until we approached the gangplank and my imminent departure that he addressed once again the situation I had witnessed. In his usual way, he did not have much to say, and I knew then, as I still do now, that a great deal had been discussed in that stateroom that was not being, and not going to be, passed on to me. I figure that Frederick thought I should not have to be burdened with a lot of details more or less irrelevant for my limited role in this matter. But he did make the point in several terse remarks that the parties to the original compact were bound, among others, by two fundamental understandings: by a promise of silence and by an agreement that only he himself, under the condition of consulting with others and informing them in advance of what he was doing, was granted the license either to break that silence or to alter the terms with which the silence was maintained. His governance in this affair, he asserted, was commended by the possibility that he might be able to occupy the most central position in it and thereby be able to assess what was needed when it was needed. Everyone had approved the commendation.

"Even though I was not a party to the original compact and had not contributed to its deliberations, he assumed that I would consent to the first understanding; it was self-evident that I would and accordingly did. But he made it clear that it was up to his discretion how and when and if to include me on the potential developments provided by the second understanding. Here again I figure—and it would be consistent with Frederick's *modus operandi* in such matters—that it would be more propitious for me, as one not fully intimate with the plethora of personal considerations that might unfold among the original parties to the compact—simply to be the spectator of certain effects rather a contributor to their causes. He would inform me of whatever he felt at a given time was appropriate to inform me. He went on to show a great deal of concern that the arrangement never be misrepresented by anyone to anyone; a careful and judicious silence was to be observed, and, if one or another of us found ourselves being pushed into explanations by a too ambitious and invasive inquiry, we would simply have to profess that confidentiality disallowed any further discussion. There were questions that one simply should not feel, either in this particular case or in principle, obliged to answer. Our interlocutors, in such an instance, were free to draw their own conclusions; there was nothing one could do about that. The point was that no one should make claims that were false or that one day would have to be explicitly repudiated. He realized, naturally, that none of this would be easy to do; but it was an effort that had to be sustained until, or unless, there was no other reasonable choice but to reveal the actual state of affairs—and even in this case, the revelation should be made only to those persons for whom it was important to know and whose confidentiality, in turn, could be assured. It was left up to him to decide when and to whom this could happen. Frederick thought it was necessary, given my relationship to the family, for me to inform Martha, and naturally he would let the others know that he had extended the protective cartouche in this manner. Beyond that, I was, for the meantime, simply bound by the promise of silence—a provision Frederick would change later on to allow me, as trustee of his estate, confidant of his affairs, and director of the Foundation, to apprise a potential successor of whatever I thought was necessary. And this, accordingly, Edmund, I have done. That is why I have had both the liberty and the obligation to discuss it with you."

"But, Theodore," I finally inserted into his long monologue, "I thought you said that the compact in some sense was provisional. You now imply that it is to go on in perpetuity. I'm not sure I understand. "

"That, I agree, is a source of some perplexity. But here I must remind you of the central point of all of this: the compact was made, in the first place, to protect the sensibilities and interests of each party to the original compact, and, despite everything we can say about those same sensibilities and interests, its most fundamental purpose was to protect the sensibilities and interests of the child. I emphasize this with no uncertainty: its fundamental purpose was to protect the child. That was finally the *raison d'être* of all the rest. I assume, trusting the good will and perspicacity of Frederick as I do, that this final purpose has been attained somehow or another, my perplexity notwithstanding."

"Then what, Theodore, are you perplexed about?"

"Do I need to say? You said it yourself when we began this rather extended deposition. It's the question you yourself proposed, the question that defines our terms."

"You mean: What does Cornelia know about it?"

"Yes."

"And why does that define our terms?"

"Because all the original parties to the compact are now deceased. Only Cornelia is left to be protected, if protection is what she requires. And I do not know the answer to that, Edmund."

"What difference would it make, do you think?"

"All the difference in the world."

"Which is . . . ?

"Which is . . . if she knows, and, perhaps even more significantly, if she also knows that I know and, further—please excuse the extravagant convolutions of this statement—that she knows that I know she knows, the compact—the blessed compact—is no longer in force. And that is a very big difference."

"And what is that difference?"

"We need be silent about it no longer."

"And is that important for you?"

"Yes. It is important. I like to know, ideally, where things stand, where the parameters have been drawn, so to speak, even though, in some other sense, it may make very little difference, perhaps no difference at all, in how we actually communicate with one another. We may never even have the occasion to discuss it. But, by the same token, we would no longer have occasion to avoid it either. Put simply, to have that tacit understanding would mean everything in the world to me and, I presume, to her."

"In other words, you would need to be silent about it no longer; but, in all probability, you will be silent about it nevertheless. What is tacit will remain tacit, just in another way."

"I assume that is true. Of course, all of this is important for you as well."

"Then why is it important for me?"

"For what is bound for me, at this point, is also bound for you. That may change someday. Meanwhile, as is all too obvious, you must observe the same set of restraints that we observe. You will know more about that in time. But also what you have learned today is important for you right now."

"Right now? And why is that?"

Besserman rose from his chair again, walked across the room, gazed at his collection of photographs, as if consulting them about what to do next, slid his hands into his jacket pockets, and turned slowly to me.

"That is why I asked you to this meeting today, Edmund."

"Yes, you said—"

". . . it was important. It is important."

"And what is of such importance?"

"She is here."

"Who is here?"

"Cornelia is here. Cornelia is in Boston."

"Cornelia!"

"Madame de Quevillon. An unanticipated visit to the United States. I found out about it only a few days ago."

"And . . . ?"

"I have taken the liberty to set up an appointment for you to meet her—at her suite in the Regency Hotel, Wednesday afternoon at 2:30. I apologize for this. It's all a trifle sudden, and I have been, again, peremptory in my arrangements. She is on a very tight schedule. I hope you don't mind."

"I don't mind, but—"

"You must be ready."

"Ready?"

"You must be prepared. She knows all about you. She is eager to meet you. She will be prepared, I assure you. She always is. Cornelia will be prepared."

Part Three

Although my appointment to meet Cornelia was set for midafternoon at her suite in the Regency Hotel, I decided to take the entire day off from work. It was an exceptionally beautiful day—one of those mildly cool and sunny days in early April when the breezes from the Charles River are particularly exhilarating, when flowering trees blossom in profusion along its banks, and when the sky is a deep and almost startling blue. As matchless as the weather was, however, my purpose was to submit to my customary procedure, to "compose" myself for the meeting that afternoon, to prepare myself by proposing to do more or less nothing at all, to let things settle down so that new things, whatever those new things might turn out to be, would have a clearing of their own wherein to seed and ripen.

I also had the impression that the most appropriate place for me to gather myself, as well as, perhaps, to orient my thoughts and nourish my prevision of at least some measure of intimacy with the person whose acquaintance I was about to make, would be the grounds of the old Madison Street residence itself. I have held the conviction that a place says something about a person, though it is always, finally, the person who unfolds what may have been implicit in the place. Further, Mr. Besserman had told me, on several occasions, that he often went there to walk among its groves and gardens and to enjoy its contemplative repose. I also understood that the April vacation for the students at the college, now in progress, would ensure my privacy. I debated with myself later on that day, and still do, whether my initial purposes were particularly well served by such a decision, for what intercepted my prospective indulgence in a vague and solitary perambulation was, I will have to admit, a great deal more than that, yet a great deal that I was supremely grateful for. Besserman could have, maybe should have, warned me in advance about what might occur; but I am glad, on the other hand, that he didn't. I have never failed to appreciate gratuitous encounters whenever they happen. Moreover, if I did not discover the solitude I sought, I did certainly manage to nourish that aforementioned prevision of intimacy, some of whose defining features I was glad to have adumbrated so eloquently for me.

I drove southward that morning from the North Shore and into Boston, skirting the city along the sinewy dips and curves of Storrow Drive and catching a glimpse now and then of college crews in their slim shells skimming over the gently crested waves of the river. Since the morning rush hour was over and I had no schedule to follow, it was a calm and unhurried drive. Not far beyond the Harvard boathouse, I directed my automobile westward towards Newton. At nine thirty in the morning, the Boston suburbs looked lush and colorful; the leaves had budded on the trees, lawns had been mowed for the first time, and much of the drab residue that accumulates over the winter had been either raked into neat little mounds or already carted away. As I approached the neighborhood of Madison Street, I noted many fine old frame houses with rambling front porches and narrow lawns bordered by long-established shrubs and towering hardwood trees whose wide and robust branches would soon support full heads of foliage. It was an old neighborhood, I could see, but its upkeep was striking, and its appearance, as manicured as it was, suggested, as is so often true of old suburban neighborhoods, something of a partial reconciliation with the natural world that has grown deeper and more ample with the passage of time—which natural world itself has reclaimed, over and above the works of man, a few of its ancient prerogatives.

On Madison Street itself, I began to look for a landmark—a gatehouse or something equally grand—that would signal the entrance to the former Schefflin estate. The houses along the street were of a later vintage than what I had seen already; they no longer featured the expansive front porches, were farther back from the road and more isolated in that sense, and were approached by lengthy driveways that wound through spacious though modest grounds fringed by hedges and copses of spruce trees. They were often constructed of masonry—brick or stone—and had impressive garages and garden houses attached to them. As I drove along a lengthy stretch of road that curved through a wooded park, I happened upon a fieldstone bridge arching over a brook to my right. A sign announcing "Saint Hroswitha College" informed me that I had arrived at my destination.

After crossing over the bridge, the driveway curled through a grove of tall, shady evergreen trees, out over a well-trimmed pasture arrayed fleetingly for the season in a sunny blaze of early wildflowers, and up a slight hillock or knoll. The knoll was surmounted by a single oak tree, of great age, one could presume, reaching out and spreading its gnarled and shaggy boughs in all directions. A faint haze of pale green seemed to float like a mist through its early budding branches. From here one could gaze downward into a small hollow scalloped out between two or three other low and mildly undulating knolls. In the middle of the hollow, several redbrick buildings were clustered around three sides of a lawn—what I assumed at once to be the campus of Saint Hroswitha College. The lawn itself had been formerly bordered, one could easily surmise, by an oval drive. This drive had long since been converted into a promenade rimmed by hedges, flower beds, and a few park benches, so that now the road dipped down into the hollow, veered off to the left past the buildings, and wound, as far as one could yet see, immediately around to the back, where, presumably, parking lots were located. At the center of the green was a small, hexagonal, Italianate cistern carved out of what looked like a limestone block; an elaborate arc of wrought-iron tracery was anchored in its coping and was poised delicately above it; a tiny pulley and chain dangled from a hook at the cusp of the arc.

On the left side of the green, and facing it, was a chapel—a long, slender brick edifice with high front doors and, along its sides, tall, thin windows flanged like a series of slits or gills. On its roof, a spiny, metallic steeple rose sharply and looked, regrettably, like a tall, pointed spur or stiletto of some sort, almost as if it were a radio antenna or some other oversized electronic gadget. Although replicating some of the aspects of the redbrick character of the other buildings, the chapel was instantly recognizable as a fairly woeful product of contemporary ecclesial architecture, less offensive for its putative starkness than for the gawky intersection, here and there, of sharp angles tilted discordantly in various directions and unresolved by, or into, any larger architectonic conception. To its rear were several smaller buildings. On the right side of the lawn was a large, rather squat building, made of the same red brick, with broad granite stairs rising from the promenade to a façade marked by a row of glassy ornamental portals. It was surmounted by a short, even rather stubby, cupola, in this case located at the center of a broad, flat roof and, I thought, painfully disproportionate with it. It had all the grace of a thumb protruding from a hole in a worn-out glove. I figured—and later found out that I was not mistaken—that the building was the college library. Again to its rear, and partially hidden by it, was a packet of other buildings: dormitories, no doubt, or classroom buildings and laboratories, all made of brick and looking more or less the same.

At the far side of the green and facing the knoll stood what was clearly once a private home with a flagstone terrace bordered by a balustrade along its front and a pillared and scrolled entry portico leading to its front door. The residence looked diminished in size by the larger college buildings in its proximity, but its brick façade had a notably rough-hewn and weathered appearance. It stood out from them as something pointedly different, however, something compact and textured in contrast to the others, though, most evidently, having to some extent set the style and tone for all of them. I was pleased, even at this initial glance, to see that an effort, not altogether successful, to be sure, had been made to reclaim a modicum of unity in style for the entire establishment, having seen so many academic campuses where every individual building had pandered, in one way or another and at one time or another, to a different architectural fashion, each or any of which might be reasonably satisfactory in itself or not, but, as contributing to a whole, did little more than offend the eye, if not the spirit. I was also pleased, on this occasion, to note that an equal effort had been made to retain the focus of the original estate, however much under altered circumstances, for what was exceptional—and immediately recognizable as exceptional—had been, in the end, underscored and preserved as the exceptional thing it was.

Exceptional? Some critics of domestic architecture might, especially at first impression, disagree. It would not be difficult to understand why. After I had parked my car in an adjacent area designated for visitors, I wandered back to the house and took my first real examination of it. Those familiar with the expansive and opulent mansions of the affluent might consider it small, for it was, in a sense, almost—if I may use the words—"compressed" or "chiseled" or something to that effect, not just by comparison with the nearby buildings of a more flaccid and sprawling institutional character but also by comparison with what one may have expected to find. It almost—and this is strange to say—gave the impression of being something like a "cottage," for, as commodious as I would soon find it to be, it appeared to draw itself into a conformation so tightly knotted, so cohesive, that any awareness of its actual size was displaced in favor of its understated, though impregnable, modesty. I am well aware of how a term like "cottage" has been appropriated in the past, in some locations and apparently without irony, to describe the grandest and most pretentious of domiciles. But in this case I was confident that the designation was warranted, for the house had nothing overtly "grand" about it. It did not stand outward from its setting, like a foreign object deposited randomly on a plot of turf but rather "stood into" it, less as an obtrusive artifact than as something naturally and deeply enrooted in its setting, as an ice-age boulder might be embedded in a New England hillside.

My first cadre of critics could very well find this modest stature disarming, as I did at first; they might even find it disappointing in the sense that some portentous opportunity for a grandiloquent statement had been lost. Other critics might, I imagine, object to the setting itself, to how the house, rather than having been raised magnificently on the grassy prominence above it, had been implanted in the hollow behind it, whose mildly undulating declivities hid the house from the road and even from most of the approach along the driveway, whence its virtues, once one had agreed on what those virtues were, might perhaps be more justly displayed to its advantage and more justly admired, though such a decision would have required the loss of the great oak tree that lent such a majestic aura to the scene. We are accustomed, one could contend, to "great houses" perpetuating even today vestiges of what was once important in the martial genesis of their type, occupying high ground and commanding far-seeing and defensible crests around it. In this case, however, it looked as though the oak tree had, to some extent, determined the placement of the house, rather than the house being used as a nub to configure, or reconfigure, whatever natural features were preserved to surround it.

Still other critics might argue that the building was excessively plain and simple; that it showed no particular architectural flair or ingenuity, it being, as clearly it was, of a somewhat normal, though slightly wayward, Neo-Georgian design, with its medley of square and rectangular brick walls, its white painted trim, the occasional rococo touches here and there on its cornices or facings or ornaments over doors and windows. As I strolled around the house, I could see that even the landscaping in the immediate vicinity was conventional for the time of its building; it was embowered on all sides by stone terraces and balustrades intermingled with mature rhododendrons, yews, holly trees, and other evergreens. Under and around the sturdy groves of trees, the ground was carpeted with broad stretches of leafy pachysandra, now all lushly daubed here and there with clusters of spring daffodils and violets.

For all that, the edifice was exceptional. When seen up close, the house was revealed as a startling profusion of sculpted details. Among its abundant regular lines, its right angles, and its well-delineated symmetries was an ever-present reticulation of irregularities, irregularities superimposed over irregularities, an effusion of irregularity at every level of structure, from the entire house right down to each brick, it seemed, and to each cranny between a brick and its neighbor. Nothing was smooth or bland or flat. A jagged roof of thickly ratcheted slates, multihued by rain and sun and varying in hundreds of different sizes and shapes, cascaded downward in overlapping and serrated rows like a great shaggy cliff lowering over the eaves of the house. A mottled verdigris crest with curved spikes and knobby finials bristled along the ridge of the roofline and was intersected, in curiously asymmetrical ways, by three towering and many-fluted chimneys of varying heights and dimensions, each of which was capped by a crowded mélange of chimney pots, streaked and blackened with the soot of winter fires. It looked as if the entire house had been hewed, piece by piece, bit by bit, with hammer and chisel out of some extraordinary natural thing.

"It's the bricks above all," a voice interrupted my thoughts.

"The bricks?" I asked, not knowing whom I was addressing and where the voice was coming from. I glanced around, looking for its source.

"Yes, it is the bricks that give the place its savor, don't you think?"

I turned directly around. I faced a nun, or a person I assumed was a nun, dressed in an ankle-length black habit or jumper, perhaps, with a black sweater and a white collar. She wore a small white veil or coif at the back of her graying dark hair. She looked as if she might be in her late middle years, was petite and spare in build, and stared at me with her somewhat inquisitive but smiling face. She struck me immediately as a brisk and energetic person, full of sparkle and wit. Her serene visage disguised, in its own way, what I would soon come to recognize as an adventurous and exuberant spirit.

"Allow me to introduce myself," she said. "I am Mother Madeline d'Agneau, professor of English and dean of Saint Hroswitha College—well, dean for the time being, as these things go; and, as I am sure you know, things have a way of not going on too long. *Sic transit gloria mundi.* And you are . . ."

"I am Edmund—"

"Ah, Mr. Edmund Schofield. Yes, I know. I just wanted to be sure. I have been expecting you." She approached me with a little jump in her stride, thrust out impulsively from her shoulder and tilted at a slight angle to her body a rather high, straight arm with a tiny, bony hand, similarly tilted at the wrist, and we shook hands. It was all just somewhat ungainly, as if somehow we were not really shaking hands but rather engaging in an obscure modification of some ceremonial gesture with whose rubrics I was unfamiliar. I have never met a countess, but I imagine that, if one ever should, or would be permitted to, shake hands with her, that is how one would go about doing it. For that matter, I had never met a nun before, at least at such close quarters. Meanwhile I pondered why, once again so soon in my life, my appearance should be so confidently and unfathomably anticipated.

"I am honored, to be sure," I remarked, wishing I had some apposite Latin phrase to append as a rejoinder, "but how could you have expected me? A few hours ago, to tell the truth, even I didn't know I was coming here."

"I didn't say I was expecting you today, Mr. Schofield," she explained. "I was expecting you someday. Mr. Besserman forewarned me of the eventuality that I might see a roguish-looking chap poking about here and there, 'casing out the joint'—to use his expression—but appearing, for all that, rather distracted. I don't think you look the slightest bit roguish—though I make allowance here for Mr. Besserman's 'poetic license'; but I dare say that you look distracted enough to fill the bill."

"Why 'distracted,' I wonder?"

"I gather that is another, perhaps indirect way of saying 'attentive,' when one is attending closely to things that one normally does not pay much attention to. I can tell you from professional, as well as professorial, experience that the greatest challenge mounted by students to the exercise of their own lovely intelligences is the refusal to pay much attention, long and lovingly, to lovable details."

"Then, there is a lot to be distracted about," I returned. "I imagine everyone needs to do one's fair share of concentrated gaping at things now and then."

"If what is gaped at is worthy of being gaped at. I think, in this case, it is. You have picked a fine day, Mr. Schofield, to do your gaping. Let me have the pleasure of showing you around, if you don't mind."

"I wouldn't mind at all. It would be my pleasure."

"I will not detain you for long, so don't worry—I have nothing like the tedium of a campus tour in mind. Furthermore, I know you have an appointment later today in Boston."

"I assume Mr. Besserman filled you in on that too?"

"Mr. Besserman fills me in on everything—in due time. That's his way. But he was not my source for that particular item of information."

"Then someone else who likes to fill you in, no doubt?"

"That's one way of putting it. You will discover that for yourself soon enough. My source did not know for sure that you might drop by but rather guessed you would. That's why I did not necessarily expect you today but was keeping a lookout for you anyway. My source does have a way of guessing accurately what people will do."

"I don't know whether to take that as a promising or an intimidating prospectus."

"That, too, you will discover for yourself soon enough."

"I guess I will. But meanwhile, about the bricks . . . you know, the bricks . . . before we move on."

"Yes, about the bricks." Mother d'Agneau turned her attention to the house and studied the wall closest to us, as if to consult the subject of her discourse before presuming to speak about it further. "Well, they are very old, much older than the house, 'recycled' bricks, one might say, using the contemporary mode."

"And just how were they 'recycled'?" I inquired.

"The Schefflins were traveling in England—both Frederick and Agnes Schefflin enjoyed visiting the cathedrals and the great houses there. Frederick Schefflin also, so I have been told, was engaged in exploring, at their invitation, some technical innovations developed by the Cadbury chocolate people, while his spouse combed some nearby villages in search of those curiosities that so enthralled her. One day, purely by accident, she happened upon an old manor house about to be demolished by a wrecking crew. It necessitated no little effort and no little ingenuity to forestall that great steel ball on its imperiously swaying crane from swinging into action. I understand that free provisions at the local pub were very helpful in this regard. She brought her husband to the site on the following day. They concluded, after some hefty debate and a great number of calculations, that it was worth the trouble and the expense to save those old, hand-made bricks, etched and mellowed by three hundred years of wind and rain and snow, of nesting birds, of coiling ivy. So they purchased them, had them carefully dismantled and brought to Massachusetts, and made this house out of them. They did not try to replicate the original house itself, or even its late Tudor style—the obstacles to that prospect were simply insurmountable, not the least of which was that the original interior panels, window casements, and doors had already been removed and sold off independently before Agnes Schefflin found the place. Hence, the bricks were really all that was left and were accordingly incorporated into an entirely new kind of structure. The result, especially the interior, is admittedly eclectic—composite, but guided by a single sensibility, I think, rather than a random jumble. I will let you be the judge of that. Nevertheless, this ancient masonry erected in a new land veritably sings its age. Don't you think so?"

"And you most lyrically sing its praise," I responded. "But wasn't that all rather extravagant? And for a private retreat hidden by that knoll from the eyes of the public?"

Mother d'Agneau considered that statement for a while in silence. She pursed her lips, folded her hands together in front of her, and raised her index fingers side by side, touching the tips like a little steeple. It dawned on me at once what I had already intuited might very well occur: that I had directed my question to a college professor, and one does not direct a question to a college professor without incurring, for better or for worse, the inevitable and sometimes ambivalent consequences.

"Extravagant?" she echoed. "I suppose so. But then all beauty, even in the natural world, it seems to me, is extravagant; leaps, as it were, well beyond the bounds of whatever is necessary and practical. And, if one loves beauty and exercises the proper prudential judgments in allocating one's resources justly, why spare the cost, especially if part of the cost entails the rescuing of something very precious from being lost? Indeed, without such sorties into the extravagant, all learnedness and wisdom, all grandeur and celebration could be readily cashiered as well. I think that the Schefflins were conscious of fashioning a place where others could gather and participate in a kinship, not only of lineage but of humane cultivation, a place infused by the numina of civilized and beneficent presences. I think it was always appreciated as such. We today still appreciate it as such. It is a contemplative place too—just right for us, you know—so sequestered and solitary and hushed."

"Can we go inside?" I asked.

"That's why I am here," she answered, "to show you at least the principal rooms of the ground floor. In the past we have used those rooms for receptions and other public functions when we have them. We don't really use them for very much anymore, since we now have facilities in other buildings more attuned to the general—if I may say so—blandness of our collegiate purposes. I might mention that the two upper floors of the residence are our convent rooms, so I can't take you there."

We walked around to the front door of the house, passed through its ornate portico, and entered a large entrance hall with a staircase at one end and two smaller halls opposite one another and leading off to the left and the right from the main hall. Along the entire far end of the main hall stood a row of tall, two-story-high windows that flooded it with such a spacious and breezy resplendence, and framed and partitioned so exquisitely the view of the terraces and the trees beyond the windows, that the interior of the hall itself seemed transformed into a marvelous extension of the natural scene outside. It reminded me of the large glass wall in the Schefflin Foundation in Boston. A small statue, with the light coming in from behind, stood silhouetted on a pedestal in front of the windows. I could not see it clearly, but it had the stiff and somewhat crude contours of an early medieval woodcarving.

"Saint Hroswitha," my guide informed me. "Do you know of her?"

"I can't say I do."

"Few people have ever heard of her. She was the abbess of the convent of Gandersheim, late tenth century. She wrote plays; comedies actually, but too didactic for my taste, in imitation of the Latin poet Terence. Some scholars claim she was the first playwright to appear in Europe after the decline of the classical period. We are proud to have her as our patroness."

I didn't know how to respond to that. How does a person who lived a thousand years ago act as one's patroness? We lingered there in silence for a few moments; then Mother d'Agneau directed me to the hallway on the left. She had little to say initially, as if everything that needed to be said was said by the house itself. We were surrounded by a gallery of passages and chambers of polished, deep-grained wood, heavy-planked and dark-stained. Tall paneled walls at our sides were shaped into a multitude of thin-spiraled arcs and flutings like medieval choir stalls, often surmounted by trefoil or quatrefoil designs. Overhead, white plastered ceilings displayed elaborate floral moldings in patterns that circled around decorous central rosettes. Though the hallway itself was dark, even cloistral in its aspect, intense sunlight poured into it through massive open doors from the adjacent rooms so that its darkness was penetrated by slanted shafts of misty light, and the polished wood became dazzling and translucent with the reflected glow. What seemed capacious and even monumental at one moment was secluded and intimate at another. As we walked and as our footsteps echoed in the silence, I could peek into the series of rooms to either side of the hallway. Here and there were niches hollowed into the wooden panels; little statuettes and the occasional crucifix had been placed, obviously by its contemporary residents, in these shallow but ornate concavities.

"It looks more empty than it did when the Schefflins occupied the house," Mother d'Agneau finally spoke up. "Except for these high-backed Queen Anne chairs placed at intervals along some of these walls, most of the original furniture is gone. I should like to have seen it as it was originally, though I have seen some photographs, and Cornelia—the Schefflins' daughter, whom you are going to meet, presumably, this afternoon—has described to me in detail what it was like. There were once two full-length and rather massive seventeenth-century Gobelin tapestries hung on either side of this hallway. I have seen photographs of them. One depicted the sort of pastoral scene so favored in those days of the Sun King and his retinue; it showed a bevy of shepherd boys spying on some nymphs who were bathing in a mountain pond—not the sort of decor appropriate for a convent, Mr. Schofield, as you can well imagine, though I am sure it was rather innocent, as those things go, certainly a great deal more innocent than the literary works I routinely assign to my often reluctant protégés. The other tapestry showed a scene from an Arthurian romance, where, amid the broad-leaved foliage of a woodland, two plumed and armored knights on their horses salute one another peacefully from the opposite banks of a dappled stream. I don't know who the knights were taken to be—Lancelot and Galahad, perhaps, father and son, according to some versions, neither knowing who the other was, meeting for the first time under such auspicious conditions. I assume you know the story."

"I think I once knew, but the details are hazy," I acknowledged.

"Well, no matter," she sighed. "We really must get you 'up to speed' someday, Mr. Schofield. But those old tapestries must have been delightful to behold—lending these rooms just the requisite flavor of chivalric grandeur. There was another old tapestry in the living room, but I know really nothing about it. In general, my impression is that there never was much furniture in these rooms, at least from what I can discern in those old photographs: some chairs along the walls, as there are now, side tables, lamps, of course, a variety of oriental and other kinds of carpets, sconces and chandeliers aflame sometimes, in the evening, with candles, a few paintings on the walls, all somber-hued and rather Netherlandish, from what I can make out, as well as a few German and American romantic landscapes. But one sees few of the usual appurtenances of the modern parlor or living room. These, I believe, were reserved mainly for the small sitting rooms upstairs adjoining the bedrooms, many of which were arranged in diminutive suites or apartments.

"Downstairs, the parlors and the library were sparsely furnished, except, of course, for the dining room which was outfitted the way dining rooms usually are—a great oaken table with matching chairs and sideboards and silver candelabra and a rather amazing chandelier, still there, about which we will simply have to defer comment until we have a chance to see it. It seems odd to say this, but these rooms really didn't need furniture, or at least much of it. Each room is a spacious but intricately wrought enclosure with little bays, embossed and fluted, recessed into its sides and provided with upholstered window seats and benches carved into the walls themselves. These rooms furnished plentiful space for private conversation or for those priceless individuals—you know, the sort who want to be at a party but also don't want to be—who discover in a host's library a book they have always dreamed of finding and just want to be left alone with it for a while as the festivities proceed."

"You do seem to know that sort rather well, Mother d'Agneau," I ventured.

"I don't go to parties, Mr. Schofield. But, if I did, I confess I probably would be the type, though I don't know how 'priceless' I am. I certainly find our own official social functions insufferable enough and always summon up the readiest pretext at hand to flee precipitously from them."

"So, you prefer a life without festivities ..."

"I didn't say that. It depends on the kind of festivities you have in mind. Every day is a feast day, and every feast day has its banquet."

"So too much festivity ...?"

"There is no such thing as too much festivity, once we recognize what there is to be festive about. And doesn't it say somewhere, in the Book of Proverbs, I think, that for a festive mind, all of life is a festival?"

"Forgive me, but I shall not try to understand that."

"Perhaps not now. But I hope someday you will. *Ubi caritas gaudet, ibi est festivitas.*"

At the end of the hall we strolled into what certainly was the largest room in the house, bordered on three sides by full-length French windows looking out over the balustrades of the terraces and the abundant vegetation beyond them. At the center of the far wall, between two sets of windows, was a large fireplace. It was framed by a mantel of what looked like aged cherrywood carved into intricate patterns of vines and clusters of fruit. An oblong rectangular carpet, of unusual length, vibrant color, and flowing sinuous patterns, lay on the floor. In one corner of the room was a grand piano.

"The original piano," Mother d'Agneau pointed out. "Cornelia left it here for us. It's a wonderful instrument but in need of some restoration, I'm sorry to say, and since Sister Emilia became incapacitated, it is rarely used nowadays, at least in a serious way."

"I assume this was the setting for the Sunday musicales I have heard so much about," I said.

"Indeed," she answered. "How Mr. Besserman loves to come here sometimes, and sit by himself in one of those chairs for hours and listen to that music in his memory. It's very sad. But it is also very good that he has such a memory and can cherish it as he does."

"And the carpet?" I inquired. "It is, I dare say, somewhat different from what I am accustomed to, as far as carpets go."

Mother d'Agneau was familiar with the carpet and began, with no little professorial acumen, I would add, to expatiate upon its details. "It is an Ottoman work, late sixteenth century, of western Anatolian provenance; rare, I have been told; illustrating a design unique to the so-called Oushak tradition."

She pointed to the various medallions and the patterns that emanated from them. I was surprised by the complexity of its conception and execution. She continued, "I'm told that the original weavers aimed to assign a certain cosmological import to it: one might propose that the design, in each direction, extends into something like eternity; that all designs, of whatever complexity, exist independently of our minds and continue forever; and that the particular embodiment of one of these designs in a specific rug constitutes but a minute and limited version of it. It's a sublime idea, don't you think, a kind of aesthetic Platonism in an exotically Levantine mode."

It took me a few moments to digest these rather engaging pronouncements. Then I said, "I have also been told that many carpets coming out of the Near and Middle Eastern tradition have some kind of deliberate imperfection in them—an imperfection introduced so that the perfection of the Deity, and hence His approval, is not challenged by a claim to perfection by human beings." It struck me immediately as strange that I, as a confirmed agnostic, should, under these circumstances, be the first one, in a religious house, to invoke one of the synonyms of God, even if in its most abstract form.

Mother d'Agneau fixed me in a meditative gaze, her head tilted slightly, her lips pursed again in that expression that signaled a lecture in the offing. Then she declared, "Well, Mr. Schofield, I don't think I can vouch, in one way or another, for the accuracy of that observation, either as an historical generalization concerning the weaving of rugs and whatever motives may have influenced that weaving or for whatever trend of theological thinking such an unwarranted anxiety may represent; but I would think that, if what is considered an imperfection is introduced deliberately, it is done to highlight some aspect of what is putatively perfect, a touch that sets off the whole and helps to make it a whole—in which case it is hardly an imperfection, but rather part of the perfection. When I study this carpet carefully, as I have think I have done, I find a hundred little modifications, asymmetries, eccentricities of the weaver's hand in stitching this or that miniscule knot, or this or that little nodule, variations in the timbre of the dyes, spreading a thousand irregularities over its surface like little gemstones; and all I can say is that such multiplicity lends, most majestically, to the splendor of the whole.

"Further, as far as the theological observation is concerned, I cannot speak for the traditions you allude to, but I think it's worth mentioning that all the theological sources of which I am aware insist on making the claim that God wants us to be perfect as He is perfect and to make things that reflect His perfection. A much wiser voice than mine has said, many centuries ago: 'To detract from the perfections of created things is to detract from the perfection of the divine nature.' "

"Then I am surprised about how little perfection there is in human life," I lamented.

"I understand what you are saying," she conceded. "For all that, I am equally surprised about how much perfection there is, once you are willing to take the time to look for it, to pay attention to it, and to admire it. There is enough of it, I can assure you, to keep us busy for several millennia of lifetimes."

"Something to be festive for?" I pursued.

"Indeed," she professed, "one of many things to be festive for."

"I hope your students are able to share some of these perspectives of yours."

"I do what I can in that regard. I have always thought that one of the greatest acts of love is to help another learn how to love. Juliana of Norwich said that if someone loves a thing well, he or she will want to help everyone else love and delight in that thing too."

We passed into what was once the library—and still was a library. It was a wide, richly paneled room surrounded by a multitude of shelves, all inside closed cabinets with glass doors. The shelves were filled with books. Otherwise it was a characteristically institutional library in very much the conventional sense.

"The original Schefflin and now our convent library," Mother d'Agneau announced, with a slightly wry tone in her voice. "We have some decent collections here, and a lot of dross as well, I'm afraid to say. We also use this room for retaining the few volumes we possess that could be dignified by the term 'rare book,' though most of what we have in that regard would be of interest only to a very few specialists. A professor from Louvain once came here to study several of our volumes—early Renaissance *incunabula* mostly, but of a narrowly devotional nature. A young lady interested in antiquarian book bindings also came here once to look them over. I would have loved to see what the Schefflins collected here. I don't know where the collection went, and I don't think any records of it survive."

"Perhaps Agnes Schefflin collected here 'many a quaint and curious volume of forgotten lore,'" I said, convinced that my literary allusion would not go unappreciated. If Mother d'Agneau was impressed, she didn't say anything about it.

"I wouldn't doubt it for a moment. Frankly, I wish we had them here. She loved, Cornelia told me, all sorts of wonderful and enchanting old things:

the medieval romances, fairy tales, novellas full of strange and otherworldly events. All of that was an artistic taste that she rather carefully cherished."

We passed from the library into the hallway again and from there across the large central foyer to the hallway that led off to the right. We took a brief look at the former dining room. It was outfitted in the same style as the others, with a capacious hearth that resembled the one in the living room. Otherwise, the room was furnished with several nondescript circles of small sofas, chairs, and coffee tables.

"We use the dining room as a place to entertain the visiting families of the sisters," Mother d'Agneau informed me. "It would be futile to try to imagine the sort of banquets hosted here once upon a time by the Schefflins."

But I scarcely heard what she said, for my eye was drawn upward to the large chandelier that hung from the center of the rosette on the ceiling. I noted at once how out of place it was amid the present furnishings of the room. It was even difficult to grasp at first sight exactly what I was looking at. It was a dazzling, iridescent bramble of creamy porcelain boughs and twigs, spiraling around one another and sprouting gilded blade-like leaves and lustrous flowers of a dozen tints. On the branches abounded a vivid aviary of glazed songbirds of the most awe-inspiring lightness and brilliancy. Some seemed poised, with outstretched wings, to soar into flight; others nibbled at branches or tiny insects; others reposed in shelters of nests and crannies. I could not identify what species of birds these were; I recognized some jays and woodpeckers and larks, but most were unfamiliar to me—European variants of familiar species—but I was transfixed by the translucent blues and reds and greens of their pleated feathers and golden beaks glimmering out from the depths of the foliage. Mother d'Agneau seemed to assent to what was implied by my silence. "It does leave one rather speechless, doesn't it? It was left here by Cornelia, who didn't want to move it from its position above what was once the great dining table. She says little about it, as if it is too precious to talk about. It's Meissen rococo, as you can see, excessive perhaps and possibly not to everyone's taste. Cornelia had an uncle, Uncle Aloysius—I'm sure you have heard of him by now—who had a predilection for it. He was a physician and, like some physicians, was especially keen not only on the realities but also on such vivid representations of animate life.

Thank goodness we have one sister in our convent who is willing to risk her life once a month, perched on a teetering ladder, to keep it dusted and polished. But, despite her heroic efforts, we have succeeded in turning its surroundings into an excessively drab room."

Crossing the hallway again, we entered into a smaller room, a kind of pavilion, an annex almost. Its floor and ceiling were covered by interlocking lattices of mosaics and tiles. This, I was informed, was the "garden" room, or solarium, often used as a breakfast room by the Schefflins. Its walls were frescoed in the most riotous and eclectic way, with depictions of a fantasy landscape that featured lush scarlet flowers blazing among palm fronds, peacocks and other brightly plumaged birds, pyramids, a sphinx, classical ruins, and snowcapped tropical mountains along a distant horizon. And, among other exotic fauna dotted in tiny clusters across the vast savannahs, giraffes!

"Giraffes!" I exclaimed with some surprise.

"Yes, giraffes," Mother d'Agneau repeated. "Agnes Schefflin's signature representations, you might call them, for better or worse. And the whole room is Agnes at her most uninhibited. It is her own work, you know. She does bring it to the brink of excess, don't you think, but manages to hold the line. I think it's the use of pastels that tones it down."

Beyond the windows of the pavilion I saw a small walled-in garden. It featured a number of trellises and flower beds, and many old vines coiled up and over the brick walls. At the far end was the door to a greenhouse. We walked out into the garden through a door at the side. It was sunny and cool there.

"An herb and spice garden originally, as I understand," Mother d'Agneau said. "We call it now 'Our Lady's Garden.' "

"That may be," I affirmed, noticing the statue of the Virgin Mary safely ensconced under a protecting trellis. "But I recognize this garden somehow. I have seen a painting of it. Something is missing."

"What is missing," Mother d'Agneau went on to inform me, "is the fountain that used to be in the center of the garden. The fountain is, as I am sure you know, in the courtyard of the Schefflin Foundation in Boston."

"I have seen it there," I replied. "The painting shows Cornelia sitting on the rim of the fountain. She looks very young in the painting."

"I have also seen the painting. Cornelia brought the painting here once so that we could see what the fountain looked like. I've never seen the actual fountain itself. I understand Agnes designed it. It was, to some extent, I've been told, originally intended as a scaled-down replica of the fountain in the Piazza Madonna dei Monti in Rome. It was carved from a delicate ivory-tinted travertine marble. Its bottom basin was often filled with water lilies. They called it the 'ivory fount.' The ivory was a reference, actually, to the magical ivory of a unicorn's horn—just the sort of thing Agnes Schefflin would think up. I should love to see it someday."

Mother d'Agneau pointed to the greenhouse at the far end of the garden and told me a few things about Agnes's horticultural efforts and collections. But we didn't enter it. "A terrible disarray," she confessed. "In our early days here, some of the older nuns maintained the tradition of growing medicinal spices and a variety of vegetables for our refectory. But they have passed on, and the younger generation no longer has the time or patience for that kind of activity. Anyway, the greenhouse is now used to store the equipment for the landscaping company that works for us."

She also indicated that the remainder of first floor of the house consisted of pantries and larders, a large kitchen, a facility once referred to as a "powder room" but still convenient for their guests, a staff's dining hall, now used as a small refectory for the community, a workshop, laundry, and so forth. She didn't think I would be interested in seeing any of that. We strolled gradually back toward the front door. I hesitated at the threshold with a question—a question I was diffident about asking. But I asked it anyway. I started off by saying, "I have been informed that your college came into the possession of this property as a gift."

"It did," she answered.

"And the donor, technically speaking . . . ?"

"The Schefflin Foundation."

"And who do you think made that decision?"

"Its board of trustees . . . to use your expression, 'technically speaking.' That would have been the only source of authority to do it. But I think it was at the behest of Cornelia—of course, she was a member of the board of trustees. She still is. She also made the decision to leave certain items here."

I had another question. As I struggled to formulate it, Mother d'Agneau intruded and asked it for me. "You are wondering, I presume: If some aspect of the 'old faith,' as some call it, has retained, almost in spite of itself, a part of the Schefflin character in maintaining this residence as it was, did the Schefflins themselves, or some part of them, retain a residue of the 'old faith,' having fashioned as they did, though without realizing it, a fit environment wherein that 'old faith' could find a home conducive to its own distinctive ends?"

"Yes, I think that is what I was wondering, though I am not sure I could have expressed it in the complicated way you did. It seems strange that an edifice built for one purpose can so successfully be adapted for another purpose."

"I will accept for the moment the premise that such a successful adaptation has actually occurred—you compliment us, really, when you say that. But I will do my best to answer you. I assure you that I don't know too much about the Schefflins' backgrounds in that regard. I can, perhaps, piece together various items I have picked up over the years from Mr. Besserman and from Cornelia herself. Frederick Schefflin's father, Benjamin, may have had Lutheran origins; his mother, Marlena, came from a neighboring principality—a largely Catholic section of Germany. I think that the influence of her father, a schoolmaster deeply in conflict with local authorities, as Mr. Besserman tells the story, may have loosened her ties with a Church too entrenched in a residual feudal order in which the bishops served the barons, first and foremost, or were, in many cases, the barons themselves. Both Benjamin and Marlena arrived in America independently, as you probably know, but without religious ties, I understand, and that was the environment the young Frederick grew up in. As for Agnes, she was from what was originally a Belfast Presbyterian family, but I have the impression that even here not much of a traditional connection survived.

"I do not think that, under those circumstances, Frederick or Agnes retained much of a denominational identity or allegiance, at least not in any public way. I do not know what they may have thought about in the recesses of their hearts. Frederick, if I have a sense of who he was at all, was a man of *pietas* in almost a Virgilian sense, a natural *pietas*, to be sure, reflective and resolute and taciturn, though probably so interior to his character that he was scarcely aware of it. Like many another Nicodemus or Joseph of Arimathaea in the passage of time, he has stood to the side yet tendered to, as deeply as can be tendered to, what might be authentically called 'the heart of the matter.' As I have heard, he was always open to and sympathetic with, and even rather curious about, the religious convictions of others. It's as if he was making a serious effort to understand them. Most of the workforce at Schefflin's was Catholic—Irish, Italian, Slovak, Polish, Portuguese, and others; and he encouraged, accordingly, communion breakfasts in the great dining hall of the main factory, often celebrated by the cardinal archbishop of Boston himself, and the observance of saints' feast days important to the different ethnic groups. Frederick was also deeply respected by the members of Mr. Besserman's synagogue and was an honored guest at many of its functions. About Agnes I can say nothing other than mention again her fascination with mystical books of various kinds, which may mean something or may mean nothing much at all. Curiosity and fascination do not always lead to conviction. She liked to read Hadewijch of Antwerp and Hildegard of Bingen, among others."

"But not Saint Hroswitha of Gandersheim?"

"Perhaps she did, but that is a rather specialized interest. I do wish I had known Agnes. I think we would have been close friends. We share, in a way, the same name: the lamb."

"The lamb?"

"Agnes. D'Agneau. If we had ever dined together, we could have called it the Supper of the Lamb."

I didn't understand, at the time, the allusion, nor the pun it apparently justified.

Mother d'Agneau added, "I don't know what direction all that reading led her in, or whether it led in any direction at all. But I rather suspect it did. Cornelia once made a rather cryptic remark about it which I didn't understand."

"And Cornelia?" I asked. "What about Cornelia? You seem to know her well."

Mother d'Agneau mused for a moment. "I wish I knew her a great deal better than I do. One always does want to know her better. In this matter, however, I do know something about her, but I will refrain from saying much of anything since you will be coming to know her, and she can speak for herself. But allow me to suggest this much: Cornelia will be visiting us in a few days, after she returns from a rather harried trip to Hartford and New York and someplace in rural Maryland. Her visits are always a treat for us, and our sisters will make an earnest effort to prepare a suitable luncheon for the event—an effort, I'm afraid to say, that will not succeed too well, since our kitchen staff is not reputed far and wide for its culinary skills. Our specialty, I tremble to reveal it, is okra gumbo—please, don't ask any questions about that gastronomical incongruity in boiled-beef and codfish cake New England! Let me say—indirectly but relevantly to your inquiry nonetheless—that it is we who shall most likely have something to learn from her, and not the other way around, though she will take in a great deal while she is here, as she always does."

"Then she tells you what to do?"

"Cornelia never tells anyone what to do. The independence of mind she always exercises is what she expects of others. However, it is true that one cannot speak with her for very long without being offered a commission of some type. It's not always clear what that is. She just seems to make anything one is doing already a much more serious and important thing to continue doing. And sometimes, I have to confess, she seems to understand what we are up to better than we often do. There is something in her that tells me that, despite her active life in the world, her family, her many associations, she may well have a better understanding of the life of a convent than many of those who actually lead such a life. Cornelia has one of those minds that takes in a whole picture, not just parts of it. And she knows there are no easy answers—at least not to the questions that matter."

"That seems to me to be a discouraging state of affairs!"

"Oh, there is nothing discouraging about that at all. I said there are no easy answers, Mr. Schofield; I didn't say there are no answers. To make up one's mind that there are no answers is, in itself, the easiest answer of all. It shuts down all further questions; it shuts down questioning altogether."

"And how does Cornelia give her answers?"

"By pointing a way, by revealing a promise, by defining, in terms as pliant as they are precise, a task to be undertaken; by encouraging one to do it; and all of this in as indirect a manner as is possible to do. It's up to the listener to bring things to a conclusion—granted that a conclusion is what things can be brought to in a given case."

I demurred in my consideration of this point. Finally, I said, "All of this reminds me of someone else I have heard about."

"Frederick Schefflin, I would venture?"

"Exactly. Which is certainly, in its own way, a most wonderful commendation of her. Still, I am mystified by what you are saying. I don't understand how she could genuinely fathom the values you represent. Wouldn't it all be too foreign to her?"

"You mean . . . ?"

"I mean that you have elucidated for me something about the religious backgrounds of the Schefflins. Wouldn't such a background preclude much in the way of being deeply knowledgeable about your way of life?"

"Ah, Mr. Schofield, I see what you are driving at. I guess I should say that there is more in her background than the Schefflins. I approach this subject advisedly, for there is a great deal I do not know or understand about it. There was the uncle I mentioned to whom she was deeply attached."

"Uncle Aloysius?"

"Dr. Aloysius Fitzgerald. 'Uncle Aloysius'—as they called him."

Mother d'Agneau wondered whether to continue or not. But she did continue. "He was married to Agnes's sister, Bernice. Cornelia often mentions him in her conversations about life at Madison Street. Mr. Besserman has brought him up to me on occasions too. Uncle Aloysius must have had a significant influence on her life. He died young. I can't help but think that there is some mystery about him that even she may not understand. Mr. Besserman sometimes speaks about him, but in such a reserved and tactfully qualified way, as if there is something he would like to disclose but is held by some promise not to. But Dr. Fitzgerald was, if I may use that rather inaccurate expression again, of 'the old faith.' I don't know much more than that; what I do know is that, in her college years, whatever it is that converges in a person to induce the recovery of a very ancient covenant of faith converged in her. Dr. Fitzgerald, somehow, was an important part of that convergence—that much I can make out, even though it didn't happen until a number of years after his death. What may have happened before his death is a matter about which I know very little. As for the rest, Cornelia will have to tell you. I doubt very much she will. She is not inclined, except in rare instances, to talk about such matters."

"And what else can I expect from her? You and Mr. Besserman have thoroughly terrified me."

"Don't be overwhelmed!"

"She will try to overwhelm me?"

"She will try nothing of the sort. But she just may overwhelm you anyway. She really is a simple person, as clear and bright as a sunny day. That, alone, is enough—rare enough even—to be overwhelming."

"And, in a nutshell . . . ?"

"Cornelia in a nutshell? In a nutshell?" Mother d'Agneau declared. "I don't know what to say. I think I must object to the question. It's difficult to think of her, or of anyone, being in a nutshell."

"Then don't try. Objection sustained. I withdraw my question."

But Mother d'Agneau was not to be deflected from the effort. After a moment's thought, she said, tentatively, "If you fall into a well, she will try to pull you out."

"Fall into a well?"

"Yes, if you stumble and fall—especially into a well."

"Why a well?"

"I don't know, actually—it's just a metaphor that seems right at the moment: something deep and slippery and obscure and difficult to get out of: like the ditches in the psalms that people manage to tumble down into and need to get hauled out of; like the narrow, dark places we sometimes find ourselves in—find ourselves cramped, airless, benumbed, suffocating. That's all. That's plenty. In some ancient Egyptian inscription, from who knows which of their multitudinous dynasties, a departed soul pleads for entrance into paradise by claiming that he has given food to the hungry, drink to the thirsty, clothes to the naked, and ships to the shipwrecked. We have, of course, the initial triad in our own sacral *écriture*, but I rather like that part about the ships. Our ships often go down, as well outfitted as they are. It's like the wells. We need somebody else's help. We must be willing to give that help; even more, we must be willing to accept it."

"Then I will try not to fall into a well. Indeed, I will avoid assiduously the proximity of all wells."

Mother d'Agneau nodded somewhat skeptically at me. "Perhaps so, Mr. Schofield. But I have a curious feeling that, in spite of yourself, you enjoy 'stumbling' into things, though maybe not always into wells."

"Now, what gives you that impression?" I countered, amused by this observation.

"The very fact that you came out here to the college in the first place. If Mr. Besserman is, in some sense, the reason, however remote, of your 'stumbling' into here, it is precisely, I suspect, because he has recognized this proclivity in you, as ingenuous as it may be, and therefore can be confident, as well as eager, in this case, to set you loose upon those things that matter most to him. He depends on your stumbling."

"An extraordinary hypothesis, if I may say so," I protested, surprised a bit by such an assessment of my own character. I wondered if it were true. I decided to turn the discussion back to her. "In any case, Mother d'Agneau, you seem to know something about falling into metaphorical wells."

"I do. More than I really want to know."

"So your faith must be a great comfort to you."

Again she looked askance at me, tilting her head, pressing one narrow finger into the side of her cheek. "It's funny how people say that. I speak only for myself in this matter, but I wonder if it is altogether comforting to know that one has chosen to do what is difficult all of one's days, that all the thickets one wants to hunker down in, all the hiding places, all the burrows where one can dig down into and escape, will inevitably be found out and ripped asunder, and that one will be embroiled in a no-holds-barred wrestling match with a wily contender for the remainder of one's life, even to, and especially at, the termination of it. I do not deny that faith is a comfort, but it is also work—difficult and demanding work, a task that never lets up. Sometimes the bottom of wells can look pretty inviting by comparison. At the bottom of the well there is nowhere left to go. Dead zero. Nothing more, you could say, to worry about."

"And at the mouth of the well . . ."

"The entrance into everywhere. Everywhere to go."

"And maybe that's a comfort?"

"It is. When we have nowhere to go, then we really are in trouble. We seem to be creatures designed to move on, not stay where we are, to move beyond even ourselves."

"And that wrestling match? What's the point of that?"

"To move us beyond the paralysis that thwarts and binds us. To make us flexible and hale and venturesome. To make us the loving creatures we were meant to be."

"You have a great deal of counsel to give. I appreciate that, Mother d'Agneau."

Our, by now, lengthy colloquy at the front door, had finally led to exiting the house. We stood together on the terrace, surveying the oval green in front of us and the immense oak tree spreading its boughs over the knoll. Mother d'Agneau indicated that I should feel free to explore the rest of the grounds or visit other buildings if I wanted to. I said I did not have much time left. Then I turned to her and said, "I hesitate to tell you this, but you do remind me of someone I know—someone we know in common."

"Now, do I? Who could that be, I wonder? Not Mr. Besserman, I assume!" She laughed. "You flatter me, but do I really remind you of Mr. Besserman? Is that because I am indulging my irrepressible bent for giving little lectures? I would hope it is more than that, for to be told that I remind someone of Mr. Besserman is a compliment of which I am scarcely worthy. I know him personally; he often comes to the campus for one of his 'periodic ambles,' as he calls them; he drops in to visit for a spell, has a cup of our abominable convent coffee, nibbles at one of our equally abominable biscuits, and is a fund of wonderful stories."

"But you never offer him a bowl of your okra gumbo? He has an adventurous, if not a foolhardy, spirit where cuisine is concerned, as I am learning, much to my chagrin."

"Well, the gumbo will come in time. As for his lectures, I am sure you know by now, Mr. Schofield, that he is a man of vast erudition and discrimination; his lectures are always worthwhile. Have you heard the one about Sung landscape painting yet?"

"Please, I implore you, no syllabi in advance. But I might say that the other day he expressed some shock that I was not familiar with a certain violin partita of Bach. He was aghast; he threw up his arms and wailed, 'What a misfortune! What a deplorable thing!' I know that, at times, he is being somewhat bumptious with me; still, I took him to task for it, and he just chuckled. So I decided to get my revenge. I had mentioned to him at my first meeting that I had an interest in Cajun music and could even perform some of it on a banjo. On this occasion, I brought the subject up again and asked him how much he knew about that tradition. He confessed to utter ignorance of it. So I threw up my arms, groaned in anguish, and parroted his words, 'What a misfortune! What a deplorable thing!' "

"Did it work?" she requested. "I hope it worked. After all, how can one get through life without some acquaintance with a Cajun jig or two?" I was flabbergasted by her response. Was she being sarcastic? But I answered her question. "I guess it did. When I met with him a week later, and while he munched on one of his fiery dragon sandwiches, he discoursed learnedly on Cajun music and asked me all kinds of searching questions. I was rather hoping that his sandwich would bite back, but it didn't, or at least not that I am aware of. He even asked me if I could perform for him."

"And did you perform?"

"I didn't have my banjo with me."

Mother d'Agneau smiled. "I shall have to remonstrate further with him on this issue, Mr. Schofield, now that you have, as it were, 'breached the wall' on this important subject. Do come back to Saint Hrothwitha College someday, whenever you feel the desire. It's nice to be alone here for a while. But bring your family too. Have a picnic! Bring your banjo! Be welcome. And watch out for me—there are a lot of good places to lurk around in these gardens—you never know from behind what leafy bush I might suddenly spring. Further, I very well might join you in your musical offerings, if you don't mind my engaging in some partially unintelligible bayou *patois* as I do it."

"You mean ... you mean you yourself have a Cajun background?"

"As Cajun as a flood in the Mississippi delta. A number of my sisters here have the same background."

"So that is where the okra gumbo comes from?"

"I'm afraid so. But it is really very good. You should try it someday. Ah, Mr. Schofield, you would have marveled at how I once, perhaps at the age of twelve, could pole a flatboat through an alligator-infested swamp. And Mr. Besserman knows that. It's about time for him to familiarize himself with this aspect of what is important to you … and to me … and to us. I won't detain you any longer. Give my best—my very best—to Cornelia."

"Rest assured, Mother d'Agneau, I shall be most pleased to do that."

"And we will be sure to remember you at our conventual Mass tomorrow morning."

"Please don't bother. It won't do me much good."

"Oh, yes it will. It will do you a great deal of good. It can't do otherwise. Goodbye, Mr. Schofield."

"Goodbye, Mother d'Agneau."

Part Four

She was tall; strikingly tall; taller than I had expected; tall enough, one might say, to require, for me, a readjustment in the angle of my accustomed "sights" ever so slight, yet sufficient to make a world of difference. She was slender, poised, observant; one of those miraculously ageless people who look younger than they are, yet who are possessed of a dignity and zest that only maturity itself, in its most rarefied embodiments, can confer. It is difficult for me to describe her apparel; I have neither eye nor verbal provender, especially where feminine habiliments are involved, for that kind of thing; but I am impelled in this case to make an effort. There was nothing, as far as I could make out, distinctly "high fashion" about her attire: she wore a tailored jacket and skirt of fine woolen tweed, of heathery lavender hue, a white high-collared blouse with a thin golden chain hanging down from around the lace ruffle at her neck. At the end of the chain was suspended a diminutive pectoral cross, antique Byzantine or Russian in design, roughly hewn and asymmetrical rather than smooth and even, with a small baroque pearl embedded in the tip of each cross-piece. Her earrings, of a single pearl each, were suspended from rusticated golden hasps.

She had large, watchful eyes, as I had expected, of startling bluish green settled deeply and meditatively beneath dark black eyebrows; and full jet-black hair, streaked here and there with incipient silver strands, coiled up at the back of her head in an elaborately braided chignon. All of this was elegant yet natural, I must profess, insofar as I am qualified to make such a profession; old-fashioned in a way, the *signum* perhaps of an earlier generation but without any overt mark of a fashion held over through negligence or eccentricity or the need to make a "statement" of any kind; meticulously curried, yet without fastidious excess, of *trompe l'oeil*, of whatever it is that calls attention to itself apart from that self of which it is a part. Simplicity, yes. Aloof; refined and delicate of line and hue as is a solitary and finished jewel in its setting and amid its dazzle of refractions; yet prehensile, supple, pellucid, a source of resilience out of what appeared to be a depth of personal gentility. In another sense, some might say, ordinary in the blended patinas of a life lived well and fruitfully; a life sifted and firmed by a panoply of rich experience.

I am glad that at least in this regard I had been admonished in advance. I had seen photographs of her. I had seen the painting of her sitting by the "ivory fount." I had heard sufficiently about Uncle Aloysius and Aunt Bernice so that I could see both of them brought to a kind of summit of attainment, sumptuously, one could note, in her. If astonishment is what I felt when first ushered into her presence, it was an astonishment that did not overwhelm me, did not stun me into some speechless discomfort. Would that such composure had stood me in good stead throughout the duration of our strangely ordained and, to use another poet's expression, "fatal interview"!

As I said, I was "ushered" in. A young woman, short and stocky, olive-skinned and muscular, with a short-cropped toque of boyish blonde hair, to whom Cornelia spoke now and then in French, seemed to be, and later I found out was, acting as her secretary, her factotum and traveling companion. It was she, Liselle by name, who had intercepted me in the foyer of the Regency Hotel and brought me up, in a manner of speaking, to the small suite of rooms occupied by her employer and patroness. I had to struggle to keep up with her swift strides through the carpeted hallways of the hotel and to avoid the robust swings of her elbows as she walked. My feeble efforts at small talk in the elevator met with polite, though curt, replies. I was not sure she understood much English. She left us soon thereafter in that rather tight-fitted sitting room, everything in it crammed together, especially in its having been converted into a temporary office of sorts, a kind of "field office" in the military sense, with stacks of paper piled randomly here and there and suggesting a brand of mobility poised for sudden retreats and advances. A tea service rested on a table in front of a sofa, where, after we had introduced ourselves, Cornelia sat down. I took a chair to the right of the sofa, facing her.

I don't remember much else about our physical circumstances. It was an ordinary room, decorated with those vapid prints and watercolors that one finds only in hotel accommodations and dentists' offices; behind the sofa was a large window that looked out, through gauzy drapery, toward the towering mirror of the Hancock building in the distance. I also don't remember clearly, for some reason, whether we partook of that tea and pastry that aromatically invited our future refection. Actually, I had not had any lunch that day, and as frivolous as it is to recall this detail in such a circumstance, I was very hungry. But I do remember those brief moments wherein I, as I mentioned, adjusted my "sights" and, conversely, sensed her, in her way, adjusting her own, sizing me up, I would grant, seeing how I fit whatever preconception she may already have formed of me or how I stood among the assemblage of those she had known in her life, an assemblage, no doubt, infinitely more variegated and even distinguished, in those multifarious ways in which humans can be distinguished, than certainly what I had known in my own more circumscribed, more delimited, ambits of daily life.

How does one cope with being summarily recast onto a larger and grander compass of the world stage? Well, one way is to deflect one's mind into the most banal of concerns. I am not normally too conscious of my clothing; but, in this case, in the specialness of this case, I might add, I experienced a most sudden surge of anxiety about what shoes I had put on that morning. I couldn't remember and was too flustered, despite my deeper composure, to look down and find out. On top of that, what atrocious necktie had I mindlessly snatched on the way out of my house, as I usually do, depending upon the rearview mirror in my car and some prolonged red light at an intersection to provide the finishing touches for my negligent ministrations? I regard all of my neckties as atrocious, but some are more atrocious than others, and I couldn't help but think, on this occasion, that I might be judged by my necktie. All such worries vanished in a flash, however, and I was soon enough put at ease.

Our conversation began, not unlike my first conversation with Mr. Besserman, with the customary rehearsal of subjects that always appear, at first hand, to be trivial—trivial because customary, perhaps—but are not trivial at all because they touch upon those things that actually are of singular import in our lives. We discussed our families: spouses, children, homes, interests, the usual sorts of things. She seemed to show a very special concern for—I will call it what she called it—"education," though the term, as she used it in what I take to be a rather more European than American mode, inferred much more than what we usually mean by "education"; I suppose we would be inclined to use the words "upbringing" or "formation" as reasonable substitutes. For her, as I could make out, it was much more than a matter of schools, of vocational choices, of egregiously conventional benchmarks, of professional training; it was more a matter, I guess, of everything that gives inimitable shape and meaning to a person's life, of everything that makes at least part of life an end in itself rather than a means to an end, of everything that would be involved in bringing to fruition the possibilities not only in the private enclave of one's soul, its inviolable inwardness, but also in that entire nexus of relations with the human family, the soul's equally inviolable solidarity with the rest of the world. For her, I assume, "culture" (though she never used the word itself) would not mean some collective entity one grows up in and inadvertently absorbs; to the contrary, it would be a spiritual ideal to pursue and a carefully considered process with which to pursue it, if one were sufficiently privileged to do so.

As we discussed each of my children in turn, I could see she was interested in discrete details, not so much in the conventional milestones along those road maps we follow in our lives and which we impose, in all innocence, of course, on others—you know, this or that degree or award or program, those socially approved catch-alls that are as convenient as they are ultimately empty and uninformative. For example, after having been told about my daughter's piano lessons, Cornelia seemed to be much more interested in what pieces she was trying to learn than in hearing me continue a catalogue of other activities my daughter was engaged in, and, having been informed about several pieces (as much, frankly, as I knew or could recollect), she wanted to know how my daughter was confronting a particular Debussy composition—in this case, "*La fille aux cheveux de lin.*" It was as if the particular thing gave access to what was important about the general state of affairs in my daughter's life more than the general observations themselves could give. Unfortunately, I was unable to address her question on this matter satisfactorily, which was a confession of just how much attention I was actually paying to what my daughter was doing in this regard. Cornelia, obviously, knew the works of Debussy rather well and did mention that a number of them were part of the repertoire of pieces she could perform on the piano ("more or less" perform, as she put it, "more," as she explained, for her own enjoyment and "less," at least thus far anyway, for the pleasure of others). She spoke briefly about her children—three boys and a girl—again accentuating in each case the "piquant" detail and remarking that all were now living "independently," wondering what exactly that meant and if people, especially people in one's own family, ever were actually "independent" of one another.

She also filled me in on what had brought her "stateside" in this particular instance: her annual meeting with Mr. Besserman—though under these circumstances somewhat organized at the last moment—to discuss matters of the trust and to review the activities of the Schefflin Foundation; an urgent conference in New York of a minor, largely unheard of, and now somewhat tottering (I got the impression) international commission in which she was a participant; most importantly, visiting a friend from her college years who lived in Hartford and who was dangerously, possibly terminally, ill; least importantly, in the scale of matters, a horse show in Maryland in which she was to be one of several judges; and others that she adumbrated briefly but did not explain. She regretted that she would have to forgo some of the usual but important "rounds" she would make ordinarily on such a journey, many to old friends and various relatives. Even then, she admitted to having taken on too much—the commitment to the horse show had happened by mistake (some confusion in communications)—but it was too late to back out of it gracefully; and she was also in a hurry to get back to France.

She told me she was glad to have brought along Liselle, who was of boundless help in navigating through the reefs of a complex itinerary and a crowded schedule; without Liselle's precision and acumen, she would not be getting things done in the rather convoluted order she was required to follow. Cornelia could not commend Liselle highly enough; she mentioned that Liselle was also a farmhand, a very good one at that, of wiry

Norman peasant stock, who could easily wrestle any unruly or recalcitrant bullock to the ground if the situation demanded. I assured Cornelia, that, without subscribing to any implied taurine analogy, I would do my best to be neither unruly nor recalcitrant, though I own to having perceived Liselle more as a staff officer, or better yet, as the female reincarnation of a Napoleonic field marshal, than as a livestock wrangler, no matter how adept she might be.

When the conversation turned, finally as it must, to me, Cornelia was dismissive of any protocols I might have anticipated in a situation like this. As I soon gathered, I was not to be "interviewed" in the usual sense as a job applicant. As Besserman had warned, she was indeed "prepared," touching upon my "credentials" in a manner just sufficiently oblique and allusive enough to inform me of the depth to which she had studied and assimilated them, so that further reference to them was no longer obligatory. Instead, I was being—and I revert to the concept "education" here—educated to the task offered me, as if the choice were primarily mine and I were being asked, indirectly and in whatever fidelity of heart could be presumed of me, whether or not this was indeed a task I was able and willing to undertake. Once again, as with Besserman, it was not a question of those professional technicalities whose mastery I was assumed to have attained reasonably well; it was much more a question of entering into an effectual "consanguinity" of some kind, if not comprehensive, then at least partial and receptive, with those persons among whom I would work, whose dispositions could be at least partially intelligible and even acceptable to me, and whose purposes I could help to perpetuate and prosper.

As I consider this process of initiation, as I look back on the several stages I advanced through while trying to grasp it, I should under no circumstances, now or ever, want to mitigate the challenge such a choice presented me with. I had strayed into a landscape whose features were distinctly unfamiliar to me; whose inhabitants confronted me, however ingenuously, with perspectives that sometimes "dumbfounded" me, not because of their oddness but because of the level, one might say, or the degree of their deliberative and humane seriousness, which was simply not the order of business in the world I was accustomed to. However gridlocked in routines and standardized objectives my professional life might be, it was a world without "ritual" of the sort I had detected in Besserman's office; it was a world of technicalities and timetables, of procedures and deadlines; it was a world, for whatever good or ill might be predicated of it, largely without a reflexive order of priorities and principles both ordered to something higher than itself as well as, in that respect, susceptible to being applied to changing events that compelled the most scrupulous ethical attention to adjudicate their perplexities.

As I said, the challenge was real, for I did not put it out of question that someday, in some preemptive fickleness of heart—and we never know when our hearts shall be tempted to betray us—I could end up using the very moral preeminence that I was witnessing here, and the unique standards it might exact from me, as a weapon to defend myself against it. I could in time, as is all too common in human affairs, come to contemn for some self-serving reason or another, everything I had been summoned to understand and to act upon. How often an unsolved difficulty in one's life manifests itself as an assault directed, irrelevantly and capriciously, at precisely those whose consummate fineness is construed as a reproach to one's own personal disaffections. We have a way, under stress, of cutting down others to fit our own size. Here again I had to tread warily, for I could sense already that the preeminence of which I spoke, and the unfamiliar heights that it occupied and that in turn nourished it, were grounded in something, in some overarching architectonic impetus that still was well beyond my ken. I was being asked to cope with all of that, all of those unknowns.

I knew that there was no financial inducement for me to seek out this attachment; in fact, such an attachment might very well mean jettisoning that vague and rather surreptitious aspiration I had harbored for so long of an early retirement to an airy, hibiscus-garlanded villa in Florida with a gleaming white yacht moored on a canal at a boat slip notched into my fondly imagined, all-encompassing veranda. Nor was it a question of prestige conferred by representing a foundation that, it was all too clear, zealously safeguarded its own anonymity. My professional ascent had been easy, dictating no unseemly stratagems, no foraging or rapaciousness, bidding only that I do my work and meet my deadlines. Indeed, I was always surprised when the proprietary taskmasters of my firm motioned me upward to larger and more remunerative responsibilities. I left behind me, as far as I knew, no trail of injured sensibilities and displaced, envious colleagues.

Hence I had no conventional incentive to change anything, to pursue new projects. Even my family was, it was prudent to assume, content with the way things were, though I kept my spouse and children informed at every step of the process I was going through now, and, it was equally prudent to conjecture, both their curiosity was aroused and their support reasonably well assured. My problem was—our problems always are, are they not?—to be supremely just: to be just in this particular case, to be willing to repose ultimate confidence in those who proposed to place their ultimate confidence in me. And, in order to do that successfully, I had to have confidence in myself. I could not simply "bluster" into an unknown world and think, necessarily, that that was all it took to be part of it. "Bluster," in any event, was what I had to do; I had no other choice. But then I had to understand what I had, indeed, "blustered" into.

"Well, Mr. Schofield," Cornelia had commenced when finally turning her attention, for the moment, to more professional matters, "my inclination at a moment like this might be to ask you to tell me all about yourself, but I suspect that such an inquiry has already been precluded by Theodore's efforts, and I should not want you to have to labor through an interrogation of that sort again. I assume he has been very thorough in that regard; he always is."

"I don't think I was ever really interrogated," I said, "but I doubt there is much more to say—about myself, that is."

"Oh, there is always more to say, Mr. Schofield, if not just about everything, I'm sure especially about you. I have received the full report; of that you can be sure. Theodore is thorough in what he communicates to others, but only, as I am sure you know by now, about those things that are relevant to whatever point is at hand. There is always more that he knows that he doesn't say—not to conceal it but to let it wait until it is pertinent to mention. That seems like a simple enough principle, doesn't it? But with Theodore it is not simple at all; he will sometimes wait for twenty years to say something, until, that is, the right moment has come at last. And the problem is that he has been saving it up all that time, waiting for that moment and judging with precision that the occasion has finally arrived. I have found it, at times, just a little unnerving, I'll admit, but he would not have it any other way; nor would I."

I nodded. "I think you are right, but I have to confess that I am still arguably at the 'unnerving' stage."

She smiled. "You will get used to him soon enough. He is formidable at first sight. I have known him all my life, and I still find him formidable."

"Indeed!" I responded, "I imagine there are a few other 'formidable' critters lurking about the territory."

"So you did visit Madison Street after all!" she exclaimed. "I suspected you would. Well, I am so glad. It is a memorable place with not a few memorable 'critters' to go along with it. Which particular one did you happen to meet?"

"I'm not sure if 'happen' is the most accurate term, but I met Mother d'Agneau."

"Memorable enough. I have had a most wonderful friendship with her over the years."

"She sends her best regards. She is looking forward to your visit. She says you are of great help to them; you keep them on track."

"Actually, I don't, "Cornelia corrected. "I just do a little to remind them of what they know already."

"Then they get lost now and then?"

"No more or less than anybody else. People just often need a little nudge to get them back on track. It's a privilege to be able to give that nudge, as long as one is reasonably confident that one knows what one is doing. Anyway, what's wrong with getting lost now and then?"

"What's right with it?"

"Getting lost has a purpose. It forces us to think. It forces us to reconsider for a while the lay of the land and how we are moving through it. We do have a way of trying to get through life without thinking. But it is what we, as the kind of critters we are, are most designed to do."

"I'll try to remember that," I said. It was comforting for me to know that I had a few acquaintances in common with Cornelia—persons who had "primed" me well for my initial discussion. Given the trajectory of our conversation, as it would turn out, some of Mother d'Agneau's "imagery" would later stand me in good stead. I asked Cornelia about her "education," though I felt I knew, in some sense, about much of it already. She focused, as I would expect her to, on a single aspect: in this case, her interest in the Middle Ages and especially in the decorative arts of the early period.

"I was a student of Eleanor Duckett at Smith," she began. "It was she who, more than anyone else, awoke my interest in medieval things, especially in the 'formative' period, as some consider it. Perhaps you have read some of her works?"

"I'm sorry to say I haven't."

"Oh dear, what a . . ."

"Misfortune?"

"Yes . . . of course," she hesitated, "how curious!"

"Why curious?"

"That you should have taken the words out of my mouth." I didn't bother to explain.

She continued. "I am preparing a short monograph on a local monument of some antiquity—a convent chantry situated on a ridge not far from our *petit demesne*, dating from perhaps the mid-tenth century. It is all that is left of that particular convent. The chantry, even though partially in ruins and having been used as a stable on and off for several centuries, is a fine work of late Romanesque architecture. Its original windows are all gone, but the paving tiles are still intact and their designs are some of the best I know of. You won't find the place on tourist itineraries, and the only visitors are the occasional and rather particularly—and, perhaps I should add, peculiarly—specialized medievalist, a young couple now and then on bicycles looking for a secluded place to have a picnic, and the birds that roost in its cornices."

"A small thing then?" I remarked.

"Yes, small. Very small. But not for that reason negligible. And it is located in my neighborhood, and neighborhoods are never unimportant, don't you think? If there is going to be any intimacy with the earth in its largesse, it will be both in and with what is close to us; for that is all that we can really get to know, more or less, with a fullness from which we can infer the largesse of the creation as a whole."

"I hope you will show me these paving tiles someday," I asked. Paving tiles would be a novelty in my life, even as an Ouschak carpet had been that morning. But I was not ready to cope with the "creation as a whole."

"I would love to show them to you. It is an easy and picturesque horseback ride from our farm. Can you handle a horse, Mr. Schofield?"

"Well, in a manner of speaking. I learned something of it at a summer camp when I was young. My most vivid memory is of a rambunctious palomino running off with me, out of my control, after having been scared by a rabbit. Mind you, I didn't blame the horse. The rabbit scared me too. In any event, I am not sure how much I would trust my skills."

"We can find a gentle enough horse for you. But, I warn you, then you will have to endure my forays into a pedagogic mode. I love to 'decant' the past; I use that word deliberately. Much of the past is like a fine old vintage wine; one wants to pour it in a thin, wavering stream, ever so patiently, from its musty old bottles, in the muted glow of candlelight even, to distill the best from what is dross. I find that decanting the past is genuinely humbling, if for no other reason than that it reveals how desperately little we know about it, how much of a mystery it is, how different it is from the threadbare stories we construct to explain it, to 'put it in its place.' Anyway, it is fun to talk about such matters, even if I do rattle on a bit."

"Don't worry. I think I am growing accustomed to lectures. I have heard part of your—perhaps introductory—lecture, and it sounds all terribly erudite to me. One day, I imagine, you shall be offered a professorship in some renowned seat of learning."

"Really? I don't think so," she objected. "I doubt that there are more than a few dozen people in the world who would be seriously interested in the subject of my monograph. Well, add to that a few hundred readers, maybe, who might want to spend a few hours with it as a minor, if ancillary, adjunct to some larger project they are pursuing. So I don't think the academic world would have much use for me. Further, what advantages would it give me that would not at the same time exact a price I was unwilling to pay? My monograph is one of those deferred projects, Mr. Schofield, one of those things that is put off from time to time because the fulfillment of other and more important obligations claim priority, as difficult as it is to acknowledge that sometimes. I am here in the United States for just such reasons. And I am in a hurry, I think I told you, to return to Normandy, but I didn't tell you that one of my mares is shortly to give birth to a foal, and I insist that I, to say nothing of Liselle, be there to assist with the delivery."

We discussed other matters, mostly touching upon life in Madison Street. I figured that, in her sundry, richly woven accounts, often responsive to my questions and pointed, as far as was possible, in the direction of my interests, she was trying to accomplish what Mr. Besserman had set out to accomplish: to limn for me an account of that multicolored legacy whose threads I was being asked to trace. But what was most striking for me, more striking indeed than the account itself, was the tone in which it was delivered. I might have expected to find nostalgia, and perhaps I did find some of that. I might have expected to find shadows, no matter how deeply hidden or suggested, of those deep recesses of regret we all conserve in our hearts, of a struggle with a past whose lost opportunities are regarded as irrecoverable, whose benumbing shortfalls still extend their tenacious privations into our present lives; but I found none of that. Nor did I find a need—any need at all—to justify, to placate, to reproach. What I did find was a gently sloping concavity of tenderness—a tenderness for others, for the loss of others beveled downward with such depth into that broad-rimmed, bejeweled cup of her life that it shone, out of that cup, not like loss but like a fullness, like a vessel filled to the brim and running over, evoking in the glow of its very receptivity a gratitude welling up and fructifying everything she touched upon. It was extraordinary indeed to be in the presence of such a grateful human being, whose gratefulness and liberality were annealed and illuminated by those same unspoken sorrows of her life. Even when she spoke of herself, it was not drawing attention to herself but, to the contrary, was engaging with me at the deepest level and depositing an invaluable keepsake into my custody, with all the depth of trust such an act implied.

Then again, as I spoke to her, another quality of intellect began to emerge with unusual force. She took joy in exercising a passionate logic. She delineated principles and priorities; with sharp, clear analysis, she knew her reasons and understood her perceptions; she delighted, almost "devoutly," I would say, in the way that particular details both grounded and displayed some higher and more universal order of relations that she was affectionately privy to and did not for a moment shy away from or ignore. It's as if the world, despite all its heavy mystery, had a form and a shape that one could, with effort, with enormous effort in some cases, understand and take pleasure in. It's as if the world manifested a succession of circumferences, one broader and encircling the previous one, extending into outer horizons whose limits, if it had limits, we could just barely begin to envisage. I had a sense, in talking to her, that this is what it must have been like, in some respects, to converse with Frederick Schefflin.

She talked about her visits to Concord, to the house of Uncle Aloysius and Aunt Bernice. "I had, you know, a room of my own in the attic, a sort of garret—'Cornelia's roost,' it was called. I spent many a vacation there and sometimes entire summers. It was like another home for me. During the summers, especially when we were joined for a while by my parents, we drove up to the lakes and went out for canoe rides and climbed the mountains and camped in the national forest. Father seemed to know everything about setting up wilderness camps. I can't tell you how lovely it was. Mother was especially fond of wild blueberries. How often we went on forays into the Squam Range on sunny days, sharing a picnic while gazing over those pristine waters and islands of that too precious lake and picking several buckets of berries and bringing them back to Concord. Father liked to take some of them to the carriage house in the back, and we would make blueberry ice cream. I got to crank that old machine until the ice cream thickened up so much I couldn't turn it anymore. Then Uncle Aloysius would take over from there. It was fun watching Father and Uncle Aloysius preparing food together. Mother was not especially good at cooking (decocting strange ointments and bizarre elixirs was another matter), and Aunt Bernice could, as far as I remember, scarcely boil an egg. It's good she always had local farm girls who could make some money by coming in and tending to the Fitzgeralds' kitchen.

"It was something of a tradition, for many years, for Uncle Aloysius and Aunt Bernice to visit us at Madison Street for Christmas. The house was wonderfully adorned with holly and candles and a lovely but antiquated style of decorating the Christmas tree. We had many guests who would drop in for a visit during the day at different times—a kind of open house, as one might call it nowadays, but often persisting throughout the holiday season. There was always a Christmas musicale at one point, and a flourishing buffet that was replenished with new enticements all day long and well into the evening. Aunt Bernice inevitably would manage to arrange for producing one of those old mystery plays from Wakefield or York, or sometimes from France or Italy or Spain. We would ransack the attic for costumes, the kitchen for glimmering pots and pans that could be donned as knightly armor, and the garden shed for staffs and spears and whatever else we needed. I remember one year poor Father being dragooned into playing Noah—he was reticent about taking on dramatic roles—while several guests were pressed into service as animals being herded on to the ark; Aunt Bernice taught them the basics of bleating, mooing, hee-hawing, growling, and the like."

"Was Mr. Besserman also there at these festivities?" I interrupted.

"Theodore? Well, of course he was there, and Martha too," she answered. "Theodore was a lion in that particular performance."

"A lion!"

"He did a very good job at rolling his head and roaring. He could not have known more than five minutes beforehand that he was going to be cast as a lion; so his skillful performance would suggest that, for whatever arcane purposes he had had in mind sometime previously, he had studied the MGM lion rather carefully—you know the one that sticks his head through a garland of film strips that has *ars gratia artis* inscribed on it. Martha, on the other hand, provided background jigs with her violin. She could make her violin sound like a bagpipe—the medieval kind, not the Scottish military bagpipe with the big drones on it. We also had a sonorous, primitive old sheepskin drum from backcountry Connemara that Uncle Aloysius kept thumping away on. We would all join in a rambunctious dance at the finale, a kind of *estampie*, perhaps. It all went together very well."

"But what were you?"

"Mother did me up as—well, as a giraffe, if you must know."

"A giraffe?"

"A baby giraffe. I was still pretty young then. The body of the giraffe from the waist down. The rest of me was neck—giraffe neck from the waist up. It was all a rather ungainly role to be playing."

"She had a preoccupation with giraffes, I understand."

"Yes. Mother loved to climb trees now and then. It was one of the riskier things she enjoyed doing. She said it gave her a 'giraffe's-eye view' of the world. Father could never get her to desist from that rather peculiar and dangerous practice."

"And Aunt Bernice—other than being producer and director, what role did she play? I assume she made all the decisions."

"She certainly did. Hence, she liked to assume the role of God, and a very convincing God at that. She could wrap up her waist-length hair around the front of her face and make it look like a beard. In other plays, she delighted to take on the role of the devil. She would braid her hair into two great cones on top of her head so that she looked as if she had horns. I never knew her to do a lick of garden or farm work, but as Sir Lucifer, and having appropriated the requisite tool from the garden shed, she could wield a pitchfork like, as they say, a 'pro.' Some of the neighborhood children would get so frightened that they would run into the dining room and hide under the table."

"But you didn't?" I interposed.

"Didn't what?"

"Get frightened and hide under the table"

"I didn't hide under the table, but I did get frightened. We all were frightened of that pitchfork being brandished all over the place."

Cornelia finally took notice of the tea service in front of us. "I'm afraid that will be cold by now."

"No matter," I said.

"Are you sure? I could order a fresh pot of tea."

"Really, don't concern yourself with that." I don't recall what happened to the tea service after that. I think I may have nibbled on one of the pastries.

"At New Year's," Cornelia went on, "we would join the Fitzgeralds at their house in Concord. That was a much more modest affair, I can assure you. I don't think Mother and Father ever had much interest in New Year's celebrations, but they appreciated getting out to the country for a while. Back in those days, Mr. Schofield, if you can imagine it, most country backroads in New Hampshire were still unpaved and there was an abundance of horse-drawn sleighs still around so that one could race along those only partially plowed roads, bundled up in blankets, the frosty wind in one's face, the dazzling sunlight breaking through the frozen silence of the winter forest, and the muted tromp of the horses' hooves while the runners slid swiftly over the snow. I wonder if there ever was anything in the world as exhilarating as that. We made it a tradition, when weather allowed, to hire several of these sleighs, along with their cavorting horses and sometimes excessively cavorting drivers, and to gallop in tandem to the Shaker Village in Canterbury, just north of Concord. It was a welcome destination; bowls of hot, steamy soup and gritty cornbread and sweet, fresh butter always awaited us at the guesthouse. There were not too many of the original Shakers left at that time, but there were enough to allow the community to continue their work. We welcomed their kindly attention. Father admired the quality of their craftsmanship—he loved everything that human beings make, the products of human industry and inventiveness, but he picked out their work for special attention. Further, he had a fascination with their way of life, rather especially with the humane and decorous efficiency of their operations so that maximum time was left over for what they regarded as 'higher' concerns. Father himself was, in a way, obsessed with such stark good order, but good order directed finally to providing what he felt that he, and others around him, needed in order to endue life with all those spontaneous things, the life of sport, of learnedness, of joyous sociability, of all those things whose ends lay, as he would say, 'delectably in themselves'—'higher concerns,' as he, by and large, seemed to understand them. On his European travels, he enjoyed visiting the old Cistercian monasteries too, which he compared with the Shaker village at Canterbury; I think he had, in spite of himself, a lively sense of the higher contemplative modes to which these habitats were ultimately devoted.

"The rest of us were there for the adventure of the ride. Aunt Bernice was never reticent about assuming one of her multitudinous and ordinarily flamboyant roles. Wrapped in an utterly barbaric cape of what I assume were rabbit pelts, she became, for the nonce, a Cossack princess out of a Russian novel, throwing kisses to farmers we passed by and singing out in a slightly unintelligible voice something or other that was contrived to sound like Russian. I don't know what the farmers thought about all of that as we pranced past their fields and orchards, but I would not doubt that they had seen stranger things in life. In my various exchanges with New Hampshire farmers, I have never known one whose life was not replete with prodigies, real or fanciful, and I imagine this one might have been high on their list. At night, especially if it was New Year's night, Aunt Bernice would put on an entertainment in her little improvised theater at the back of the house. A few neighbors and several of Uncle Aloysius's medical associates might join in as well; but it was not much more than a kind of vaudeville show, each person presenting what he or she could or was willing to do. Father would play a short gigue on his cello; Mother would sing a Scottish or Irish folk ballad, *a cappella,* sometimes in Gaelic: always so sad and so beautiful. Uncle Aloysius had this little comic piece he repeated from year to year about a hard-of-hearing doctor trying to understand his patient's symptoms (I was often the patient) and getting everything wrong, and Aunt Bernice would do an outrageous satire of a Miss America contestant trying to perform Lady Macbeth in the mad scene from *Macbeth.* It was all very remarkable ... as long ... as long as it lasted."

Her voice dropped. "It didn't last too long."

"Nothing does," I murmured, wondering why I felt the need to say that.

I thought I should perhaps change the subject, but I should not have thought, as I think I did, that Cornelia would have any difficulty recalling these early memories and maintaining her so exquisitely tempered equipoise. I asked her about her husband, Colonel Maurice de Quevillon. I immediately divined that this avenue of discussion was laden with obstacles, not in the sense of some personal entanglements that I had unwittingly broached but rather in the sense of a range of historical and cultural complications whose import I could scarcely be assumed to understand without a great deal of prior explanation. I knew already from my conversations with Besserman that the Colonel was descended from a very old French military family; that that fact itself, in the history of modern France, was fraught with a constellation of political ambiguities and discords difficult for us, with our simpler, ostensibly less compromised history to fathom—though some might argue that our own Civil War generated just such ambiguities; that the career of the gentleman himself, and indeed the course of the married couple in its earlier years, had been embroiled in the chaos of postwar France, in Dien Bien Phu and Indochine, in the interminable Algerian crisis and the crucible of the Gaulist republic;

that Cornelia's foreign nationality had added another dimension to the ordeals they had had to endure. She said nothing of this; perhaps one day she would.

But she did speak of her husband's love for horses; for their ancient manorial *demesne* deep in the Pays d'Auge, with its half-timbered *logis*, its craggy towers and barns and dovecote, embedded in rural traditions extending back to the feudal period of Normandy; for his collection of nineteenth-century military prints; for the thriving retail cooperative he had helped to establish in the local area. She did mention her marriage ceremony of many years ago: it had taken place in an old medieval church, a full military marriage, with her husband's fellow cadets in attendance. It had been rather a privilege for them to have had such a setting made available to them, and it had been a beautiful affair. Frederick had been long since deceased, but Agnes had come to it; Cornelia did miss the presence of many of her American compatriots at the time, for they would have loved it. Aunt Bernice was still active but made it a point not to travel much of anywhere at all, as far as Cornelia knew, outside the closed circuit, as it were, of New York and Cape Cod that she had prescribed for herself soon after the death of Uncle Aloysius.

A lapse in the conversation ensued. I broke the silence by asking, "Then you were married in the Church of your husband, I assume?" I am not sure what caused me to take this particular tack at the moment—I guess I had recalled some of my discussions with Mother d'Agneau—but, in any case, I had introduced, inadvertently, and with no other initial intention than a partially idle curiosity, a subject that at once I regretted, that I should regret even more as it developed, but that I came ultimately not to regret at all. Had I approached an issue of too personal a nature, too inappropriate for social chatter? Cornelia did not seem to be perturbed at all by my inquiry and answered in the affirmative. She had indeed married in the Church.

"And as a member of the Church?" I persisted, not knowing at this point what else to do but pursue the inquiry, especially since, the more clearly I remembered my conversation with Mother d'Agneau, the more I recalled that I was already in possession of some of that information even as I asked about it.

"Why do you ask?" she returned, without exactly answering me, but addressing me with a tone that implied both an affirmative answer to my question and a genuine interest about why I was bringing up this matter.

I thought for a moment before I answered her. I made a conscious effort not to assume the all-too-frequent patronizing tone that persons of my perspective often adopt when entering discourse of this kind. "It's just that the Schefflins did not have, as I have been led to understand, any particular, or maybe particularized, religious attachments."

She mused in silence about my observation. "About such attachments in others one never really knows, I think," she responded. "While I was growing up, Mother and Father did not have denominational ties, if that is what you mean by 'particularized.' I don't know what they actually thought about such matters. It is inconceivable that they would not have thought about it and not have had convictions of some sort. But I cannot vouch for what those were. They just didn't talk about them, as far as I can remember. I knew how they acted relative to the beliefs of others."

"Tolerant, I would think," I averred blithely, with exactly that sort of fatuity I was trying to avoid.

"I wonder ..." she demurred. "I wonder ... if that is the correct expression. Sometimes I think that to be 'tolerant' is often to place ourselves in a superior position, to 'know better' and yet deign to hear out something we would not otherwise countenance except as justified by those generous impulses we are gratified in imputing to ourselves when mistaking etiquette for civility and condescension for respect. Furthermore, tolerance can be motivated by disdain. Tolerance is scarcely accurate to describe at least how Father interacted with others on these matters. His attitude, as far as I saw it, was always one of studious and genuine interest in what others held to be true, a kind of humility, you might say, in the presence of things he could not claim to understand. In these, as in all matters, he exercised a meticulous reserve of judgment; he was circumspect, detached, but never sarcastic to, or contemptuous of, the persons to whom he spoke. If it is correct to describe him as interested and willing to trust the good faith of people, he was also simply too aware of how one's interlocutors, however well-intentioned they might be, could misrepresent respectable positions without knowing that they were doing that, could presume to know more than they could possibly know, to arrogate to themselves, arbitrarily, the authority to represent groups and bodies of established opinions without much of an entitlement to do so, and to display greater self-assurance than a given topic could justifiably warrant. Father had his own convictions, naturally, the fruit of much thought and consideration, and when the occasion for doing so was appropriate, he was rarely diffident about stating what these were; after all, that in itself is a kind of gift to others. But he never advanced such ideas, as we are all so inclined to do, with the presumption, the self-assuming tone, that those whom we address already comprehend the terms of our discourse, consent to its presuppositions, and share the same sardonic stance to those who stand outside our circle, as if nothing else were possible to an intelligent human being.

"He had a similar attitude in regard to other matters. In business, for example: in his position, as you can well imagine, he had to contend with persistently exhorted schemes and propositions whose cogency (to say nothing of motives) he had to assess, even when they came from individuals or institutions with ostensibly irreproachable qualifications. I'm not sure Father ever engaged in an altercation with anyone. I was told once—by Theodore, I believe—that a self-appointed delegation of business-school professors, representing (so it could be construed) a most prestigious institution indeed and purporting to bestow upon him their well-meaning but unsolicited counsel, visited him one day in his executive offices unexpectedly and ended up bringing down upon themselves an unwonted and most peremptory dismissal. Father, swiftly thereafter, sent each of them a conciliatory note, thanking them for their desire to be helpful and palliating their presumably wounded sensibilities with gift boxes of cherry cordials and brandy truffles.

"Now, I must say, Mother was rather more of an enigma; her inveterate courtesy, her affection for mystery, always made it difficult to discern exactly what was going on in her, though things would and did change in her lifetime, particularly in her final years."

"What happened then?"

"Eventually she followed me into the Church. Well, what an absurd way to say it! She followed me only in a temporal sense. She followed her conscience."

"Then, I take it, you—the two of you finally—constitute something of a new direction in the family tradition," I proposed.

"More of a recovery than anything else, perhaps," she qualified, "a recovery in several different senses. And then . . . and then, there was Uncle Aloysius. He was 'family' too."

She gazed at me rather intently at the moment, as if waiting for a signal from me as to whether or not we should change the subject. I don't remember, frankly, what I did, what signal I gave. But I didn't want her to stop, and she must have seen that, somehow. After all, I was eager to understand who she was, and, to that end, I wanted to know more about how she perceived her connection with Uncle Aloysius, now that she had introduced that subject.

"I am sure you realize, Mr. Schofield," she began, "that there are many things in life that one cannot readily talk about because talk itself simplifies too much matters that are, in all their ramifications, extremely complex and, conversely, complicates too much matters that are, at heart, extremely simple. I shall not try to unravel that paradox, even if I could. What I have referred to as a 'recovery' was enkindled most overtly in my college years. I think that some of my interest in the early medieval period was part of that concern, or certainly ancillary to it. I say 'overtly' because I am not too sure it wasn't there long before in some nascent state, as so many things are in us long before they blossom. The road I followed thereafter was fraught with difficulties—I cannot tell you how many and how demanding these were; and one continues thereafter to struggle with those same difficulties perhaps for the rest of one's life; but when I arrived, as I eventually did, at the stage of a more explicitly 'catechetical' induction, I realized something very curious. Now, I know this will seem very obscure to you—most initiates to the faith are baffled by the welter of discriminations, definitions, categories, modes, and everything else that bristles at every juncture of the theological scene. I won't try to justify any of that, except to assure you, if I could, that such distinctions are intended, in principle at least, to do justice to the complexity of the human condition. In the midst of confronting all these 'canonical' items, I discovered something of special interest to me. According to some provisions of ecclesial law regarding the sacrament of baptism, and according to a memory that these same provisions awoke in me, I discovered that, technically in a manner that most people could not help but feel is excessively bizarre, I had been, arguably, a member of the Church since my childhood."

I think I must have shaken my head in disbelief.

She laughed. "You are an attorney, Mr. Schofield, and therefore you must understand, better than most of us, the manifold ways in which some human beings can, and do, take on the task of representing others, both institutions and persons, and are authorized to act on their behalf. Someone did, you might say, act on my behalf and on the behalf of others. It's a complex picture and not always with the clearest boundaries we could desire. Good 'jurisprudence,' should we say, takes into account such ambivalent matters. But, rather than attempt to explain some of the fundamentals of what is called the sacramental life, I will tell you a story. There is much that is rather bewildering about this story. But I will tell you this story, Mr. Schofield, if you have the patience to hear it, and I guarantee you that, other than my catechist, the ordinary who received me into the Church many decades ago, and my husband, I have never told anyone else."

"You honor me," I said, not being too sure how or why I was being thus honored.

"It was a hot, sun-drenched afternoon in Concord," she began. "I was nine years old at the time and spending the summer with my uncle and aunt. As I often did, I accompanied my uncle on his rounds of house calls. He had this wonderful old automobile—a convertible with wire-spoked wheels and commodious running boards—and we would trundle up and down hills and dusty roads, going from farmhouse to farmhouse. Often I would stay in the car while he entered a house and attended to his patients. It was such lovely countryside in those days, and people were so happy to see him come, though often the strain of illness and grief showed all too manifestly on their sun-browned faces. While he was in the house, the children of the family might come out to see me—I got to know many of them over the years—and would lure me out of the car and conduct me into the barns or sheds to see a newborn lamb or a frisky calf or a gaggle of ducklings on a nearby pond.

"On this particular day, we concluded our rounds, as we sometimes did, by returning to Concord, parking the car at home, and strolling to an ice-cream shop on nearby Main Street. I can't tell you how much fun this was. Everyone in town seemed to know Uncle Aloysius and waved at him or stopped him on the street and told him funny stories—or I think they were funny stories, because everyone laughed at them. After the ice-cream store we wandered farther southward along Main Street, going nowhere in particular, just walking, as we often did, and enjoying whatever cooling breezes managed to make their way through the tall vault of elm trees that, in those days, towered over and shaded the street. We looked at the spare traffic making its way down the street and, once we had entered a residential section, said hello to people sitting on their front porches with fans and icy containers of lemonade. A few blocks farther down we passed a church, a tall, thin brick church standing back from the street and surrounded by trees and a lawn, which I later came to know by the name of Saint John the Evangelist.

"Uncle Aloysius suddenly decided to go into the church—it would be cool in there, he said, and we could rest for a while. So we went in. I had never been in a church before, so naturally I was curious. We passed through the vestibule and into the dark silence of the nave and sat for a while in a pew toward the back. I was fascinated by the golden tabernacle and by the little red candle glowing at its side, by the brightly colored windows, and by the sculpted figures in the front, standing under what I would later know to be their pinnacled Gothic canopies. But we were both silent and reposed there, without talking, for about ten minutes, it seemed. It was nice to be there. Then we stood up and walked back into the vestibule. In the vestibule was a marble basin of water, a 'stoup,' as such items were once called. Uncle Aloysius stood for a moment by the stoup. He seemed to be thinking about something. I looked up at him and pulled on his left hand. It was time to go, I thought. Suddenly, with his right hand he reached into the basin and scooped out a handful of water. The next thing I knew he had uttered some words I didn't understand, and the cool water from the stoup ran in rivulets down my head and over my face. I remember laughing. It was the best game of all. Uncle Aloysius wiped my face with his handkerchief. He was smiling. He did give some explanation of what he was doing, but I don't think I understood a word of it, and I certainly didn't remember much more of it than the cold water dripping down over my face.

"I did not understand until years later that he had escorted me, as it were, through the portals of his faith; into what had been, as I would come to see later, the 'joy' of his youth, the hearthstone of his ancestors; into what we can only surmise he regarded, or which he came to regard most acutely at that moment, as the sole proper domicile for the breaking of bread—the bread of remembrance, of thanksgiving, of sacrifice. He had acted, as best he could under those perplexing circumstances, as the representative of that domicile. As later events should soon demonstrate, the conferral upon me had also been an act of recovery for himself, and he would live out the fidelity for the rest of his days, as limited as those days would turn out to be."

"So he rediscovered his 'roots'?" I inquired.

"That, yes; and so much more than that," she replied. "He rediscovered something in the context of which he also recovered his roots. One's 'roots,' provided one can actually distinguish about them what is authentic and what is, in some negative sense, merely and not always beneficently mythological, can sometimes, among other things, point the way, just as sometimes they impede the access one needs. The point is, so often, to find a threshold so that the real exploration can begin. That baptism, however bewildering it must seem to you, Mr. Schofield, was part of Uncle Aloysius's legacy to me, part of my threshold too, though I should not realize it as such until later in my own life. However, one can hardly deny that it was most unusual, the sort of thing that gets done, according to ecclesial sanctions, in the breach only when the normal requisites and conditions are, for whatever snarl of reasons, unavailable. Further, such an act bears with it certain obligatory consequences. I can well imagine Uncle Aloysius had to struggle with that, not knowing exactly in what his authorization—or authorizations, I should say, derived perhaps from several different sources—consisted and how far they extended. I have little doubt that he thought time itself would unravel some of the issues and point in the proper direction; it turned out that there was not much time left.

"Meanwhile, whenever I visited Concord thereafter, I was often his companion, though ordinarily silent and uncomprehending, in his exercise of religious observances. He opened a dozen different doors for me to peek into, even if he didn't say much about them, as if those things could, and would, speak more convincingly for themselves in the course of time than he could manage to do. It might simply be something as simple as setting up, as we so often did together, a Christmas *crèche* as he related the story that went along with it. And he was right, as far as I can discern. Those observances did speak to me, more eloquently than the words that sometimes accompanied them. Aunt Bernice had no interest in this matter but no objections to it either. And Father and Mother, who hardly, in any case, would have disapproved, stood back and let happen whatever was going to happen. In any event, I am deeply grateful to have been, as innocent and ignorant as I was in the situation, at least a partial occasion for the restoration of Uncle Aloysius's own birthright. I guess one could also claim that it was the attainment of a birthright for me in several ways. It's not the only time that would happen in my relation to Uncle Aloysius. He gave a very special life to me, and I was glad to return, in whatever way I could, a very special life to him."

"And all of this commenced," I said, "on that hot afternoon in Concord, in the vestibule of that church, when your uncle poured those cooling waters over your head?"

She laughed. "I'm sorry," she said. "I laughed when it happened, and I laugh whenever I think of it."

"So do you laugh whenever you approach one of those basins of water in the vestibules of your churches?"

"I probably should. We bless ourselves with that water every time we enter or exit a church in order to remind ourselves of our initiation. But, admittedly, customary practices can just as often blunt as hone our memory."

At this moment in our conversation occurred one of those incidents, perhaps propelled by my own inadequacy to know how to respond to what I had been hearing, whose very cataclysmic turn was, conversely, the escutcheon of its inexpressible magnificence. I embarrassed myself; it was not what I said that was so embarrassing but that I faltered as I said it and then was embarrassed by my faltering. Even as I recount it, the sting of my mortification returns in its initial intensity. Again, what I said was innocent enough, though inept in its own terms, which is why the gush of remorse, of self-reproach, that swept over me even before the words were out of my mouth invested my statement with a significance that it did not need to have.

"So Uncle Aloysius baptized you!" I quipped (yes, that is, unfortunately, how I need to describe it). "Then Uncle Aloysius was your godfather too!"

It's the "too" that really did it. I tried to stop it, but it came out. It did not have to mean what I made it mean by stumbling so monumentally over it. Had I—oh my God (excuse the expression!)—violated, through a flippant and maladroit tongue, the confidence that had been placed in me? How could I reconcile myself to this indiscretion by spinning some improbable web of apologetic disingenuousness?

I felt as if I lost all presence of mind. I felt as if . . . as if . . . I had tripped over a stone and toppled into . . . into a well. Yes, I am bound to recur to Mother d'Agneau's imagery here, for I have no other way to say it. I felt as if I must have had a particularly droll expression on my face, rather like a raggedy Punchinello pinioned in the midst of a tragic-comical cartwheel that had hurtled him downward into a dark well. A dark well? Had I hit water? Had I splashed down and sluiced into the bottom of its murky depths? My eyes filmed over, and my ears were deafened by a massive rush of fluid into my head.

I don't know how long this lasted. Maybe a second or two. Maybe not even as long as that. Then I detected a hand on my forearm, a firm, delicate hand, grasping me, catching me in my fall, bearing me upward. When my eyes cleared, I was looking straight into those amazing blue-green eyes of Cornelia, who was leaning forward from her sofa toward me.

"Yes," she affirmed, pointedly and serenely, repeating my words as if it were the most natural thing to do, "Uncle Aloysius was my godfather too."

A numbing silence followed, as thick and as palpable as a starless, moonless night in which, without a lantern or other light, one seems to be walking blindly into a wall of black soft wool that nevertheless recedes mysteriously before one's steps. Thoughts raced through my head. If the ambiguity of my indiscretion could be tilted potentially, by an emphasis on one word, in one direction, without necessarily resolving it, could not the equal ambiguity of her repetition of my statement likewise be tilted potentially, now by a lack of emphasis on the same word, in a different direction, without being resolved? It was that word "too" in both cases. What, in effect, had she told me? For all I could discern then, and still discern now, she had told me that, in one way, nothing had happened, that all was in place, that everything was in the same place it had been, and that the potential resolution of ambiguity had been put in abeyance—where it should, and would, remain, until the proper occasion to resolve it could arise. But, in another way, not the words themselves but the fact of the incident had been of major importance.

She had withdrawn her touch on my forearm and had rested back into the sofa again. Then, through that silence, she suddenly, gently, gratuitously remarked, "I have a favor to ask of you, Mr. Schofield. I hope you will not find it impertinent of me to make this request."

"I am more than willing to accommodate your wishes, Madame de Quevillon, if I am able," I consented stiffly, with just the slightest crook of my head, sidling for refuge into the momentary role of an officious clerk in an old, leather-bound novel from another century that was now, without loss or regret for anyone, forgotten.

"As I have told you," she resumed, "I have a number of matters to attend to while I am here in America. It would be a great relief to me if you could look after one of them for me. I am thinking that your legal background might be of some utility in this matter, since there may be papers or documents among the files I would like you to review that have some legal status or another. I doubt that there is much there of that nature, if any at all, and what's there would be so long out of date that it is unlikely to have much legal force left in it. Still, one is always surprised at what may turn up. I think you would be the best judge. I would like to put this matter thoroughly in your hands. How you judge is how I shall judge too, and what you decide to do is what I would have decided to do."

"You flatter me indeed," I protested, still ensconced deeply in my role of embarrassed servility. "Just give me the appropriate instructions, and what you will, I shall will too."

She smiled. I thought of my undergraduate days; of reading Dante in the hellish burrow of my dormitory room—a not unlikely facsimile of some pestilent pothole in the Inferno itself; and I thought of Beatrice at the portals of Paradise, her eyes filled with sparkling light, her hand and her fingers beckoning to something beyond herself, gesturing, directing, urging me onward.

"Well, Mr. Schofield, we need not be too solemn about this," she said, luring me cheerfully out of my protective, if officious lair. "Uncle Aloysius had a cousin of some sort, maybe a second or a third cousin, and I don't know how many times removed. The Fitzgerald family tree is enormously complex, and I'm afraid one would have to engage in a feat of scrambling, squirrel-like, up and down and along the boughs of that tree and into the boughs of other family trees that interlace with the Fitzgerald tree before one would finally alight upon Clotilde Carey. So I won't try to. Clotilde lives in that house once occupied by my uncle and aunt in Concord. Somehow, it got passed on to her though the medium of several other owners and residents, all more or less of the same lineage. Now, over the years, we have kept in touch, and I have visited her a number of times. She is a delightful person—a retired kindergarten teacher and as full, I am sure, of as playful a spirit as her former wards ever were. She informed me by letter recently that she will have to give up the house. It's much too large for her, and her advanced years are enticing her to a more salutary clime. In any event, there is no one else in the family who is interested in the place; hence, before selling it, she feels the obligation to clear out family remnants that have collected over the last half century and been abandoned and forgotten. In her 'mucking around,' as she calls it, in the attic, cellar, old carriage house, and other places where things have collected, stirring up dust and cobwebs while sporting some 'feral face mask' in order to protect herself from all that 'lethal fluff,' she has come across a number of boxes containing documents and files that belonged originally to Uncle Aloysius. She doesn't know what to do with them and feels ill at ease in ignominiously consigning them to the city dump. She had hoped I would visit and decide what to do with these materials. I consented; but now, under the pressure of trying to do so many other things, I would welcome your assistance in looking after these papers."

"I would be honored to do so," I affirmed, my wits having been finally restored, by this time, more or less to their normal function. Moreover, I did feel honored, having almost the sense that the request had something in it of a bequest, an invitation to enter into something actually rather more personal than it seemed at first sight, a bestowal of confidence in the insight and steadiness of my judgment. I wondered at its implicit approval of who I was. I hoped that I could be as confident as she was in the surety of my judgment; I had good reasons, given the immediately preceding event, to doubt its steadiness. I could not help but feel that my foundering steps were exactly what she most appreciated about me when the threshold of something that might really be important to her was being crossed.

She wrote down on a pad of paper the address of the original Fitzgerald house and the telephone number of Clotilde Carey. I scarcely needed directions to Concord, since I had either been in, or passed through, Concord a multitude of times in my life, usually for brief moments on my way to somewhere else but enough to give me a sense of the city. It is a small city, anyway, one in which it is easy to find things. Cornelia told me that she would call Clotilde and inform her of my coming. There was no hurry, but perhaps sometime in the next few weeks would be good. I myself should call Clotilde, when I was ready, and tell her the exact day and time. I said that I would have to consult my schedule but that late the following week would probably work out for me. Cornelia was pleased. She said she would be back in Europe by that time.

My departure from the Regency was simple enough. Cornelia rose from her sofa to shake hands with me and bid me farewell. Liselle, who entered the sitting room unaccountably as I made motions to leave, offered to accompany me downstairs to the lobby, but I told her that I could find my way without a guide. I couldn't help but entertain anxious notions of being wrestled to the elevator floor, hapless mooncalf that I might well turn out to be, after perpetrating some unintentional misdemeanor or blurting out some sure-to-be-misinterpreted phrase, by that energetic and thoroughly intimidating young woman. Meanwhile I glanced backward at Cornelia as I left the suite. She was already, as it were, "contained" in some other project, directing the full steady gaze of her attention upon it. I couldn't help but feel a little lost, for just a moment, as I departed. I don't know why or to what end. Maybe all departures make us feel somewhat lost. Our convergences both diminish and enlarge us: in our separations, especially from those who have made an effort through their attentiveness to make us one with them in some way. We leave something behind us when we go; yet we also take something with us—in spite of all, of all loss and all gain, we linger together as one soul together, one heart, one spirit.

It was late afternoon. The rush hour traffic was just beginning. I was famished. I darted into a coffee shop and purchased a searing-hot cappuccino and a cool, moist slab of lemon-frosted pound cake, which I saved until I had found my car in the hotel parking garage. I sat for a while in the garage, in front of the steering wheel, sipping warily at that coffee through the little aperture in the plastic lid and gobbling down my desultory tidbit, giving little thought to it and spilling crumbs all over myself. Indeed, I don't think I was thinking much about anything at all. I just gazed into the dimly lit hollows of the parking garage and watched people come and go. Still in a daze, I started up the car and drove it out into the downtown traffic. I don't know how long it took to get home. I didn't care either. I wanted to get home but wasn't in a hurry. I felt altogether too contented at the moment for that.

Part Five

I lost very little time in making my next appointment with Mr. Besserman. In fact, I tried to see him on the day following my conversation with Cornelia. He was not available, or so he insisted on the phone; he had a luncheon meeting with the board of directors of a theater project in Maine that sought to initiate a Shakespeare program and was looking for financial backing. But would I like to come? No, I wouldn't, I protested; I had too many other things on my mind. Would the promise of a sandwich entice me to the meeting? He was having Tram conjure up a virtual "tempest" for his Shakespearean friends, he chuckled. I could pose as Caliban, or so he taunted me; it was always good, he added, to have at least one dyed-in-the-wool Philistine at confabs with "cultural" types—it kept things from going too far overboard, from getting potentially "shipwrecked." Now I had even more reasons to turn down his invitation. The last thing I needed in my present state was to contend once again with a tentacle, however profusely garnished. And, simulating as much ironic chagrin as I could, I thanked him for his all-too-thoughtful compliment about Caliban and the Philistines. He laughed. Then he said to drop by at about three o'clock. The group had a long drive back to Maine and would be gone by then.

I arrived at the foyer of the Foundation offices just as the delegation from Maine, a rather elderly group of men and women—bedizened, bejeweled, lathered and lotioned and largely befuddled—was trying to figure out, desperately and volubly, how to get out of the glass-paneled elevator. There were a few too many of them for that tiny elevator, so they were rather wedged into it—a condition that did not help very much in their effort to pry open the narrow glass doors (whose panels folded inwardly, unfortunately, and against which, in their haste to exit, they were rather tightly compressed). Poor Mr. Dougherty had heard already the ascending decibels of consternation as the group struggled and squirmed. He rushed to their aid as fast as his aged limbs could carry him and, with no little shuffling of bodies and becalming of souls, managed to extricate them one by one from the packed compartment of the elevator. I think they were relieved to be out and on their way.

After they had gathered their coats and left, Mr. Dougherty turned to me and mumbled, "Well, I did divide them into two groups and sent them up that way. I don't know why they decided to come back down together. On the way down they all seemed to be yelping complaints at the unfortunate fellow assigned to drive the elevator and telling him, in no uncertain terms, that he was doing everything wrong. I can't imagine what he could have been doing wrong, but I guess that didn't matter much. He was still doing it wrong. They don't seem to like one another very much." I commiserated with him; he shrugged his shoulders and, angling his long, arthritic limbs with all the care of a daddy longlegs, picked his way back to his little retreat in the cloakroom.

I rode the elevator up to the fifth floor and entered, unannounced as usual, into Besserman's office. He sat in his great chair looking rather wan. I took my accustomed place, sinking into the cushions of the divan.

"Perhaps I really am getting too old for this kind of thing," he said, without greeting me first, "or maybe that was a particularly difficult group. First of all, they were all disagreeing with one another practically from the start and seemed bent upon enlisting me on one side or the other in quarrels about which I hadn't a clue as to what they involved. Second, they seemed put out by any questions about their plans, as if plans, heaven forbid, were relevant to what they were doing. Third, they thought I was obliged to commit the Foundation to a grant on the spur of the moment. It all went rather badly. They didn't even like the sandwiches. I don't think they will have a pleasant ride together back to Maine."

"Well," I commented, "they didn't have a very pleasant ride together down in the elevator."

"Don't tell me about it!" Besserman threw up his hands. "It's a shame: what they have in mind is good, if they could focus on a few essential preliminary matters. One old gent bickered with a lady about whether they would rent costumes or make their own—all before they have even settled on what they would use as a theater."

"I'm glad Caliban wasn't there to make things worse."

"Caliban would have been most useful; as it was, was I presumed to be Prospero, droning incantations from his enchanted book and making things happen by magic?"

"I thought you did make things happen by magic."

"Well, now, come to think of it, I do almost make things happen by magic—or at least that's the way it looks from here when my bumbling ventures produce unexpected and sometimes preposterous results."

Besserman required some reprieve, I figured. I was not wrong. He slid down from his chair, ambled over to his desk, and, pressing a button on an intercom, ordered coffee and tea from the café. While he was doing that, he looked in my direction and asked me if I wanted any pastries to accompany our afternoon snack. He inquired as to whether I "still" enjoyed ginger cookies and would like to have some, since they were available, were made from the "original" recipe, and were just as good as ever. I declined the offer, puzzled then, as I would be for a while afterward, as to how he possibly could have known I had once enjoyed ginger cookies—and this when I was a child. His reference to an "original" recipe defied, for the moment, all cogent explanation. In any case, deciding not to pursue the matter, I declined the offer. He seemed disappointed but finished the call, returned to and mounted his chair, and tapped his lips with the forefingers of his folded hands in that ritual way he had before delving into some new subject.

"So, Mr. Schofield, what can I do for you today?" he asked.

"What do you mean, Theodore, what can you do for me today? You know very well what you can do for me today," I complained.

"You met Cornelia yesterday?"

"Of course, I did; you know that very well."

"And you are all in a 'stew' about it, no doubt?"

"A 'stew'?"

"A great commotion. An upheaval ..."

"'Stew' will do, I guess, depending on how one qualifies it. I can't imagine anyone who could put a person more at his ease than Cornelia."

"Agreed. But anybody, in a proper frame of mind, should be in some kind of 'stew' after meeting Cornelia. She enlarges life; she confers a blessing on it, an amplitude, makes it, at once, more bountiful and joyous. One's head is spinning for a while afterward, even if one has also been put, as you said, at one's ease."

"Yes, I know. I have also heard another describe her in roughly those terms."

"Ah, so you did visit Madison Street yesterday!"

"I did. Another one of your little ambushes, Theodore?"

"You describe Mother d'Agneau as an ambush?"

"How else would one describe her?"

"Come to think of it, ambush is an appropriate term. It's good to be ambushed now and then."

"But it would be nice to be warned in advance. How did you arrange that?"

"I arranged nothing at all. Just part of my magic, I guess. Unless I had arranged something, I could not have warned you. If I had arranged something and had warned you, it would not have been an ambush. Be that as it may, I assume it was a busy day for you."

"Maybe too busy. I should have stayed where I was, in my vitreous office, treading water like a contented goldfish and writing billion-dollar contracts for hostile acquisitions—you know, something paltry and down-to-earth like that."

"But certainly you enjoyed your visit to Madison Street, didn't you, ambushes or no ambushes?"

"I did."

"And I gather you learned a few things about Turkish carpets."

"I did that too. Toward the end of our conversation, Mother d'Agneau and I did discover a common interest in which we are conspiring to re-educate you. By the way, have you ever deployed your taste buds upon the esculent delights of okra gumbo?"

"I've never heard of it! Well, I've heard of okra and I've heard of gumbo, but never of okra gumbo."

"What a misfortune!" I mimicked. "But now you have. Get ready! It's in your future somewhere. You see, I can match the lot of you, when I want to!"

"You will get used to us, I can assure you. But I did meet Cornelia this morning for an early breakfast. She, and her inimitable sidekick, Liselle, are already in Hartford by now, I imagine. They had to rent a car in order to transport all that stuff they had with them. She apparently enjoyed her '*petit entretien*' with you yesterday. She gave you some special task to do, but she didn't say much about it."

"Well, I shall not say much about it either. But it does involve … it involves Uncle Aloysius."

"I guessed as much. I figured by your tone that your particular 'stew' might be simmering more intensely than an ordinary 'stew.' What did the two of you talk about?"

"That's private counsel, Theodore. I am unable to divulge our conversation. Attorney-client privilege, you know."

"Oh really, Edmund, let's not resort to our professional tricks. Anyway, you are not her attorney yet, nor is she your client. What did you say there? I am dying of curiosity. It must have been really quite awful to provoke such a delighted response in her."

"Confidential. Sorry, Theodore, you don't get to know about this." I was glad to be able to cover my conceivably ill-contrived traces with a conveniently invoked code, though I knew very well that I was scarcely involved in something technically called counsel. I was also glad to be able to have something of this story that I knew and that he didn't.

"Very good, Edmund," he replied. "But I return to my original question, 'What can I do for you today?' "

"I think you need to update me."

"Update you?"

"Tell me how this whole thing developed."

"How what whole thing developed?"

"The story of Uncle Aloysius."

"That could be a tall order. And why do you need to know?"

"Because, as probably you do know, I am being sent to Concord. I am to be a special emissary of a sort."

"That much I know."

"I am being sent to go through … to go through some things."

"Things?"

"Uncle Aloysius's things."

"That much I did not know."

"A second cousin of Uncle Aloysius, or third cousin, or something to that effect, lives in the original house. Her name is Clotilde Carey."

Besserman took a moment to consider this information. Then he said, "Yes, I am familiar with the name, though I have never met her. I am also familiar with the house—but from a long time ago, I should mention."

"Well," I resumed, "she discovered, in the carriage shed near the main house, a sizable stack of boxes containing records of Uncle Aloysius's medical practice. There may be other items as well. Cornelia wants me to determine if there is anything of importance among them. Clotilde Carey needs to move with haste in this matter. Cornelia simply is too pressed for time to attend to it right now, and she also thinks a practiced legal eye might be good for the process."

"It all sounds rather routine to me. Scarcely a matter to be in a 'stew' about, if I may say so."

"You might be right, Theodore. But the context in which this request was made, the fortuitousness of it, the spontaneity—all of that has me puzzled."

"What was that context?"

"That's exactly what I am not going to tell you about."

"Then how can I help you?"

"By filling me in, by updating me. If I am to understand what I may find, I need to have more of a context to understand whatever that is."

"As I am sure you realize, there is no way to predict what you will find, and therefore I am not confident that I will succeed in giving you a context that will be helpful."

"I know. But anything would be better than nothing."

A knock on the door announced the arrival of our tea and coffee. Tram entered the room, and all was served with pleasant formality. He deposited a plate of cookies on the table and departed, closing the door silently behind him. Besserman tended first to our refreshments. I was always surprised, in my dealings with Besserman, by the attention he paid to minor details. So often his manner appeared piecemeal, vague; yet it was anything but that.

To the contrary, what one observed was a succession of highly deliberative moments, each a feat of tenacious concentration as one thing after another was scrutinized with exacting care: the coffee—its warmth and color; the dazzle of light from the window against a vase; the tilt of a flower in that same vase. After finishing his "saucer" of coffee, Besserman leaned back in his chair.

"In some respects," he began, not looking at me but rather gazing now inward with that same concentration into the remote world of his impending narrative, "not much changed after those momentous decisions had been made regarding the birth of the child. In lives as interwoven as those of the Schefflins, new responsibilities, even rather amazingly new responsibilities, were effortlessly spliced into patterns that already existed. In other respects, everything changed, and I would conjecture that an observation of that sort hardly needs much in the way of illustration. It would be tedious, I think, to document the ins and outs of how matters were arranged at first. The Schefflins embarked on their trip to Europe, returning about a month and a half later. Subsequently, Agnes retired into the privacy afforded by Madison Street itself, and for a while all those lively 'continental' Sundays, with their buffets and string quartets, were suspended and the ordinary social rounds deferred. This was no undue burden for Agnes since she had inherited some of the reclusive habits of her mother and was content to be engaged with those avocations that so delighted her.

"Aunt Bernice discovered for herself a picturesque spot in a village in nearby Vermont, just across the Connecticut River from New Hampshire, with an equally picturesque old housekeeper in attendance. It was easy for Uncle Aloysius to visit her almost constantly, and, if I am to trust what little I can decipher from what I have heard about it, the period of expectancy may have been the closest that the two ever had together, exceeding that of any other time, even in their later marriage. At least, in a manner of speaking, the 'three' of them were together for the time being, as they would be later on in the future on various occasions, but without the imposition of formalities and titles and arrangements that would, in some official way, divide them. It was, moreover, perhaps the only time that Aunt Bernice fully accepted, in pleasure and pride, not just the role but the reality of being a mother and of bearing a life that united all three of them. But it was the role that remained primary for her. It is logical, if one takes into account who Aunt Bernice was, that she would have chosen to enter into this role with a fervor perfectly tailored for the deepest levels of its enactment, distilling to its finest point the dramatic sense of her self-styled 'confinement,' while drawing the father of her child as deeply as she could into this drama and engaging with, genuinely, the universal experience of women in child-bearing. Further, there were the provocative exigencies of her own particular case. One of those exigencies consisted purely in the determination, whose very contour gave the interval devoted to it its keenest and most delectable tang, that the episode would have its fitting, its indelible, closure. As we have noted, Aunt Bernice loved terminal things, 'once and for all' experiences, and she made the best of this. As with anything in life, an awareness of a terminal point often intensifies the experience that leads up to it.

"The child was born, an infant girl, Cornelia, in the crisp, cool milieu of a New England spring and, bearing the Schefflin name, was immediately and seamlessly engrafted into the Schefflin household. I had a limited role in this, addressing those matters where the law must, for better or for worse, stake its claims. Aunt Bernice, having concluded her carefully apportioned engagement in this affair, took her bows, most deservedly in this case, and turned her attention to other and, for her, more compelling interests.

"I doubt that the rhythm of life for Aunt Bernice and Uncle Aloysius did not assume its accustomed character and pace for a period of years thereafter, except that, of course, there was now all the more reason, at least for Uncle Aloysius, for dropping in on the Schefflins at every suitable occasion, and if Aunt Bernice was usually in tow, it is because Uncle Aloysius insisted on bringing her there. I don't want to suggest that she was not, for the most part, delighted to accompany him; she always went primarily because she wanted to be with him but also because she took, unquestionably, a limited pleasure now and then in seeing Cornelia, in watching her grow and hearing her first words and all those other things that parents enjoy in their offspring. But here again, there was just so much time she was willing to allot to such events, and she was eager to be off to meet that elusive appointment, that prevenient 'entrance' that awaited for her somewhere, one might be inclined to say, beyond the beckoning horizon. Uncle Aloysius, on the other hand, took these occasions as the crowning pinnacles of his weeks and months, his seasons and years; never, one could assert who did not know the facts of the case, did any man frame the relationship of an uncle to a niece with greater compunction and attentiveness. One should not conjecture that there was any difficulty with Frederick and Agnes in this regard. When Uncle Aloysius and Aunt Bernice joined them for the Sunday buffet and the musicale, or for the extended Christmas festivities, or for any number of picnics and boating events, the Schefflins knew when and how to withdraw and yield the young child into the care of her real parents for the time being. It is perhaps unnecessary to point out that Cornelia became deeply attached over the years to Uncle Aloysius, not only because of the particular marks of his regard but also for that more general enthrallment that so often children develop for the kindly and always especially welcomed visitor to the parental house.

"As for Cornelia herself—what can I say? She was a bright and imaginative child, happy, full of play, admirably suited for the fantastical proclivities of Agnes, who found in her an enthusiastic initiate and companion for those wonderful literary worlds that Agnes inhabited—from the simple children's books to the more complex realms of the ballet and the theater and the proud old legends of ages past. Cornelia looked a great deal like Aunt Bernice, with the same refined features, the thick black hair, the intensely white skin, the startling aquamarine of her eyes, though she did not bear the same high-strung carriage or temperament of her mother, and her eyes were mellowed by the reflective depth and shadows that so defined the appearance of Uncle Aloysius.

"It would be otiose to assert that the nurture of Cornelia constituted for Frederick and Agnes the most sublime happiness of their lives, a point of devout focus for them, a joint venture whose every detail elicited the most searching considerations and scrupulous application. And yet they did not hover over the child or inhibit, as they could have been tempted to do, that delicious freedom a child needs for pursuing her own petite projects, however capricious and endearing. It would be equally otiose to claim that the Schefflin household did not amount to something like an ideal environment for the young Cornelia to grow and prosper in. Moreover, inheriting somewhere in her chromosomes a strain of irrepressible and rugged sociability from the Fitzgerald clan, she delighted in the round of social activities that went on in the Madison Street enclave; she soon had many friends of her own age who came to Madison Street for the parties, for the marionette shows Agnes orchestrated and produced, often with Cornelia's persistent and somewhat awkward help, and drawing liberally upon the inexhaustible cache of the Brothers Grimm and Hans Christian Andersen, and for the frequent children's cinema entertainments that Frederick, possibly the first owner of a home 16-millimeter movie projector in his neighborhood, was proud to present. He also had a moving-picture camera so that he could direct and edit his own films, like a virtual 'movie mogul,' he liked to boast, silent films filled with scampering boys and girls engaged in chivalric charges on hobby horses or fending off pirates in an imaginary tropical sea.

"Cornelia often visited her friends' homes too and even their summer retreats by the ocean in Maine or Cape Cod or in the mountains of New Hampshire or Vermont. And, of course, the whole routine of schools and lessons unfolded as Cornelia advanced in age. From Frederick she learned to love music and took up the piano; from Agnes she learned to love not only the literary but the fine and decorative arts as well; from both she grew enamored of paddling canoes, of swimming, of hiking in the mountains; and, on her own, as she matured, she would discover the equitation whose mastery she would cultivate when she was much older. If also, in later times too, the culinary genius of the Schefflin branch should flourish in her, it was not, as well we know, by virtue of her chromosomes in this case but by virtue of traipsing around in the Madison Street kitchen after Frederick, who, often in zealous though vivacious competition with their Swedish chef, Greta, produced gustatory masterworks for her to emulate in future years.

"It was sad, certainly, that Uncle Aloysius was not able to interact with Cornelia as he would have liked to. But he came to Madison Street as many times as he could, to recitals and holidays and school events. It was also a matter of deep regret that he could not introduce his own daughter as who she really was to the Fitzgerald clan and, especially, to his parents. The little 'niece' was welcomed, naturally, to the few events to which it was convenient for Uncle Aloysius to take her (usually without Aunt Bernice); Cornelia was treated by the adoring clan as a prodigy, as a kind of 'fairy child' whose mystifying appearance and beguiling ways afterward provoked many a lively discussion over a frothy mug of Guinness. I think it is fair to hazard that Uncle Aloysius's kinfolk never stooped to untoward speculation, but there seemed to be, for them, a 'surplus' of something in this child, a bond, a connection with them and theirs, something more strange and wonderful than all the apparent circumstances could warrant. This obviously fanciful designation of 'fairy child' was not without foundation, more subliminal perhaps than conscious, in an ancient and almost mythological perception, however modified from its original Irish origins to meet the present circumstances, of the mystical child, the somehow 'exchanged' or 'substituted' child from another domain.

"Uncle Aloysius's mother, especially, found herself frequently doting upon the child with the deepest wonder and remorse in her heart; found herself wanting to reach out and press that child to herself with a forcefulness she could not explain; found herself constantly wishing that this were her son's offspring, with such fervency that at times she would convince herself that she was. That she had a throng of other grandchildren to command and distract her attention is probably the only reason she did not dwell sufficiently on that striking resemblance the eyes of the child bore to those of her own son in order to draw the conclusion that this indeed was her grandchild. I don't know, Edmund, whether or not she, or any of them, ever found out the truth. And for Uncle Aloysius, the recognition that this chasm must exist could not have been for him anything less than a source of inconsolable pain.

"The day did come when Uncle Aloysius and Aunt Bernice got married. Who could possibly explain the reasons for this turn of events? At some point is it possible that Aunt Bernice knew that further delay was her adversary and that she must do what she could to move things along? Or perhaps she had realized that a future in the theater for her had to retract its more ambitious prospects and confine itself to more limited objectives. As usual, we can safely conjecture that it was she who made the decision and who directed the procedures. In this matter, as in so many others, Uncle Aloysius deferred to her wishes; it was part, we can infer, of his unalloyed chivalry. But practical considerations intervened as well. Not only deferring to his future wife's preferences but also wishing to avoid social embarrassment for his parents, Uncle Aloysius consented to a private marriage before a justice of the peace. Nobody, not even the Schefflins, were in attendance; they didn't even know it was happening; and they, like everybody else, didn't find out for some time afterward.

"Only Cornelia, ironically, 'knew,' in a sense, of their marriage the day it happened, and, in an odd sort of way, celebrated its occurrence. At the time—it was summer, and she was six years old—she was staying for a few weeks as a guest at a summer 'camp' in the Berkshires belonging to the parents of a young pal from home. After the early morning wedding, Aunt Bernice, perhaps feeling a momentary surge of maternal sentiment but also delighting in an escapade so giddy and impulsive and, under any rubric, consummately dramatic, conceded to Uncle Aloysius's wish to drive out from Boston to the Berkshires that very day and inform Cornelia about their marriage—which they did. Cornelia, naturally, had little or no understanding of what was actually going on, but then, and then only, for an hour or two, in front of the bewildered eyes of the hosts, who watched from the porch of the house, they hugged and laughed and held hands and played in a nearby arbor, husband and wife and child, father and mother and daughter, pretending to be what they really were, a family together. Despite all the time that Cornelia would spend with her natural parents in later years, she was never to experience that exhilaration again in that same exhilarating way. And, if I am to believe what I have been told, she never forgot.

"The marriage itself solved nothing and did little more than augment and exacerbate Uncle Aloysius's dilemma. Aunt Bernice found, for the time being, a respite from her wanderings and a center for her life, though she remained as active as ever in the pursuit of her goals. But she now had that stationary but revolving stage, as I have described it before, and what she could not go to anymore, she brought to herself. Uncle Aloysius was deeply glad to have her with him, to share her days and nights, to delight in her inexhaustible plenitude of beauty and charm. And he, as he ever did, threw himself with remorseless energy into his work, his medical practice, earning, as he went, a reputation for passionate service that bedazzled Concord and its surroundings and won him boundless admiration both for his skill and for his humane public spirit. Furthermore, after several years in Concord—for reasons we will never fathom—he resumed his connection with his ancestral faith and became an active member of his local parish. Aunt Bernice, of course, had no interest in that aspect of his life.

"For all that, at some very deep level of the affective life, one could surmise that a vacancy seemed to hover between them, between husband and wife, now even more intense than ever before, as if their residence together, and the official designation conferred upon them by the marriage contract, served only to accentuate, in some distended sense, the presence of the 'missing person' whose very being, whose identity and source, represented the paragon of their union into a single, composite whole. Don't get me wrong about this, Edmund; the two of them were as riveted together as any two human beings ever get. If you saw one, you also somehow saw the other, even if the other was not around. I have never experienced anything like that before. It's as if they lived within one another. Still, if I may be so bold as to use in this case a mathematical metaphor to express the deepest matters of the heart, they were like the two sides of an equation but without the equal sign between them. Both sides of the equation share the same ultimate sum, the same numerical identity; yet, without that one, sole, irreplaceable cipher of their ligature, or better, without that substantive ligature as a sign, without that 'two in one flesh,' they are suspended by themselves, paradoxically one and yet separate, indissoluble and yet detached. One might query, at this point, if some effort was not expended to fill the gap by trying to produce further embodiments, both exemplary and substantive, of their unity. About that we shall never know. As I have said, one can assume that Aunt Bernice knew where to draw the line. They never had any more children together.

"Under the circumstances, almost anyone would have thought that a woman like Aunt Bernice had had to contend with an irrepressible appetite for glittering things: for palatial homes, for cellars stocked with the finest wines, for a milieu of opulence and luxurious self-indulgence, of classy boutiques and high-fashion expenditure, of fastidious attention to what was invariably *comme il faut*, excluding, with no degree of either hesitation or uncertainty, anything with even the faintest pallor of the vulgar or meretricious. Well, from everything I was ever able to learn about her, she was, in her own way, as parsimonious as Uncle Aloysius was. She conformed herself willingly to the austerity pertinent to maintaining the household of an ill-paid, and sometimes only sporadically paid, country doctor: attending, as apparently as she did, much to our surprise, to its expenses, managing its budgets and schedules, conferring, by any measure, well-calibrated oversight upon its days. Though she herself did not possess that impetus toward the healing arts that so impelled her husband, she understood its often single-minded challenges and yielded to its imperatives. For she, too, conceived of her own work, her theatrical 'mission,' if I may presume to call it that, as a project that invoked a certain degree of professional 'asceticism' for its proper realization and that extended, in its own way, its sovereign balm of laughter and good cheer to the spent and frazzled souls of her fellow citizens. To this effect, she willingly concurred with her husband to surrender the better part of their simple residence to the 'lame and halt' of the earth who, among others, hobbled across its threshold and bundled down in its parlor; and, if her tastes nevertheless required of her that fastidious attention of which I spoke, she never allowed them to come between herself and those whom she welcomed, with all due deference and amiability, into her home.

"Frankly, I don't think she ever missed the luxury that simplicity of life denied her. She had not known it in her youth; she had never aspired to it in her young womanhood, however frequently a coarse and invasive voice would try to prevail upon her to do so and to assure her, with a wink of a bloated and lubricious eye, of its voluminous success; her years 'on the road' (if one presumes to dignify her minor and short-lived "gigs" in that way), were never even remotely lucrative to her; were, to the contrary, spent in run-down hotels and barely inhabitable rooming houses. Even after her marriage, the more limited range of her theatrical activities probably cost more than the pittance they earned. She never felt somehow diminished by the contrast between Uncle Aloysius's and her way of life and that of the Schefflins, for she perceived well that, if the accoutrements were decidedly different, the goals were somehow the same, were vested in the metamorphosis of personal virtues and skills into public goods and benefices. She resisted—well, they both resisted—all efforts of the Schefflins to subsidize their style of life, as often as this was offered to them. They were intent upon making things work on their own.

"Furthermore, she knew all too well what not many are willing to acknowledge: that it is the woman who makes clothing and jewelry beautiful, rather than vice versa; and, with just the slightest stitch here, or dab of color there, she could transform the most ordinary garment into something that could make all but the most willfully obtuse of *grands couturiers* crimson with envy. High fashion, as such, might be taken, by some observers, to have passed her by, if she had not so adroitly passed by high fashion itself. Her sense of style had most likely been practiced by years of patching together costumes for low-budget productions from materials found fortuitously backstage; these costumes could revamp her in a moment from a staid and indomitable duchess into a fluttery and voluptuous soubrette. From Uncle Aloysius she found an unwavering support for her vocation; and he found in her an equally unwavering support for his medical practice. He loved her need to be loved, to be admired, to be, in any case, spectacular, both as an individual and as an iridescent stage presence; she loved in him his capacity to do this, with all the determination and modesty that this love required; she, in turn, was more than willing to enfold him, as far as it was in her nature to do so, into the depths of her own soul so that he might find the peace and renewed vigor to serve afresh the needs of his patients.

"The situation may have been slightly altered when Frederick and Agnes, perhaps somewhat anxious about what they felt could emerge someday as a crisis in the marriage of Uncle Aloysius and Aunt Bernice, went out of their way to draw the life of their adopted daughter ever closer to the lives of her real parents. They need not have felt any anxiety on that account. Uncle Aloysius and Aunt Bernice were as close together as anyone ever is. Nothing would have driven them apart. But the Schefflins, as attached to Cornelia as they were, once the Fitzgeralds had purchased the house in Concord and set up housekeeping together as a married couple, encouraged Cornelia to spend extended periods of time with them, especially during the summer vacations. It is difficult to ascertain what the Schefflins may have been thinking at the time. Perhaps it was just a question of justice, as difficult as it is to figure out what is actually just in a given situation—justice to Cornelia, justice to the real parents. Perhaps they thought that an assumed parenthood had to give way as much as possible to the real parenthood, since that was near and available; even had to give way to what might, in the end, be its own final renunciation and to prepare the ground for that. I don't think we will ever know all the motivations involved, though it would be like Frederick to prepare for possible contingencies and unforeseen circumstances.

"In any case, Concord became a kind of second home for Cornelia. The Fitzgeralds lived in a steep, gabled frame house with a front porch and a lawn girded by a rather traditional picket fence. As I have already intimated, part of the house, the front rooms, had been converted into Uncle Aloysius's medical facilities, while the couple lived in the back of the house, especially in its roomy, wide-planked kitchen and in a small but modish second-floor parlor with an adjacent bedroom that looked out over a rose garden to the carriage shed at the far end of the backyard. A woodshed attached to the house had been converted into a makeshift little theater of sorts; it was used solely for somewhat spur-of-the-moment family productions. On the first floor, next to the medical facilities, was a small library; that is where Aunt Bernice collected her mail, her scripts, her production notes, and other paraphernalia associated with her theatrical projects in the region.

"Aunt Bernice, naturally, was busy during the summer with those projects as well as the work she contributed to the medical practice. Cornelia spent a great deal of time with Uncle Aloysius, a regular little 'helper,' you might say, accompanying him on house calls, comforting the sick (when this was possible or advisable), filling out, now and then, some of the easier paperwork, working with his assistant nurse in the office, running errands to the pharmacy, and generally being a boon companion. I often wonder how much about medicine she may have picked up during those years; later emergencies in life, both touching her own circle of family and friends as well as those with broader social ramifications, have always brought out in her the adept hand and sensitivity of a potential physician, ready to be of service and demonstrating in many situations an uncanny sense of what to do.

"I don't need to dwell on all the particulars of this time. But I do know that it came, abruptly and tragically, to an end. I will try to be brief about this, Edmund, though I scarcely know where to begin. I received a telephone call from Frederick late one afternoon. It was early November and was just beginning to get cold outside. I was at work. Frederick was as terse on the phone as he could be. Uncle Aloysius was ill—typhoid fever, as it turned out. An epidemic of it had spread through the mills of Manchester just south of Concord and through much of its circumjacent area, including Concord itself. All the medical personnel of the area were converging to see if they could stem the tide and tend the sick. The demand was enormous; the doctors and nurses were working long hours and exhausting their resources. They were also running incalculable risks of becoming infected themselves. I had read about all of this in the Boston papers. In the midst of this turmoil, and after weeks of almost uninterrupted activity, Uncle Aloysius had come down with the disease. Aunt Bernice notified the family. The prognosis wasn't good. One of the medical rooms in the house, his dispensary, had been converted into a sickroom. Frederick announced that Agnes, Cornelia, and he would depart at once for Concord. He asked me to join them, if possible, the following morning. I told him that I would be there. I have to say that all of this happened with a suddenness none of us could have anticipated.

"I am not sure what I expected to find when I arrived at the Fitzgerald house late the following morning. I guess I expected to enter a scene of alarm and confusion. I should have known better, for it all looked rather composed, or even 'settled,' in some ominously unsettling way. It was, at one level, the way the Schefflins ordinarily did things; yet I could detect that more than that was involved. Once again I had stepped, as far as I could make out, into a situation in which portentous decisions had been made, agreements reached, action resolved upon, though still not taken, apparently.

"It was a sunny day, and sunlight streamed through the house with an exceptional buoyancy as windswept clouds passing overhead cast their intermittent shadows through the windows of the somber rooms. Only the dispensary was darkened, though even here occasional shafts of sunlight broke through the curtains that shifted in the draft of one slightly open window. The room was being kept cool and fresh. I could see the bed where Uncle Aloysius lay, his assistant nurse close at hand, sitting at a nearby chair, wearing a surgical mask, and watching him intently and monitoring his fever. Through a door at the end of the entrance hall I could see into the kitchen, where Agnes and Aunt Bernice were sitting opposite one another, silently, at the table. Agnes grasped Aunt Bernice's hands firmly in her own, while Aunt Bernice stared at the windows, as if she was searching for some explanation that lay beyond them.

"For the first and perhaps the only time since I had known Aunt Bernice, she was 'out of character' and had divested herself of her customary role-playing for the occasion. She looked genuinely 'crestfallen' in some old original meaning of that word, as if some plumage she normally disported had been stripped from her and left her without the repertoire she ordinarily drew from to engage with any situation. This is not to say that she looked shrunken, despoiled, denuded; if anything, she looked as sublimely regal and poised as she ever did, except that it was a personage I had never seen before—a person whose unmasking revealed a visage possibly even more extraordinary than what her simulated masks had portrayed. I wonder, Edmund, in all justice to Aunt Bernice, if all of us don't have our hidden wardrobes of dissembling frocks and vizards we don when we see fit, mainly to deceive ourselves, as if the mirror were the primary audience of our mimicry; and then the prospect of death sneaks up behind us and strips them away from us while our eyes blink, not at its menacing darkness but at its mordant light, its unflinching clarifications.

"Agnes, I should say, steadfast in the redoubt of her spirit, as we would soon discover in the subsequent hours, held tight to Aunt Bernice, kept her from faltering, kept all of us, even Frederick in all his steadiness, from being vanquished by what was happening. Meanwhile, Cornelia stood by the door of the dispensary and gazed in at Uncle Aloysius. The room was considered quarantined and Cornelia, as I learned later, had had to be restrained several times from entering. Frederick was sitting in the waiting room. He rose when he saw me, shook my hand, and drew me to the side. I recognized by this very gesture that there was some serious news to be imparted, and I braced myself for it.

" 'Dr. MacMahon has just departed, only a half hour ago. He has come a number of times during the night,' Frederick announced.

"I asked, 'Shouldn't Uncle Aloysius be in the hospital?' I knew already that, if Uncle Aloysius was being treated here, it was for good reasons. But I wanted desperately to contribute something, whatever it was.

"Frederick answered, 'The hospital is already overflowing with patients. This arrangement is what, under the circumstances, Uncle Aloysius requested. We are following his wishes. Anyway, a hospital would be of no further use now. He is not responding to treatment. Dr. MacMahon informed us that Uncle Aloysius is dying. He may survive until the evening. There is nothing we can do now.'

"We were silent together for a minute, listening to winds soughing through the tree boughs outside and watching the refracted sunlight bend and sway through the tall windows and into the interior of the house. Then Frederick said, 'I am glad you came, Theodore. You are always a great comfort to us.'

" 'Is there anything I can do?'

" 'You have been with us at other crucial moments. I welcome your presence and appreciate your judgment. But, now that you are here, I need to attend to my heaviest duty.'

" 'Which is . . .?'

" 'I must tell Cornelia what the rest of know about Uncle Aloysius's condition. Agnes is really the one who is in charge. I don't know what we would do without her. But she is occupied at the moment. When I take Cornelia aside, we must not be disturbed. Be so kind as to shield our privacy. There may be people coming to the front door, making inquiries, seeking admittance.'

"Frederick left me in the reception room and approached Cornelia, who was standing by the dispensary door. She was getting tall now, though she still had a lean, girlish figure. They spoke for a few moments. Then the two of them withdrew into the library and closed the door behind them. My job was to attend to the front door and to any comings and goings that might occur and to ensure that Frederick and Cornelia were not interrupted.

"In about ten minutes Cornelia emerged. Frederick had followed her to the door of the library and stood there. Her face was curiously set, her bright blue eyes downcast but steady. She bore herself like someone with firm assurance, preparing herself to assume a heavy load. I was startled by what I saw. She bore herself like Frederick and had his expression on her face. She walked directly to a small writing desk in the hallway beneath the stairs, sat down, and withdrew a sheet of notepaper and a matching envelope from a drawer. I remember it well; the notepaper and envelope, selected from a set belonging to

Aunt Bernice and reserved for special, ceremonial messages, were of a subdued roseate tint and were embossed around the edges with delicate white tendrils and ornate volutes. The flap of the envelope was bordered by a kind of white lace-like brocade or frill. Cornelia took up a pen. I watched her as she wrote. It didn't take long. She folded the sheet of notepaper and slid it into the pink envelope, wrote something on the envelope, then carried it to the door of the dispensary. She didn't seal it. The nurse came over and received it, nodded at some word of Cornelia, and took the envelope to Uncle Aloysius.

"I am not sure of how much I was able to see beyond that. The dispensary was dark, though spurs of sunlight fretted back and forward through the depths of the room. Cornelia had resumed her post by the door and blocked some of my view. But I knew that the envelope was delivered to Uncle Aloysius. Despite his weakness, he must have been able to open and to read the note, for he gestured to her — I could see his hand, only his hand, momentarily illuminated by a fret of sunlight, rise and fall; and he must have smiled at her, for I saw that she smiled back. She continued to stand there — stood there indeed until the end. Frederick, meanwhile, was on the telephone, calling the Fitzgerald parents. They arrived later in the afternoon, just in time to say goodbye to their son before he died."

Besserman mumbled, "*Consummatum est.*"

"What was that?" I asked.

"Something Uncle Aloysius's father said. He was a physician, you might recall, and was able to attend his son in his final minutes. That's what he said when he stood by the sickbed and saw his son draw his last breath. It was he who pronounced him dead."

"What does it mean?"

"It means 'It is finished,' 'it is done,' something like that, in Latin. But it has a context or a significance that I don't fully know."

"Was anyone else with Uncle Aloysius when he died?"

"Yes, Aunt Bernice was with him. At one point she defied the quarantine and stayed with her husband until it was over."

"How old was Uncle Aloysius when he died?"

"About thirty-eight. Still a young man in every respect. A very great loss for everyone."

"I imagine the obsequies for him were remarkable."

"'Remarkable' is hardly the word for it," Besserman mumbled. "Nobody had anticipated the sheer extent of it. I drove to Boston that evening to pick up Martha. Our plans were to come back to Concord the following morning, which we did. When we arrived, we discovered a queue of visitors a block long, many carrying flowers or gifts of food and filing slowly from the street and into the house. Uncle Aloysius had been placed in the reception room. The arrangement was simple and decorous. Many bouquets and wreaths of flowers had already arrived and were disposed neatly around his coffin. He looked as spare and virile in his death as he ever did in life, dressed in a dark brown herringbone jacket and a white shirt and a dark blue tie fixed with a golden clip, his eyes closed, his light, wavy hair combed directly back from his forehead. On his chest, and tucked aslant into the folds of his jacket, lay that anomaly, that delicately brocaded envelope, that pink envelope, with his name inscribed upon it."

"The final communication between Uncle Aloysius and Cornelia," I said.

"Such as it was," Besserman added.

"And do we know who put it there?"

"It was Aunt Bernice who put it there, I was told."

Besserman waited, considering that point, then continued. "Naturally, the Fitzgerald clan had come *en masse*, from Boston, from elsewhere too, I imagine, wherever they were, a goodly crew who served almost, in a sense, as a guard of honor for the deceased. Perhaps it is worth noting that the circumstances of the death and the constitution of the immediate household were not conducive to the traditional Irish wake, and that particular formality was dispensed with. The funeral Mass, that afternoon, at the Church of Saint John the Evangelist was so filled with mourners that a sizable crowd had to be satisfied by gathering outside the church to await the cortege that would finally emerge. It was an impressive and moving ceremony. An impromptu chorus, gathered for the event, performed several parts of Mozart's Requiem, and Frederick provided an especially haunting and solemn rendition of the sarabande from the Bach's Second Suite for the cello. The officiating priest gave a sermon in which he reminded the congregation of the young Italian saint, Saint Aloysius de Gonzaga, Uncle Aloysius's namesake, who died of the plague while tending to the afflicted populace of Renaissance Rome. He mentioned Damien of Molokai and read the final sentence from Robert Louis Stevenson's eloquent letter defending Damien's work among the lepers: 'The man who tried to do what Damien did, is my father . . . and the father of all who love goodness; and he was your father too, if God had given you grace to see it.' The priest said that Dr. Fitzgerald had joined ranks with the thousands, with the tens of thousands, with the hundreds of thousands, of those who had given up their lives over the ages to tend to the sick. A decision was made to inter Uncle Aloysius in a Concord cemetery, since this was the community he had served with such constancy, although for too short a time.

"I am not sure how much more 'updating' you require, Edmund. The Concord interlude, if I can call it that, was over, and Aunt Bernice transferred ownership of the house to one of the Fitzgeralds. I'm not sure she even sold it—just signed some papers, transferred the title, gathered a few of her personal items, and left. She departed for New York City. Life for the Schefflins resumed its normal pace, though, as you know, Frederick himself died prematurely not long afterward—less than a decade later, and in a similar, unexpected way: sudden, little or no warning, taken out peremptorily in his prime. Two hardier men I have never known: stalwart, sturdy, like two oak trees felled to their roots by spurts of a storm so powerful that nothing could have resisted them; each leaving behind him in the lives of others a lacuna so gigantic that the very crater of uprootedness itself became, not a valley of perdition but rather a vessel of fortitude for all generations. They were among those courageous persons who regard other persons as being more important than themselves and who make the setting of a single stake in a single portion of this sacral earth an act of generosity for the entire world. What else is there to say? I think you have been, in one way or the other, apprised of what has happened since then."

"I suppose so, though I have many questions. I am curious about Aunt Bernice. What happened to her in the end?"

"I'm not confident that I can give a satisfactory answer to that, Edmund," Besserman replied. "She disappeared, as it were, into another world, one that I do not know or understand much about. Sometimes I'm not fully convinced that Aunt Bernice ever had a truly professional calling, though she gave certainly the overt impression that she thought she had. But I refrain from too definitive a judgment here because I am aware of how important a function fortuitous events play in the unfolding of a career and even of one's life, and the opportunity for showcasing and expanding her talents, such as they were, simply may never have been granted to her. She did have experience in amateur theatricals and played a number of minor roles at summer stock theaters in the Berkshires or on Cape Cod and in the White Mountains. Nevertheless, it was I, or maybe it was really Martha, after all, with her own exacting eye for who among her students was serious and to be taken seriously, who detected in her a certain negligence about how she confronted the more technical aspects of her calling—tedious, though indispensable prerequisites for its performance—as well as a reluctance to sustain both the painful apprenticeship and the occasional humiliating rebuffs that any serious practitioner of an art must be willing to undergo. Aunt Bernice may have been one of those people, gifted as they actually may be, who, if they do not arrive quickly at their destination, are impatient of the delays and setbacks and are unwilling to abide the arduousness of the trip. Furthermore, the infectiousness of her own personality and her attractiveness may have betrayed her into thinking that that was enough, that that is all she had to do, thereby missing the deeper point that the art of acting required just the opposite: to be someone one was not. Or maybe there is another explanation: that she really was the genius that some, and especially Uncle Aloysius, thought she was, but the roles she played with such gusto, such nuance and finesse and vividness, were the roles she composed for herself, solely for herself; in some larger sense, it was her role to play roles in and through the daily experiences of life itself. When she was confronted with the exigencies of stagecraft, of doing and being what others expected her to do and be—those others being directors and fellow actors and audiences and critics and the like—she found such tasks too reductive, shallow, limiting for her, too repressive of the latitude she felt she required. She was so acutely chiseled for the panoply of roles she fashioned for herself that they seemed 'natural' to her, whereas the roles that drama afforded were, by contrast, 'artificial,' if I may use a term whose paradoxical import in this context must be all too obvious. Well, we could entertain any number of hypotheses.

"Of this much I am sure: she loved the theater and blossomed eventually, like some species of nocturnal or crepuscular flowers, more in its shadows than in its light. I think you can get the picture easily enough: a world of restaurants and dinner parties and salons where theater people and their sponsors congregate, make connections, gossip about one another, exchange news, and so forth. She came to love all of that, so I have been told: its milieu rather than its work; its style rather than its substance; its being a stage itself whereon she could respond to her own cues and make her own self-choreographed moves, rather than submit to the demanding practice of theater itself. I assume, likewise, that such a world, like any other world, needs people of that sort of ancillary calling to support it in very necessary ways: who have the requisite apartment in the requisite neighborhood; who know the right sort of people to invite to the right sort of *soirée* with a caterer entirely apposite for those whom they are serving; who can introduce so-and-so to so-and-so, from which introduction a cornucopia of benefits do sometimes genuinely flow; who display, in a limited fashion and without asking for anything in return, a patronage perspicacious of talent and generous with opportunity that others are sincerely grateful for. I think she flourished at this task to the end of her days. And she was, I assure you, always well looked after."

"She, then, had her patrons as well . . ."

"Well, naturally, Frederick did step in after Uncle Aloysius's death and, over her objections, provided a modest endowment for her, adequate for her needs, which were, as we have seen, never excessive. Her years of abstemious economic self-discipline stood her in good stead; just as she could transform ordinary clothing into fabulous apparel, so she could squeeze out of a small budget a way of life supremely vibrant and varied. She had no overtly familial obligations to compromise her funds, and what she gave to others, as she had always given, was her charm, her beauty, her personality, her active and sympathetic engagement with the convolutions of others' careers. She was, as far as I know, deeply appreciated for this, and no other demands were made upon her. Her independent means were sufficient to give her the liberty she needed and to provide for the hospitality she extended to others without attracting too much attention from the darker side of the theatrical *demimonde* that otherwise may have been tempted to prey upon her (though I think her own sharply honed mother wit would have rendered her immune from such adverse blandishments).

"Hence she lived, by any standards, well. Cornelia has filled me in, at times in the past, about some of the details. Aunt Bernice had a small *pied-à-terre* in New York City, close to the theater district, for the winter season and a one-room studio, built into a sunny and high-ceilinged loft in an old barn in Cape Cod, overlooking the bay during the summer. It was not much, in a way, but it was more than enough to live the kind of life she wanted to live. She kept up her connections with the family, though always in that somewhat detached manner she had. Perhaps it would be more accurate to say that the family kept up connections with her. Cornelia, especially, was attentive to her, kept in touch, always made a point of visiting her when she was in America and of making sure she was provided for and in good health. As her children grew up, she would bring them to see their 'Grand-Aunt' Bernice as much as possible. Aunt Bernice, as I have heard, was always cordial to them and pleased by their homage, though she was equally prompt in signaling that their visit, as pleasant as it had been, had run its course. Nor did she go out of her way to reciprocate much of anything; I am not aware that she ever made a journey to France to attend important family milestones or events. She rarely, if ever, as far as I know, deviated out of that intensely narrow circuit she made of her life. It absorbed her fully, though I have been told that she made her occasional, perhaps secretive excursions to unknown places and destinations, gathering up perhaps from time to time scattered blossoms into the floral basket of her life."

"In any event, for all that," I contended, "she managed to dock her maternity in a haven, and leave it there for others to care for."

"I guess you could say that," Besserman cautioned me, "though I don't think we know all there is to know about that. Your expression 'haven' perhaps says what needs to be said. Her child was placed in as good a set of circumstances as one would ever wish for one's child, and in that, arguably, the solicitations of her maternity were expressed. No one could ever accuse her of having abandoned, in some utterly thoughtless way, her obligations to her child. Moreover, how could we know to what extent, under sundry guises and attenuated circumstances, out of the corner of a steadfast and vigilant eye, she kept watch on the upbringing of her daughter and took pride in every step she took, took pride even in that new generation of lives, Cornelia's children, whose *fons et origo* she knew she was, despite her ostensible esteem for terminal scenarios? Further she had the benefit, if one is always disposed to call it a benefit, of knowing who exactly she was, what she could give and what she could not give, and acted accordingly."

"Yet, what did she have to give up, as a result, in order to pursue a chimera, a false hope . . . ?"

"If a chimera was what she did pursue. Because our aspirations end in failure doesn't mean there was anything false or illusory about them. Most of our aspirations, or at least many of them in some way, end in failure. That does not mean it was wrong for us to aspire to them. Anyway, we cannot be certain, as I have already indicated, about what Aunt Bernice's aspirations really were. In the 'little theater' of her own life, she may have been preeminently successful. Only she would know that."

"But about Uncle Aloysius . . . where did all that stand with her in the end?"

"There was, Edmund, how shall I say, no grand portrayal of the grieving widow, no mourning Electra. What could have been, according to some lights, her greatest role turned out to be no role at all. She never made a public display of her grief. Perhaps tragedy, in the end, was not her *métier*. At least that is one way of interpreting what happened. What I saw on that day of Uncle Aloysius's death, and for several days afterward, was the figure of a woman still unimpeachably '*couturièred*,' though self-possessed and with an identity of her own, so compounded and inviolate that it took all of us by surprise. Perhaps this was the real Aunt Bernice that only, finally, Uncle Aloysius had been able to see and love and that only the devastation of his loss granted the rest of us the fleeting privilege of seeing as well. I don't know if any of us ever were granted that privilege again.

"I should add that, as far as we know, Aunt Bernice never looked seriously at another man for the rest of her life. Having had Uncle Aloysius, she never had need for anyone else. It's as if that particular space in her, that particular need we all have in different measures, got filled to completion. Also—and this may be another paradox for you, Edmund—I wonder if it may not be true that for some people, the deepest grief arises from the deepest love; is, thereby and in itself, the best witness there is to that love and thus is known simultaneously as the deepest joy. I imagine that Aunt Bernice mourned, but it was a kind of mourning few of us could be expected to understand. Further, I think that Aunt Bernice lived out her life thereafter as one who needed, in the final analysis, nothing, because she had had the best there was to have and knew that. I could also mention that, at her written behest, she was, in the end, reunited with her husband in his resting place in Concord."

"With that, Theodore," I said after a short pause, "I feel 'updated,' at least for now. I still have many questions . . ."

"A great many, I am sure. To be answered in time," he agreed.

"Then I embark on my mission, with your blessing, I hope."

"With my blessing, if that's what you think you need. I also note you have not touched those divine cookies I ordered for you."

"I did not actually request them."

"I ordered them anyway. Try one."

I did. They were ginger cookies. I recognized the taste and quality. Once again I experienced one of those shocks of memory, one of those palpable and startling eruptions out of the past. Why did those innocuous little pastries renew for me an incisive and rapturous flavor? In any case, whatever they were and wherever they came from, they were very good, very good indeed. I pocketed several for my journey home and made my departure.

Part Six

There was no particular hurry about my excursion to Concord, yet, as was becoming habitual in this case, I couldn't help but detect, once again, something auspicious in the moment, something demanding that all things else should be shunted aside and the moment, in its classical formulation, be "seized," be acted upon in accordance with its auspiciousness, the intimation of which, as it should turn out, would be irreducibly confirmed. How can it be, I wondered then, and wonder still, that a set of ordinary protocols, in one set of circumstances, will be quotidian and tedious to the point of inducing numbness while, in another set of circumstances, it will be invested with a template for marvelous happenstance that no romance out of antiquity could ever hope to emulate?

My journey to Concord was, at best, in its broader outlines, a secretarial mission of the sort that, with full confidence, any of my clerks in the law office could have been assigned to do. Yet this mission was differentiated, ineluctably, by the source who initiated it and whose intent, as spontaneous and probative as it was, was also, in some perplexing way, equally premeditated and decisive. After all, it was her job, Cornelia's job, that I was doing, and her responsibility that I was assuming; and it would not have been transferred to me without a special, if obscure, purpose in mind. I was acting not only as her envoy but, more significantly, as her representative with both the license and the restrictions that accrue to a representative in the proper sense; and I should not have been asked to do so if there had not been a matter of a distinctly personal importance attached, potentially anyway, to my venture.

Furthermore, I had the sense that I was being sent, somehow, not as counsel, but as a friend, for there was nothing germane to the situation that would encourage me to keep a log of my hours or a record of my expenditures (as negligible as these would have been). I was not sent forth to execute the task of a filing clerk. I was sent to discover, not necessarily some particular thing as I saw it, but whether there was some particular thing to be discovered and, if there was, to exercise the appropriate discretion in knowing what to do with it. And I knew that if discovery awaited me, it would take the form of a recovery, a repossession of something whose significance would open gates and cause walls, as robust and legendary as the walls of Jericho, to come tumbling down.

I also think that it is worth mentioning—though one might reasonably debate its relevance to the task at hand—that a drive northward out of Boston and into New Hampshire, since my childhood, has always evoked in me a certain rather acute anticipation, a heightening of senses, a readiness to react to something different, even something extraordinary. To be sure, I had already a lot to anticipate under these particular circumstances, even without a childhood attachment once again obtruding into my affairs. I am not sure whether I can define exactly what it is I used to anticipate in those early years, and still do anticipate, nor whether the evasive object of my anticipation has been over time purely idiosyncratic, or imaginative, or grounded in some measure of apprehending what is really there to be anticipated. Some might insist that it is as conventional as any mystique of place or time seems, when put to the test, to be conventional; in that I am no different, in this regard, from the ordinary tourist or seasonal resident. In any case, as odd and as anachronistic as it may seem, trending northward for me has always been, and continues to be, tantamount to heading toward a "frontier" of some kind, a "wilderness" whose forests, whose mountains, whose lakes and ponds have both held out, and delivered on, again and again, the promise of what is primeval, capacious, grandiloquent in its generous silences, monumental in its rugged boulders and granite cliffs. If even today I find myself catching my breath at these wonders, I am doing no more than responding to the remnants of those glaciated ages whose polar breath still lingers in the great notches and valleys and the marks of whose icy talons still score the cascades and gorges so massively entrenched in the landscape.

Those who have known New Hampshire from other perspectives—and there are many other perspectives one could have—might find themselves sufficiently mystified by my description. After all, much of the southern tier of the state has become but one more expansion of the insatiable Boston exurbia; big highways now induce a plentiful flow of commercialized tourist traffic through the state; and even the original and early-nineteenth-century industrialization of its urban pockets is old enough to have witnessed its cycles of rise and decline and rise again, so much so that its antiquated brick factories, once abhorred as hellish devices by the Luddites and transcendentalists of a previous age, are now considered tokens of an invaluable heritage and lodge art museums and recital halls where once mechanized looms shuttled and throbbed and where farm girls, anxious to muster meager dowries so that they could return to the farms and to marriage, groped through noxious clouds of dust and lint.

Perhaps what I discern is a memory from my childhood, a memory actually of the fantasies I entertained, or even a memory of others' memories; memories, like all memories, selective and constructive of what they purport to remember; memories perpetuated by my forebears and passed from generation to generation to be, finally, congealed, in some curious fashion, in my own. For all that, New Hampshire remains for me, anachronistically, I'll admit, the small villages, the dairy farms, the lumberjacks with their teams of horses, the stone walls, the mountain trails afresh with the brisk edge of alpine air and the heavy scent of balsam fir, the harvesting of ice from frozen lakes to cool the quinine drinks of English officers in far-off India, the kennels whose huskies made possible Admiral Perry's traverse of the polar ice caps, the college whose "winter carnival" was once the most celebrated collegiate festival in the nation, as its colossal snow sculptures rendered homage to the imperious beauty, the breadth and freedom, of the "hill winds" in its, as yet, primordial "veins." Yes, all or much of that is now shrunken, diminished, gone, irretrievable; yet venturing across that border, "north of Boston," as Robert Frost would have it, is still for me the prow of a canoe headed into the glassy calms of a glacial lake with its skirt of lichened rocks and its shoals of wooded islands.

Such reflections were occasioned, in this instance, simply, I guess, by the force of habit; more pertinently, perhaps, by the conviction that I was entering a domain deliberately, and not arbitrarily, chosen as a favored domain at various times by the various protagonists of the drama that unfolded before me. I cannot dispel the notion that the places we inhabit in our lives, even sometimes for brief periods of time, those indissoluble matrices of points wherein actions we have pursued are defined and sustained, do not, in some sense, retain our presence; it is as if the *genius loci*, the indwelling of the place, becomes part of who we are, even as we, in turn, leave something of ourselves behind to enrich its contours. It would be futile to argue for the validity of such an abstruse observation in the face of its skeptics. I won't try; but such a supposition has guided, again and again, my own perambulations among the sundry and miniscule fragments of the past. Places are important; places are part of our identity as the lucent though substantive creatures we are; places are sanctuaries, rendered numinous by what has been inimitable in our lives and are worthy to be meditated and venerated as such, as all the great civilizations of the past, in their own ways, have realized and done. It was certainly out of this recognition that I recalled that Frederick Schefflin, in his early manhood, frequently came north, accompanied by friends, to engage in his occasional fishing excursions by the streams close to the Canadian border. He was even reputed to have built a small log cabin from timber that he, and his companions, had felled—a transitory resurgence, perhaps, of what lay dormant in his Black Forest origins. Indeed, it was not without significance that the Schefflin family gravesite, environed by so many grandiose and chiseled mausoleums in Mount Auburn Cemetery, outside Boston, was sequestered, concealed even, in a grove of evergreens and was marked by no other monument than a single mossy boulder lifted out of a glacial brook and transported from a New Hampshire mountainside expressly for that purpose.

In Uncle Aloysius's case, the situation was, I figured, a great deal more complicated; from all accounts as I heard them, he had not simply responded to an opportunity offered to him by an available medical practice; rather, he had found a venue that he envisaged as suitable for the kind of both professional and personal life he felt obliged to live. To depart from the bustling ethnic neighborhood of a great, though not yet depersonalized, city to a more remote, and even, in a way, a "foreign," place (though it is strange to describe Concord in this way) must have represented a conscious choice whose multiform implications could invite a great deal of speculation. At the time, and even now, I was not, and am not, inclined to pursue these speculations except to note that Uncle Aloysius wanted to be both close to yet far enough apart from whatever he came from, so that what was, by any standards, innovative in his life could be given a fresh and uncompromised place to thrive and a new and unfamiliar set of conditions to meet. He must have thought, and Aunt Bernice ultimately consented, that this was the right place for her too, or at least for the kind of relationship they shared together. In some respects, the Boston connections, if invaluable for both of them, were also too many and too deep to allow them to discover the terms on which they could live well together. If, as Besserman expressed it, the very intensity of that relationship might have been the heart of its weakness, fine-tuned adjustments of this sort were necessary. Like the string of a violin, a touch too much—or a touch too little—of tension would undo it. Apparently, and almost miraculously, they were always able to make these adjustments.

I assume there must have been something about Concord in those days that answered whatever needs the young couple may have had. It was a small, almost miniature, city, retaining well into the first half of the twentieth century the character of the exemplary nineteenth-century American provincial metropolis, with its river, its dowager train station, its elm-lined main street, the front porches of its sprawling, firmly jointed frame houses, its cluster of churches (my mother, on our journeys northward so many years ago, used to refer to it affectionately as the "city of spires"), the palatial granite façade of the state capitol, with its imperial golden dome, its modest industry.

If it was, in those days, an intimate city, it was at the same time neither huddled nor cramped but rather a locale of broad prospects and leisurely elegance; its wide, shady, bucolic streets led out, and merged seamlessly, into the lanes and byways that laced through the immediately adjacent hills and farmlands; it looked to the south, where the Merrimack River flows downward and bends, just beyond the Massachusetts border, eastward toward the ocean; and it looks to the north, out of whose upland valleys its river flows and where the first sentinels of the White Mountains arch their craggy spines along the far horizon. It was, in its prime, a serene and solemn city; a city of parks and groves and running streams; a city, in another, more spiritual age, worthy to have sponsored, in its midst, a sacred shrine, a locus of pilgrimage and spiritual renewal.

Needless to say, Concord has changed prodigiously since then, so much so that my description will hardly be recognized by my contemporaries; its voluminous and magisterial corridor of elm trees along Main Street, for example, has fallen victim to an arboreal disease; its ornate train station has been replaced with a shopping center whose inanity defies all description; if it ever had much of a river traffic, such traffic has been irremediably cut off by dams both up- and downstream; its spires are now overshadowed by buildings in their vicinity; its adjoining farmlands are now submerged under parking lots, governmental complexes, shopping malls, and industrial parks. But its former blend of intimacy and spaciousness, I take it, was just the proper home for Uncle Aloysius and Aunt Bernice. Furthermore, though I must forbear to ascribe to Uncle Aloysius—or to Aunt Bernice—my own longings for the "frontier," for what is conceived as lingering within the unmediated and unmitigated vitality of the natural world itself, I cannot help but see something like this in the aboriginal force of whatever it was that brought the two of them together, where the most intensely natural is exactly the thing that looks most unnatural to the rest of us and where its exuberance replicates, at its best and most expansive, the powers of nature itself. Such an extraordinary bloom would require, I would think, some reticulated, trellised niche, bursting with leafy sunlight, to guarantee its sustenance, and the freshest of rural breezes to foster its growth. And, as sheltered as such a niche might be in a modest and unassuming civic order, it also required in its immediate proximity, I would think, that vestige of a "frontier" I just described, elemental and vital, intrepid and inexorable.

Moreover, if I have ever understood the social ethos of New Hampshire at all, it is the most remarkable measure of good neighborliness tempered by an almost religious consecration to minding one's own business; it is, in a way, an ethos of communally sanctioned and supported solitude; it is a place to be left sublimely alone—which is why, I think, it has had such an unusual attraction for literary people; it is an ambiance of cultural cenobitism wherein the eremitical inclination can be embedded in a socially solicitous yet disengaged skein of observances and gestures. For something about the relationship of Uncle Aloysius and Aunt Bernice had the character of a solitary mountain, whose lofty configuration is set off most appropriately by the range of which it is part. My various hypotheses about these matters are supported, I believe, by Aunt Bernice's departure from Concord and from New Hampshire almost immediately after Uncle Aloysius's demise. Without him, the setting no longer made any sense to her at all.

I could add to this account, finally, whatever it is I am able to divine about what in later years continued to draw Cornelia and Agnes northward to New Hampshire, northward to Concord for visits to a revered home site and an ancestral grave, and even further northward to the lakes. For Cornelia, such a gesture necessarily had the character of a return, a repossession for a while of a terrain endeared to her by her memories; and it was natural that Agnes should have shared the same memories and accompanied her. But, for all such considerations, I also suspect that such visits, even as seasonal and recurrent as they were, had motivations not unlike that lure of a paradigmatic prow that I once envisaged cleaving the limpid surface of a sunset lake, the same plash and clatter of paddles, the same call of loons over the dusk-enshrouded woodlands that thrilled and magnified the days of my youth.

Well, for all of that, I must own up to what actually turned out to be the somewhat uneventful drive northward I took that day, a drive now divested, unfortunately, of much of its former magic by my being too preoccupied to pay much attention to what was passing by. It was at least a sunny day, warm and springlike—like the day in the previous week when I visited Madison Street, though, as I could well expect, the New Hampshire spring was delayed from what I was accustomed to in the suburbs of Boston. Still, I saw a few apple trees beginning to bloom and was glad to have confirmed for me thereby that some orchards had not yet fallen prey to the rapacious claw of modern commercial development. Even so, as the highway passed over or beside an exceptionally hidden or steep gulley of one sort or another, I could spot shrunken snowbanks, often littered with pine needles and other forest debris, still lingering in deep shadows with damp or swampy fringes around them as they slowly melted away. I noticed, too, with no little pleasure, the crocuses and snowdrops just beginning to protrude through the damp soil, the violets and clumps of fiddlehead ferns coiling tenuous sprouts, so rudimentary and delicate, out of the spring thaw.

The approach to Concord, like the approach to all cities, has become the usual depressing sight; automobile dealerships, strip malls, and fast-food restaurants abound. But I was pleased, as I always am, while steering on to Main Street, to see the remnant of the old Concord coach factory, looking like a large inverted egg cup made of brick with a tippy little cupola on top. That the renowned western stagecoaches had their origin here has never ceased to thrill me. Further up Main Street I was startled when I saw a church on my left as I was driving by and then noticed a sign that indicated that it was the Church of Saint John the Evangelist.

I have driven up this street a dozen or more times over the years on those rare occasions when I have visited Concord, and, though I have known, as I mentioned before, that Concord was a city with many churches, a "city of spires," in my mother's terms, I have never paid much attention to any particular one, what denomination made use of it, or what architectural style it displayed. They simply faded into an indistinguishable background of assorted oddities, agreeable enough, but eliciting no special notice. Now this one suddenly thrust itself out at me, and, please excuse the expression, "punched" me, as it were, "in the eye." It wasn't the architecture, I can assure you, though that was fine enough—redbrick, neo-Gothic, more Canadian in tone than northern New England, as a number of things in northern New England are, by virtue of the extensive French Canadian immigration into these regions; moreover, it stood, stands, alone, not immersed in a row of other buildings, so that, if it has reason to call attention to itself for some other reason, it is ideally positioned to do so.

In this case, it certainly did have reason to call attention to itself. I had expected that at some point I would see it, but not so soon; I expected I would have to seek it out, to find it as one more landmark on my journey into the repository of Schefflin memories, and prepare myself emotionally for taking it in; I did not expect that it would pop out at me with that surprising quality of the solid-rock ordinariness that physical objects in this world invariably have. Part of the astonishment is the asymmetry between the kind of diaphanous significance that has been mentally conferred upon a thing and the abrupt revelation of the concreteness of the thing itself. What happened to me then and there happened in a flash, in that second or two of lateral vision one can spare while driving past something down a busy road. But it was more than astonishment for me: a quick, torrid shot of that flush, that distress, instigated by the story of that edifice, renewed itself instantaneously for me, made me wince, distracted me for a moment, causing just the slightest swerve in my driving and an angry honk from a motorist behind me.

Soon I turned left where Main Street and Pleasant Street form a kind of crossroads at the center of the city and began to search for the address Cornelia had given me. Once again I had looked forward to a leisurely drive around the neighborhoods west of Main Street, doing my usual "testing of the waters," getting "the lay of the land," absorbing what I could, before introducing myself at the door of the original Fitzgerald house. Do I have a certain morbid propensity to do this kind of thing? And is it always to be quashed by an arrival too early, too abrupt for my sensibilities? Anyway, I had just barely made my turn and gone a block or two when I realized I was there! A tall, thin, white-clapboarded house with its front porch and lawn and white picket fence and gate on the corner so close to the downtown, hemmed in by recently constructed condominiums! It was exactly what I had been led to expect, and it was not what I had expected at all. I had to remind myself that more than a half century had passed since the occupancy of that house by those people whose histories now absorbed my attention. I figured it was a miracle that it was still there and even more of a miracle if it should survive much longer. That it would soon be on the real estate market did not hold out much promise for that. I have seen, again and again, the fate of old and fine dwellings in Boston and on the North Shore, where I live, when the land on which they sit has become more valuable than the building itself. I immediately began to look for a parking place, realizing with some chagrin that the area bristled with parking meters and clusters of signs promulgating complex rules for parking on certain days and at certain times. However, as I edged past the Fitzgerald house, I saw that a long, perfectly straight driveway on the far side of the house passed from the street and along the side of the house and a backyard to what must be the carriage house I had heard about, sheathed in white clapboards identical to those of the main house and handsomely situated among some arbors and flower beds. I directed my car into the driveway and pulled up close to the carriage house, being conscientious, as I always am in such matters, almost to the point of the ludicrous, about not wishing to block access to anyone else. I then walked back the length of the driveway, turned at the front of the house, mounted the wooden steps to the front porch and knocked on the door.

I didn't have to wait long; I was expected, having spoken to Clotilde Carey earlier that morning on the telephone. She didn't come to the front door, however; I heard a voice calling out to me and moved back to the side of the house next to the driveway, where I saw her leaning out of the kitchen door—a door I had just walked past—and waving rather energetically to me. Remembering that kitchen doors are generally how one enters into older households of New England, I quickly joined her, and she brought me into a spacious, old-fashioned room lined with beaded wooden cabinets and appliances that clearly came from another era. The refrigerator was a slender white enameled box standing high on four legs, with an immense, round, drum-like condenser mounted on top and a kind of door and door clasps I had never seen before except on meat lockers in traditional butcher shops. Next to the refrigerator was a relatively modern electric range; on the opposite side of the room, a ponderous elbowed pipe connected an ornate iron stove to a chimney right behind it. Its highly polished and untarnished nickel fittings and the empty woodbox nearby suggested that the appliance hadn't been used in years. A large rectangular table, with a blue-checkered calico tablecloth covering it, occupied a substantial portion of the kitchen. Several slightly battered wooden chairs were lined up along its sides, and a vase of fresh daffodils adorned its center. I couldn't help but think that the daffodils had been placed there for my benefit. The room was flooded with sunlight streaming in from a brace of windows facing out toward the driveway and arrayed above and along the kitchen sink and its adjacent counters.

Clotilde Carey herself was an elderly woman; tall, lanky, trim in what I took to be the Fitzgerald manner (however remote that particular gene pool might be in her case), silver-haired, partially stooped, but limber for all of that, slightly erratic in her movements, with a cheerful voice and animated eyes. I recalled that she had been once a kindergarten teacher, though it was difficult to imagine such a towering figure channeling around some bantam brood; and I quickly learned that she had the inclination, one that I have known among other kindergarten, as well as early elementary school, instructors, of sometimes speaking slowly and relapsing into carefully chosen and methodically phrased monosyllabic words addressed even to adults, at least at first acquaintance, and of initiating any kind of activity by first spelling out, in a somewhat singsong voice especially adapted for its purpose, the simple rules and procedures of the activity, as if it were a new and especially delightful game. She took obvious pleasure in having the prospect of showing me around the house, for it seemed that, with the exception of the few rooms in the back that she actually made much use of, the rest of the house was about as remote and alien a place for her as it might be for me. She began by spelling out in some detail the itinerary we would take and the order of presentation she would follow. My instinct, my spontaneous impulse in this circumstance, might well have been to flee; but such a reaction was deflected by the charm of her personality, by my desire to see the house, and by my willingness to play the delightful game she was proposing.

There was, is, not much to say about the house: old, yes, but well-maintained; late-nineteenth-century frame construction, with high ceilings and plaster walls often covered with timeworn but spruce and attractive wallpaper, painted wooden moldings, well-polished hardwood floors and staircase and mantelpiece, and even ornate cast-iron radiators, of a type I had not seen for years, their serrated flanges coated with a light pastel yellow paint and, despite the obvious care, chipping here and there at the base. Like some New England houses, built no doubt in what, at some time, was considered the "cutting edge" of fashion and adapted ideally, according to some now assuredly outdated school of thought, to the vagaries of the New England climate, the residence was tall and narrow and stretched thinly along an east-west axis so that the southern side of the house, with its high, wide-paned windows, was maximally oriented to absorbing the warmth and light of the sun during the winter, while the rest of the house, with the proper ventilating apertures opened up, would be a natural breezeway for cooling in the summer. A row of maple trees had been planted along the southern side of the house, bordering the entire length of the far side of the driveway, so that the winter sun could find its way through bare branches even as the full glow of the summer sun would be deflected by leafy crowns. It was, in any event, a bright, comfortable house, though one could not help but wonder how the surrounding buildings, of much more recent provenance and casting their long shadows, now might impair the efficacy of its original design. Not everything was so positive, however. As was mentioned earlier, Clotilde Carey was not a close relative of Uncle Aloysius, had never actually known Uncle Aloysius or Aunt Bernice (outside of what may have been a few chance encounters, hardly remembered at all, at "clan" gatherings in Boston when she was very young), and the house itself had had several other occupants between the original Fitzgeralds and herself.

Consequently, as she made a point of reaffirming, her knowledge of how the house had been used by the couple was limited to the few things she had heard at various times from those, and especially Cornelia on the occasional visit, who were better informed than she was. But she told me, what I knew already, that the two front rooms of the house, both parlors with a hallway in between, had been used by Uncle Aloysius as a dispensary and a waiting room. Two smaller rooms to the rear of the parlors, not much more than a deep closet in one case and a small butler's pantry in the other, served respectively as a nurse's station for Uncle Aloysius's assistant and as what must have been a cramped private office for himself.

All of these rooms, at the time of my visit, though outfitted sparsely with fairly artless furniture and kept scrupulously clean, looked unused for years. I knew that front parlors in New England houses generally were reserved for seldom and typically ceremonious duties; but, in this case, it was difficult not to think of the pageants of suffering that certainly did pass through these chambers in their time as a physician's place of work and of their final task of providing a site for that same physician's sickness, death, and subsequent obsequies. I noted, too, the modest room adjacent to the front parlors (Aunt Bernice's library, I presumed), from the door of which Cornelia must have emerged to communicate with Uncle Aloysius for the final time. Other parts of the house, with the spur of my tour guide, sparked memories of the stories I had already heard from Theodore and Cornelia herself, though I made no effort to allude to these stories. This was, after all, Clotilde's tour and was being played out according to her rules, and I didn't wish to interfere.

I saw the back sections of the house, where the couple had actually lived (and where I surmised Clotilde lived as well), the bedrooms and the snug sitting room on the second floor, and the woodshed, which had been converted to, and still was, in effect, a tiny theater, though now with a dusty stage and an unevenly faded curtain drooping to one side, as if it had been drawn open one last time, ages ago, for the actors to take their bows and remained fixed ever since in that position. A large number of boxes and old furniture had been stored up in every corner of the theater. A single, rather small window, high up on the far wall and almost opaque with dust and accumulated cobwebs, admitted an intense stave of sunlight that slanted through the dusty air and illuminated, like a spotlight, one corner of the stage. Had the little theater ever been used again for its distinctive purposes? I wondered. It is peculiar, too, that I had no sense here of something blighted, foreshortened, or abandoned, despite the disarray I witnessed. It just looked dormant somehow, in hibernation, as if it could arouse itself into vibrant life again; had indeed done that already, it said in some strangely silent way, not here but somewhere else, and only the cocoon of its former phase of life had been, decorously and gracefully, left behind to turn in the breeze suspended from a single gossamer thread. I tried not to imagine the dramatic skits themselves, the actors involved, the applause of an audience that probably numbered fewer than those on the stage. I will be candid: I had to do everything I could to keep this moment, and in fact the entire tour itself, from devolving into an excessively maudlin experience for me. I had to struggle to put my normal emotional responses into a deep freeze for the duration. I was glad to be led around by my newly found preceptor, whose tall, stooped shoulders sheltered me, in a way, "in the shadow of her wings" and whose playful detachment helped to bind me in the dazed and speechless wonder of a bewildered five-year-old.

After our brief tour was completed, she offered me some coffee, which I readily accepted; and a doughnut, of course—what would life in New England be without the periodic doughnut? We sat at the table together in the enormous kitchen. After her usual explanations and instructions, all carefully and slowly and monosyllabically worded for my presumptively infantile intellect (I fully expected a carton of crayons to be produced for my "project"), she rose, opened up a large pine cabinet, and drew out a cardboard box full of files and papers, which she placed on the table before me.

"That's the first of seven boxes, Mr. Schofield," she announced, now unaccountably addressing me as a fellow member of the adult world, "I fetched them several days ago from the carriage house. I didn't want you to have to grope through all those cobwebs and sawdust and 'souvenirs,' if I may be so bold, of the various forms of animal life that have occupied it—you know, the barn swallows, the rodents, both aerial and earthbound, and other residents more or less cantankerous and funny—skunks, raccoons, woodchucks, barn cats, and heaven knows what else. I even found, buried under some loose floorboards, the skeleton of a fox with scraps of fur and a furry red tail still attached. I am sorry about it and about the condition of all of the outbuildings—but that is the way I found them, and I have never really known what to do about it. Only recently, when I decided I would have to put the house on the market, have I tried to burrow through them, resembling I am sure, some of those secretive residents whose tunneling habits I just decried. I have even contrived a special protective mask for the job. Anyway, since it's all old family stuff, I feel some obligation to see what's there. That's when I discovered the material belonging to Cornelia's uncle. There's a lot of it, so I hope you won't find this process too tiresome. I think it needs a more skillful eye than I can provide for it."

"I guess that is one of the reasons I am here, Ms. Carey," I insisted, "though I wonder if my eye is as skillful in such matters as people would like to think."

"Well," she replied, "I am confident you will do an expert job. I have looked through some of them already. Of course, I cannot really judge if the materials have any importance. Most of it, I am sure, if not all of it, could be disposed of without much of a problem. I don't know why any of it is still here. I think that Bernice Fitzgerald must have felt, at the time of her husband's death, unable to deal with it—so often the recently bereaved are like that; others didn't know it was there, nor did I until I discovered it tucked away in a dark corner under some musty old horse blankets."

Clotilde dipped a portion of her doughnut into her coffee, lifted it to her mouth, and, manifestly proficient in that genteel art, gingerly sheared off the dripping part of it. After a chewful silence and a leisurely, methodic swallow, she resumed, "You just cannot imagine how many things are packed away in the carriage house, and the garden shed, and the attic and cellar and the old theater. Since the house had been, in a sense, passed along in the family, nobody has ever seen fit to clean it out. I guess they always thought that they eventually could come back and retrieve the things they left behind because such things would still be there and still retrievable. But they never came back and in effect either forgot or just ceased to care about those things. I discovered a misshapen clunk of old, oily machinery in the carriage house the other day. I simply couldn't budge it, it was so heavy. Mr. Hazelton from down the street dropped by and, after poking it and turning it around and over (and getting his hands and forearms thoroughly besmirched with grease), identified it as the transmission of a Model A Ford. He told me that there are some people who would pay good money to have something like that. I can't imagine why. Really, an old piece of junk like that! He told me that there are people who will give good money for practically anything, so I should be careful about what I do with things. But none of it really belongs to me. How can I sell it?"

I paused, considering her query. I really did not have much experience in this kind of thing, but I offered my opinion anyway. "I assume that you have title to the house."

"Indeed I do."

"Well, then, it seems to me that the things you describe fit, in one manner or another, into the category of abandoned property. In a few days, when I am back in my office I can find out if there are any statutory provisions in the State of New Hampshire pertaining to abandoned property. I will get back to you with that information. In any case, it may be worthwhile, if you do find something of genuine value, to see if you can locate an original owner, or the heirs of that owner, though I rather doubt that you have a real legal obligation to do so. But that will make you feel better about it and might be the just thing to do in some cases, as you have done with the records of the Fitzgeralds. But I don't think you have the moral obligation to go through unusual efforts to dispose of these things—you might spend the rest of your life doing that, and you could open up some serious contention among competing claims—claims that otherwise would never have been made. Even the most trivial things—hubcaps, lanterns, sugar spoons, a whiskey decanter, a set of sherry glasses—can provoke the most dreadful quarrels, unfortunately. Again, I doubt much in the way of any strictly legal obligations is involved, but I will find this out for you; after all, as you said, these things have been abandoned and were abandoned a long time ago. In effect, people have renounced their claims, and you have as much right as anyone to consign or transfer such claims to whomever you will. You could have a grand garage sale, and, if anything comes of that, donate the proceeds to a charity."

"You put me at my ease, Mr. Schofield. My thanks," she nodded. "But I detain you too long with all my chatter. Regarding the material in these boxes, Cornelia, as I understand, has consigned them to your keeping and left all decisions up to you."

I took an initial peek at the contents of the first box. A somewhat delirious thought entered my mind. "It might be useful if I could have something to mark these files and boxes in some way as I go along. That will help me to remember what I have already seen and also to sort the contents if I find that sorting is necessary."

"Yes. Wonderful idea!" she exclaimed with a twinkle in her eye. This could be a game after all. "What do you think you need?"

"Something with different colors," I replied. "You wouldn't happen to have some crayons around, would you?"

"I certainly would!" she proclaimed. "I have about a million crayons. I have whole crates full of crayons."

"Four or five would do," I responded, "of different colors and brightly hued."

"Crates or crayons?"

"Just the crayons would be fine."

When Clotilde went off to fetch the crayons (it turned out that I never really needed them), I began my work. I realized soon enough that it would be improbable to find much of anything worthy of retention. Most of the records were handwritten, most by Uncle Aloysius, I assume, though several other hands were evident—various assistants over the years, I figured, Aunt Bernice certainly, and, on a few very simple documents, a childish but deliberate handwriting. At a certain point a somewhat crude typewriter had been used, though what I found were extensive reams of carbon copies rather than originals. It was curious indeed to shuffle so deeply through the accumulated paperwork of an age, so sparse, so efficient in its own way, before a series of electronic revolutions, promising a reduction of paper, would bloat such procedures into the omnivorous glutton of forests we know today.

Before I had spent too much time with the first box, I decided to pull the other boxes out of the cabinet and to examine them briefly so that I could make some preliminary assessment of what I had to do. Meanwhile, five crayons of brightly colored hues had been delivered, along with another cup of coffee, and Clotilde disappeared into some other part of the house. I chose a red crayon to start marking the outsides of the boxes but discovered that the boxes already had labels, however faded and almost illegible, and that everything, to all appearances, was already well organized. I did have to confront the occasional derelict mouse nest, to say nothing of a few dehydrated mouse corpses, squashed between a file here and there, but I soon enough felt equipped to cope with that inconvenience.

Although I was touched certainly by perusing these detailed and daily testimonials to a man's professional life, I could not see much value in preserving them. Perhaps a social historian might envisage in them a potential account of a medical practice, or at least of one aspect of a medical practice, as it was conducted more than a half century earlier, but there would probably not be much to distinguish it from the practices of thousands of other physicians of that time whose records might be more informative than these. I recognized that no patients' medical records were kept among the boxes, indicating that they had, most likely, been passed along to whatever physician it was who took over the practice after Uncle Aloysius's death. I did rifle through a number of financial transactions, orders and bills pertaining to pharmaceutical and medical-service companies, receipts of many kinds, communications with various hospitals in the region, bills and contracts involving a telephone and other equipment and a fairly sizable accumulation of insurance documents (but no claims or claim disputes among them). I also discovered several batches of income-tax filings, being surprised how small the sums and simple the returns were in those days. I saw nothing that would have, in our time, much legal significance, no special titles to anything, no court transactions, no licenses or certifications that would have any significance so long after they were issued. Of course, I knew I had been sent here to exercise just this kind of discrimination, though one hardly needed much legal training to be able to do it. The only difficulty was to know how best to dispose of it. It seemed odd just to throw it all into rubbish containers and have it hauled off in the weekly municipal collection.

Clotilde solved that problem at the small lunch she later prepared for us and served at the kitchen table. She knew a local contractor who could pick up such things and give them a proper and discreet disposal. He could shred all the paperwork and bundle it up for recycling. I consented and offered to seal the boxes, to help remove them to a place, perhaps back to the carriage house by the entrance doors, where they could be picked up conveniently, and to pay for the services of the contractor. Clotilde at first insisted that she could handle the bill of the contractor but, in the end, was agreeable to all my suggestions.

Except for that minor piece of business, our lunch together was very pleasant. First of all, it was delightful in its simplicity—just the sort of thing for (as Besserman would chide) a "ham and cheese on white" fellow like me, although the rather viscous yellow pudding (rice or tapioca?) she offered me for dessert was not terribly enticing. I discovered in conversation with her that she knew fairly little about Uncle Aloysius and Aunt Bernice, despite her occasional visits from Cornelia, and I figured that, if Cornelia had refrained from filling her in on much of that history, she must have had reasons for doing so, and it was my job to respect those reasons. Sometimes, perhaps, it is good for the occupants of an old and much used house not to know too much of its history. Although Clotilde had to come to Concord several decades after the demise of Uncle Aloysius, she was aware that his reputation lived on, both in the city at large and in the parish where he became, in his life, an esteemed parishioner and, in his death, something of a revered figure conferring an added blessing to the local scene. She also said that she felt that the house itself seemed to have something special about it, as if important things had happened there. People in the neighborhood regarded it with deference; when Cornelia came by every two years or so, she seemed to relate to the house with a pronounced concentration of spirit, as if it were, in her mind, a sanctuary of some kind and to be reverenced as such.

Clotilde deeply regretted that she had to sell the house; she regretted even more the bulldozers that would quickly reap the harvest of the sale. But she did have one story to tell me about the house. For many years—intermittently and often years apart (Clotilde could not be certain that she always noticed this occurrence from inside the house or was at home when it happened)—a woman unfamiliar to Clotilde would appear in front of the house, enter through the old picket gate, and sit down for a while on the small wrought-iron settee located nearby. She never seemed to be reticent about engaging in such unusual behavior nor disposed to approach the owner of the house about the propriety of her sojourn there. She was always dressed in an outfit both dazzling and simple at the same time, almost "homemade," it would appear. She sat straight up on the settee, her hands folded, her gaze fixed tenderly on the house, her deportment perfectly molded and poised. Clotilde, on those occasions when she attended to what was happening in her front yard, had been sometimes tempted to step out on the front porch, to introduce herself, and to invite the stranger into the house for a chat and a cup of tea or something to that effect. But the woman's finely honed attitude, her tone and posture, deterred her from interrupting what was so overtly the unmistakable solemnity of the occasion. Furthermore, the bizarre "visit," perhaps better described as a "ritual" than a "visit," never lasted very long. Suddenly, unexpectedly, the woman would rise, exit through the picket gate, and walk away, only to reappear several years later and do the identical thing. Clotilde never knew who she was, but she conjectured that this woman must have once been what would have been called "a great beauty" in her prime. Then, after a while, a decade or more in the past, she never came back again.

"It sounds," I ventured, perhaps a little too blithely, "like a rather dramatic performance." Naturally, I was able to identify, almost instantaneously, who this woman might be and to apply to her what I had been told about her character.

Clotilde considered my comment for a moment, tapped her index finger lightly on the kitchen table, as if bringing her pupils to order, and politely disagreed: "I can understand why you, Mr. Schofield, or anyone, would be inclined to describe it like that. I might very well be inclined to do that too. But that's not the way I interpreted it. I cannot attest to anything about this lady, except that her 'visit,' or 'visitation' or whatever it was, was about as genuine as anything ever gets to be in this life, without so much as a hint of affectation or imposture. I had a sense of a person who knew exactly who she was and what she was doing, and who was doing it for nobody else except herself and for the sake of some priceless memory she harbored deep inside her. It was, indeed, a most extraordinary thing—which is why I felt I could not intrude, even if in the most friendly and solicitous manner."

"Did you ever mention this to Cornelia?" I inquired.

"I never thought to," she responded.

Although it would have been easy enough for me to do so, I did not feel it was appropriate to advance any information about this mysterious personage, and I let it pass without comment. I already felt a little morose about the rather glib comment I had made. Though I certainly felt moved, deeply moved, by Clotilde's account, I didn't see how I could try to explicate it for her without reducing it to something both trivial and sensational at the same time. To address it properly would require having to fill in all the details that would underscore its distinction and safeguard what I could now clearly see was its dignity. There would be a time to do all of that, but this was not the right time. I also thought that what Clotilde had witnessed was the same sort of thing Besserman had described for me about Aunt Bernice in the days immediately following the death of Uncle Aloysius: a different Aunt Bernice, not the theatrical artifice but the real woman in all her self-possession and poise. Clotilde had been privileged to see such a vision and understood, in some way, what she was looking at; I couldn't help but be a little jealous of that.

Hence our lunch concluded—somber and inconclusive after all. But then Clotilde smiled. I could see she was well trained to assuage feelings and redirect sensibilities. She jumped up from the kitchen table with her usual vigor, went to the pine cabinet, and pulled out another container. It was a kind of small carrying case, a black leather satchel, rather scratched and frayed by time. She brought it to me.

"I found this," she said, "tucked in along with the boxes under the horse blankets. I haven't looked inside—you will have to pry off the lock to get into it. I assume the key to it disappeared a long time ago. It has 'things' inside it; you can hear them moving around when you shake it. It is intriguing, isn't it? One loves little mysteries like this, rather like wrapped presents, don't you think? But it goes with the other medical things, and I thought you should take care of it. Call me if I can be of any help." Clotilde dismissed herself again, after clearing off the luncheon dishes.

I was soon finished with the final two boxes. There was nothing of significance there—they included some applications for a nurse's assistant that told me, anyway, something about what was expected as the daily routine of the office. Also I found some contracts and bills related to a local cleaning and laundry service. All of this was in very good order. It was clear that Uncle Aloysius supervised his own billing and that someone else took care of most of the receipts. It was also clear that there was some system of pro-rating in the assignment of charges, that a whole class of patients were assessed fees so negligible as to be more symbolic than real, and that even a substantive number of these patients were unable to pay the bills, as miniscule by our standard, as they were; moreover, there was nothing to indicate that they were pressed to pay. Copies of their bills were maintained, often with little notes from the patients stapled to them, apologizing for the failure to pay and promising to do so in the future. It was evident that few such promises were fulfilled. Unpaid bills were noted and simply filed without follow-up or further reference. There were indications that some bills had been paid in kind: a dozen eggs, a rhubarb pie, a quart of strawberries, a brass buckle, a bundle of firewood, a set of horseshoes from a local farrier. How could the Fitzgeralds have used a set of horseshoes? I wondered. These were all duly noted. I knew a physician once who confided to me that a truly serious dilemma of his profession was taking money from the impoverished ill. I recognized in Uncle Aloysius an inveterate healer who shared this same compunction.

I turned then to the leather satchel. I'll admit I was a little intimidated by this. Prying off the lock did not present much of a problem. I rose from the table and sought out a kitchen knife for the purpose, but I found, when I returned to the table, that the material of the satchel was so degraded that the entire locking mechanism literally tore off with little effort. I opened the satchel. My first impression was that I had opened up the sort of case that physicians once carried with them on house calls—and indeed it may have been one—for I saw medical instruments packed rather neatly in place: several stethoscopes with different attachments, a small pen-type flashlight, a rubber mallet, a thermometer in a narrow glass tube and a blood pressure monitor, a case with a device for examining ears and eyes, again with different attachments, and various other mechanisms I would be hard put to define. I found a scroll bound with a ribbon. I removed the ribbon, unrolled the scroll, and saw that it was a diploma from Harvard Medical School. I wondered if Uncle Aloysius had simply never gotten around to having it framed and mounted for his office. I rolled it up again. Several other documents appeared at the bottom of the case. One was a license from the State of New Hampshire to practice medicine. It was small and flat and clearly had once been framed for public view. Another document certified membership in a medical academy of some sort. I wondered who may have packed up this satchel; it all had a curious flavor of something impersonal about it, as if some stranger to the family had assembled these things and put them together in a rather piecemeal manner. I was also puzzled by what to do with these things. I decided that I would bring the satchel and its contents back to Boston and have Besserman help me to decide. Perhaps Cornelia would like to have them. It was difficult to know.

I realized then that there was one final object remaining in the satchel, almost invisible to the eye but evident to the hand. I lifted it out. It was a small, dark brown, velvety pouch whose opening was pulled together tightly with a golden-threaded cord. It had something in it, so I loosened the cord, opened it up, and gently tipped it to the side to empty the contents onto the kitchen table. Out fell a curious miscellany of things: some cuff links, a tie clasp, a golden watch chain with a vest pocket watch attached to it, a fountain pen of gracefully tapered design, a gold ring, a pair of wire-rimmed reading glasses in a case, and a religious medal on a chain. It took a few seconds before I realized that what I was looking at, what was gathered in the pouch, were the sorts of things, the personal effects, an undertaker might remove from a body before sealing the coffin. These items had adorned Uncle Aloysius in his final viewing by the world. How deeply, in a way, they signified part of who he was and the kind of life he led.

But something else was in the pouch, pushed somehow into its far corner. I turned the pouch over again and shook it. Nothing came out. I shook it again, this time more violently and impatiently. A small pink envelope flew out so impetuously it almost made me jump. It slapped down on the table in front of me, its flap side up. I immediately regretted my precipitance. The corners of the envelope were bent and frayed, and a finely embossed scrollwork along its edges was browned with age. It was unsealed and its flap was creased and partially bent open. The lace-like brocade along its border was crinkled and torn here and there. I realized that my rough treatment may have caused the flap to project upward in that condition. I picked it up, now with utmost care, turned it over, and laid it flat on the table. On the opposite side, in large, careful letters, in a hand I recognized from the rare pieces to be found among the old medical files, was inscribed the name "Uncle Aloysius."

I panicked. I'm sorry. What else could I do? Reverting back, once more, to type, I shoved, almost maniacally, the envelope back into the pouch, as if I had stumbled upon something I was not meant to touch or see, and hastily gathered the other objects and stuffed them back into the pouch like a jewel thief about to make off with a forbidden heist. I think, at one level, that I did not want Clotilde to see what I had found in that pouch. I dreaded, at that point, in such a rush of discovery, having to browse around through the various objects, more or less dispassionately, with another person, commenting upon this or speculating about that. And what would I do, in just such a circumstance, with that envelope? I simply did not want to have to explain what little I knew about it to another while I was still in high dudgeon about how to treat it. What if that person insisted upon opening it and reading it! But, more than anything else, I just had not expected this sudden immediacy to occur, this overwhelming impact of something so internal, so intimate to the persons whose destiny I had been tracing all these days. Had I inadvertently violated some taboo by being so matter-of-fact, by being an intruder, by so crudely shaking out from that pouch a precious reliquary to which a very special sort of reverence had been due? I tightened the cord that sealed up the pouch and packed it back into the medical satchel along with all the other things I had found there. Then I closed the satchel, folding together as best I could its frayed and torn edges. Finally, I stood up from my place at the table, sought out Clotilde, and announced to her that I had finished my work and was ready to go.

It was midafternoon. After we had repacked the boxes and wrapped them up with packing tape, Clotilde exited the house and showed up soon thereafter at the kitchen door with a sizable wooden wheelbarrow, an old-fashioned type with a big metal wheel in front, a flat bottom, and removable side panels. The wheel was bent and its axle was loose, so it wobbled precariously under the load we conveyed upon it. We worked together to bring the boxes to the carriage house. She swung open the wide door, painted black and creaking on old, rusty iron hinges. I am embarrassed to confess that this refined lady in her eighties displayed rather greater physical strength than I did in hauling around those boxes and stacking them by the door. She had even insisted, on our second trip from the kitchen, on pushing the wheelbarrow herself, as if to spare me from excessive strain. She apologized again for the interior state of the carriage house, but I did not doubt for a moment her ability to contend with whatever challenges it might present.

At one point I became diverted from what I was doing by peering into the dark, tangled, and heaped interior, making some effort to sort out the disarray before me. I wasn't very successful in doing this. I noticed a child's sled, the frame of a bicycle whose wheels had been removed, and an old, hand-cranked ice-cream machine in a corner. I was gazing upon this for a few moments, thinking of Agnes and her buckets of wild blueberries, thinking of Frederick and Uncle Aloysius cranking that old machine, when a sharp, bony finger stabbed me in the shoulder. I glanced around and practically cried out. Over me hovered a figure with the most terrifying face I had ever seen — it looked like the engrafting of a First World War gas mask into the most bulbous space helmet to be found in a science-fiction film. Its great blank and glassy eyes and the two wavy antennae sticking out of the crest of the helmet gave it the appearance of some gigantic formic mutation: a huge queen ant bending over me and ominously grinding her mandibles. Clotilde, reacting to my alarm, pulled off the horrifying appurtenance and grinned at me, the way one rapidly pulls off a mask in front of a child so that the child does not get scared and is reminded of who is actually behind it.

"When I work in here," she chuckled, "I wear this. It protects me from all the dust and other residues."

Was I—I guess I was—comforted by this information? She replaced the mask on a hook by the door, laughing delightfully all the while, and swung the door shut. "She would be all set," I thought to myself, "for preparing her protégés, if she still had any, for next Halloween." What would I wear? The image of some sort of pirate garb uneasily floated through my mind. I had, after all, my little treasure, which I had to ferret out of there and safely home.

Before I departed, I retrieved the leather satchel from the kitchen and gave Clotilde a brief account, without too many details, of what I had found in it. I described it as consisting of physician's instruments, some old diplomas and certificates, and several "personal effects." She was satisfied with that. As I prepared to leave, I asked her about Saint John the Evangelist Church. She replied that she knew it well, being a member of the parish it served. It would be open if I wanted to visit it; it was always open during the day. She asked me, if I should visit it, to say for her, in her words, a "little prayer before the Blessed Sacrament."

"I . . . I shall . . . I shall do that," I stuttered. Should I have said no to her? Of course not. But I didn't have the slightest idea what I had agreed to.

As she waved goodbye to me from the kitchen steps, I couldn't help but muse that it would be nice for me, and my family, on our way to the mountains someday, to pay her a social call. I knew we would all enjoy such a visit, even if we ended up around the kitchen table drawing pictures with crayons. But I also knew that she would probably depart for sunnier climes long before that could happen. I backed up my car along the driveway, and, with some delay, into the busy street behind me. As I departed, I noticed the gate in the picket fence and the wrought-iron settee at its side, facing the old house.

I stopped at the thin-steepled brick church on Main Street only for a few minutes, only long enough to park my car and to step through the front doors and take a brief look around inside. I felt like a trespasser on someone else's consecrated ground. I noted a water stoup to my right as I entered. Everything was so much smaller than I had imagined. Even the interior of the church, neo-Gothic, as I had expected, was taller, narrower, more compact than the exterior of the church let on. I was alone, but, for all my anticipated disquiet about what I might find alien and suspect, I felt safe and at my ease. Here, I couldn't help but feel, was a shelter where one could put life, or something about life, "on hold"—not suspending or immobilizing it, but rather realigning it along some set of coordinates where events and places could be viewed from an entirely different perspective; where one could just possibly blend stark and anfractuous accents into tacit harmonies; where one just might, for the moment anyway, be unhurried, clearheaded, recollected.

I decided to sit for a minute or two in a back pew, wondering if, by any chance, I was sitting where Uncle Aloysius and Cornelia had reposed so many years ago. I stared at the sanctuary lamp, as I guess they call it, close to the little door at the center of the altar, and I did manage to deliver, albeit ever so maladroitly, on my promise. I silently asked whatever presence it was that was assumed to be living somehow in that glittery domicile to take care of Clotilde Carey; then, while I was at it, to take care, as I considered my request further, of all of them—yes, all of them, those living and those dead; of Cornelia and her family, of Liselle; of the Schefflins; of Theodore and Martha Besserman; of Aunt Bernice; of Uncle Aloysius; even of old Mr. Dougherty and the evanescent Mr. Gleason, wherever he was flitting to (perhaps Ariel-like) in his sundry escapades. I was swift to reassure the recipient of my address that I was there purely as a proxy, a surrogate, speaking not *in propria persona* but as an attorney, an ersatz suppliant only, and that my supplication should be taken wholly in that spirit; that the presence posited to reside in that little brassy tabernacle should not go around leaping to any conclusions about exactly where I stood. For I fully intended to stand my ground, even if I stood upon another's ground at the moment. But when I found myself unexpectedly too absorbed in this unwonted mode of discourse and exceeding altogether the perimeters of my commission, when I began to get the oddest glimmer that, advocate that I was, another advocate was presuming to dispossess me of my charge and talk both for me and through me; in short, when I began to include members of my own family in my supplications, as if all of this was, after all, a serious business, I realized that it was time to be going. It is one thing to step over a certain boundary; it is another to linger there longer than one should. I paused by the stoup on the way out and, compulsively, jabbed my hand into it. Is that what Uncle Aloysius did? Is that what all of them did most of the time? Or just the fingertips? Then what?

I left the church and shook the water off my hand, spraying myself accidentally in the process ... and shook something else out too, out of my head or out of my brains maybe, like a dripping retriever shaking itself after loping out of a pond—dispatching what is foreign to it into a nimbus of watery spray, yet wagging its tail, nevertheless, refreshed and invigorated by what it had shaken off. I was soon on the highway headed southward into Massachusetts.

I had just crossed over the border into Methuen when another unpredictable and unruly impulse made me take an exit off the highway and begin to seek out a place where ... where what? It was such an uncharacteristic move for me that at first I couldn't fully decipher what I was up to. Then I understood. I needed to "cool off." I needed to relax. I needed a drink. A drink? When did I ever "need" a drink? I don't know. But now I needed a drink. I also found it comforting to be back in Massachusetts. A familiar place, I guess, where things get done the way I expect them to get done, whatever that means—and I am not too sure I have the slightest idea what that means—or whatever value that might or might not have. And I needed to limit myself to one drink at most. I still had a long drive home.

I found a place—there seemed to be no shortage of them: a restaurant, of a slightly disreputable appearance, that advertised over a side door, with a green fluorescent light curved around in the shape of a tipped martini glass, a cocktail lounge. It was provocatively called "The Tippy Tipler Lounge." The sky was just beginning to darken, and the fluorescent light had been turned on and was blinking so that I could notice that part of the light no longer worked and left a dark spot along the stem of the glass. I can't say that I found that too promising about what this place might turn out to be. But neither was it discouraging. There is a certain comfort sometimes in something being pleasantly broken. I pulled the car into a nearly empty parking lot, locked it, and began to walk to the door of the lounge on the side of the restaurant. Then I stopped, returned to the car, in the bemused, seemingly aimless daze with which I had exited the highway, rummaged through the satchel, dug out the little pink envelope from the pouch, put it in my pocket, and approached the cocktail lounge once again.

It was dark and cool inside. Muted greenish lights at regular intervals along the tops of the walls shone upward at a high curved ceiling. A mechanism of some sort caused the lights to alternate in degrees of brightness and dimness, resulting in undulations flowing across the ceiling and merging with other undulations from the opposite side. Low, round tables were surrounded by equally low, soft chairs upholstered in some thick, languorous fabric, conceivably brownish red, though it was too dark to tell. Small lamps with red shades glowed at the center of each table. At the far end of the lounge was a bar, lit up by a row of small floodlights mounted just above it. It had a few barstools in front and the usual array of bottles on mirrored shelves behind it. To the side of the bar, a yellow fluorescent tube traced the image of a large champagne bottle, tilted jauntily to the side, just like the martini glass outside, but filled with little round bulbs blinking on and off in patterns that simulated bubbles rising to and through the neck of the bottle. Soft saxophone music played in the background. I was, as far as I could see in that darkness, the only customer in the lounge—too early, I figured, for usual business or for the evening "happy hour," if they had one. I made my way to a table in the back of the room. As I weaved in and around those low slung tables and chairs in the darkness, I felt like a tropical fish, rainbow scales aglitter in the vermilion glow of those little lamps, with scalloped fins trailing long, satiny threads behind me, undulating through the sun-speckled hollows of a coral reef and in and around half-hidden sea anemones whose lush filaments brushed softly against me as I passed by. I finally sank deep into a cushiony-soft chair.

I didn't see the waiter until he stood above me at the table. It was a shock—how high up he was, how low down I was, how silently and stealthily he had approached me through all that maze of furniture. I couldn't really see him clearly in the darkness except as a long, lank shadow poised eerily between me and the soft green waves of light ebbing and flowing overhead. It was like being a diver confronted in the lonely depths of the sea by the sinister figure of a shark hovering between himself and the surface above. The lamp on my table was reflected in a row of pearly buttons on his shirt front that peered at me like a thin line of tiny, predatory eyes. But his voice was kindly enough, that consoling voice that bartenders always seem to have, or that we always think they have. I placed my order; it was a martini. What else would it be? I was informed that it would be accompanied by a side order of potato chips, "on the house," a special available only in the late afternoon.

As I waited for my drink, I slipped again into that rather benumbed state of not knowing what to do next and either refusing to think about it or acquiescing into thinking, as so often we perhaps delude ourselves into doing, that some indefinable interior process will make a decision for us, that we will discover our intentions somehow in the unfolding of their application. The waiter returned, served the drink and the chips, and disappeared just as silently as when he had originally approached me. I almost wished he could have joined me. The martini, however, was cool and finely blended and delectable; a high quality of gin, I thought, after I had taken my first sip; and just the right combination of vermouth for my taste. I had expected something watery and insipid and lukewarm in this "joint"; but I was pleasantly surprised. I would have to give the fellow a generous tip. Frankly, I had no interest in the chips.

I thrust my right hand into my pocket and drew out the envelope. How fragile it seemed in my hands. I could hardly see it; how could I dare to touch it? I hoped I hadn't damaged it more than I already had. I laid it on the table in front of me, directly under the glow of the lamp.

I examined it again: its brownish edges, its bent flap with its tattered embroidery, its richly textured but delicate rose-tinted paper, its faded scrollwork. I turned it over to study once again the name "Uncle Aloysius" inscribed on the front and the long, high-lettered, careful calligraphy with which it was written.

I took another sip of my martini. Then I opened the envelope and slipped out a thin sheet of paper—the same kind of paper as the envelope. It was folded in half. I was no longer thinking about anything; I was running now purely on whatever that interior impulse was telling me to do. I unfolded the paper and turned it over to read. It was framed by the same scroll-like embossing that I saw on the envelope. The lamp shed just enough pale ruddy light over the paper to enable me to see what was on it.

I was surprised how little was there—just a few words, inscribed in the same calligraphy, but taller somehow, and grander and more deliberate in its rendition. It said:

"Father, I love you. I will always love you. Cornelia."

Part Seven

"Rapscallion!"

"What?"

"Scoundrel!"

"But, Theodore, whomever can you possibly mean ...?"

"You ..."

"Me? I protest!"

"*Schlemiel!*"

"At least you could insult me in a language I understand. I still protest!"

"Perfidious scamp! Well ... that will suffice ... yes, for the moment anyway, perfidious scamp!" Besserman skipped back and forth along the floor in front of me in a jaunty little dance, tapping the grin on his lips rhythmically with one stubby finger and stopping for a moment in a brief interlude of amused distraction, as if the search for the most precise term of amiable opprobrium had displaced, momentarily, the rather more urgent matter at hand. He seemed altogether delighted with himself. "You see how I am at a perfect loss for just the right word. How can I give vent to ... my utter disquiet! Perfidious scoundrel!" He commenced his dance once again. He gestured now and then at Frederick's portrait, so much so that I wondered if he were engaged simultaneously in some sort of mute obloquy directed against that august personage.

"I thought you had settled on 'perfidious scamp.'"

"Well, yes, I did ... but as I said, 'for the moment anyway.' That moment has passed. I seek ever new horizons of reproof. In any event, does it really make a difference? Let it be 'perfidious scamp' if you insist."

"I didn't insist. I was just reminding you."

"I stand ... as it were ... reminded."

"You don't implicate Frederick in all of this, do you?"

"Frederick? Of course, I don't implicate Frederick! Don't confuse the issue! I implicate no one but you ... though, there can be no doubt, we are all implicated in one fashion or another, including Frederick!"

"And in just what sense have I been perfidious?"

"Do you always open other people's mail? Do you always disclose, as you have disclosed to me, the content of distinctly private communications? Is that how you treat your clients? Is that how you dispense with the sacred canons of confidentiality?"

"How the tables are turned!" I exclaimed. "Now you invoke, as spuriously as I did only a few days ago, a code that is not even remotely relevant here. Anyway, it was hardly mail, Theodore, and it had already been opened up! Actually, it had never been sealed. And there are no clients, technically speaking, involved here; and certainly no communications, no confidences addressed specifically to me. In fact, I can't get around the hunch that I was required to open it, that I had been sent there specifically to find it and to open it. It asked me to open it! In any event, I am hardly ready to excuse what some, including myself in the right circumstances, might regard as inexcusable, except to point out that I could not have been ready to recuse myself from what was irrecusable. Don't forget: I had been appointed to be, in a sense, her ... her persona, her proxy. That was my charge. She opened it; she presented it to you. Think of it that way. Meanwhile, as I should not have to remind you, you now have read it too and already, I take it, enthroned it, on your own prerogative, prominently, for the time being, among your invincible memorabilia. I know it sounds ridiculous, but I regard your objections, Theodore, as overruled."

"Objections overruled? Are you both judge and attorney in this case? I shall have, in time, to address your objections, especially that presumed 'hunch' of yours. In the meantime, what is there for me not to object to? ... That it should befall you—you, a stranger to our affairs, a neophyte, an impudent Johnny-come-lately—to impart this ... the capital point ... the point that makes all the difference, all the difference in the world?" Besserman retorted.

Despite his effort to simulate outrage, he sauntered playfully—almost capering, as it were—back and forth before the ornate hearth, fists now uncharacteristically tucked deep in his jacket pockets, his head lowered, with the slightest lilt in his stride—strange enough in a person of his deportment, but it gave the impression of one who was, at any moment, about to leap into the blackened orifice of the hearth with both legs simultaneously lifted into the air, to stomp on the base of the hearth, and then, with a puff of ash, to bounce right up the chimney. "Jolly old elf," one was inclined to think. But I knew by that racy little dance and that glint of irony in his phrases that Besserman was having a perfectly wonderful time—the best time in the world. I could expect that he would compress his delight into a series of thrusts and swipes—a feline propensity perhaps, not incongruous with his role, once upon a time apparently, as one of Noah's lions; for my part, I was prepared, with just as much delight, to parry whatever might come my way. After all, we had something to celebrate. We could afford to badger one another as much as we wanted to. The pink envelope with the brocaded frill on its flap and slightly brownish scrollwork along its rim had been propped up on the mantelpiece over the hearth—it had not been easy for Besserman to reach that height without perching himself, rather precariously, on his tiptoes, but he managed it anyway; it occupied a place of unusual prestige in his miscellany of curios. Meanwhile I sat, somewhat at an incline, rakishly even, lolling in an unforgivably *fin-de-siècle* style, in the low divan opposite the hearth. I could expect Besserman to deliver, among whatever business he had to conduct, an entertainment, royal and furbished, in all its felicitous dimensions.

"But, Theodore," I exclaimed, "I thought you knew everything already!"

"I do know everything! Well . . . just about everything."

"Still, you missed this—my goodness, just imagine—this, as you yourself referred to it, 'capital point'!"

"Well, I did, and I did not, and . . . in either case, Edmund, even if I did miss it, it's because I know just about everything."

"A capricious answer, Theodore! Explain yourself!"

Besserman desisted from his gnomish promenade, backed himself up rather imperiously toward the great winged chair, and, with a little bound, followed by an equally rapid little descent, plumped down into the cushion of the chair. He gazed for a few moments at the multicolored blaze of the mullioned windows, which a late afternoon sun lit up into a dazzle of bright golds and rubies and greens; his lips were pursed, and, turning to me, he raised a hand as if to signal that an altogether fresh, if rugged trail through the wilderness of his excogitations was about to be initiated. "In some sense, after all . . . now don't be hasty in concluding that I am trying to 'upstage' you in this matter or to dispel the importance of what you have found out . . . but, after all, I did 'know'; that is, I had made that inference, and I had inferred on as good a warrant as inferences generally get made that Cornelia understood the actual relationship between herself and both Frederick and Uncle Aloysius; had, indeed, understood that relationship since the time of Uncle Aloysius's demise.

"Granted all of that, though, there were, and still are, as I ascertain, a great many particulars I did not and still do not know, and from which it has been and is impossible to draw responsible conclusions. But, in the end, to be in possession of such a total configuration does not matter. There are mysteries in people's lives, a great number of them, that we are not meant to penetrate; and some we are meant to penetrate—obliged to, in a sense—if the way should be open to us, not in order to forestall further wonderment or, in some peremptory fashion, to close 'the case file,' but rather to mount the threshold of even further mysteries whose very presence is enough to evoke the intimation that there is just always so much more, so very much more, to it than we ever suspected—the sense that one question now, let us say, satisfactorily answered, has just burgeoned into a multitude of new ones. But, in such a situation as this, I was bound by confidences, by promises both articulate and tacit, not to broach the question, not to ask, not even to transgress the boundaries of what had been conveyed explicitly to me by Frederick and which I was careful to safeguard even in what I imparted to you.

"Of course, you guessed, I am sure, what the true state of affairs might be; right off, you guessed; made the same inferences I had made, drew the same conclusions, circumstantial speculation such as it was. I knew that as well as I knew anything about you. But it was not our business to discuss the nature and ramifications of those conjectures. So much was given to me;

so much could I then justifiably pass on to you. Correspondingly, so much had been passed on to you; and consequently, just so far could you press me to join you in your speculations. The 'capital point' of which I spoke previously was precisely the confirmation of what I had inferred, of what otherwise, and in so many respects, was all too obvious, because so much did not really make a great deal of sense without it. My case stands, however; I could not ask and, hence, could not receive the confirmation that I sought. I guess what I am trying to say here is that the inference remained exactly that: an inference and no more."

"But Cornelia," I countered, "certainly she was free to settle the matter for you."

"About that I do not know," Besserman answered. "The fact that she did not suggests very strongly that she did not have that license. Under any circumstances, she would have not known just how I had been 'bound' in this affair, since it was clear that indeed I had been bound in some fashion or another. Nor did I know how, and in what respect, she had been 'bound' as well. Not infrequently I have attempted to visualize what sort of occasion would be appropriate for her to bring up the subject, perhaps between the courses of a Sunday dinner at the Regency . . . somewhere, let us say, between the *sautéed langoustines* and a *crème brûlée*? Needless to say, it would never have been opportune for me to bring the subject up. And what overture would be necessary before we could raise the curtain on such an extraordinary thing, which at the same time, in another sense, would not have been actually extraordinary for either of us because, if I have gauged the situation correctly, it was so much interlaced into the very fabric of all that we did and understood, even if we never talked about it? If she suddenly disclosed the entire matter, what would I have said, given the inferences that I had already made? How could she have grounds to expect from me anything but a stunned silence that should inevitably occur—stunned more by the act of disclosing than the disclosure itself—since nothing else would have been possible?

"Is there anything in this world more dumbfounding than when the deepest mystery turns out to be, upon its verbalization, what has been the most conspicuous thing of all? Into such a discomfiting situation she would never have presumed to thrust us. Moreover, it is difficult for me to know what kind of place this entire matter occupies in her heart. Among the many things we never genuinely fathom are the sorrows, the losses of others. I could never really expect Cornelia to tell me of it, perhaps for that very reason; it would be too unlike her to make her own sorrows a burden to anyone but herself, to reduce them, in her view, to an instrument with which to belabor the rest of the world, to corral its sympathies, to leverage its indulgence. Once again, I avow, it was not my business to ask and not her business to tell. Beyond that, though, in a sense, there was something—important enough, in any event—that we had to say to each other, but we could in no wise discover the occasion nor decipher the rules that would govern our saying of it."

"Then it was nobody's business."

"Not exactly," Besserman suggested.

"Then whose business was it?"

Besserman bent his head at a slightly cocky angle, rolled his eyes in my direction, and grinned. "It was yours."

I bolted upright from my semi-reclining, decadent position on the divan, my stint as *fin-de-siècle* aesthete brought to an abrupt halt. "Now, Theodore, really, there are limits! What are you trying to say?"

"Not a great deal, really."

"Not a great deal? But it sounds like a great deal, and most confounding at that. The implication is that somehow ... that somehow my hunch was right, that she sent me!—yes, that she sent me in order to make that discovery and to disclose for your satisfaction the confirming evidence!"

"Upon reflection, I think she did just that."

"And you too, no doubt, had your self-styled 'omniscient' hand in this invidious plot?"

"Plot? Invidious? Now who among us is masquerading under the articles of reproof?" Besserman laughed, "I hasten to assure you that there was no plot, no unwritten script into which you were cast as an unwitting actor. And invidious? Hardly a term to describe what you yourself so deftly, or was it so ineptly, and at so many stages, initiated, though I should bless your soul all my days for your having done so. I would not doubt for a moment but that Cornelia had no 'designs' upon you when you entered her suite at the

Regency. By the end of the interview, however, or perhaps somewhere in the midst of it, she had, for whatever reasons, decided to shift, to transfer, or better, to share a responsibility with you—that is, the task of finishing up whatever minor details were left in Uncle Aloysius's affairs, since Clotilde Carey had apprised her of them. You can imagine how important, how personal, that would be to her. What she had intended to do, she asked you to do—not because she sought to avoid the pain involved, for she, of all persons, would never act from such a motive. I don't know what you did to merit, in that instance, her decision to pursue such a course of action. I don't think you have told me everything about your interview with her, and I wouldn't expect you to. There are now things between you and her that are none of my concern. And I am glad about that. Moreover, I have little doubt that your commission was effected in genuine ignorance of everything you might find. Such ignorance, however ingenuous it might be, could cut both ways: it opened up a possibility, and only that. It was certainly, as I would understand it, a rather characteristically Schefflin gesture—a kind of gift to you, a portioning out of something that could make you part of us, that could, in the end, make your story our story as well."

When I tried to speak, Besserman forestalled me with a wave of the hand. "Cornelia," he resumed, "has always been, in my judgment, a woman of supreme prudence and forethought—that is, and this may surprise you very much, Edmund, she doesn't make plans in the usual sense; she doesn't have designs. For her, prudence has a just and singular place to go, which in turn gives a direction, or more accurately, a range of directions all more or less adjusted to that same end, for it recognizes, with startling honesty and clarity, that very little is, in any real sense, under our control, under our 'management,' as we should phrase it in contemporary terms. To be more specific, I don't think that she knew with any certainty that the pink envelope would be there amongst Uncle Aloysius's effects; she suspected it might be, even though there were excellent reasons to figure it might not be there. One could, for example, have the impression, as I certainly did, that the note had been left where it was at the time of the obsequies and had been enclosed in and buried with the coffin. Further, if it was not there but elsewhere, tucked most probably in heaven only knows where, virtually irrecoverable, again she did not, and could not, know; but she did surmise that, if you found it, you might open it and, having opened it, report back to me with what you had discovered.

"In all of this I see nothing more than her situating of things in terms of a potential occurrence—a potentiality, I would add, not somehow imposed upon but rather inherent in those things thus situated. It takes both generosity and trust to allow things to happen in that way; it takes grace and simplicity to accept when things don't happen in the way one wants them to happen, and most of the time they don't. I might also add that, unless you so decide to inform her, Cornelia will never know the results of her action. If I can claim to know anything at all about who she is, I can presume to say that she is not sitting somewhere waiting for a result. She did what she thought was proper. Beyond that, she would be the first to recognize that such things pass into others' hands; it is up to them to make of them what they consider fit. Furthermore, if I can claim to know anything about who you are, you will decide not to inform her of the outcome, because to do so would be, in some sense, to divest the affair of precisely—how should I call it?—the trustful audacity with which it was so spontaneously offered."

"Shall I take that statement, Theodore, as an observation or as an injunction?"

"An observation certainly. If it had been necessary to counsel you on such a matter, I should have said nothing at all."

"But we shall, shall we not," I said, "transfer the satchel to Cornelia, whenever it is convenient to do so. After all, if it belongs to anyone, it belongs to her. I would think that the proper time to make that transfer would be in this office when she again visits the United States. I can't fathom sending it through the international mail and having some perplexed customs officials browsing through its contents. And when we hand it over and she searches through it, as we can be sure eventually she will do, she will find, among those other things, the pink envelope that we shall have replaced by that time. She is likely to ask me about it."

Besserman disagreed. "I think it is just as likely she will not ask you about it. Having given you the commission she did, she is the last person who is apt to enjoin you for a report on your findings. If she does ask, then just tell her exactly what has happened. Whatever she wants to know, let her know. You are not dealing with a vulnerable or a captious personality here."

"And if she doesn't ask?"

"If she doesn't ask, which, as I said, I suspect she won't, then she has elected to leave the matter alone, and therefore it is well to act accordingly. If that is what she does, she will have good reasons for doing so. She will draw, I am certain, the right conclusions."

As I think of it now, I was reassured by this minor exchange with Besserman. Still, there were matters—a number of them—that needed clarification. I presupposed that we would get to each in its proper order. Nevertheless, I pursued the immediate subject further: "So things might not have happened as they did. There may have been no pink envelope. I may not have had the predisposition to snatch it away as I did, and then to open the note and read it."

"To be sure," Besserman replied, "as you say, things might not have happened as they did, in which case we would have been where we were heretofore, which was all right, wasn't it? But they did happen, and we are still all right, even a great deal better off, as I see it. And, this is what is so prodigious, it is all brought to a kind of completion—as much completion as ever really happens in this tatterdemalion life of ours. That old rapscallion himself would have been glad to know."

"Now, you do mean Frederick, don't you?" I queried.

"Yes, I do mean Frederick. Edmund, don't you see the beauty of it all—a beauty the like of which only Frederick could have envisaged? Yes . . . finally . . . it's all his work in a way, his setting up of the potentialities, his mode of action. I am not thinking simply of our more immediate discovery, our confirmation. But rather consider the original event itself: the house in Concord with the sun streaming sporadically through the great, tall windows, the deathbed, the fourteen-year-old child drawn aside into the library, the pink envelope, the final gaze exchanged between Uncle Aloysius and Cornelia after he had read the note and as she stood by the door looking in at him—Cornelia so immensely collected in her grief, containing all she was being asked to contain in an unsurpassable reserve of emotional power and restraint, as if that moment of discovery configured for her, in a single *aperçu*, both the saddest and happiest recognition in her life. What a moment, Edmund! How much more sense does it make to me now! What a consummation of a humane and decent happiness in the very purview of death itself!

"As I reflect upon it again, I realize that when I entered that house it was not unlike entering the stateroom in the *Mauritania* a decade and a half earlier: I was entering a situation in which a whole series of decisions had been made and agreements concluded. The constituency had altered and would alter even more before I would leave the house that same afternoon. How thoroughly, it seems to me, and with what portentous resolution did Frederick have to renounce his most important claim, one of the most important claims he had in this whole wide world, so that Uncle Aloysius could become in the fading hours of his life what he had always been in the deepest sense—the father of his own child. For Frederick had not just one but three important things to do: to inform Cornelia that a deeply beloved person was soon to die; to surrender in this act his own deeply cherished paternity to this other person; and, what's even more—and how acutely he must have realized this—to open up for Cornelia that staggering opportunity of bringing peace and completion to Uncle Aloysius's life. And she did just that.

"Edmund, I could not believe for a moment that Frederick had instructed her to do what she did. It was her own decision. She did what she did in as pure and as simple a manner in which it could have been done—in that immediacy of death to confer life, life flourishing with all its durability and plenitude. I cannot even begin to imagine the happiness that the note must have brought to Uncle Aloysius, and the depth of knowledge, of understanding, of intimacy in that final look between father and daughter. Uncle Aloysius would die in the ineffable peace of that acknowledgment. And Cornelia also, having entered into that acknowledgment, would now understand it in its totality—a totality that would remain with her, with all its pain, with all its sorrow, with all its joy, for the rest of her life.

"But that's not all, Edmund. For now I understand that another most extraordinary thing had simultaneously occurred. Up to this point, don't you see, Cornelia had been brought up in many ways more by Uncle Aloysius than by anyone else. In a paradoxical sense, even in his role as uncle, he had been her father in a moral as well as in a physical sense; through the years,

Frederick had, indirectly, already given her over, in some subtle way, to her uncle's paternity, for though he loved her deeply, he realized—with what inner anguish on his part we can only guess—that Uncle Aloysius had, in spite of everything, the prior claim, the authentic claim, which he could in no wise gainsay or inhibit, though certainly Uncle Aloysius never pressed the claim.

"In consequence, as Cornelia grew up, she was not, in those early years, really much of a Schefflin at all in any genuine sense. She was a Fitzgerald occupying a Schefflin household. But, through the years, she had been absorbing the Schefflin identity as well, and when she emerged from the library that afternoon, and how sharply I remember it, she emerged with all that seriousness and clarity and composure that was above all the hallmark of Frederick's character. In renouncing his assumed fatherhood, Frederick became for the first time a real father in the most spiritual meaning of the term. She came out of that room genuinely and forever after his daughter. When he passed on to her that momentous word, that weight of moral resolve, she, in taking it up in the way that she took it up, became a Schefflin as well as a Fitzgerald, became a Schefflin in this regard to the very depths and roots of her character, and has remained so ever since. She was, as it were, reborn in Frederick, to bear in the utmost dignity and in the utmost secrecy of her heart that great mystery of suffering that she was witnessing and that she would now forever share. That is the Schefflin legacy right there, Edmund, to elevate inconsolable loss into the promise of immeasurable fecundity. Out of that promise arises, again and again, renewal, rebirth, not just the continuity of life but its perpetual freshness and vitality. Do you not see, Edmund? The last wonder is greater than the first!"

Besserman hesitated again, as if pondering which way to develop his train of thought. There were still loose ends, as I considered it, yet to be accounted for. I had little doubt but that these were now the elements of his meditation. And so they were. But I would act as catalyst again: was that not my role? I decided to confront the matter indirectly. "And what we know now—that, too, is part of the story, as you say?"

"Very much part of the story, yet in such a surprising way, the more I reflect on it," Besserman added. "Cornelia's silence all these years, Frederick's silence—how many tasks did that perform, after all, especially when one takes into account that there were, of course ... others ..."

"To be considered," I said, completing the sentence for him.

"To be considered. Yes, most eminently! Agnes ... there was, above all, Agnes. How central she was to all of this! Knowing Frederick as I do, I know that he would have acted purely in consort with her on a matter of such grave importance; they would have—I can just see it now—weighed every word together, every gesture, every eventuality, insofar as such things can be weighed—combining his analytical caution with her synoptic verve, her oversight. She may indeed have hovered above all of us in that instance, silent, watching, rueful, elegantly but volubly mute. The more I think of it, especially now that we are in no uncertain possession of the key factor, the more her remarkable presence on that final day of Uncle Aloysius's life becomes strikingly clear. You could also say she was, in a way, the 'hostess' of that event—if you will forgive such an inadequate and rather trite analogy—but she made things happen, was sure that everything was in its right place so that others could act on it.

"She had to renounce something that day too—something of inexpressible importance to her as well—and her renunciation may have even been more difficult than Frederick's. Agnes was, in some sense, the real maternal presence in all of this, in whose circumference of warmth and breadth of spirit everything was given birth and substance. At a moment when, as we are told, the most deeply rooted instinct in the maternal heart is to grasp tight and hold on, she let go—let go with a graciousness we can hardly describe. Perhaps there are times when we need to understand that the generosity we associate with the maternal impulse can operate at levels and in ways we can scarcely imagine. Perhaps she had been preparing herself for this contingency for years. Perhaps in what may very well have been for her a mounting succession of painful adjustments in 'sharing' Cornelia's childhood more and more over the years with another household, she had inured herself to what she foresaw as an inevitable realignment of her maternal attachment. But I rather doubt all of that. She knew very well, I'm sure, that no matter when and how such a realignment should occur, no matter how much the grounds for its support would shift beneath it at one level, at another level nothing would happen at all. Her—what did we call it—'synoptic' vantage understood too well the personages involved, the steadiness and pertinacity of their relationships. But even such a confidence could scarcely allay the pathos of her consent. As I see it now, in no respect was her maternal presence more manifest than in the way she suborned her own loss to the losses felt by others, transmuting their losses into what she took on as her own most distinctive loss, gathering them up into one 'synoptic' whole. Is there any more magisterial way that, in the realm of the spirit, one can 'ensoul' the souls of others?

"There may have been another renunciation on her part—one that is perhaps not too easy for us to understand: to surrender such an enactment, in fealty and trust, as she did, into Frederick's hands. She had to commission him to be the agent of their mutual consent. How she had to 'deplete' herself of what was most cherished for her we can only surmise. In the end, though, as we have said, she lost nothing at all. She too, like Frederick, simultaneously lost and gained a daughter. Of that you can be sure. From everything I have been able to discern, Cornelia, if nothing else, made certain beyond a shade of doubt, that Agnes's role in her life would be sustained and nourished as exactly as it had been in the past, and yes, as it would be, even more fully than ever before, for all the days of Agnes's life. Again and again, Agnes was replenished out of the boundless gratitude and affection of Cornelia's heart. I might mention in passing, what may or may not be of significance to some people, that in the course of events, sometime after Frederick's death, Agnes followed Cornelia's journey into the faith of Uncle Aloysius. Cornelia helped her to gather up all that lay dormant in her over the years in that respect and to bring it to fruition. That may not mean much to us, Edmund; those doggedly encrypted scotomas in our field of vision yield little else but an obdurate blindness in these matters. But I have good reason to be convinced, over and over again by so many I have known, that to those whose hearts flower within the compact of a sacramental life, as they understand it, its radiance and moral depth is never to be underestimated. What more can we, in good faith, add to this?"

"Except for one more detail . . . !"

"One more detail?"

"One rather critical detail."

"Ah-ha, Edmund, now I think I anticipate you; I am ready for all your moves. And that detail? Be certain that I had not proposed to neglect it, but I shall allot you the privilege of pronouncing it. It is, after all, your move."

"Aunt Bernice."

"Aunt Bernice," Besserman echoed. He leaned his head back on the chair so as to take in the long, evening glow that had gradually filled the room with its muted and delicate hues. The myriad mementos of his life scattered about on the tables and bookshelves and mantelpiece seemed to cast long shadows over the room. In the peace and silence that followed his invocation of her name, I glanced again over those precious things: the violin in its showcase, the pink envelope enshrined above the hearth, the old photographs, the pictures of Frederick and Agnes, of Cornelia sitting by the "ivory fount," of Besserman holding his tennis racket. I saw the picture of Uncle Aloysius, too, recessed in its own shadowy niche. And there was Aunt Bernice herself, standing by her bicycle, her long white dress gathered around her knees, her head angled so winsomely as she smiled at the camera. Besserman, now almost fully shrouded in shadows, finally remarked: "You always come back to Aunt Bernice, don't you? I rather think you have a special place in your heart for her. Perhaps—now, would it be too extravagant to plead—you identify with her in some fashion?" He chuckled to himself, as if immensely pleased with this suggestion.

"Well," I proposed, "she is the one who really doesn't fit in all of this. She is the outsider, isn't she? She is there, inadvertently or otherwise, but by the same token she is not really there either, a visitor from a foreign world, a stranger, an alien even in the enchanted kingdom you have so methodically unscrolled for me. And so, oddly, am I. Both she and I have rather transitory, if not altogether cameo, roles in this complex production, wouldn't you agree?"

Besserman drew a deep breath. "Aunt Bernice would have loved your theatrical metaphors. You would have done her proud. I have no doubt of that. But, since you have brought yourself so unequivocally into the picture at this juncture, I will start with you and get back to Aunt Bernice."

"That sounds good to me," I consented, wondering what direction this would take us in.

"You might recall that earlier in our conversation you took some … perhaps offense at the implication that you were 'set up' by Cornelia to make the discovery you did. Further, you asked if my own—now, how did you say it?—'omniscient hand' were involved. I think I may have satisfied your curiosity as to the first point. But the second point remains to be discussed."

"Yes," I responded, "though my 'offense' was rather more simulated than real. In any case, I did wonder how you might be involved. A conspiracy perhaps?"

"Well, hardly! But why, Edmund, if I may revert to an earlier question, why *did* you open Cornelia's note?"

I was silent. What really could I say to that? How does one exculpate one's occasional forays into impulsiveness?

He went on, "After all, it was, arguably, none of your business. Do you always open other people's most intimate communications? Explain yourself."

"Well … I was just curious; that's all." A puerile excuse, I realized, even as I said it.

"Is that all?"

"All right, I was dying to know."

"Is that all?"

"All right, you said it yourself, I wanted to be part of your story! I wanted to be able to bring to you what might very well be the finishing touch."

"And what a wonderful moment it must have been for you: that cocktail lounge, as you have described it to me, with its indubitably shapeless music, its soft lights, its plush furnishings, its acquiescence precisely in what has no line or form or measure. I know that sort of place and have not been, at times in my life, altogether immune to its attractions: an environment where one can, for the time being, submerge oneself in its gratifyingly narcissistic fragrances and ill-defined opiate dreams. Who has not wanted to be, at junctures in their lives, transmogrified into a florid seaweed combed back and forth by surf and current in the tepid waters of a tidal flat? And then, by way of contrast, a projectile thrusts itself out of a different era, so sharp, so absolute, in a sense, that would carry you back into the heart of the story itself, that would give you an unparalleled intimacy with it. Your eyes were, with the greatest likelihood at that moment, the first eyes after Uncle Aloysius to read that communication; and probably the only eyes other than his to do so. Don't you see, you were an outsider, but you made yourself central. You have a wonderful propensity for bolting through doors, Edmund, though not the wrong but the right doors."

"But what does all of this have to do with your 'omniscient hand,' Theodore?"

"I shall make an effort to explain. First, Edmund, you mentioned in our first interview that, as a child, you frequented the Boylston Street Schefflin's every Saturday during the winter with your family. It was for dinner, following a matinee at one of the downtown theaters. It was something of a ritual for your family. A very nice ritual, I would think, and the kind that adults, years later, remember very fondly."

"Well, I suspect anyone could ascertain these facts from the little I said about it, as clearly you have. And yes, my memories of that are especially affectionate. It was a warm and hospitable place, as I recall, where one felt very much at home."

"That memory might also be especially fond because your perhaps over-indulgent parents allowed you to cap off, systematically, every dinner with a chocolate sundae as well as to gallop over to the pastry counter to pick out the sweets for the drive home, a task you undertook with no little panache. And why were you granted the privilege of making those choices when apparently your brother and sister were not? I think it was because you simply enjoyed so much what you were doing and had the temerity to do it."

"Theodore! Don't tell me you have done research on my childhood eating habits! And you even have a charge to bring against me! A usurpation of sibling rights, perhaps? Did you simply divine all of this, having read the telltale signs in some revelatory wrinkle on my forehead? Or do I bear some suspicious crumbs and stains perpetually upon the cuff of my shirtsleeve? Or, better yet, have you employed a private detective to follow me from the days of my infancy?"

Theodore shook his head. "No, Edmund, none of that! It's really all quite simple. You see, I was there; or, rather, we were there."

"You were there!"

"It just so happens that Martha and I had our rituals too, pretty much the same sort of thing for a few years, in this case. But it was not always the cinema matinees we attended—though sometimes we did. We were childless, and perhaps that had something to do with the delight we took in watching your family going through its 'dinner out' antics. My goodness, but all of you were a lively troop! We even came to know your names and would say hello to your parents as they passed our table. We were, I would think, for you and your siblings merely part of the adult scenery that children are so skillful at ignoring. But I particularly remember you, your excitement at being 'out,' your impulse to want to do the unusual thing, to take the chance, your willingness, as both Martha and I conjectured, to barge through any door there was to barge through; to try anything new and exciting."

"So that's how you knew about the ginger cookies!"

"I did remember, didn't I, that poignant detail. I had good reason to. On one occasion, your parents actually sent you over to our table to offer us some of the confections you had picked out. We were just enthralled. I had a little conversation with you. I asked you which ones you particularly recommended. It was the ginger cookies all right. Unlike most children, you were perfectly happy to talk with complete strangers, although I don't know if you were perfectly happy to have to surrender some of those favored morsels. Often, you liked to grab a whole bunch of them from the parental purchase and stuff them in your pockets. Actually, you did the same thing just the other day."

"Did what?" I interrupted.

"Stuffed your pockets with some ginger cookies as you were leaving. Anyway, Martha was so thrilled. On the way home that night, she said, in some wistful flight of fancy, I'm afraid, how nice it would be to have a little son like you. My word, how she did dwell on that now and then in later years! She would imagine the two of us taking you to the circus and watching the elephants and the clowns. We would load you up with cartons of popcorn. Alas, we never did go to the circus; we didn't have anyone to take with us."

I didn't know how to react to any of this. Then I said, "So I did have, as you say, a 'little conversation' with you?"

"Indeed."

"Maybe that's why I thought, when I first entered your office, that somehow I had seen you before. "

"I wouldn't be surprised."

"Except that I couldn't place you. I thought that maybe you reminded me of our Lebanese grocer back when I grew up in Somerville."

Besserman shrugged his shoulders. "I have, I must confess, always enjoyed washing and fluffing out heads of lettuce. Sometimes I have regretted not having a pushcart somewhere to sell my wares. I used to be very good at growing my own tomatoes. I might mention in passing that there is someone else who joined us for dinner one evening whom you probably didn't notice, but who noticed you."

"Don't tell me!" I pleaded. "Okay," I cried, "tell me!"

"Well, a teenage girl, spindly, tall for her age . . ."

"Cornelia!"

"You said it. We had made a point of drawing her attention to your family and to you. Really, Edmund, that's partly why you are here. Yes, we did our research. I had had a list of possible candidates submitted to me by one of my associates. I found a number of persons with fine credentials—such fine credentials indeed, as is so often the case in a search like this, that it is difficult to distinguish one candidate from another. But your name happened, incidentally, to appear on that list. Marvel of marvels, after all these years, I recognized your name, with some surprise, I might add, and I knew that such a connection for me was enough to make you different from the others, at least in that limited respect; and that the association of the Foundation's name with something out of your family and personal history, however tenuous it might be, would be sufficient to attract your attention once we had contacted you. Naturally, I made further inquiries, and, as soon as I had settled on you, I figured that you would hardly be able to refrain from exploring the offer—not that you would remember me, which I would not have expected at all, but that you would remember the ritual that had been part of your family's life together. You see, you would have the attachment, the 'fond memory,' that would make all the difference; and you would have, indeed did have, what I will call, for the moment, the 'pluck' to act on it. Most people in your position wouldn't have done so, would not have been so willing to step out of the 'mainstream,' especially once their careers had crystallized into a successful posture that would be difficult to reconfigure. Imagine, to countenance, with perfect composure, I assume, that mercurial apparition of Mr. Gleason suddenly sprouting up before you at the head of your desk with a summons held out in his spatulate hand, then to venture up this somewhat derelict street and to sally through that all-too-monumental archaic door downstairs, even to ride a glass elevator almost a century out of date, knowing not a great deal in advance but already committed, in some way, to taking up the challenge, to finding out what it was all about, but even more to becoming part of it, if that were possible."

"And this, Theodore, you knew from the start, as it were!" I railed.

"Nothing of the sort, Edmund," Besserman tossed back. "I am as innocent as Cornelia in this regard. But I had ascertained, what apparently she also had ascertained in her interview with you, that your response to things could be unpredictable—and yet in only the most complimentary sense. She knew that you had something in you that tipped her off, something you tumbled through or stumbled on that ensured … that ensured …"

"Yes, that ensured …?"

"You would do it again, if and when the opportunity to do it again gratuitously presented itself. I guess I shall never know, shall I, with what intrepid faux pas, with what dauntless gaffe you plunged through just the door that needed to be plunged through."

"Indeed you shall never know!" I stammered.

"Granted. Meanwhile, we have our confirmation, and we know what we know by means of you, which makes you really central after all. Yes, both of you."

"Both?"

"Yes. Hence we come back to Aunt Bernice. Like you …"

"An outsider."

"In a way; yet central. I mean, even more central, some might be willing to contend, than anyone else. Aunt Bernice is, after all, the hidden genie in this story, the spirit in the lamp who glows at surprising moments with unsurpassable incandescence and disappears again into obscurity, who is the heart and soul of so much we have addressed. I will not deny that, in some sense or other, there may have been shadows that darkened, at least in the most conventional sense, her own particular destiny—some might be disposed to call it a self-absorption, a lack of some horizon that all of us need to live our lives with the breadth of responsibility appropriate to them. But I shall forbear from making any definitive judgment in this matter. There is simply too much about her we do not know. In any case, it was she who, as they say, drew the 'bottom line,' as stunning as it was to our sensibilities and yet so consonant with that complex vision she had of herself, and who could not be deflected from her aims. It was she who gave Frederick and Agnes the most important gift they ever had, who conferred, in her way, parentage upon them, thereby bringing forth from them an ever greater measure of all the determination they could, and would, garner to make things good in the lives of those around them. It was she who gave us, all of us, Cornelia—no, not just in the pure physical sense, though that in itself would have been enough to sing her praises through all eternity—but also in a spiritual sense. For all that we can say about how deeply Cornelia may have been forged in, and by, the hearts of Agnes and Frederick and Uncle Aloysius himself, she was, she remained, in the core of her being, the daughter of her own mother: a child, and then a woman, whose incomparable éclat, whose sheer brilliance of spirit, came from Aunt Bernice and would inspire the cavalcade of loyalties and admiration everywhere she has gone and in everyone she has known.

"But I am sure you are wondering, at this point, Edmund, in the event, in that most crucial event, in Concord so many years ago, what else happened? A revelation of fatherhood was, as well, a revelation of motherhood. That may indeed have been the most difficult line to cross for everybody in this case. For Uncle Aloysius, the journey was at an end; for Aunt Bernice, the journey was just beginning, or at least taking a radical turn. But, to all appearances, it did not work out that way. We will never know what may have passed—as certainly something did—between Aunt Bernice on one hand and Frederick and Agnes on the other in those minutes before Cornelia was drawn aside into the library while Agnes held on tightly to Aunt Bernice's hands as they sat together in the kitchen. Just what was passing between them, their hands knit together in that heartrending silence, as motherhood itself was being conveyed from one sister to the other in the adjoining room? We may surely guess that prior consent had been sought and won, and that some other agreements were reached as well. Frederick, as you may recall, had reserved for himself the privilege of initiating the moment and nature of whatever disclosure had to be made; but he attached that privilege to the corresponding obligation of seeking and abiding by the consent of others. You can be sure that Aunt Bernice's consent was, in any event, the decisive factor. Can you imagine her dilemma? Fourteen years earlier she thought that the curtain had dropped on the act, or the *entr'acte*, or whatever it was, of her natural motherhood, only to see a new act beginning and the curtain rising again. She was caught on the stage with no script prepared, no costume, no scenic background. She had to depend, this time, on what others would do. That is why the agreements they made were more important than ever for her, though the nature of those agreements will ever elude us; but then they would have been made, under any circumstances, for Cornelia's sake, and hers alone—giving Cornelia, in the end, as I am certain, the range of possibilities necessary to act as she saw fit.

"We can only presume to know the terms of those agreements by observing their consequences. And their consequences, from what I have ever been able to observe, were to retain an understanding already reached, already in operation. Hence, there was no radically new journey commencing for either mother or child in their relationship to one another, at least as far as any of us could see—just a transition, notable enough, but conferring barely a tremor in its occurrence. Every bond of fidelity was preserved precisely as it was, precisely as it had already been defined. And all official titles were preserved as well. Cornelia made that choice; she knew how to make that choice. It was an act of consummate generosity to everyone she loved. And that was all the more reason why there were matters about which we could not speak; why, in the passage of years, we had little other choice than to abstain from any direct discourse about it. A subtle equipoise of humane fidelities could not be abused by the inevitable abrasiveness of speech itself."

I remarked, "Do you mean, Theodore, a fiction of a sort? Or perhaps a fiction of a fiction—almost, as it were, a double negative, each side, in a sense, canceling out the other, making, in the end, a positive?"

"No, I should not call it a fiction. I should call it an understanding nuanced and flexible enough to alter its features as necessary and yet remain tacit, a finely tuned arrangement that had worked and would continue to work as it did, that had preserved a certain dignity and balance in a complex human situation and could continue to do so; where the truth is known but is a silent truth, a premise always acted upon but never spoken of. One could say that, if the substance had changed, even changed as radically as was possible, the original scaffolding of its conformation remained securely in place. Aunt Bernice remained thereafter 'Aunt Bernice.' Maintaining the outward forms of the original compact ensured that the very carriage of Aunt Bernice's apparent indifference, the reserve her particular genius needed to feed upon, would in itself be the vehicle through which that genius would be mediated and her maternal solicitation, as far as that went, sustained. It would allot the 'space'—if I may use such a contemporary expression—to Cornelia to be both niece and daughter at the same time: to respect, as niece, her mother's reserve, and to meet, as daughter, the obligations, now mutually recognized more than ever between them both, of caring for her in a special way.

"I take the liberty of conjecturing, with confidence, that whatever Aunt Bernice gave Cornelia, Cornelia returned a hundredfold, fashioning for her mother, especially in her final years, even, as it often had to be from halfway across the globe, a domain of peace and dignity. However we may want, in the end, to ascertain the strengths and weaknesses of Aunt Bernice, this we must acknowledge: that she thrived, nowhere more fully, certainly not even in that life she perhaps projected for herself, than in the glorious certainty that she was loved; that she was loved in a very special way by the person, by Cornelia, who was, as now could fully be acknowledged by both of them, the fruition and sign of a prior love; that, in that prior love, she had been loved, unconditionally, not just by anybody, but by a person most capable of love and most capable of appreciating who she was; by, in short, the most exceptional man she had ever known. Perhaps unable to love in that same way, she had needed this love more than anything else to make her life meaningful and complete. And when he was gone, there was someone whose love could, up to a point, take the place of his; someone who was the living embodiment of the two of them together. I imagine that Cornelia was not alone in fulfilling the demands of this project; that she would inform, enlist, encourage, at varying levels, her spouse, her children, all her new connections, in this effort, can scarcely be doubted. All of this sublime and bountiful mimicry would have pleased immensely Aunt Bernice's dramatic bent, the perpetuation of a role she had so well mastered, even as Cornelia's children would have found it delightfully arch and *bien amusant* to refer to someone they knew was their *grand-mère* by the altogether gamesome title of 'Grand-Aunt Bernice.'

"What, naturally, remains—will remain, I figure—a conundrum for us, now that we have had confirmed for us the true state of affairs, is how Cornelia negotiated a course through what must have been an uneasy passage regarding the understandings and perplexities of her paternal Irish family. I could never address this subject with her, obviously, because I did not have the confirmation that would authorize me to do so; nor did she volunteer anything about it, probably because she did not know what I knew and felt she could not ask me about it. But I rather suspect, knowing her as I do, that she found a way, that she would not let this issue rest until she had fully met the demands of justice and integrity in this case. I have no doubt, given the heartfelt acceptance of her among her Fitzgerald family members and her deep associations with them over the years, that she had succeeded in placing herself firmly among them as one of their own and in fully vindicating the honor and fidelity of her real father, as if, in any real sense, he had needed such a vindication in the first place."

"Which brings us back, finally, to Uncle Aloysius himself...," I said.

"... even to that, even to him, just, if you recall, where we began," Besserman finished my thought. "You wondered why, when you first asked about him, his picture was so strangely placed, in a niche by itself, set off from all the rest. We are not always prepared to give explanations for matters of that sort. Why do we arrange things on a tabletop the way we do? Or in a bookshelf? Or in an album? Why do we give prominence to some things and less to others? Why do we place one item close to another and far from yet another? Sometimes our reasons are clear; sometimes not. For me, I guess, Uncle Aloysius is set apart too, but in a special way; he is the tragic presence among us, the protagonist, the scholars would say, of the story I have had to tell. The purpose of his niche is not to hide him but rather to gather us all, to funnel us into the depths of his bounteous and beautiful soul. It is the calm gravity of his great suffering that has given dignity, finally, to all we have preserved. And it is that love, his love, that stupendous love, that has given us, in this case . . ." Besserman hesitated again.

I repeated for him, ". . . that has given us, in this case . . . ?"

"Everything—yes, everything. He, above all, as I referred to him once before with you, Edmund, is the chevalier of the heart, the paragon of gallantry, the knight errant who has, for the sake of others, broached the darksome forest, emptied himself into the abode of desolation, and emerged, in the end, embowered in an accolade of triumph, an accolade of light. And what more could we have than that? What more could we want than that? And what more could we say about it?"

Besserman withdrew into some private meditation, his head lowered and his lips pressed against his cupped hands. He spoke again: "Nevertheless, I still wonder, all this being said and done, that Frederick never breathed a word to me. I can imagine, as consonant with Frederick's way of doing things, that he figured I would simply have to find out for myself. Maybe his early and unexpected demise in a faraway place prevented his telling me what others had agreed he should finally tell me, and then they thought he had followed through on that; and my own confidentiality within that circle would have never disabused them of that notion."

"Theodore, if he had told you, what then?"

"Well . . . I think that is difficult enough to say. A counterfactual hypothesis like that can lead to limitless possibilities."

"But some possibilities do get excluded necessarily."

"Such as . . . ?"

"Such as me."

"You, Edmund?"

"And my part in this story."

"Ah!"

"And your part too, if I may say so, Theodore!"

"How's that?"

"You have been granted the privilege of telling it—of telling it all."

"I don't understand."

"Wasn't that item, that 'capital point,' finally the question, the big question that tethered the circumference of the story? Because of that, and that alone, you have had the opportunity to relate everything—everything from beginning to end, just as you have done; to put it all together, just as you have done. In our review of the case—and what a supreme juridical brief it has been—we have given an account of all the participants in this story, except, finally, for you. And you, Theodore, your task, commission, was to put it all together. That was your job. That is what you wanted to do, wasn't it? "

"Ah!"

"Wasn't it?"

"Yes, it was."

"Not just what you wanted, but what you felt obliged to do."

"Yes."

"Frederick bequeathed to you, among so many things, just that privilege—a privilege to fulfill that obligation. And you have exercised that privilege and brought the circle to a close."

"Ah!"

"That's why Frederick never told you. He never told you so that you, in the end, could tell it. It would be your story. You might recall in our conversation of a few weeks ago how you described for me the final hours of a soiree at Madison Street when Frederick played a cello solo for the remaining guests and how the tones of that composition seemed to weave all the facets of your lives together. Now you have performed, for me, on the cello of your soul, as it were, a work of your own improvisation, a cadenza for a cello, mellow and wise, diaphanous and resonant. And now it's done."

"And now it's done!" Besserman echoed. "I hope I have done it as well as you suggest in your marvelous metaphors. But with that, don't you see Edmund, with that the covenant has been fulfilled, has reached, indeed, its completion, its termination. The pink envelope has revealed the mystery and opened it up like a glorious blossom. Now you, too, can tell the story, Edmund. You are free to pass it on, to tell whomever you want, to tell all the world if that is your disposition!"

Besserman clapped his hands together; he clapped them so forcefully that it almost seemed to thrust him off his seat.

"How blessed are we!" he cried. *"How goodly our portion! How pleasant our lot! How beautiful our inheritance!"*

He arose with a sudden motion from his great armchair and extended his massive hand toward me. "And now you will, I presume, accept what I formally offer you, Edmund—to be a partner in the trusteeship of the Foundation."

"Theodore, isn't this a rather sudden change of subject? I'm not ready for this yet!"

"Not at all! As you said, 'now it's done.' My work is completed. My days of stewardship may now happily draw to a close."

I arose to grasp his hand, perplexed by the immediacy of his gesture. "Of course I accept. But you sound a bit final in all of this. We will have much business to do together. And doesn't your decision need to be approved by the board?"

"It already has been. Its final pronouncement was simply contingent upon our finishing up certain unfinished business. Yes, we have much to do, but only what is necessary to effect a few alterations in administrative details. You will do it all the more efficiently the sooner I have made, to use a lovely Shakespearian word, my 'quietus' from these noble lodgings." We sat again in our respective seats.

"But what will you do, Theodore? I can't imagine . . ."

"Then don't imagine. I have settled my accounts, and my accounts are good. Only I wish to doze before I sleep. I have things to think about, to remember in the proper sort of way; and I have some thank-you notes to write. They must, you know, be written with the most requisite care."

"Isn't this all, if you will pardon the expression, being just a trifle lugubrious?" I chided.

"Well . . . if you insist. I had no intention of broaching such a matter. I can assure you of that—it's all unpremeditated. But I do have, nevertheless, a timetable to observe that is as benevolent as it is decisive. But 'lugubrious'? Perhaps you mock me, Edmund, but I don't think so. Oh, there are times when I wish I were a man of the desert and that I could speak with the lips of one who has fed on locusts and wild honey. I have on occasions some clue of what my forebears were said to know—the rank aroma of camels, the distant bleating of ewes and braying of she-asses as they nibbled at the sparse tufts of grass in a desert wadi, the herdsman sitting at the entrance to his tent in the cool of the evening. But that is all in the imagery, Edmund, and I suppose finally that it is as remote to me as it is to you. Nor, for all the solitary aloofness of my domicile here, am I a dweller upon a mountain fastness; I have pitched no pavilion, and I await no revelation. This is not something, you understand, that I boast about. My home is the *civitas*, the city of man, and I must speak out of both the limits and the richness which that fact affords me. You must know, too, how much I love it, the vast and multiform paraphernalia of it; yet, and here I most earnestly admonish you, if for a moment we should entertain the notion that all of it—our courts and universities and museums, our theaters and hospitals and libraries, our conservatories and churches and businesses and institutes of a thousand kinds, our workshops and studios and farms and a multitude of other things that constitute the human project on the face of the earth—that all of it, jointly or severally, is somehow what finally counts, why then we shall have diminished the good it can represent into nothing but sheer, irreclaimable rubbish. We shall do nothing, in that moment, but debase it and divest it of meaning and order."

"What is it, then, that counts, Theodore?" I asked, surprised by this disquisition, prophetic in spite of itself, the speech of a man who does dwell on lofty mountain fastnesses.

There was a long pause in our conversation. Besserman seemed to be mulling over something of import, a reply to my query, however tentative, however groping it might be. "What counts?" he murmured. "Well, you don't really expect me to answer that, do you? Then again, I suppose you do. It is a righteous question. Maybe, in the end, it is the only righteous inquiry we can make. And it is likewise just to think that we must, in the end, give an account of ourselves, however limited and limiting that may be.

"Would it be altogether too arrogant of me to venture that what counts is . . . after all, whatever it is that defines the purpose of those all-too-human, all-too-fragile arrangements we value so highly? That perhaps they bestow, in principle at least, the hub for a community of mutual deference, of generosity, of a civility so deep that there is no aspect of our lives that is not penetrated to its very core by it, a civility so tenacious that it bears up under the most outrageous opposition without compromising its principles and without succumbing to the tragic incivility of others? Yet even that civility, in turn, that ethical substratum of all that is vital for us, depends upon how we conceive of what is even prior to it, what makes it possible in the first place.

"I hope you can forgive the ruminations of an old man, Edmund, but you know, as one gets older and older, one's awareness of the world just keeps getting larger and larger. One realizes how much more there is to see, and how very little of it one has actually seen; how much more there is to understand, and how little of it one has, finally, understood. How little do we ever know about one single human life, including our own.

"When one recalls the good things of one's life—the persons, the happenings, the things one admired so deeply—that were so inexplicably 'there' for us, in precisely the configuration they took specifically for us as who we are; when one considers that one has experienced only the most miniscule portion of all that is, of the inexpressible richness of things; then one must be struck dumb by the recognition that this is, can be, nothing other than something delivered to us, delivered into 'our innermost keeping.' It has an 'address' on it: an address with our name written on it, our one and only name. Think of that, Edmund. A postman—yes, how odd to say that, a postman—comes and delivers a parcel and that parcel is the universe itself, the womb and cradle of life.

"What counts, Edmund, what counts, if you can recognize that 'parcel' for what it is, is the sheer giftedness that is its only explanation. Oh, don't think for a moment, Edmund, that I am blind to the rancor, the fraud, the violence that besets the human condition, the gargantuan forces that befoul, envenom, desecrate, smother what is good in our lives; I have seen enough of that. I have contended with it; I, too, have taken my irretrievable losses. But I also know that I can identify, that I can mark those devastating lacunae for what they are because I am able to grasp, in some slight sense, the boundless plenitude they impair. Only by looking into the abyss of desolation can we have the courage and the wisdom to take the full measure of what we have been given. I know it is a good deal easier to talk about these things than to live though them or to console the sorrows they incise so deeply in our lives. I know, too, that I have been blessed with a beneficent life. The greatest benefice of all, I am convinced, is the ability to love and the concurrent bestowal, almost too miraculous to be true, of all those things upon which we have conferred, and can confer, that love. If I have come to recognize anything at all in my life, I have recognized that the love with which I have loved has ever been the gift of a love that has loved us.

"If I am right about this, Edmund, then the civility of which I spoke has both its roots and its buds, its habitation and its summons, in that love. And if I dwell on it, as I have, it is not simply to possess and to savor it, but rather to preserve it for others, to gather it up as a harvest, as a blessing for others who will follow us and who will add, if their eyes are open and their hearts are faithful, their own measure to it. The shrouds of all that grief we have shared will furnish forth the raiment of our sacrificial praise. O my God, Edmund, what will it amount to in the end! What most inexhaustible banquet bestowed upon us in the course of our lives can we justly anticipate as the disclosure of our destinies! But I have said too much. I have said much more than I should have said."

"You are being too opaque for me, Theodore," I exclaimed, being rather overcome by all of this. "I preferred the talk about those pungent dromedaries, the braying jennies, the desert wadi . . ."

"That makes perfect sense, Edmund. It's the particular things and persons we have known in our lives that make the difference. The little we can say about them is always bound to be opaque. As for the dromedaries, the jennies, the wadis, the nomad in his real or in his memorialized tent—yes, the most apparently insignificant things, things in their discrete times and seasons, things in their imperishable uniqueness—these are what intimate to us, at every juncture of our lives, the largesse of our origin and purpose. I leave it to you, Edmund, I leave it to you to work out the details."

"If I can work out the details, Theodore. I think you give me much more credit than is my due. And what shall we say of you, in later days, those of us who are your successors? Where shall we hang your portrait, Theodore?"

"Whatever for?" Besserman demanded.

"You began with him!" I pointed at the portrait of Frederick Schefflin.

"So . . . ?"

"So when it behooves me to do what you have done, where shall I begin?"

He declared. "No memorials of me, Edmund, until all that is left of me, from your perspective, is a distant memory, growing dim with time. Your memorial, if memorial there be, will be a story."

"But have you not been, for us, for everyone else, the 'master' of your 'house,' the 'prince' of your 'dominions'?"

"Of my 'house' and my 'dominions'? And then, to top it all, 'master' and 'prince'? Scarcely. You know me well enough by now, Edmund, that it is not my presumptive modesty that forbids such flattery. I should indeed glory in it if I could. But I must assume some modicum of precision. I have often thought that one of the greatest gifts we receive is the sum of the obligations conferred upon us by the very particular circumstances of our lives. How little inclined we are to think of obligations in that way. But that is who we are in our own dense particularity. We are what we are bound to do in the highest sense, in our highest aspirations—even, I might add, accompanied, as they often are, with every conceivable obstacle that can arise to prevent and discourage and deflect us from doing them. Even these obstacles are part of the circumstances and tell us what to do, what direction to take. 'Master' and 'prince'? If I have been a faithful servant, I shall have been all that I was asked to do and all I have wanted to be. As I said, I have some thank-you notes to write, not just a few but many, and not just to the living but also, copiously and eloquently, to the dead. And not just to those whom I have known but, if only in principle, to those countless unknown thousands who have made my life, and the lives of those whom I have loved, meet and just. It will take the rest of my life to do it."

He demurred for a moment. Then he waved me away brusquely with the words, "We will have a great deal to do. Let's begin tomorrow early—nine o'clock?"

"Excellent!" I knew I would have to cancel some appointments. There would be no difficulty with this. This would be where I would go from here. As I rose to leave, Besserman stood up suddenly, almost as an afterthought, looked at me with an expression both gruff and tender at the same time, and extended his hands to shake my hands once again although the gesture had something in it, not so much as a farewell as of a benediction. "*Shalom,*" he uttered. "And bless you … bless you … my son, if I may be so bold as to call you that, call you my 'son,' even if in the figurative speech of a daft old dotard gathering up, at the end, as the poets have said, his sack of 'rags and bones,' beloved as each and every one is to me. How Martha would have liked to hear me address those words to you! How very much she dwelled on you those many years ago. She would have liked to hear me call you 'my son' as if you really were. I hope you don't mind."

I nodded my approval. I looked up again at the portrait of Frederick, now scarcely visible in the shadows that filled the room, yet still so alive with those eyes turned so mildly outward, gathering in all that was good about the past and contemplating what lay beyond the horizon. Did I seek his approval as well? I then turned and waved back to Besserman as I departed through the carved oak door that led into the hallway. I glanced upward for a moment at Agnes' giraffes, their round, black, quizzical eyes gazing at me through the foliage. I resisted the impulse to wave goodbye to them too. That glass-paneled gilt elevator, which I had found so daunting on my first visit to Besserman's office, stood at the landing, but I decided nevertheless, as I did on my first day, to walk down the marble staircase, dimly lit by the bronze and crystal sconces along its descent. The building was strange and silent, now that the staff had returned to their homes for the night.

On the ground floor I stood for a moment by the partition of ironwrought tracery and etched glass. The fountain, the "ivory fount," with its basins and runnels and spouts still visible in the gathering darkness, splashed gently in the middle of the garden. The cluster of lilies in the bottommost basin had begun to bloom with small jewel-like flowers. I thought for a moment of Cornelia, still in her girlhood, sitting by that fountain as it once was in the breakfast garden at Madison Street and as it was portrayed by the painting in Besserman's chambers. And I thought, too, of Uncle Aloysius by that same fountain, perhaps on some visit from Concord, perhaps waiting for Cornelia as she prepared to spend an afternoon with him. I wondered what they would do together—maybe a matinee followed by dinner at the Schefflin's on Bolyston Street—the same Schefflin's I had known in my youth—where, from a table by a window, they could trace together the long evening shadows, on just such an evening as this, extending languidly over Boston Common and the Public Gardens from the surrounding buildings. Aunt Bernice?—she might be off at an opening with her theater friends somewhere else in the city. And that was good too. It was all very good.

"Uncle Aloysius," I murmured to myself as I stood there. It made me sad to think of him; yet I smiled inwardly too. I watched the pinnacle of the fountain spray and dazzle in the fading light. I gazed at the basins' calm lucid waters curling over their ivory and amber tinted rims, gliding from one basin to the next, in ever widening circles, ever deeper and deeper receptacles below gathering in the overflow from above. I gazed at the gentle undulation of the lily pads and their diminutive blossoms as tiny ripples moved back and forth across the surface of the water. What fullness, I thought, what abundance of life! What passage of love and what allotment of devotion, in this world, shall we ever truly comprehend?

My reverie was interrupted by Mr. Dougherty, who asked me if I would like to have a cab sent for. I declined the offer. With an elderly and cordial garrulousness, concerned as ever with his favorite subject of the Red Sox and their favorable—most unlikely, I would add—"prospects" for a pennant this year, he accompanied me to the door.

Outside, the street lights had just come on and the one or two basement shops still left on the street had lit up their display windows; but very little traffic, pedestrian or otherwise, moved up and down the street, though I could hear in the background the immense chirr, the bustle and energy, of Boston, its homeward-bound rush hour now in full progress. As I turned the corner into the adjoining avenue, I looked back at the slender, almost miniscule façade of the Schefflin Foundation, which seemed still to me, after all this time, so out of place, and yet so inexplicably in place and irreplaceable, as if all its surroundings could come and go, leaving it untouched.

The evening sun was just dipping down behind the darkened buildings to the west and shed one final blaze of sunlight through the street, which caught, full and golden, the high oriel windows of the top floor. Once again I marveled at it, as I had done that very first day when I answered Besserman's note. I marveled at—how did Besserman put it?—its "imperishable uniqueness," which now glowed afresh, as if it were reborn, as if it were born anew before my eyes. I marveled, too, at the imperishable uniqueness of its vitality and purpose. For having been vouchsafed the richness of its memory, I could now live the life of its promise—its promise having become my own simply because it would now be my particular commission to pass it on to others beyond me—which to this very day, and to this very hour, and to this very moment I have done.

Finis

About the Author

Johann M. Moser was born in Cambridge, Massachusetts, in 1940. He grew up in New York City and later in New Jersey. At Dartmouth College he majored in philosophy and studied with the poet Richard Eberhart. In 1970, he received a Ph.D. in comparative literature from the Catholic University of America in Washington, D.C., where he specialized in poetics and medieval literature. From 1970 until his retirement in 2000, he taught literature and philosophy at St. Anselm College in Manchester, New Hampshire.

Moser published a volume of verse titled *Most Ancient of All Splendors* with Sophia Institute Press in 1989, as well as edited and translated for the press both an anthology of classical Nativity verse and, in collaboration with a colleague, Robert Anderson, an edition of St. Thomas Aquinas's hymns and prayers.

Although familiar with many areas of the United States and having lived several years abroad, Moser spent his early summers in the Lakes Region of central New Hampshire, where he has now resided for over half a century. In these decades, he has formed an intimate bond with northern New England, whose mountains and lakes and lively populace have been a source of inspiration for him, even as he has devoted himself to a sustained pursuit and emulation of world literature in all its dense historicity and its universal aesthetic achievements.

www.ingramcontent.com/pod-product-compliance
Lightning Source LLC
Chambersburg PA
CBHW030131010826
48973CB00002B/514

9781964001135